Alison Booth
STILLWATER CREEK

BANTAM

SYDNEY AUCKLAND TORONTO NEW YORK LONDON

Permission to reproduce words from *The Power and the Glory* by Graham Greene courtesy of David Higham Associates and Random House UK.

Permission to reproduce words from *Waiting for Godot* by Samuel Beckett courtesy of Faber and Faber Ltd.

A Bantam book
Published by Random House Australia Pty Ltd
Level 3, 100 Pacific Highway, North Sydney NSW 2060
www.randomhouse.com.au

First published by Bantam in 2010
This edition published in 2011

Addresses for companies within the Random House Group can be found at www.randomhouse.com.au/offices

National Library of Australia
Cataloguing-in-Publication Entry

Booth, Alison
Stillwater Creek

ISBN 978 1 86471 125 7 (pbk)

A823.4

Cover photography by Corbis & Getty Images
Cover design by Natalie Winter
Internal design and typesetting by Midland Typesetters, Australia
Printed in Australia by Griffin Press, an accredited ISO AS/NZS 14001:2004
Environmental Management System printer

10 9 8 7 6 5 4 3 2 1

MIX
Paper from
responsible sources
FSC
www.fsc.org
FSC® C009448

The paper this book is printed on is certified against the Forest Stewardship Council® Standards. Griffin Press holds FSC chain of custody certification SGS-COC-005088. FSC promotes environmentally responsible, socially beneficial and economically viable management of the world's forests.

To my family

'*There is always one moment in childhood when the door opens and lets the future in.*'

GRAHAM GREENE, *The Power and the Glory* (1940)

Jingera Township, 1957

1957

CHAPTER ONE

Ilona's first impression was of light. Light glancing off the water, light sluicing the valley, light shaping the folds of the green hills that tumbled down to meet the sea. A golden light, for the sun was sinking fast. Surely the bus must soon arrive at Jingera. She and Zidra were the only passengers left after a sun-dried woman, wearing a floral dress and a miscellany of string bags, had alighted several miles back. Before long it would be dark but not before they saw the cottage, pray God not before then, for Ilona couldn't bear to reach a new place after night had fallen.

There had been too many arrivals after dark. The first was in that cold Latvian winter at the concentration camp near Riga. And after the liberation, a series of displaced persons' camps, and ultimately her arrival in England. Only in Sydney had she disembarked in daylight, this time with her husband Oleksii and small daughter Zidra, the three of them walking down the ship's gangway, in the harsh morning light of a summer's day.

But she would not dwell on the past when today's journey was looking so promising; when the light was streaming down the valley and illuminating Zidra's face, so that her sallow skin assumed an unusual radiance. Ilona examined her daughter: only nine years old but already she was striking with that combination of upturned nose, short upper lip and disproportionately high forehead. And the pretty dark curls that were just like those of poor dead Oleksii.

'Look at the sign!' Zidra pointed to a white sign at the side of the road. *Welcome to Wilba Wilba Shire,* and underneath, in smaller letters, *Drive Carefully.* This was ignored by the driver, who swerved the bus into the next bend in the road.

Ilona peered through the front windscreen, at the road snaking down in front of them. There at last was the town of Jingera, a haphazard collection of weatherboard cottages clinging to the hillside. It was smaller than she'd expected, although the McIntyres, her friends in Sydney whose Jingera cottage she had arranged to rent, had warned her that the place was a bit of a backwater. But full of such friendly people, they'd said, who are crying out for a piano teacher.

'Just look at the sea, Mama!'

Below the town lay the river, widening into a lagoon that seemed to be connected by the thinnest thread of water to the ocean beyond. Ilona put an arm around Zidra's shoulders. Her face was starting to acquire that pinched look it took on when she was tired.

'Pickin' up the key from the butcher's shop?' The bus driver twisted his head round to look at them and grinned. 'Not a bad place, luv. Could be worse, there could be more people!' He restored his glance to the road just in time to negotiate another of the hairpin bends. 'Cadwallader shuts up at five sharp, so it's lucky we're on time, or youse might've bin campin' under 'is awning!'

Opening the bus window slightly, Ilona inhaled deeply. The air was fresh and salty and she felt her spirits lift. She had left

Sydney behind, she had left Europe behind. Maybe it would be possible to forget the past and start a new life in Jingera, this sanctuary by the sea. Unclasping her handbag, she felt inside it for the reassuring shape of the Latvian–English dictionary. While it hadn't been needed so far today, she did not know what linguistic challenges the evening would bring.

The bus turned sharply off the main road and into Jingera township. Past a white-painted hotel and a corrugated iron hall, around a war memorial in the centre of an open space ringed by buildings, and at last shuddering to a halt in front of a few shops sheltered by wide awnings. On the fascia of the middle shop was the name she was looking for: 'Cadwallader's Quality Meats'. They had arrived.

Only after alighting from the bus did she notice the middle-aged man standing on the pavement outside Cadwallader's Quality Meats. Above his head, a large black and white cow, painted on the shopfront window, seemed to hover like a cloud over his thinning dark hair. When he stepped forward to shake her hand, she noticed his slight limp and the newspaper-wrapped package he was holding.

'Welcome to Jingera,' he said. 'George Cadwallader's the name.' He clasped her long-fingered hand in his own – a butcher's hand. His fingers were scrubbed and clean. 'Let me take your suitcases. It's just a short walk from here to the McIntyres.' They asked me to show you how the stove works and the fuse box. And this must be your daughter,' he added, smiling at Zidra. 'I hope you had a good trip. Bus not too bumpy for you?'

'It was terrible, especially from Burford,' said Zidra, who was rarely at a loss for words. 'The bus went really fast round all those zigzag bends. Poor Mama was so frightened!'

Cadwallader laughed.

Taking Zidra's hand, Ilona followed the butcher across the open area in front of the row of shops. Past the war memorial they went, an obelisk covered with a surprising number of names and elevated on a square plinth several steps high; past the post office at the lower corner of the square and into an unkerbed street leading down the hill to the lagoon. Zidra had now become quiet and was gripping Ilona's hand tightly.

Weatherboard cottages lined each side of the road, some of them semi-concealed by hedges, others with no gardens at all so that it was possible to see into the front room without even trying. Please make it a house with a hedge, Ilona thought, for privacy.

The butcher stopped when he reached a gate several hundred yards down the hill. On each side of the gate was a dense glossy-leafed hedge and Ilona sighed with relief. The salty air was overlaid with a scent of something unknown, sweet but not sickly, that might have been from the small white flowers growing on the vine entangled in the hedge.

'Such *delectable* flowers, Mr Cadwallader!' But from his grin, she knew that *delectable* was not quite the word she was looking for. Later, she would look up its precise meaning. Perhaps she should have used that all-purpose word, *nice*.

'Call me George,' he said. 'Don't know what those flowers are. They grow like weeds around here.' After struggling for a moment with the gate, he ushered them through the opening.

A brick path led up to the cottage, or what Ilona supposed was the cottage. It looked more like a support for the vines that tumbled over the verandah roof and fell like swags from the guttering; brilliant orange, trumpet-like flowers growing in bunches. Zidra jumped onto the verandah and bounced up and down on the splintered grey boards that squeaked under her weight. George now had the front door unlocked. Inside, the hallway reeked of stale air and dust and Ilona could hardly bear the smell after the loveliness of the garden.

'No one's lived here since the end of last summer,' George explained, as if the neglect were his fault. 'We don't get too many holiday lets this time of the year, even though September's a mild month here.'

The initial reservations she had melted away when Ilona looked up and saw the wooden fretwork forming an arch halfway down the hall, and the carved shelving running along each side at about picture-rail height. The floorboards, though scuffed and in need of polish, were warm red and of some timber that she had never seen before. She knew then that she could make this place into a home.

At the far end of the hall was the kitchen. A fuel stove occupied most of one wall, and an ice chest and pine dresser stood opposite. On the kitchen table, covered in red-and-white checked oilcloth, sat a black bakelite wireless set. She touched it lightly.

Catching sight of the view from the window next to the stove, she held her breath. There was so much space in front of her, so much space. George was saying something about the ice chest but she couldn't speak, she couldn't listen. Beyond the lagoon, now the colour of pewter, lay a strip of olive-green bushland and beyond that again was the dark blue of the ocean smudging into the paler washed-out blue of the late afternoon sky. It was this view of ocean and bush that lent the McIntyres' cottage a sense of openness. Although the cottage wasn't big, it didn't seem cramped; she couldn't abide confined rooms although that's what she'd lived in for years. Even in Homebush, space had felt restricted. And right outside the kitchen door was another little verandah that overlooked a garden that would be perfect for Zidra to play in. Seated in that rickety-looking cane chair, Ilona would be able to watch the lagoon and the sky, and she and Zidra would be safe.

Collecting herself, she mumbled some response about the ice chest, and tried to concentrate very hard on what George was explaining; the workings of the wood stove in the kitchen and the location of the septic tank, and the fuse box and the kerosene lamp in case of emergencies, and the days on which the ice man came.

'My piano will be arriving tomorrow,' she said, once George had finished his instruction. 'I shall need to find a piano tuner.'

'There's one in Burford. He fishes here sometimes. He's a reasonable cove.'

'I want to give piano lessons. I must advertise somehow.'

'Cherry Bates might be interested. She said only the other day that she wanted to learn the piano.' He bent down in front of the stove and made a slight adjustment to the kindling.

Ilona wondered who Cherry was. It was an unusual name and she knew of no Latvian equivalent. She was about to ask George about her when he continued, 'She works in the pub. Married to the publican. You could put a notice in the post office window about the lessons. The town isn't as small as it looks. There are more houses along North Road – that's the road next to the pub – and there are some behind the headland. There are farms too, mainly dairy.' At this point he became quite animated, talking at some length about cows and milking and cheese, and even the local abattoir. It would have been better not to hear about that, although she knew that meat was his job, if not his vocation.

Before leaving, he handed her the newspaper-wrapped parcel. 'Just a few things you might need tonight. Nothing much really.' As if embarrassed by his kindness, he avoided meeting her eye.

After he'd gone, Ilona opened all the windows of the cottage and unwrapped the parcel. It contained half a loaf of bread, butter, a twist of tea, and half-a-dozen sausages. How considerate he was; she hadn't bought any meat when she purchased a few groceries in Bomaderry and she would cook the sausages for their supper.

Opening the door in the front of the stove, Ilona put a match to the kindling. The flames flared and soon the wood was blazing. Mesmerised by the flickering flames, she forgot for a moment where she was. Four months had passed since she'd last lit a fire. That was in the incinerator at the back of the flats where they'd lived in Sydney and several weeks after poor Oleksii's death. She'd decided to burn the shabbiest of his old clothes, the ones that the opportunity shop wouldn't take. For several days she'd agonised about whether or not she should enlist Zidra's assistance with this. It might help her come to terms with her father's death. She had seemed almost unaffected by it, so much so that Ilona had wondered if the girl might be finding it a relief to be without his oppressive presence in the evenings. She no longer withdrew to her little bedroom, as she used to when Oleksii came home from work, but stayed with Ilona in the kitchen, chattering as much to herself as her mother.

In the end Ilona had decided to burn Oleksii's clothes by herself. Late one evening she'd put them into a cardboard box with some newspapers and crept out to the incinerator, a square brick construction a few feet high. A large red globe of a moon had bobbed up over the roofs of the houses behind the flats. Its jauntiness contrasted with the neglected look of the yard. After crumpling up sheets of newspaper, she'd fed them into the incinerator and piled the clothes on top. One garment she kept out though, a faded blue-and-white-striped shirt, frayed around the neck and cuffs. Raising it to her face, she sniffed: not even the faintest scent of Oleksii remained.

This was the end and her eyes started to fill with tears. Angrily she'd brushed them away and retrieved the matches from the cardboard box. Her hands trembled so much that striking the match proved difficult and it was only at the fourth attempt that the newspaper ignited. Small blue and orange flames licked and crackled around the edges of the paper, and were soon united in a golden plume of fire of such intensity that Oleksii's clothes also began to burn. Onto the top of the pyre she'd flung the blue-and-white-striped shirt; there was no point in being sentimental over an old rag. The flames leapt up several feet into the air. In ten minutes it was all over and only the smouldering embers remained. Soon even these were reduced to a pile of ashes.

But that was all in the past and here she was in the kitchen of the McIntyres' cottage in Jingera, with Zidra hungry and tired, just as she was herself. Picking up the poker, she prodded the burning wood. Surely the stove would soon be warm enough to cook on. She watched the flames flare up and then shut the stove door. After removing a dead fly from the frying pan, she rinsed it at the sink before starting to fry four sausages and then some tomatoes. The stove top was greasy. The place would require a thorough clean-out in the morning and tonight she should make a list of what to buy at the little general store.

After they had eaten, Zidra said, 'Can't I go outside now?'

'Tomorrow, darling. It is already dark. And the garden could be full of spiders and even snakes and whatever else might be found in a neglected Australian garden.'

'It's not fair. We've got a garden here and you said I could play in it. You never used to let me play outside in Homebush.'

'You can go outside tomorrow morning.' But first Ilona would check the garden carefully, something she couldn't face this evening, not when there were all those other things that needed doing. 'Anyway, it's late and you're tired and you need a wash.' Suppressing a sigh, she started to scrub at the inside of the bath. The brown marks appeared to be stains and would not come off. Harder and harder she rubbed while Zidra continued her litany. At last the bath was sufficiently clean, or at least none of the marks would come off with further rubbing, and she began to fill it with water.

In the little bedroom that was to be Zidra's, she made up the bed. Straightening up, she caught sight of her reflection in the flawed glass of the mirror: a slender woman of medium height with a drawn face and usually exuberant fair hair now badly in need of a wash. It was undeniably the case, she decided, that she looked far older than thirty-seven years. She gave the mirror a quick wipe with her handkerchief but unfortunately this did nothing for her appearance.

'There's a spider behind the toilet!' Zidra called from the bathroom. 'Quick!'

But she wasn't quick enough and the spider had gone. 'It was there,' Zidra pointed behind the pan. 'You were too slow.'

Ignoring the scowl, Ilona looked instead at the dark smudges under her daughter's eyes that were from fatigue rather than the dust that lay everywhere. Tears could not now be far off. After the long day it was no wonder that she was becoming a little excitable and in a way Ilona was glad of it after her calmness in recent months. 'There is nothing here,' she said gently. 'Only a few old spider webs.' She contemplated the high toilet cistern that was connected to the wall by metal brackets and skeins of dusty webs. 'In the morning I'll brush all those down, but not now. I'm too tired and so are you.' She pulled the chain and water gushed into the pan and swirled away. 'That will frighten away any insects,' she said more confidently than she felt. 'And now you must have your bath.'

When Zidra had at last fallen asleep in her narrow bed, Ilona put on a warm jacket and took a cup of tea out on to the rickety verandah. The dark shapes of overgrown shrubs defined the lower boundary of the backyard and, below this, the smooth water of the lagoon palely reflected the new moon. Although she couldn't see the breakers, she could hear their regular pounding. Perhaps one day that sound might become an irritation, or maybe it would always be as soothing as it was now, when she was able at last to leave behind the anxiety of yet another journey that had ended. It was a far easier ending to the journey this time. Everything had seemed less difficult once she had seen the inside of the cottage and its outlook, and observed Zidra's joy at the prospect of the garden.

She would wait a few days before advertising piano lessons. After retrieving her notebook, she stared at the figures written in it: one hundred and sixty pounds, three shillings and ninepence was all that was left. Provided she was frugal, this was probably sufficient to live on for a while. It had come from her piano teaching. There had been none of Oleksii's money left after the funeral expenses had been paid.

She remembered how affronted Oleksii had initially been by her decision to give piano lessons after they'd settled in Homebush. Before the war she'd done nothing but practise the piano and take exams, for her father hadn't wanted her to earn a living either, but those days were long gone. Oleksii had clearly forgotten that she'd worked in Bradford when they'd first met. Eventually she'd persuaded him that she would be unhappy if she didn't teach but it hadn't been easy. On no account was the money she earned to be used to supplement his meagre earnings at the biscuit factory, he'd said, insisting she open a bank account in her own name.

Until she'd started teaching the piano in that dreary western Sydney suburb in which there was hardly a tree to be seen, she'd felt lonely and alienated. It was because her English was so poor and she had so little to do. In Bradford she'd mainly spoken Latvian, surrounded as she was by other refugees, and she seemed always to be working or caring for Zidra or sleeping, with no time left for music or for improving her English. It was their hope, when she and Oleksii left England five years ago, that they would have more spare time in Sydney. And for her there had been more time. Too much time, until Oleksii had bought the second-hand upright piano.

After beginning to play again, she'd been surprised to discover that little had been forgotten, although her fingers were clumsy and stiff, and a part of her that she'd thought was dead began to send forth tender new shoots. That was when she'd hit upon the idea of teaching the piano. Once Oleksii was persuaded, she'd begun to teach and her English began to improve too. Oleksii's death had changed this fragile equilibrium. Soon afterwards she'd decided that Zidra should grow up somewhere else, somewhere sheltered, a small town rather than a big city. When the McIntyres had mentioned their vacant cottage, she'd jumped at the opportunity.

Welcome to Wilba Wilba Shire. That sign outside Jingera was surely a portent. But before she could start teaching the piano again, there was a lot to organise, not least enrolling Zidra in the local school and taking delivery of the piano and arranging for the piano tuner to come.

She began to make a list of things to do the following day. She always made lists, had done so ever since being released from that last camp. They helped her impose order on her days, helped maintain a fiction of sorts that she had some control over the future.

CHAPTER TWO

A few days later, Zidra, hiding under the hedge in the front garden, watched the small boy as he lobbed another stone at the skinny black girl with the torn dress. Her legs were scratched and she was wearing grubby sandshoes with no socks. 'Cowardy cowardy custard,' the boy chanted.

The stone hit the girl hard on the thigh. Zidra winced in sympathy. After picking up the stone, the girl hurled it back at the boy. It hit him in the stomach and he doubled over, moaning. The girl, not content with the success of her attack, strode towards him and shouted, 'Shut up yer bloody bum!' She shook her fist at the boy. Zidra watched in admiration from her hiding place and muttered these new words quietly to herself.

Just then her mother came out of the cottage. Zidra crouched lower in the shrubbery. She couldn't bear to be spotted. Her mother would call out something in the thick foreign accent that had embarrassed Zidra so much from the moment she realised Mama spoke differently from most other people. Zidra herself could pick up accents wherever she went. Mostly she chose to speak Australian English but sometimes she would put on a Bradford accent. Now, hidden in the bushes, she remained silent as her mother stomped down the side of the house, calling, 'Zidra, Zidra!'

'Zidra, Zidra!' the small boy mimicked once her mother was out of earshot, and then for good measure he added, 'Bloody wogs, why doncha go back home? Boongs not wanted 'ere neither.'

What a boong or a wog was Zidra had no idea, although she realised they couldn't be words of endearment. The skinny girl grabbed the boy by one of his jug-handle ears and dragged him, whimpering, up the street. After twenty yards or so they were joined by some white children. Abandoning her ear-hold, the skinny girl raced up the hill, leaving the others far behind.

'Cowardy cowardy custard!' the small boy called again, and was joined in his chanting by his friends as they marched up the road towards the schoolhouse, high on the headland.

The school bell rang and Zidra felt her stomach lurch. These children would be her classmates when she started school on Monday week. Until then she could stay at home to get used to the place, Mama had announced, but after this it was back to lessons. Zidra didn't want to go to school though. She'd rather spend all her time in this paradise of a garden.

'Zidra?' Her mother was now running up the side of the house.

Emerging from her hiding place, Zidra couldn't resist trying out the expression she'd just learnt. 'Shut up yer bloody bum,' she said softly. Afterwards she was glad that her mother didn't seem to hear.

<hr />

That afternoon, Zidra hid under the hedge again to watch the children going home but she couldn't hear any voices. No sounds at all apart from a faint rustling as a breeze lifted the leaves of the hedge and the distant thump of the surf.

'Wotcher doing under here?'

Zidra gave a little squeak. The voice was coming from right next to her, and there was the skinny black girl, crouched under the hedge not more than a yard away.

'Did I scare you? Didn't mean to.' The girl smiled, showing all her teeth. They were very white. Zidra liked the way she smiled so you couldn't help smiling back. The girl's wavy hair was cut in the same style as Zidra's but prettier; Zidra hated her own curls.

'I saw you this morning throwing rocks.' Zidra tried to keep the admiration out of her voice.

'That was just at Barry,' the girl said. 'He started it. Gotter stick up for yerself at school. No one else will. Anyway, I knew you were under the hedge. The others didn't, but I did.'

'How did you know?'

'Saw your face. Couldn't miss that little yellow moon shining out of the bushes.'

Zidra laughed. She liked this image and the kindliness she felt in the girl. 'What's your name?'

'Lorna Hunter. I know yours already. Heard your mum call you this morning.'

'Bet you don't know my last name though,' Zidra said, and then wished she hadn't. Kids sometimes laughed when they heard it.

'What is it?'

'Talivaldis.'

Lorna didn't laugh. 'It's nice,' she said. 'Sounds like a song. I've heard music coming from your house. Do you play the pianner?'

'I'm learning but I hate it. She's a teacher.'

'Who?'

'My mother. She sings too.'

'I love singing.' Lorna broke into song. Her voice seemed to come from somewhere deep inside her. There were no words to the song, just pure sound. I've never heard anything so beautiful, Zidra thought, even Mama singing.

'You've got a lovely voice,' she said.

Lorna gave her infectious smile again. 'I can show you some really good places to play,' she said. 'Maybe after school one afternoon.'

'What sort of places?'

'Bush places, swimming holes in Stillwater Creek, that sort of thing. Why doncha go to school?'

'I'm starting a week on Monday.'

'They might gang up on you, some of them. 'Specially the boys. I'll look out for you, though. Miss Neville will too. She's tough but she's nice when you get to know her.'

'I met her yesterday and she wasn't all that nice. Put me right off the tables.'

'She's got a thing about multiplication tables. Gotter learn them off by heart.'

Zidra was just about to reply when her mother came out of the front door and down the front path. 'Zidra!' she called. 'Who are you talking to under the hedge?' She bent down, smiling.

'My friend, Lorna.' When Zidra looked around she saw that Lorna had gone as noiselessly as she had arrived.

'Is that a pretend friend or a real one?'

'A real one, of course,' said Zidra, embarrassed in case Lorna was in the street, listening. She wriggled through the hedge and peered out the front but Lorna was already at the bottom of the hill, almost as far as the lagoon.

'You will make lots of friends when you start school,' Mama said, when Zidra crawled out of the hedge. 'And now we must remove all those leaves from your hair before you come inside.'

'She was here a minute ago,' Zidra said, scuffing at a stone with her foot. 'She's not pretend. You frightened her away.'

'Of course she was here.' Mama put her arm around Zidra's shoulder and gave her a little squeeze. 'Try not to damage your shoes, darling. I polished them only this morning.' Together they inspected the shoes; they were dusty and scratched.

'I need sandshoes for playing in,' said Zidra. 'Like Lorna's.'

Zidra refused to go into the post office with her mother. Mama was going to ask Mrs Blunkett to put her advertisement for piano lessons in the window. There was a queue inside and waiting in that couldn't possibly be as interesting as hanging about outside.

A rickety old picket fence surrounded the small square of garden next door to the post office. One of the pickets had fallen sideways. Zidra thought it would be easy to get it to stand up straight again. The picket was only held with one rusty nail at the bottom but there was another poking out of the crossbar at the top. Wiggle, wiggle. If only she could get the hole in the top of the picket to line up with the nail, then it would stand upright. The nail and the hole just wouldn't align, no matter how hard she struggled. The picket was soft and splintered at the top so maybe she could just ram it onto the nail. She pushed hard with both hands and then let go. The picket fell off the nail at the bottom and landed at her feet.

'Having a spot of bother?'

Startled, Zidra looked around guiltily. A large fair man a good bit older than her mother was looking down at her. She'd seen him in the street the day before. It was good that he was smiling. It meant that he was one of those forgiving grown-ups rather than the other sort.

'Let me fix it.' He picked up the picket and managed to reattach it to the crossbar by dint of a bit of wriggling and pushing. 'There. No one any the wiser now, except you and me.'

She smiled at him. His moustache was several shades darker than the hair on the top of his head and golden hairs sprouted out of his nostrils. Zidra could see them glinting in the sunlight.

'I'm Mr Bates,' the man said. 'Would you like a rainbow ball?' From a pocket he took a small white paper bag and held it out. She wasn't supposed to eat anything but apples between meals because of her teeth. Her mother said they were as soft as chalk and at great risk of decay, and she'd already had three fillings before they left Homebush. She peered into the bag. Big round sweets; the loveliest looking gobstoppers she'd ever seen. Mouth watering, she still hesitated.

'Go on, be a devil,' Mr Bates said.

She wasn't supposed to accept anything from strangers either, but this man was hardly a stranger, she'd seen him only yesterday. Anyway, Mama was still talking to Mrs Blunkett inside the post office and couldn't see what she was up to. She reached into the bag and took out one of the rainbow balls.

'Take two and don't tell your mother,' Mr Bates said, winking.

She winked back and took another. One went into her mouth and the other into her pocket for later. Sucking hard, she didn't feel in the least bit guilty anymore. The illicit nature of this treat was almost as enjoyable as its sweetness.

'I hear your mother teaches the piano,' Mr Bates said. 'What do you want to be when you grow up?'

Answering his question when her mouth was full of rainbow ball was difficult, and anyway there were so many years between now and adulthood. They seemed almost infinite.

Infinity bothered her, especially at night when she was trying to go to sleep. It filled her with panic. When she died she was supposed to be going to heaven and life there went on forever. That was even more bothersome because then you had to think of life here ending and how could you realise it had ended if you were dead and in infinite heaven?

'Maybe you'll be a mummy with lots of children,' Mr Bates said encouragingly, in the sort of voice grown-ups sometimes used when they were talking to children.

Zidra cringed. Pushing the sweet into one cheek with her tongue, she managed to say, 'Not a mummy or a daddy. I'll probably drive a truck rather than teach the piano.' Even she was surprised by this choice. What she really wanted was to have adventures and roam the world, and return to Mama from time to time when she felt like a rest.

Mr Bates laughed, before strolling on. Zidra stood up and idly kicked one foot against the kerb. One by one people came out of the post office, but not her mother. To amuse herself, she read the advertisements stuck to the window. Most of them were dull but there was one for puppies who were looking for a good home. Although her home was a good one for puppies, her mother would think otherwise. Peering between the advertisements, she saw that the queue had now gone and her mother was talking to Mrs Blunkett. Mrs Blunkett had curly white hair and so many freckles that she looked orange. She was nodding vigorously and holding the white card over which her mother had worked so hard the night before to find the right words to describe her skills as a piano teacher.

The piano tuner had come that morning, all the way from Bega, to fix the piano. 'It no longer plays plinkety-plunkety but plays as it is meant to sound,' Mama had said in an overexcited way to the piano tuner. Immediately she'd dashed off a short piece that involved much movement up and down the keyboard. The piano tuner had clapped when she'd finished. 'I was showing off a little,' Mama admitted later. 'But one does not know to whom the tuner will relay the information about my prowess. Mighty trees from little acorns grow. We must never forget that, my darling little Zidra.'

Zidra took the rainbow ball out of her mouth and inspected it. It was whitish-grey with swirls of colour. After putting it back in her mouth, she wiped her sticky fingers on her skirt. When she was a little girl she used to wipe her sticky fingers on her hair. Mama often reminded her of this, sometimes in public.

At first her mother had been on her best behaviour when they'd visited the school the day before. The mistress, Miss Neville, was almost as thin as Mama and a bit taller. She was wearing a light grey suit with a long skirt. A pretty pink-and-blue patterned scarf was tucked into the neck of her white blouse in the same way that Papa used to wear his cravat for special occasions. This had upset Zidra, for she tried not to think too much of her father, it made her sad. Before she'd had time to recover, Miss Neville had made her recite the six times table. Zidra had been unable to continue beyond six times three is eighteen. 'She's a little behind for a nine-year-old,' Miss Neville had said.

'Ees it not enough that her Papa has died but that she must be insulted too?' Zidra's mother had said, her English lapsing as it sometimes did under stress. Zidra had blushed for them both.

Miss Neville had looked out of the window while making a minor adjustment to her cravat. 'I didn't mean to cause offence,' she said. 'But I do believe in being direct.'

After a moment, Mama said, 'Offence has not been taken. I too favour directness. You will find that Zidra ees very advanced at ze reading. In Eenglish and in Latvian.'

Although Miss Neville had made no comment about the Latvian, she'd offered Zidra a book from the shelves behind her, *Alice in Wonderland*. Zidra had opened it and read several paragraphs aloud, glad of the opportunity to prove herself. 'Very good indeed,' Miss Neville said. 'Although perhaps read with a little too much expression. We Australians are given to understatement. You will not find us an emotional lot, Mrs Talivaldis.'

Zidra had turned these words over like sweets in her mouth, while committing them to memory. Later she'd repeated them to her mother in Miss Neville's carrying but slightly husky voice. Mama had laughed and hugged her, and that more than made up for her failure with the six times table.

Now Zidra peered through the post office window again. Mrs Blunkett was gluing Mama's advertisement to the window. Seeing Zidra, she smiled and Zidra grinned back. After crunching up what remained of the rainbow ball, she swallowed the pieces and wiped her lips on her forearm just as her mother came out into the street, followed by Mrs Blunkett. In her pocket Zidra could feel the reassuring shape of the second sweet.

'What a lovely little girl you have,' Mrs Blunkett said to Mama.

'Thank you,' Mama said, smiling. 'Sometimes she's an angel and sometimes she is not quite so angelic.'

Mrs Blunkett laughed and went back inside. Zidra's attention was now distracted by a bleached-looking sea urchin shell that someone had left lying on the footpath. She kicked it and watched it bounce down the hill almost as far as their front gate. That had to mean good luck.

CHAPTER THREE

Another Saturday night. By the time George Cadwallader had finished his bath and put on clean pyjamas, Eileen was in bed. She wore a resigned expression and the floral nightdress she'd bought recently to replace that worn-out old thing she'd had for years. After climbing in next to her, he put a hand tentatively on her right breast. He could never get over the miracle that on Saturday nights he was allowed to do this. Then to unbutton the front of her nightdress and put his lips to her nipples, nuzzling them one by one as if he were a hungry baby. Soon he was permitted to slip between her great warm thighs and slide right into her. And feel, for just a few minutes, that he might be wanted.

Tonight he felt her shudder beneath him, as if he'd brought her some pleasure at last. But then she said, 'Get off me, George, you're squashing my chest.'

He rolled onto his side and she wiped between her legs with the yellow and brown striped towel that she slipped over the bottom sheet each Saturday night in readiness for her martyrdom. When she'd finished, she gave the towel to George. This was his cue to get out of bed and put the towel in the wicker laundry basket that was kept in the corner of their bedroom.

It had to be pushed right to the very bottom, under the clothes that had been accumulating all week ready for the Monday wash. Afterwards, he got a face washer from the linen cupboard in the hall and took it into the bathroom. The water had to run for a minute or so before it was hot enough. Then the face washer had to be soaked, squeezed and carried back into the bedroom. When Eileen had finished wiping herself clean of all trace of him, he took the washer back into the bathroom and rinsed it under hot running water; rinsed it until all smell of him had gone. Then he hung it on the pipe underneath the washbasin to dry. By morning it would have vanished, whipped away by Eileen to be stowed somewhere until wash day.

When this cleansing was over, George turned off the light and climbed into bed next to Eileen. 'I love you,' he said, distinctly if a little awkwardly, as he had done every Saturday evening of their married life.

'Goodnight, George,' she said, as she had done over these past six hundred Saturdays.

He felt faintly disappointed. Perhaps he had imagined that her shudder represented pleasure, but even if it had, he shouldn't have expected that she might be able to say more. That she might be able to say, 'I love you.'

Late the following Monday, George and his assistant – known locally as The Boy, although he was pushing thirty – completed their daily rites, whereby the afternoon was transformed into evening and The Boy allowed to go home. The meat was put away in the cold room, the slabs and chopping boards were washed down, and the floor was swept and scrubbed. The Boy sprinkled fresh sawdust over it and was blessed by a smile from his employer, together with a nice piece of tripe.

Now George was alone. After locking up the till, he peered out the shopfront window. The top of the window displayed the large hand-painted cow that he'd commissioned from an itinerant artist a few years ago. Eileen hadn't been happy with that cow. It wasn't normal, she'd said. Too fat, and besides, why waste good money on decoration when he had four mouths to feed? Jim and Andy were always hungry and growing too, and their lounge-room furniture was so shabby she was ashamed to bring anyone home. Why waste good money on a painting for his shopfront window when people would buy his meat anyway? They didn't need any inducement. He was the only butcher, after all, and she would have preferred it anyhow if he'd had a nice clean white collar job.

He'd guessed what she'd really meant; that she regretted marrying him instead of that spotty young bank clerk she'd been going with before she met him, before they'd quite literally bumped into one another at the Royal Agricultural Show, in front of the piles of vegetables, the marrows and pumpkins and whatever, arranged as the coat of arms of New South Wales.

It had been love at first sight, at least as far as he was concerned. He had loved her large arms and that slightly bovine face, which had so distracted him that he hadn't noticed the shelf of her hips. They jutted out so far that he had been physically knocked sideways. Then he had looked down at her solid thighs, clad in a flowered blue and yellow dress of some light fabric, although it was April and the weather getting cooler. It had made his mouth water just looking at her standing in her summery dress in front of the piles of vegetables at the Easter Show. Meat and two veg, that's what he liked then, but especially the meat.

George still loved his meat and sausages, and still loved his wife's flesh too, although he was only allowed to handle it once

24

a week. That cow on the shopfront reminded him of her; it had always reminded him of her. It was a portrait of her, though he would never tell her that. Perhaps she was right, it just wasn't normal.

———

George said to Eileen, 'The Boy's getting a bit restless.' This was his way of preparing her for the decision he'd made that afternoon.

'The sooner he starts secondary school the better. October already, so he's only got another four months.' Eileen pulled the baking tin out of the oven. She picked up a fork and used it to prod the leg of lamb rather more viciously than seemed warranted.

'No, not our Jim. The Boy.' George couldn't resist a smile at the sight of the pink juices oozing out of the leg of lamb. Prime meat, that; no doubt about it.

'Oh, you mean The Boy. Silly name. What's he done now?'

'Wants a pay rise. Said he's indispensable.'

'He's only just finished his apprenticeship.'

'That was nine years ago, Eileen, and he *is* pretty well indispensable.'

'He'd have to travel a long way to get a better boss than you.'

George might have smiled at this rare compliment if he didn't suspect that some criticism must follow. Perhaps it would be slower than usual: Eileen was momentarily distracted by the task of turning over the vegetables. She was a marvellous cook; George couldn't fault the orderly way in which she arranged the overturned potatoes and pumpkin pieces. After returning the baking tray to the oven, she wiped her hands on her striped apron and sat down at the kitchen table opposite George. The vee of her neckline exhibited that tantalising cleavage. He longed to touch her; he longed to lay his head on her bosom and hear her say, 'You're a good boss, George, and a good husband too. Give The Boy his raise, I know you think he deserves it, and you couldn't get a better helper. It doesn't matter to me if we delay by a year or two the purchase of that new lounge suite.'

Instead she said, 'You're a good boss, George. Too good, you're too easily exploited.' She didn't look at him while she spoke, but into the distance, as if looking into the future, and a bleak future it seemed to be too. 'People take advantage of you, George. You've got to be tougher.'

Looking again at her lovely bosom, George felt a deep resentment. She wouldn't treat him kindly, although he'd always treated her as a princess; she wouldn't sanction the small salary rise that he knew he must pay The Boy if he wasn't to lose him. She was being short-sighted rather than far-sighted and he wouldn't put up with it. He'd take her advice in one respect though. He would be tough, but with her rather than with The Boy.

'If The Boy goes I won't be able to run my business,' he said. 'I'm going to pay him more because I want to keep him and because he deserves it.' He articulated his words more clearly than usual but the tone in which they were spoken was as gentle as always. 'I'm running the business and I'm going to run it my way.'

After getting up from his chair, he pushed open the fly-screen door slowly, as if inviting her to say, 'Shut the door, George, you're letting in the flies.' For a moment he hesitated. Then he let the door slam shut before descending the steps from the back verandah and limping across to the wood pile.

He'd done it. He'd stood up to Eileen. Later he'd have to pay for this; he had in the past on those rare occasions when he'd dug his heels in. At least The Boy would be kept happy. At least Cadwallader's Quality Meats would be able to carry on as before. The Boy deserved a raise, George had absolutely no doubt about that. He sat down on the chopping block and smoked a cigarette while watching the chickens scratching around in their yard.

After a while he pulled out of his pocket the little book about the constellations of the Southern Hemisphere that he'd carried with him everywhere since the war. Once the Japs had bombed Darwin, the army no longer cared about the gammy leg he'd got pranging a motorbike at seventeen. They'd sent him to the Northern Territory where he'd found that being a mess orderly suited him. He didn't mind the heat and his genial nature meant he was well liked. He'd taken to gazing at the stars on the nights he could get away from the camp, limping off into the spinifex, away from the racket of the generators and the dim yellow lights. There he would find some quiet spot and gaze heavenwards. He'd carried on doing this even after the war had ended, even after he'd been demobbed. The celestial hemisphere was how he referred to it. Only to himself, of course; he would have been laughed at if he'd ever mentioned anything so grand to anyone else.

He smoothed down the tattered cover of the book with his big hands before opening it carefully. Soon he'd need to put a new jacket on it; perhaps in plastic next time. Although he knew its contents off by heart, and could tell anyone who cared to listen all about the constellations, looking at it was almost a religious experience. With great concentration he flicked through its pages.

Some minutes later, he closed the volume. He felt calmer now, as he always did after contemplating the stars, whether on paper or in the sky. The kitchen was empty when he returned to the house. Eileen was sitting in the lounge room ostentatiously turning the pages of *The Women's Weekly*. For a moment he stood in the doorway. Then the telephone in the hallway stuttered into life.

'You answer it, George,' Eileen said, 'instead of holding up the doorway. I'm sure it won't collapse if you let go.'

He picked up the receiver. It was Pat Neville. Once the exchange of pleasantries was over, she said, 'I'd really like to enter your son Jim for the scholarship exam at Stambroke College.'

'That's good news.' George spoke deliberately slowly. He didn't know quite what to think and needed a moment or two to absorb what she'd said. 'Where is it?'

'In Vaucluse, in Sydney. My brother's a teacher there and Jim could stay with him and his wife in Rushcutters Bay while he sat the exam. So the only expense would be getting him there and back. He's a really bright lad, the best I've ever taught and I think he'd have a very good chance. The exam's in early November.'

A glow of pride seemed to start in George's toes and travel slowly up to his chest, where it began to swell and threatened to lift him off the floor. 'Very good of you to think of it,' he said. He almost added that he'd have to talk to the missus but then thought better of it. Eileen wasn't going to be allowed to spoil this moment. He'd present it to her as a done deed.

After hanging up, he went into the lounge room and sat down.

'You're not resting your head on the back of the sofa, are you? The covers have just been cleaned and I don't want any more greasy hair marks.'

George, bolstered up by his news, wasn't going to let this remark get to him, and anyway he knew that it was in retaliation for the incident with The Boy. There'd be another three or four put-downs at least before Eileen would feel she was even. For a moment he said nothing, savouring the words that Miss Neville had spoken.

Eventually curiosity got the better of her. 'Who was that on the phone?'

'Jim's school teacher.'

'Miss Neville?'

'Yes. She wants him to sit for a scholarship exam in Sydney.'

'We don't want any extra expense, George. He wouldn't get it and it would cost a lot to send him to Sydney and back, and to find somewhere for him to stay.'

'It's at Stambroke College, in the Eastern Suburbs.' Carefully watching Eileen's face, George was gratified to see that she was impressed. 'And she said Jim could stay with her brother's family, so there wouldn't be any expense.'

'Apart from getting there and back.'

'That's not much. It was very good of Miss Neville to think of organising all this.'

'Well, it would reflect well on her if he got in,' Eileen said. 'She's not doing it just for his benefit, or ours, you can be sure of that.'

'We've got a bright boy there. A boy to be proud of. Two boys to be proud of. You've done well with them, Eileen.' He could afford to be generous and, anyway, he meant it.

'They're good boys, George, especially Andy. I don't know where Jim gets his brains from, because it's certainly not from you or me, although he does look like you more and more as he gets older.'

George knew this wasn't intended as a compliment, but it seemed unwise to say anything else at this stage. He picked up the newspaper and opened it at the sporting pages, but he just ooked at the lines of print and couldn't focus on them. It was Jim he was thinking of, Jim who would achieve all those things that he had been unable to, Jim who would get away from a mother who – George now admitted it to himself – found her older son as irritating as she found George. On no account would Eileen be able to stop Jim sitting for the exam. George grimaced at the newspaper. Of course he wanted Andy to do well too, but Andy didn't have Jim's abilities.

George gave up all pretence at reading the paper and began to smile at his vision of the man Jim would become. Tall and handsome, the boy was good-looking already. Perhaps he would be a doctor or an architect. Or even a barrister – he had a logical mind – and eventually a judge. Or maybe he'd study science instead, and specialise in astronomy; there'd surely be lots of jobs at that new radio telescope they were planning to build at Parkes.

'I don't know what you're grinning about,' Eileen said.

'I'm not grinning.' Wiping the smile off his face, he put down the newspaper and waited.

'It's too much, George. It's not just the expense of getting Jim to Sydney and back for the exam, you know. It's the uniforms and all those other things he'd need if he got in.'

'We can cover those, Eileen. Think of the savings in food when he's not here.' His heart fluttered a little at this though. He loved both boys but there was something special about Jim that he couldn't quite put his finger on.

'And there's Andy too. It's just not fair.'

'We can't deny Jim his opportunity, Eileen. Andy has other qualities.'

'He paints beautifully. Ever so lifelike. He could do a much better picture of a cow than that horrible thing you've got on your shopfront.'

Just then the two boys burst into the room, to George's great relief.

'What are you talking about?' said Jim.

'When's tea?' Andy asked.

'Now,' said Eileen. 'You'd better both go and wash your hands.' She got up out of her armchair. After the two boys had clattered off to the bathroom, she added, 'You haven't heard the end of this, George, and we're not going to mention this to the boys just yet. And now it's time for you to carve the meat.'

'But I am going to mention it,' George thought to himself as he followed her out into the kitchen.

CHAPTER FOUR

Early the next morning, Jim Cadwallader watched his father lift the axe above his head and bring it down in a wide arc to splinter the block of wood into four smaller pieces. And then again with the next piece, and the next. In a year's time, when you turn twelve, you'll be allowed to chop the wood. That's what Dad had told him, as if it were a treat to look forward to, whereas Jim preferred watching the light sparkle off the lagoon and the swing of the axe as his father thwacked it into the wood. And listening to the sounds of the early morning, the chooks clucking in their yard at the bottom of the garden, the seagulls crying in the distance, and Mum fussing over Andy in the kitchen, just as she'd be fussing over him soon, when this business with the wood was over.

But it seemed this morning would be different. Dad wanted him to hump around a sack of kindling to the reffoes in the next street, their supply would be running out. The Latvians, he called them, although Jim knew that Latvia didn't exist. It was no good telling Dad that though; he just wouldn't accept that it was a part of the USSR.

'Mind you come back here quickly, Jim,' his mother called from inside the house. 'Your breakfast's nearly ready.' How she managed to keep track of him when she was inside and he wa. outside he didn't know. But if you kept quiet and never answered back, you could get away with all sorts of things that Andy, her favourite, couldn't. He was glad of that, for there was nothing he liked more than to roam about – alone or with a few friends – through the bush and the hills and the sand dunes along the beach.

'I want to have a word with you before school,' Dad said, handing him the sack of kindling. 'Maybe we can walk up the hill together after breakfast.' This was a rare event. Must have something on his mind, some misdeed that Jim couldn't even begin to guess at, since his mother was usually the one to make accusations and his father to defend him.

Hoisting the sack of kindling onto one shoulder, he marched along the back lane that was just a set of track marks really, with lush grass growing in the middle and at the edges. On the way he passed Old Charlie walking in the opposite direction. Old Charlie was also carrying a sack over his shoulder, a sack of bulges. Babies, Jim used to think when he was a little kid and believed all those stories the older boys dreamt up to give the younger ones nightmares. Dead babies. Old Charlie nodded and mumbled as he shambled by, but Jim knew better than to think he was talking to him. Barmy Old Charlie nodded and mumbled even when he was on his own. Shell shocked in the Great War, Jim's father had told him, and he'd felt sorry for Old Charlie ever since. Sorry, too, for the sack of dead rabbits Old Charlie collected from one or two of the local farms each week and boiled up into stews in his little shack by the creek that was stained brown with the ti-trees. Jim never could eat rabbit; it always made him think of dead babies. Not that he liked meat much anyway. As the son of a butcher, he knew too much about how the carcasses were produced.

erhaps he'd inherited some of his mother's sensibilities, although she didn't take kindly to the difficulty he had chewing and swallowing red meat. That's why he was so thin, she'd said, and he had only himself to blame.

After knocking on the front door of the McIntyres' cottage, he rocked up and down on one of the loose boards of the verandah floor for the pleasure of hearing it squeak. A moment later the door opened and a woman peered out. He'd seen her before only not close up. About the same age as his mum, she was quite a bit thinner, and wearing some strange-looking dressing-gown made of shiny black stuff with two golden dragons on the front. Jeez, he'd be really embarrassed to have his mum open the door in this get-up.

'Good morning,' the woman said in a funny accent. 'You must be Master Cadwallader, the son of George.'

Jim sniggered, and then blushed when he heard himself. 'Jim Cadwallader,' he mumbled. 'Dad said to give you this sack of stuff. Wood for your stove. Said you'd probably have run out by now and this'd make it a bit easier to light.'

The woman seemed really touched, as if he'd brought her chocolates rather than a load of old sticks. She made him come inside and would've given him a cup of milk if he'd let her. After emptying the contents of the sack into the flimsy wooden crate next to the stove, he glanced around. Only then did he see a girl about the same age as Andy, sitting at the table, regarding him as seriously as if she'd never seen a perfectly normal boy before.

'Jim Cadwallader, this is my daughter, Zidra.'

He grinned at Zidra and the formality.

'And I am Mrs Talivaldis. I would ask you to call me Ilona if I thought that your parents might approve, for Mrs Talivaldis is quite a large mouthful and so foreign-sounding. But perhaps

in the circumstances it might be more appropriate for you to
call me Mrs Talivaldis.'

'Mrs Talivaldis,' Jim repeated, wondering for a moment if
he might try saying Ilona next; it had such a lovely ring to it.
Lovely, lonely Ilona. He glanced at Zidra; brown-haired, olive-
skinned Zidra, who had colouring just like his own except for
her eyes, which were a golden brown.

Then Zidra said, 'I saw you coming down the road with
your sack, and I saw an old man going up the road just before,
also with a sack. Are you related?'

Jim couldn't restrain his laughter at this leap of logic. Zidra
looked quite put out until he explained that hessian bags were
what everyone carried stuff about in, stock feed and all sorts
of other stuff, and blimey, if everyone who carried a sack was
related, the whole place would be one big happy family. At this
the girl looked mollified and even smiled a bit, after glancing
first at her mother, who seemed to think it was a joke too; she
was laughing and exposing the pink gums above her slightly
yellow front teeth. This reminded Jim of his mother, and then
his breakfast, which would probably now be quite cold and he
hated cold porridge. Not knowing how to take his leave, he
simply nodded and said, more abruptly than he'd intended,
'Goodbye Mrs Talivitus, Zidra,' and marched out of the kitchen,
collecting the empty sack on the way.

'Talivaldis,' the woman called after him. 'It is most important that you pronounce firmly the 'dee' in the last syllable!'

'Mrs Talivaldis,' he shouted, shutting the front gate behind
him. Already he'd thought of a better name: *The Talivaldis*. It
had a nice ring to it. Only yesterday he'd been looking at a bird
book in the library. The *Spotted or Herbaceous Talivaldis* might
have been the name of one of those exotic birds he'd been
reading about. He began composing in his head, *The Talivaldis*

is a rare and wonderful creature who rears its single young, the Zidra, in a . . . but here he was surprised by a voice from right behind.

'Good morning, Jim.'

It was Cherry Bates, wearing a blue beach coat and carrying a sodden-looking towel. He wished *he* had time for a swim before breakfast. 'Morning, Mrs Bates. Got to get home for breakfast.' He broke into a trot, in case she wanted to know what he was doing visiting the reffoes' house so early in the morning.

After Jim had finished breakfast, he watched Andy run off with some friends to take the long way to school. 'Better get going now, Dad,' he said. You had to leave that much earlier if you were walking with a man who limped. Not that Jim minded. He minded more when Mum said, 'Forgetting your lunch, Jim? You'd forget your head if it wasn't screwed on.'

This morning, once they'd got out the front gate and finished discussing the weather – going to be ninety degrees today, that's a bit of a scorcher for this time of the year – he couldn't think of anything to say. Dad seemed distracted too, or maybe he'd forgotten what had been on his mind.

They strolled along the road. There was still dew on the blades of grass at the road's edge, and a freshness to the air in spite of the weather forecast. A honeyeater darted around the shrubs growing in the front garden of one of their neighbours. They stopped for a moment to watch it hover above one of the spidery red flowers. It had a pale yellowish face and its beak was covered in pollen.

'What is it, Dad?'

'A honeyeater.'

'No, what did you want to tell me?'

'Something pretty important, son.'

Jim shuffled his feet. Surely Dad wasn't going to tell him now about the birds and the bees, right in the middle of the street! He already knew all of that reproduction stuff from the times he'd watched bulls service cows, not to mention the pamphlet that one of his friends had shown him, which he'd got from his big sister when she'd started her monthlies. But still in silence they strolled into the square. Jim picked a flower from the dandelion plant flourishing in a crack between two kerbing stones in front of the bakery, and rubbed it between his fingers. Kids were now ahead of them on the road up to the school. Dad appeared unwilling to end the ordeal-by-silence and kept his lips firmly together. Then Jim glanced at his face, creased in concentration, and suddenly felt for him. 'I know all about that stuff,' he said gently.

'What stuff?'

'How babies are made, and all of that.' Jim looked away and blushed. 'Birds and bees.'

'I didn't mean that, son.' You could tell from his voice he was as embarrassed as Jim felt. 'No, I meant the scholarship exam for Stambroke College.'

'Stambroke College?' So this was what the walk to school was about! Jim had already heard a bit about the exam from Miss Neville. He hadn't bothered to mention it at home because he knew Mum wouldn't allow him to take it. *Just think of the expense and bother! Just think of all that, Jim!* He mustn't tell Dad that though. He might be offended.

'It's in Vaucluse in Sydney.' Dad was bursting with pride, Jim could tell from the great beam on his face, as if he'd won something in a raffle. 'Miss Neville's brother teaches there. The scholarship exam's next month. I said she could enter you for it, Jim.'

'You did?' Jim couldn't keep the surprise out of his voice.

'It would mean a trip to Sydney but Miss Neville said you could stay with her brother and his wife. It would be a real adventure for you.'

'On the bus and train?'

'Yes. Mr Neville would collect you from Central Station and drive you to where they live in Rushcutters Bay.'

Mum and Dad allowing him to go to Sydney – Jim could scarcely believe it. He'd been to Sydney only twice before, the four of them squeezed into the tiny Renault they used to own before it conked out and Dad had bought his van. It had been a lengthy trip along the winding Princes Highway up the coast-line and Andy had been carsick for a lot of the way. Every few miles they'd stopped so Andy could puke out the window.

'Terrific!' Jim said but then he thought of Mr Neville and his glow of excitement began to fade slightly. 'Has Mr Neville got any kids?'

'Don't know. Does it matter?'

'Someone to talk to, that's all.'

'You can always talk to Mr and Mrs Neville. I expect they'll speak fluent English.' Dad laughed. Talking to the Nevilles was what Jim dreaded most, though not enough to dampen his spirits for long. He couldn't wait to tell the other kids he was going to Sydney on his own.

They came to a halt outside the school gate just as the bell rang.

'It's quite an opportunity, son.'

'Sure is. Thanks, Dad.' He looked at his feet. His father deserved a great big hug but he couldn't do it here, right in front of the school. Instead, he simply said, 'See you later.' Then he strolled into the schoolyard close behind brother Andy and three other boys.

CHAPTER FIVE

You can't be too careful, Cherry Bates thought that afternoon as she pushed the net curtains to one side and peered into the square. After the darkness of Miss Neville's house, the only two-storeyed building in Jingera apart from the hotel, the harsh sunlight of the late afternoon hurt her eyes. The square outside was empty. It was time to make a quick getaway, as if she was some criminal rather than the wife of jovial Bill Bates the publican.

Absorbed in watching the square, she didn't see the woman and child walking up the hill until they were almost at the war memorial. The woman was slight and pale. A purple hat partially concealed her cloud of curly fair hair. She seemed to have a firm hold of the little girl's hand, as if the child might run away unless restrained. A rather brown little girl, in a brown frock, with brown skin and curly dark hair, but with such a pretty face.

'That must be the McIntyres' new tenants,' she said, 'out for a stroll.'

'Who?'

'The McIntyres' new tenants.'

'Ah, you mean Mrs Talivaldis and Zidra. I met them last week. The girl's starting school soon.'

'You didn't tell me.' Cherry moved closer to the window. 'The woman's wearing a purple hat, Miss Neville.' Although she'd known since the day she met Miss Neville three years ago that her Christian name was Pat, she never called her that. At first she'd felt it sounded too familiar. Later it had become a joke. 'Cloche hat. You must have a look, and she's the sweetest little girl.'

Miss Neville laughed but didn't move. 'Purple hat be buggered,' she said. 'And I'll be seeing more of the "sweetest little girl" in my bloody classroom before long.' Miss Neville liked to swear a bit out of school. Never in the classroom though; she'd soon lose her job if she did that.

Cherry giggled. She liked the hardbitten way Miss Neville talked when there was just the two of them. She watched the sweetest little girl and the purple hat wistfully. Her own clothes always seemed so dowdy and drab, and she'd give anything to have a daughter to look after. Bill would make a lousy father though and she couldn't afford to leave him. Never a shilling to call her own and Bill would have to die before she had any money. 'Over my dead body,' he'd said when she'd asked to be paid for the work she did in the bar.

Turning from the window as the purple hat and the little girl entered the post office, she looked at her reflection in the full-length mirror attached to Miss Neville's wardrobe door. Face not too bad for someone who was closer to thirty than twenty, but her hair was looking a bit over-bleached and it had been a mistake to have that perm. Her eyes skimmed over her naked body – small-waisted, small-breasted – before glancing at Miss Neville's reflection. Sprawled on the unmade bed that was rumpled from their love-making, she was blinking short-sightedly in Cherry's direction. On the bedside table lay her glasses and her short dark hair, usually smoothly combed, was dishevelled.

Cherry felt a catch in her throat. There was something deeply moving about Miss Neville and her clothes, or lack of them. Naked, she was like a different person, as if she threw off her outside personality with her garments. These now lay higgledy-piggledy on the floor where they'd fallen half an hour before, whereas Cherry's were in a neat pile on the chair next to the bed, waiting to be put on. Cherry walked over to the bed and smoothed down Miss Neville's hair, which felt soft and silky. So dark were her eyes that it was hard to distinguish iris from pupil. Cherry ran her forefinger over Miss Neville's finely cut nose, and traced out the line of her brow. Although now she looked far younger than her thirty-four years, in the smart clothes she wore for teaching she always seemed older.

Taking hold of Cherry's wrist, Miss Neville pulled her down onto the bed, and kissed her on the mouth. Feeling her limbs grow heavy and the resolve to leave fading, Cherry gently pushed Miss Neville away and stood up. 'I wish I didn't have to go,' she said. 'But Bill will kill me if I'm late. You know what he's like.'

'A right proper bastard. I don't know why you don't leave him.'

'It's obvious, isn't it? Nowhere else to go.' She laughed, to show she wasn't serious. After all, she could always go back to Burford to live with her mother in that shabby little fibro cottage on the river flat. She certainly couldn't move in with Miss Neville, not that she'd ever asked her to. It was all very well saying she should leave Bill but they never talked about what would happen then. There was no place for the likes of them, apart from in Sydney or Melbourne, but the suggestion for them to leave Jingera together would have to come from Miss Neville.

From the chair she took her knickers, part of a matching set of cream silk underwear that Miss Neville had given her last birthday. Miss Neville remained lying in bed but she put on her spectacles for the next stage of the performance. Without needing to look, Cherry knew she was watching her dress. She always did; that was one of the many things Cherry loved about the school mistress.

After fastening her bra in front of the mirror, she smiled at her reflection. Bill didn't know about these underclothes. He'd lost interest in her years ago. She'd been devastated by that neglect until she'd met Miss Neville. Now she was glad he left her alone. Now she felt revolted at the thought of the act of love with her husband. And revolted too by the sight of him, although everyone else seemed to think he was good-looking and good-natured. Everyone, that is, except for Miss Neville.

Cherry turned from the mirror and picked up the pale blue dress from the chair. She watched Miss Neville's face as she stepped into it and slowly did up the front buttons. Leaning over her lover, she kissed her tenderly on the mouth. 'I'm the luckiest woman in the world to have met you,' she said.

'Oh shit, Cherry, don't come over all weepy on me.' All the same, Miss Neville looked pleased.

Cherry fastened her shoes before giving Miss Neville another kiss. After retrieving a lipstick from her pocket, she repainted her mouth a bright red. Her nose would have to remain shiny. Next the usual routine: clattering down the stairs, peering out of the kitchen window to make sure there was no one in the yard next door, creeping out the door and through the gate leading to the narrow lane behind the houses. An excuse was ready if she met anyone, but so far no one had ever noticed, let alone asked what she was doing. If they did, she'd tell them how she was learning French. 'Je veux parler Français,' she would say. 'Je veux parler Français.'

Miss Neville had taught her the French word for every part of the body and had promised to teach her some verbs next. Cherry started to hum; she couldn't remember knowing such happiness as this. If only she'd met Miss Neville ten years ago at sweet sixteen; if only she'd met her before being swept off her feet by Bill Bates.

But when you came to think of it, she'd been extremely fortunate ever to get to know Miss Neville at all. They might have just continued passing one another in the town, nodding and smiling, for years. It was sheer luck that they'd both happened to be in Burford on that Sunday afternoon nearly three years ago. They'd met at the bus stop and cemented their friendship as the bus trundled along the winding road between Burford and Jingera. Just as they were descending the last hill into Jingera, Miss Neville had invited Cherry to afternoon tea. After that, there had been no looking back, although it had been some months before they'd become lovers. An unlikely friendship, Cherry always thought, between the barmaid and the teacher. And not one that Bill could approve of. He thought Miss Neville was too bossy, and that bossiness might be contagious, like chickenpox or measles. If he knew what she was really like he'd approve of her even less. So would everyone else in town. Corrupting the morals of our kids, they'd say. Just as they'd said all those years ago when she was at Burford Girls' High School when Mr Ryan, the maths teacher at Burford Boys', had got thrown out of his job and the town because he was a poofter. The humiliation if people found out about her and Miss Neville would be impossible to bear. Bill said she cared too much for appearances but it was all very well for him, he hadn't been brought up with his dad beating his mum, and poor Mum trying to pretend everything was okay until one night Dad had just slammed the door behind him and never come back again. Though life was better after he'd gone, Cherry – conventional little girl that she was – pretended to the other kids that he'd gone out west shearing. Couldn't bear anyone to know the family secrets. Thought they'd start to hate her, and so she'd developed her laughing self as a form of protection. If she smiled at people they seemed to respond by unburdening themselves. Smiling was a good defence. Being married to Bill was a good defence too.

Now she slipped into the hotel by the back door and sauntered into the bar. A dozen or so men were drinking there. Bill scowled at her and glanced pointedly at the clock on the wall behind the counter. Again she was repulsed by his appearance: big body, thinning blond hair, ruddy face and thick neck. Funny how things change. She'd thought him so handsome when they first met. Everyone had told her how lucky she was and she'd believed them.

After smiling sweetly at him, she pulled four schooners of beer for a man who seemed to be in no hurry to take them back to his mates. Then she moved around the tables picking up empty glasses. Pausing in front of a window, she peered out at the street. The late afternoon sunlight cast irregular slabs of shadow from the buildings opposite. The curtains of Miss Neville's bedroom were now drawn and there was a lamp on in the sitting room downstairs, although more than that she could not see. Further down the hill, the woman with the purple hat and her child were leaving the post office.

Bill came out from behind the bar and stood in the doorway overlooking the square. 'There are the reffoes,' he said loudly. 'Been here for over a week now and hardly been out at all. The woman's spent the whole time scrubbing out the house and playing the piano, Mrs Blunkett said, but I saw the kid hanging around outside the post office the other day.'

All of the drinkers, even the most morose or loquacious, gave up what they were doing and flocked to the windows. Cherry seized the opportunity to dash into the hallway. She took a compact out of the drawer in the hallstand. In the bar the men were now commenting so loudly it was a wonder the reffoes didn't hear.

'Jeez, have a perv at that,' said one. 'Wouldn't mind gettin'' stuck into 'er.'

'Good looker, sport. Where'd ja say they were from?'

'Didn't. Just bloody reffoes from Sydney.'

'Better than bloody Abos, eh?'

'Yeah, the reffoes work and the coons don't.'

'What're they doing down here? The season don't start till November. Don't get no holidaymakers from Sydney this time of year.'

'Dunno. Why doncha ask? Satisfy your curiosity the bloody obvious way.'

In the hallway Cherry finished powdering her face. Silly gossips, she thought as she slipped the compact back into the drawer; far worse than a bunch of women. For a moment more she stood listening as the conversation continued.

'Poor little kid looks a bit lost.'

'Sydney, you say they're from?'

'Yeah, but they're reffoes from Europe. Husband dead. She's a widow.'

The men sobered up a bit at this. Probably thinking it could have been one of them or one of their sons, Cherry thought. Could have been their widow and daughter beached up in Jingera.

Slipping out the side door onto the verandah, she found she was too late to meet the reffoes. They were walking on the other side of the road, heading down the hill towards the McIntyres' cottage and not into the square as she'd hoped. Then the woman and the girl both turned at the same time and looked straight at Cherry, who smiled and waved. The woman hesitated before waving back. The girl had an engaging grin.

She watched the pair walk down the hill and turn into the front gate of the McIntyres' cottage, a shack rather than cottage, held together more by vines than nails. A bit like the place she'd grown up in, only that didn't have the vines.

The clock struck the quarter hour. Back in the bar, she collected empty glasses and wiped down the messier tabletops. Then, putting on a bright smile, she returned to the serving side of the counter to take more orders.

CHAPTER SIX

Six feet underground were bones. Catholic bones, Protestant bones. But none of the other denominations. Ilona picked her way around the listing gravestones and the signs partitioning the faiths. The cemetery, on the top of the headland, was bound on the cliff side by a white-painted fence. Beyond that, on a narrow ribbon of land, bloomed blue-flowering shrubs of a type she'd never come across before. Standing here she could see in all directions. To the north lay the long yellow arc of the next beach, ending in another headland that looked not dissimilar to this. To the east the ocean swelled endlessly in. To the south stretched Jingera Beach, a sweep of sand rising into high sand dunes. Behind the dunes lay a wide strip of dense bush that separated the beach from the lagoon. Jingera was built in the wrong place, she thought. It would surely have been more convenient for everyone if it was at the southern end of the beach with easier road access. It must have been located here for other reasons; someone had fallen in love with the view, or the fishing was perfect, or the river convenient. Although she knew by now that not everything could be explained by logic, by one event leading inexorably to the next.

Seated on the top rail of the fence, she could see the school, where Zidra was at this moment, a clutch of houses and, beyond them, the roof of the hotel.

A headland was a strange place to bury people, she felt, with a panorama that the dead would never see. *Man is born astride a grave.* Samuel Beckett had been Oleksii's favourite playwright. There, she had thought of Oleksii again when she had promised herself she would not. Despite being in Jingera for several weeks, she had avoided the headland until today. She hadn't wanted to be reminded of Oleksii. She looked again at the signs segregating parts of the graveyard. Years ago she had converted to Catholicism in a half-hearted sort of a way, for Oleksii's sake, and now he was buried six feet under in the Catholic section of Rookwood Necropolis.

Breathing deeply, she tried to distract herself from these thoughts by listing all the good things about Jingera. When she had finished, and the list was rather long, she began again. By now tears were obliterating the view; she pulled out a handkerchief and wiped them away.

It was no longer possible to deny that she felt more lonely now than in those first few weeks after Oleksii's death. A death that had been so sudden. How could she have guessed that what appeared to be a mild cold might turn into pneumonia? One day he'd staggered home from the factory at lunchtime, lurching so much that initially she'd wondered if he was drunk, although putting a hand to his burning skin soon disabused her of this. So high was his temperature that an egg might have been fried on his forehead. So delirious, too, that his incoherent ranting was impossible to interpret. At one point he'd even become violent, imagining she was some assailant from his soldiering days, and so she'd given up trying to put him to bed. Eventually she'd convinced him to lie on the sofa while she dashed out to find the doctor. By the time she returned he was only partially conscious and struggling to breathe. The doctor prescribed sulpha drugs – pink cubes that were supposed to be swallowed in batches of six – but Oleksii had been unable to keep them down. That whole night she'd lain awake beside him, sponging him when he became even hotter, and trying once more with the drugs.

Early the next morning the doctor had visited again but it was too late. Afterwards he explained that asphyxiation had killed Oleksii. Pockets of pus around the lungs had made it impossible for him to breathe. That the delirium would have insulated him from any awareness of what was happening was at least some comfort to her. Why this illness had come on so quickly she did not understand. Most likely Oleksii had felt ill for days and had simply not bothered to tell her. His detachment had dated from soon after they arrived in Australia but it was something that he could not, or would not, talk about. Disappointment, she had guessed, that he could not get a job as a musician. Working in the biscuit factory was probably a bit like a prison sentence to him.

She dried her eyes and looked out over Jingera township. She could just see her cottage, its roof a splash of rusty corrugated iron in the dense foliage that surrounded it. A sea hawk sailed into view. It wheeled around the headland, gliding on some updraft, and drifted north over the long crescent of beach towards the next headland.

After a time Ilona retraced her steps through the cemetery and down the road past the school. Inside, children were singing to the accompaniment of a slightly out-of-tune piano. She sighed. So far there hadn't been a single enquiry about the piano lessons. Her funds were going down; slowly, it was true, for living in Jingera was cheap, but she would have to get some pupils soon if she wasn't to eat too much into her savings.

Passing the hotel, she exchanged a greeting with sweet-faced Cherry Bates, who was washing the hotel verandah floor. She would have liked to stop and talk but didn't feel able. In spite of what George Cadwallader had said about Cherry's interest in the piano, she hadn't approached Ilona about lessons. On through the town she walked, past her house, screened from the road by a dense hedge, and down the hill to the lagoon. There she turned along the track to the jetty.

It wasn't until almost reaching the end of the jetty that she noticed the man sitting on the steps leading down to the water. She stopped at once. Never had she seen a full-blooded Aborigine before and she couldn't help staring. Never had she seen such black skin.

He glanced up and smiled.

Smiling back, she rested one hand on the splintered jetty railing. Dressed in ragged clothes, he continued to look her way although not directly at her. One hand held a fishing line and next to him was a bucket whose contents she could not see.

'I am Mrs Talivaldis,' she said eventually. Her words seemed to hover rather awkwardly in the air. 'We have recently moved here from Homebush in Sydney. Before that we lived in England and before that in Latvia. We are refugees.'

'Tommy Hunter,' the man said. Although he didn't seem disposed to add anything else, Ilona realised she would like to establish some sort of communication. Why, she didn't understand; perhaps it was because she felt so lonely or because his silence seemed friendly.

'What do you do, Tommy?' This was too direct; she realised at once that it could be construed as impertinence.

'Fish, and when I'm not fishin' I pick beans.'

'Where do you pick beans?'

'Wherever they need pickin'. 'Ere, there and everywhere.' The man shrugged.

An itinerant bean picker. That was the sort of job Oleksii would have been doing if he were here with her; he would have been looking for a job as a *peripatetic* labourer.

And perhaps she would be looking for work like that soon if she didn't get any pupils. Leaning on the jetty railing, she looked across the water. In the middle of the lagoon was a white painted timber post and on the top of this a pelican was balanced. Its beak was the colour of a fragile rose, the palest pink.

She found she wanted to tell Tommy about Oleksii. The Aborigine was unlikely to spread what she had to say all round the town. 'My husband died in Sydney,' she said slowly. 'He hated it there. He was a musician, a composer. He worked in a biscuit factory though.' She hesitated and glanced at Tommy, but all she could see now was the back of his head. Dark wavy hair covered the collar of his shabby black jacket, which must once have been part of someone's best suit.

'No one cared much for Oleksii's music, either in Sydney or in England,' she said. 'He was ahead of his time. And became increasingly unhappy with his work at the factory, and with the need to feed our daughter and me.'

Tommy now pulled in a fish. Averting her eyes, she inspected the bushes on the other side of the water; she had heard them described as ti-tree. Behind that grew some stringy trees that she intended to identify one day with the tree book she'd seen in the library.

'Good tucker,' Tommy said. She understood that he meant the fish.

'My husband couldn't get work in an orchestra,' she said, when Tommy had cast his re-baited line back into the water. 'And he didn't want to teach. He wanted to write music. So he went to work in the biscuit factory, but he wasn't happy there and he wasn't happy at home. He had become a very unhappy man. That found its way into his music, and it is a strange thing how so much unhappiness can make such good music.' Perhaps one day in the future she would play his music again. But not yet, not for some time yet. The pelican was still balanced on top of the post. It looked as if it were contemplating something profound but it was probably waiting for one of Tommy's rejected fishes.

'Now I must go,' she said at last. 'I thank you for listening to me.'

The man mumbled something in reply and it was only when she had walked the length of the jetty that she realised what he had said. She turned around but he was not visible from the shore. To show that she had understood, she shouted his words back at him:

'We are both refugees,' she called. Then she saw, above the boards at the end of the jetty, a black hand waving a farewell.

It was only later, when she was almost back at the cottage, that she wondered if Tommy might actually have been offering her a fish for tea. *Fish for tea; refugee.* It was all too easy to misunderstand and be misunderstood.

CHAPTER SEVEN

Cherry Bates stood in the side entrance to the hotel and watched the children streaming down the hill. When she heard footsteps behind her, she didn't need to turn to know they were Bill's. He stood so close to her she could feel his breath on her hair. She stepped forward one pace.

'Lovely little kiddies,' he said and sighed.

'Noisy little blighters.' Cherry didn't want to encourage any sentimentality. 'I bet Miss Neville's glad to see the last of them. Rather her than me any day, even though you work me like a navvy here.' She laughed though. There were a few customers in the bar and she didn't want them to think she wasn't a good sort. Wouldn't be good for business, and the good Lord knew they could do with more business. It might stop Bill griping on about all the expenses and maybe they could fix some of the rotting woodwork and get the wiring redone. Bill reckoned the wiring was fine but she wasn't so sure. She'd always been a bit nervous about living in a weatherboard building, ever since she was a kid and the house two doors up had caught on fire, and the old lady who'd lived there burned to death. In her sleep, Cherry's mum maintained; she hadn't stubbed out a cigarette properly. So each night Cherry prowled around the hotel after ten o'clock closing, checking and rechecking that all the ashtrays were empty and that there were no cigarette butts smouldering anywhere. At least Bill didn't smoke, thank God.

'The Cadwallader boy'll be off to high school next year,' Bill remarked, as Jim Cadwallader passed by in a knot of his friends, skinny boys mostly, with legs too long for their bodies.

'Bright boy. Scholarship material,' Cherry reported, but softly because this might not be common knowledge and brightness didn't always win friends.

'How do you know?'

Cherry wished she hadn't said anything. The last thing she should be doing was over-quoting Miss Neville, whom Bill didn't like. Education and women don't mix, he was fond of saying. 'I can't remember who told me,' she prevaricated.

'Probably George's missus. She's always keen to blow the old trumpet.'

'Yes, but all she plays is Andy Andy Andy. Have you noticed?'

'Can't say I have,' replied Bill.

'I feel quite sorry for Jim.' It was his grazed knees that made him look vulnerable. She'd seen him and his friends in the late afternoon, racketing down the hill to the lagoon in their billy-carts, flimsy affairs made out of packing cases and odd bits of sawn timber they'd managed to scrounge.

'There goes Mrs Talivaldis. Only woman in the town to collect her kid from school.' Bill never had approved of what he called mollycoddling.

'I guess losing most of your family makes you cling on to what's left.'

'She lost all her family?'

'Yes, in the war. Except for her husband, who died in Sydney apparently. Of a broken heart and pneumonia, she told George Cadwallader.'

'Perhaps there was no husband.'

'You're always on the lookout for the worst interpretation, Bill Bates.' Cherry laughed again, to take the sting out of the words. She liked the Latvian woman and the funny way she spoke, as if finding the right word was an impossible battle. She could well have been running away from something but it wasn't to conceal her lack of a husband. 'I've seen a photograph of the husband,' Cherry added. 'She showed it to me when I dropped around with a jar of plum jam yesterday afternoon.'

'Does she look like him?'

'Who?'

'The daughter, of course. Does she look like the father?'

'Yes, quite like him.' Mrs Talivaldis' lounge room was dark and she'd carried the framed photograph to the window so that Cherry could see it more clearly. It was a wedding photograph. The man was short with curly brown hair growing away from his forehead. Dressed in a dark double-breasted suit, he was looking directly at the camera. He'd worn a rather puzzled expression, as if to ask what he was doing in the photograph. Next to him stood a smiling Mrs Talivaldis, in a white dress with lace around the neckline and a skirt with stitched-down pleats that emphasised the slenderness of her hips.

'Both parents with curly hair, but one dark and one fair,' Cherry said. 'Inevitable that the daughter should have curls. She's got the father's colouring. She looks more like him than her mother. Why do you ask?'

'No reason. Just idle curiosity.'

Cherry glanced at him leaning on one of the verandah posts. His eyes were slits against the glare. She could never work out what he was thinking, but now was probably as good a time as any to tell him about her decision. She took a deep breath and said, 'I thought of having some piano lessons. Mrs Talivaldis put a notice in the post office window.' Her voice quavered a bit but Bill didn't seem to notice.

'What do you want to learn the piano for?'

'I've always wanted to. Oh, please let me learn, Bill. It's something I've wanted to do for years.' Bill hesitated long enough for her to know he was thinking seriously of it. 'They're a musical family,' she added. 'The father was a pianist, Mrs Talivaldis said, and the little girl Zidra sings divinely.' This last bit was a fabrication on her part but she sensed that it might influence Bill.

'We haven't got a piano.'

'That doesn't matter. I could practise on the school one after the kids go home.' This was what she wanted, of course, but you had to be a bit devious when you were dealing with Bill. If only he would agree, she'd be able to spend four afternoons a week up at the school. Although she'd have to keep up the pretence of practising, that wouldn't be necessary all the time. Maybe ten minutes out of thirty, and that would leave twenty to be spent with Miss Neville. If she appeared too eager, though, Bill might guess what she was after. She added, 'Or maybe Mrs Coles would let me use her piano. She loves seeing me and I think she's a bit lonely living on her own.'

'Better if you use the school one,' Bill said at once. 'Mrs Coles would keep you nattering half the afternoon afterwards.'

'That's good of you, Bill.' She could have danced with joy and might have hugged him if he'd been anyone else, but instead she simply smiled sweetly. 'Mum always said I could learn the piano when I was a kid, but it was always next year. And when next year came around, it was the year after.'

'That no-good father of yours,' Bill muttered. 'Your mother was better off without him.' Then he added casually, 'Has the Talivaldis woman got any other pupils?'

'Don't know. I haven't mentioned this to her yet. Thought I should ask you first.'

'Does the little girl play?'

'I don't know, Bill.'

'You'll have to get out another jar of your plum jam and pay another visit.' He laughed, rather nastily she thought, glancing at him. He appeared as inscrutable as before but her heart lurched at the possibility that he might know where she went after her jam deliveries. She looked away again, towards the street. Just then the old lady from up by the cemetery hobbled by and Cherry waved at her.

Bill said, 'You must be just about out of plum jam. You're always running around trying to off-load it.'

'I've got lots more jars of jam left,' she said lightly. 'Anyway, I thought you liked me doing it,' she added. 'Good for business if the publican's wife is a bit sociable.' The ugly corrugated iron walls of the old Masonic hall opposite caught her attention. They had acquired two new posters. One was about the Christmas dance at the church hall and the other was about the bushfire danger. That's how you knew summer was here, when the posters started going up. Earlier and earlier every year. It was still two months to go till Christmas and already they were planning for the dance and, if she wasn't mistaken, they'd moved the date forward too.

She sighed. Surely there was no way Bill could guess what she got up to with Miss Neville. He didn't have the imagination and even if he did, she doubted he would care. Their marriage had gone beyond all that. What would concern him much more would be Cherry getting ideas above herself through associating with Miss Neville. Practising the piano at the school would afford many opportunities of bumping quite spontaneously into the schoolmistress and she needed these. They made her life here bearable. It wasn't just the physical side of things, it was the friendship.

Time to get back to work. She glanced around at Bill, who was still standing behind her. Through the open door Les Turnbull was visible, waiting patiently at the bar counter. He must have come in through the other entrance and she wondered how long he'd been there. 'G'day, Les,' she called out. 'Sorry to keep you waiting.'

She hurried inside to pull a middy of New for Les, while half-listening to his complaints. Today they were mostly focused on the Commie bastards, excuse the English, Cherry.

CHAPTER EIGHT

Zidra hadn't enjoyed her first week at school but at last it was over. While Lorna had looked after her to begin with, today she'd been away and that made things seem much worse. And now, to top it off, here was her mother waiting at the school gate again, even though Zidra had especially asked her not to. The only parent in sight, her clothes suddenly appeared odd to Zidra. She'd got on that funny straw hat without the crown and her dress was shouting *look-at-me* with its red and orange flowers and the hem dipping slightly. This afternoon she'd pretend not to know her, this strange foreign woman.

Zidra attached herself to a group of children who were pushing through the gate, laughing and shoving at one another. She would walk straight down the hill with all the other children, clutching her cardboard school-case that, although so new, had already absorbed the smells of stale lunch and musty classroom. If she went very fast, she'd be able to get rid of the sandwich she'd hidden at lunchtime in her bloomers when no one was looking, and then Mama would never find out. The bloomers had tight elastic round the legs and formed a useful pocket. The sandwich had been there all afternoon, making her hot and flapping against her leg when she moved.

She didn't know how Mama could have put nasturtium leaves on a Vegemite sandwich. 'You will love it,' her mother had said. 'Nasturtium leaf tastes just like watercress. We had it growing in the stream at home when I was a girl, and how your Papa loved it too, darling Zidra.'

Zidra knew that Your Papa, as invoked by her mother, bore no resemblance to the Papa that she'd known, or even to that other Father, Who Art in Heaven. Zidra remembered her Papa as the man who wasn't there. He wasn't there all day and he wasn't there at night either. He'd barely exchanged two words each day with her. If it hadn't been for the trip to the circus, she might almost have been glad that he had gone away. To heaven, Mrs McIntyre had said, and that had confused Zidra for a while, for she knew that Papa was not Thou Father Who Art in Heaven but Thou Papa Who Art in Heaven. There were two of them there now. But Papa had taken her to the circus and the other father had not. The one who had taken her to the circus had enjoyed it almost as much as she had, and had bought her fairy floss afterwards, lovely sticky-sweet stuff that was pinker than anything she'd ever seen before.

Zidra, salivating as she thought of the fairy floss, was brought abruptly back to the present. 'Zidra!' Mama called out. 'Look, darling, I'm over here!' She stooped to give her two big kisses, one on each cheek, right in front of all the grinning children.

Zidra flushed in anger and in embarrassment. Already she could hear red-haired Roger O'Rourke, with whom she shared a desk, imitating her mother. *Look dorlink, I am over here!* All the other boys sniggered. To give them time to move away, she bent down and pretended her shoelaces were undone. Then, looking at her mother, she saw that her eyes were swimming with tears. Zidra guessed this was her fault and took a deep breath. Mama should know better than this by now. Surely she should have learnt to hide her feelings. Zidra glanced from her mother to the other children but they were no longer looking this way. Engaged in kicking stones down the road, they'd forgotten all about the wogs.

Still she felt angry. 'I hate Vegemite and nasturtium sandwiches,' she cried, pulling at the elastic around the right leg of her bloomers and yanking out the horrid-looking sandwich, only partially wrapped in greaseproof paper. So roughly did she tug at it that the elastic snapped back on her legs and hurt. The sandwich landed on the ground in front of her mother. They both stared at it. Squashed flat, it looked like a piece of cardboard. Mama would surely strike her, her face had become so crimson. Zidra would have to act first. Hurling herself at her mother, she hugged her legs. Although unable to make the tears come, if she hid her face Mama would imagine that she was crying. How she hated school, she blurted out through the stuff of her mother's skirt. The boys were nasty and the girls all had friends and wouldn't play with her! Except for Lorna, that is, and she'd been away today. And when Zidra had played with her, the others called her a nigger-lover. That didn't sound nice, whatever it was.

'No, that is not nice,' said Mama, her face now restored to its natural pallor. She fumbled in her bag for a handkerchief, and then cuddled Zidra and kissed her hair. 'That is not nice at all.'

Zidra let her mother wipe her face, certainly reddened by emotion if not by tears, and submitted to having her hair ribbon retied. Mama, distracted by this, would forget all about the business with the Vegemite sandwich. Maybe she'd even consider letting Zidra stay away from school next week.

Her mama lapsed into Latvian, which normally she spoke only inside their house, to say, 'You must not care what people say or think. You must do only what you think is right.'

Zidra puzzled over this advice. She did try not to care what people said, but often what they said was unfair. It was surely right to stand up to people when they were unkind, but when she did what she thought was right, she got into fights. And sometimes what she thought was right was not the same as what her mother thought was right. While pondering this, she pulled at one end of her hair ribbon, and absent-mindedly fed it into her mouth.

'Don't suck your hair ribbon,' Mama said at once. Sometimes she seemed to know what Zidra was up to without even looking at her. 'If you're feeling better, perhaps we might go home now.'

They were too late. 'Mrs Talivaldis! Mrs Talivaldis!' Miss Neville was striding across the school playground. One arm was raised in a wave while the other was weighed down with a large basket of exercise books. 'Good afternoon, Mrs Talivaldis,' she said, looking quite friendly now she had caught up with them. 'Glad to see you. Wanted to let you know your daughter's had a good week.' She bared her teeth in a grin. 'And her arithmetic will improve with hard work.'

Hard work; Zidra didn't like the thought of that. Endless reciting of multiplication tables was not her idea of fun. Even worse was being dragged out to the front of the class by the ear, as had happened to Roger O'Rourke that morning. He'd then been made to recite the seven times table and hadn't been able to get beyond seven fours without making a mistake. If he hadn't deserved to be humiliated, she might have felt sorry for him, but only two minutes earlier he'd wiped snot on the wooden pencil box she'd placed in the middle of the desk they shared.

Miss Neville stopped in front of them. Beads of perspiration stood out on her upper lip. She looked at Zidra and said, 'You must ignore those more obnoxious children, my dear.

They'll be used to you in a week or two. The Jingeroids are always a bit resistant to change.'

Mama laughed but Zidra didn't. Although she was grateful to the teacher for her kindness, she guessed that what was said to parents differed from what was said to *obnoxious* children, of whom she must certainly be one. However she quietly mouthed to herself the new words. Obnoxious and Jingeroids. Later she would use Jingeroid. It made such a lovely sound and it had made Mama laugh too.

The three of them walked down the hill together. Her mother and Miss Neville chatted about somewhere called Hungary while Zidra picked flowering soldier grass from the side of the road. She amused herself by looping the stem around the flower and then firing the head by pulling the loop quickly down the stem. Miss Neville left them in the square. Zidra fired a soldier head at her backside. It missed, as she knew it would, and Mama chose not to notice.

There was a large truck parked around the side of the hotel. Mr Bates was standing next to it, taking delivery of beer. He winked at Zidra when he saw her. If she didn't have Mama with her, she was sure that he would have offered her a rainbow ball.

'He's certainly good-looking,' Mama said after they had gone by. 'But as my own mama always used to say, never trust a good-looking man.'

She must have got wind of the rainbow balls somehow.

'His wife is lovely,' she added. 'It was so kind of her to bring us that homemade jam yesterday.'

It wasn't the rainbow balls after all. Zidra started skipping. Some things you just had to keep secret and eating lollies was one of them.

CHAPTER NINE

Ilona was playing a Chopin Prelude when a tentative knocking from the front of the house caught her attention. She paused; perhaps it was just the breeze tapping the vines against the verandah roof. Then she heard the noise again. Someone was knocking on the flyscreen door. She stood up and ran her fingers through her hair; playing the piano seemed always to make it stand on end. When she opened the front door she was surprised to see Cherry Bates standing there.

'How *delightful* to see you again.' There, she'd done it once more, used a long word when *nice* would have done just as well. 'You will come in, won't you? I can make you some *nice* tea.'

'It's a really busy time in the pub just now,' Cherry said, a little breathlessly. Although she seemed agitated, she paused for a moment before adding, 'I just wanted to ask you if you'd be willing to teach me the piano.'

Ilona couldn't conceal her excitement. Her first pupil was to be this woman with the bright red lipstick and lovely blonde hair.

'I've never learnt before so it will be hard work for you.' Cherry looked away, apparently at the orange trumpet flowers hanging off the verandah roof. She picked one and twirled it in her fingers.

'I shall be delighted to teach you.' Ilona did not wish to seem too excited, for she could see that Cherry was a little embarrassed. She fought back an impulse to embrace her prospective new pupil.

'I expect I've got no talent,' Cherry said, 'but I've always wanted to learn. Miss Neville said I could practise on the school piano after the kids have gone home.'

'Everyone has some musical ability,' Ilona said with great conviction. 'It is just that some have a little more than others. Even for someone with the genius of my own Oleksii, it is . . .' She paused. She had been going to say *imperative* but that would not do. 'It is advisable,' she continued, 'that many hours are spent each day in practice.'

'Oh, but I wouldn't be able to do that.' Cherry looked shocked. 'No, I could only practise at most four times a week.'

'Practising four times a week will be enough, for a concert pianist you are not aiming to be. And of course you are not young enough to learn to play other than with competence.' At once Ilona realised she might have caused offence. No one liked to be considered too old and especially not such a pretty young woman as Cherry. 'I did not mean that as it sounds,' Ilona added, lightly touching Cherry's arm. 'How can I yet say what your playing will be like?'

But Cherry did not appear to have noticed any slight. 'Bill can spare me for an hour each afternoon. I work in the bar in the afternoons and evenings.' She laughed. 'How often should I have lessons?'

She laughed too much, Ilona decided. It was a nervous mannerism rather than an indication of amusement. 'Once a week,' Ilona said. Perhaps the piano lessons represented an escape from the hotel and that husband of hers, who must be closer to fifty than forty, but that did not matter. Music was an escape for everyone.

After Cherry had gone, Ilona danced around the lounge room to a jazz tune in her head. Cherry would become her friend, and surely news of the value of her piano lessons would spread. And recommendations would follow and then more pupils would come.

———

The following morning Ilona visited the post office. She had done this every day since her advertisement first appeared in the window. Every morning she had heard the same refrain from Mrs Blunkett: no telephone calls and no enquiries.

However this morning was different. Mrs Blunkett's voice quavered with excitement and even broke altogether at one point as she transmitted the news. Mrs Chapman had dropped in the previous afternoon to post a parcel, it must have been when Ilona was out walking. Mrs Blunkett couldn't help but notice what her neighbours were doing, with her shop looking up and down the street. And even if she didn't have such good eyesight then she'd hear from her customers what people were up to. You only had to blink an eye in Jingera and the whole town would know, though there were some things she'd never tell anyone. But she was wandering right off the point, she'd got a bit overexcited, and she mustn't forget Mrs Chapman's message. She was an important lady from one of the bigger properties inland, Woodlands, it was called, and she wanted Ilona to visit there tomorrow.

'It is short notice,' Ilona said. 'What does she want with me?'

'The piano lessons,' Mrs Blunkett explained. 'I thought I said. I would've dropped a note in to you but I was that busy yesterday. She wants you to teach her son. He's only six but

Mrs Chapman said he's musical. Been learning from a woman down Merimbula way but she's moved on. I told her about your daughter and you being a widder, like, and she said you could bring her along. A car'll collect you at four o'clock.'

A car will collect you, how exciting that sounded! Ilona beamed at Mrs Blunkett, might even have kissed her if she were not out of reach on the other side of the counter.

'She wants you to take proof,' Mrs Blunkett continued, rather officiously now, as if she, like Mrs Chapman, had doubts about a qualification from some place behind the Iron Curtain. 'A piece of paper, like. Something to show what you know.'

'I have nothing left.' But Ilona would not have this opportunity taken away from her. Some way around this obstacle would have to be found. Although she did not want to be reminded of all that was lost, she felt it necessary to explain the situation to Mrs Blunkett. 'Everything from those days was destroyed. Papers and identities and people too.' Her voice was rising; she must not get overexcited, she must not behave as she had done when Zidra was being interviewed by Miss Neville. After taking a deep breath, she lowered her voice to say quite calmly, 'But it will not matter, Mrs Blunkett, for I will play for this Mrs Chapman, and then she will see if I am good enough for her little boy.'

Ilona hadn't expected Woodlands to be quite so grand, nor had she anticipated there would be a housekeeper and maid as well as the chauffeur. After Zidra had been whisked off to the kitchen by the housekeeper, plump, pleasant-faced Mrs Jones, Ilona followed the maid along the dark hallway and into the drawing room.

'You must be Mrs Talivaldis.' At the far end of the room, Mrs Chapman was standing next to a baby grand piano. Dressed entirely in white, she extended her right arm in a theatrical gesture of welcome. She did not move to meet Ilona halfway but remained as motionless as a statue. A beautiful woman who is used to being observed rather than observing, Ilona thought as she marched across the Persian rug in her shabby navy crepe dress with the detachable white collar which, together with her purple hat, might well have slipped awry in the fracas that had occurred when she and Zidra had arrived.

Mrs Chapman's pallor was accentuated by the gash of red that was her mouth and the improbable red fuzz of her hair, and also by the long red talons that Ilona was now grasping, for it seemed she must shake her hand. Mrs Chapman simply let flesh touch flesh and then extricated herself quickly, leaving Ilona wondering if her hand were so clammy that the other had not wished to hold it for longer than absolutely necessary.

'So good of you to come, Mrs Talivaldis. Do sit down while we have our little talk. I'm sure you'll quite understand that I must ask you for your credentials.' Mrs Chapman arranged herself on a dark green brocade chaise longue and gestured towards the armchair next to her.

'You wish to know about me before you entrust to me the tuition of your son. That I do understand.' Ilona sat down and was almost swallowed up by the soft upholstery of the armchair, which was intended for someone much larger than her. She wriggled free of the enveloping cushions and perched towards the front, with her feet planted firmly on the carpet. 'It is possible that you might wish me to play something for you, so that you can establish if I have any talent. For me that would be preferable. You must appreciate that, unfortunately, I have mislaid all my certificates that indicate that I am who I say I am.' She faltered; her English was becoming convoluted and she feared she was in danger of losing Mrs Chapman.

However Mrs Chapman was looking intently at her. Her eyes were the same shade of green as the chaise longue; a woman who liked things to match would not be happy with second best. 'Mislaid is not the word for which I am seeking. Destroyed is better. My certificates were destroyed in the war and replacements I have been unable to obtain, but anyway I suspect that these would not be approved. By your Government, I must clarify. Musical people of discernment will always appreciate what they hear rather than what they see. That is why I wish to play the piano for you. If you will let me.'

As Ilona had hoped, Mrs Chapman was susceptible to flattery. But after playing several bars of a simple prelude by Shostakovich, she realised that something was wrong. Mrs Chapman's expression was pained. 'Perhaps it is too modern. Perhaps you do not like Shostakovich?'

'He is too Russian,' Mrs Chapman complained. 'I prefer earlier music. Bach or Beethoven perhaps, or even a little Schubert, in spite of their being German.'

When Ilona had finished playing, Mrs Chapman said, 'You play quite well. Beautifully in fact.' She smiled and for the first time Ilona warmed to her. 'I'll ring for my son, Philip. He's six years old and has been learning the piano for a couple of years, but his teacher's moved to Sydney. He'll be going to boarding school next year. His father insists on it, though I'd prefer to keep him here. I'd like him to have more lessons before he leaves. He loves music. It will be harder for him at school.'

Shortly a small boy entered the room. His head was bent down shyly. Ilona felt for him, dressed as he was in black velvet knickerbockers, an embroidered white shirt and black patent leather shoes.

'This is Mrs Talivaldis, who will teach you the piano.'

Philip raised his eyes. One was green and the other was brown, which gave him a slightly cross-eyed appearance. Ilona smiled at him. 'I am sure that we will get on wonderfully together,' she said. 'You have such a lovely name. Do you know what it means?'

The boy shook his head.

'It means a lover of horses. You will not play like a horseman though; you will play like an angel. It is a most beautiful piano that you have. You are a lucky boy.'

He looked bemused at this. For the first time he spoke. 'I'm n-n-n-ot l-l-l-luck-ck-ck . . .' His stutter was so bad that he couldn't finish the sentence.

She would have liked to reach out and touch the boy, or at least to suggest that he sang the words instead, but not in front of the mother. Singing what he wished to say could come later when she was teaching him alone. They could sing when they played. She turned to Mrs Chapman, who seemed to have lost interest in them both. She was inspecting her nails and tapping her foot slightly, whether to some inward tune, or because she was fatigued by the proceedings, Ilona could not ascertain. In case it was the latter, she decided to take her leave. 'I must travel home now. My daughter Zidra will be growing tired.'

Mrs Chapman looked up from her nails and smiled. 'I'll ring for the maid. So lovely of you to come,' she added, almost as if it were a social visit. 'You're welcome to bring Zandra when you come for the first lesson next week.'

'It is Zidra.'

'My apologies. Such a difficult name. I'll send the car to collect you each Thursday at four. Of course I'll pay you for your travel time.' Then she named a figure that Ilona never dreamt she'd get for just a couple of hours work. They shook hands again and the interview was at an end.

In the kitchen, Zidra was playing on the floor with some brightly coloured wooden toys. 'Oh, Mama, I thought you were Philip! We were playing with the toy animals just before he had to go in to see you. They're the most beautiful things. Just look at this little elephant!' She held it up. Painted a shiny dark green, it was perhaps just over an inch long and half an inch thick, and its trunk was raised above its head.

'It is lovely,' Ilona said.

Just then Philip entered, looking more relaxed than he had in the drawing room. 'Y-y-you can keep that if you l-l-like,' he said to Zidra.

Zidra's face glowed. 'Are you sure? It might spoil your set.'

'I've got h-h-hund-d-d- . . . lots,' he said.

'Oh, thank you, Philip!' Zidra exclaimed.

'That is very sweet of you.' Ilona felt touched by the boy's act of generosity. There was something heroic about him giving away such a lovely thing to someone he had only just met, and conquering a stutter to do so.

Looking at Zidra's radiant face, she felt a small pang. If only she could give her daughter more nice things! But no, that did not matter. They had each other, and now Ilona had some pupils as well. It was starting in a new place that was so difficult. Once the first few obstacles were surmounted, life could only get easier.

The chauffeur now appeared in the kitchen doorway. 'Time to go,' he said.

Ilona and Zidra followed him out into the little yard behind the kitchen, with Mrs Jones close behind them. As they passed through the gate, a long grey car swished around the bend of the drive. Ilona recognised it as an Armstrong Siddeley; she had not seen one of those since she left England. The driver parked next to the Woodlands car and got out. Tall, with an angular face that was so expressionless it might have been hewn from granite, he wore rather shabby trousers and a faded blue shirt. Once he caught sight of them, he looked as if he might have climbed back in again, had not the chauffeur called out, 'G'day, Mr Vincent! Mr Chapman's expecting you down at the stables.'

The man waved and his face relaxed into an engaging grin. Glancing at Ilona, he took off his hat, a spontaneous and graceful gesture. His dark straight hair was worn too long. She would have liked to remove her own purple hat, which all afternoon she'd known was inappropriate with the dress. He strode off in the direction of a collection of outbuildings further down the hill.

He is shy and does not like people, Ilona thought, and did not quite know how she had reached this judgement. A retiring *rouseabout* with an Armstrong Siddeley. Although she was not quite sure what rouseabout meant, she liked the sound of it. The chauffeur had described himself thus to Zidra earlier that afternoon. She would look it up when they got home.

'Who is he?'

'Peter Vincent from Ferndale. That's a property a few miles north of Jingera,' Mrs Jones said.

On the journey home, Zidra was overexcited and could not stop talking. Only Ilona responded; the chauffeur sat impassive in the front seat. He had put on a black peaked cap for the drive. His neck was wrinkled like that of a tortoise, and above that his grey hair was cut so short that the rolls of flesh at the base of his skull were clearly visible.

Ilona held Zidra's hand tightly, in part to restrain her but also because it was a way of showing her gratitude that her daughter had two fine matching brown eyes and no stutter. She felt grateful too for the sun slanting over the paddocks and casting long shadows, and grateful that she had the opportunity to make a living doing something she enjoyed. Perhaps she should also consider giving singing lessons. Forgetting that Zidra was talking, she burst into song.

'You're butting in, Mama. I was talking.' Zidra squeezed her mother's hand hard and looked at her reproachfully.

'How can I not sing when the day is so beautiful?'

'But I was telling you something.' Zidra removed her hand and turned away to stare out of the side window. The yellow ribbon restraining her hair had become untied and the ends were frayed and wet.

Ilona reached across, undid the ribbon and refastened it, pulling the bow neatly into shape and restoring an illusion of girlish innocence. Zidra remained poker-faced, her eyes on the passing scenery. The car rumbled over the cattle grid and Woodlands was left behind. The driver accelerated along the bitumen road leading towards Jingera. Ilona could see the grey strip over which they were to travel winding ahead of them, like a stream trying to find the path of least resistance through the low hills and down to the coast. After a time the road crossed a rickety wooden bridge and then ran parallel to the river. Ilona took Zidra's hand again and the girl launched herself once more into a narrative.

'Mrs Jones is such a nice lady. She gave me a glass of milk, and she'd just baked a whole tray of Anzac biscuits. She said I could help myself, so I had four.'

'Mrs Jones is my wife,' the chauffeur volunteered, the first sentence he had initiated on this leg of the journey. 'A very good cook, my missus.'

'She said she'd let me help her cook ginger snaps next time, and clean up the bowl afterwards. Oh look, Mama! There's Lorna from school!'

Ilona looked where Zidra was pointing, to a collection of shanties next to the river, rough constructions made of wooden crates and corrugated iron. Surely this could not be where Lorna lived. Half a dozen Aboriginal women crouched around a fire cooking in blackened cans and a few men sat smoking under a weeping willow. Some children were playing cricket in the narrow paddock between the river and the road.

'Oh, please slow down, Mr Jones, I want to say hello.' Zidra wound down the window and waved.

Mr Jones slowed the car and even honked the horn. One of the children, a slender pretty girl with long thin legs, detached herself from the game of cricket when she saw the car and ran through the grass towards them, waving.

Zidra shouted, 'Hello, Lorna!' The girl called back but Ilona could not quite make out her words. When Lorna was almost at the car Mr Jones drove a little faster. The girl ran faster too but she could not keep up. 'Goodbye, Lorna,' Zidra shrieked. 'See you at school tomorrow!'

'Is that where Lorna lives?' Ilona said.

Zidra did not answer, so engrossed was she in waving.

'The Abos have been camped there for some time,' Mr Jones said. 'Reckon the police will be coming by soon to move them on. Though maybe they'll wait till the farmers have got their peas picked and potatoes dug.'

'Move on where?' Ilona pulled at her daughter, who was leaning out of the window waving.

'Up the coast. Picking further north. Or there's work in the sawmills. But where they don't want to go is back to the reserve at Wallaga Lake. Can't say I blame them either. Though it's a disgrace the way they're living here.'

Mr Jones ran a finger between his collar and his neck as if it were chafing him, or perhaps it was the irritation of seeing the Aborigines' camp. He did not say any more, nor did she wish to probe further, especially in front of Zidra. Anyway, all his concentration should be directed at negotiating the sharp bends in the road as it descended into Jingera.

However she could not rid herself of the image of the camp. At least the people in this one were free to leave, or so she supposed. She would ask Zidra to invite Lorna home for afternoon tea. She wanted to meet this girl whom her daughter had befriended.

CHAPTER TEN

Zidra watched Lorna. Lying face down on the ground, Lorna wriggled like a snake through the gap under the grey paling fence. One sock had slipped down so that her right heel was exposed, and her sandshoes were worn and dirty. Behind her she left a small tunnel through the long green grass.

'This way, Dizzy!' Lorna's voice was a little muffled. 'Come on, you slowcoach!' Now her head peered over the top of the fence. So wide was her grin that it seemed to split her face in two. A few blades of grass were caught up in her wavy black hair.

Zidra lay down on the grass. Feeling it prickling through her blouse, she inched along the tunnel Lorna had made, and squirmed out the other side. Lorna held out a calloused hand and pulled her up.

'We'll get to the lagoon this way.' Lorna pointed along the lane, which ran behind the houses opposite where Zidra lived, and right down to the water. 'Then we'll double back to the jetty. When yer ready to go home it's straight up the hill.'

'How will you get home?'

'Around the lagoon and across the paddocks.' Lorna shrugged. 'Won't take me long. I got all afternoon.' She started skipping along the lane.

Zidra tried skipping but that was no good; she had to long jump to match Lorna's stride. Lorna imitated her and they laughed so much that Zidra got stitches and doubled over. When something hard hit her leg she thought it was Lorna but her friend was staring up the lane. 'Watch out,' she whispered. 'Get ready to run.' Looking around, Zidra saw Roger and Barry and two other boys from school running down the lane towards them, hands full of pebbles and faces creased with concentration.

'Go home, wogs! Don't wancha here, ya bloody reffoes.'

'Get outta 'ere, ya bloody Abo!'

More pebbles rained about them. One hit Zidra on her face. It hurt and she started to feel frightened. Lorna picked up a pebble and hurled it back. It struck Barry on the leg. He howled and lobbed a stone at Lorna. Though laughing defiantly, she put a hand on Zidra's arm and said, 'Run, Dizzy, we gotta get out of here.'

Zidra reeled as another stone hit her. This time it landed on her chest and almost knocked her to the ground.

'Pick on someone yer own size,' Lorna yelled.

'He is my size,' Zidra said, momentarily confused.

'There're four of them and two of us. Twice two is four.' Lorna's eyes were sparking almost as if she was enjoying the fight. Or maybe it was anger, Zidra decided, as she hunted around for something to throw. Bending to pick up a stone, she remembered her school-case on the grass several yards up the lane. Her mother would be furious if it got lost; she must get it back.

'Leave it,' Lorna shouted.

'Wogs! Dagoes!' shouted the four boys advancing towards them.

'Jeez, you want your silly heads clapped together,' said a loud, calm voice. Zidra turned to see Jim Cadwallader. Unnoticed, he'd somehow got himself into the lane next to them. 'Talk about dumb. Haven't you got anything better to do with your time?' Leaning against the fence with his hands in his pockets, he looked as relaxed as if he'd been there the whole afternoon. 'Why don't you carry on, you two,' he said to Zidra and Lorna. 'I just want to have a few words with my friends here.'

Deep gratitude made Zidra's knees wobbly, or maybe it was the shock. The morning that Jim had brought around the kindling and laughed at her, she'd thought he was just another smartypants boy. One of those who thought they were better than you for any old reason, but she'd been wrong about that; he wasn't a smartypants boy after all.

A quick glance at Roger and Barry and the others now made her feel almost cheerful. They looked as if they'd been caught out by Miss Neville. Cowish, no, sheepish, was the word she was looking for. She picked up her case and ran down the lane after Lorna. They could've dealt with the boys even without Jim, Lorna said. But Zidra wasn't so sure. They ran all the way to the jetty. Although it was deserted – and Zidra would, for once, have preferred to be where there were adults – she followed Lorna onto the planking. Lorna bounced along as happily as if the stoning had never happened while Zidra followed more slowly. There were big gaps between the boards and through these gaps she could see clear water and, below that, sand and bits of weed.

The girls sat side-by-side on the bottom step at the end of the jetty. It was a bit damp, but it was out of sight of anyone on the shore. Zidra stared out over the lagoon and took deep breaths to steady herself. Two black swans were cruising along on the far side of the water and a pelican followed them at a slight distance, as if it was in charge. The water in the lagoon was flowing towards the sea, towards the narrow mouth of the estuary that was just below the headland.

'Once the tide comes in the water starts flowing the other way,' Lorna said.

'I know,' said Zidra, although she didn't. To make up for this lie, she asked Lorna when the tide would turn. Lorna knew everything about tides and the weather, but she was even worse than Zidra at multiplication. It was because she'd moved around so much and hadn't had a decent schooling. That's what Mrs Bates had told Mama yesterday after the piano lesson.

'Got something for you.' Lorna pulled out of her pocket a small flat shell, wider than it was high, and almost as pink as fairy floss. It nestled in her paler pink palm. Zidra reached out and stroked the seashell; it looked smooth but it had fine ridges that only touching could reveal.

'It's lovely.'

'You can have it.'

A present; how Zidra loved to be given presents. She scooped up the pretty pink shell and stroked its surface again. She smiled at her friend. She'd like to give her something in return. Then she remembered it, the little wooden elephant – about the same size as the shell – that she'd been carrying around for days.

Putting a hand into her pocket, she pulled it out. Without a moment's thought she held out both her hands, palm side up. On one palm lay the bright pink shell and on the other lay the green elephant. 'Take it,' she said. 'I'd like you to have it.'

'You sure?'

'Of course I'm sure.' Although now Zidra thought about it, she was starting to have her doubts. This was no sort of a swap.

A pink shell that could be picked up from any old beach for an exotic green elephant that could only be found at Woodlands. But Lorna's hand moved so fast that all Zidra saw was a blur, and the elephant had gone straight into her friend's pocket.

It's better to give than to receive, Zidra reminded herself; one of Mama's sayings that Zidra had never thought much of. She'd rather receive than give any day.

She looked at the pink shell and held it up to the light. It cast a rosy light. She'd never seen anything quite like it before. It wasn't just any old shell but a special shell, and probably the only nice thing Lorna had to give.

'No one at school's ever given me anything before,' Lorna said, caressing the elephant. 'This is the best present ever.'

Zidra smiled. Now she was glad she'd given it to Lorna. Maybe Mama was right. Giving was better than getting. 'That's Jingeroids for you,' she said. 'A mingy lot. No one at school's ever given me anything either. Not even Miss Neville.'

'She's not allowed to whack the girls,' said Lorna, laughing. 'Glad you've come, Dizzy.'

'Me too,' Zidra said automatically. Afterwards she realised she meant it.

They sat in silence for a while. The light shimmered off the water like little light bulbs going on and off. Soon the water began to advance up the lagoon again, in small ripples that slapped against the piles of the jetty. The tide was turning, just as Lorna had said it would.

'Time to go,' she said. 'Mum'll worry if I take too long to get home.' The word Mum still sounded strange but Mama was acquiring many names. There was the indoor name of Mama and the outdoor name of Mum, and then there was what she called herself, Ilona, and what the others like Mr Bates had started to call her, Elinor. Four words for the one person:

Mama, Mum, Ilona and Elinor. 'Mum's still not used to me coming home on my own.'

'She'll learn.'

Zidra wasn't so sure. It would be good to have a sister like Lorna, or maybe even a brother like Jim, to share some of Mama's attention. Though at least she had some friends now. And a present too – Lorna's beautiful pink shell.

Lorna headed off around the edge of the lagoon and into the bush, while Zidra trudged up the hill. When she was almost home she heard shouts from the top. Boys with billycarts were milling about in front of the war memorial. Her hands started to tremble and she wished Lorna were with her. Hoping the boys wouldn't see her, she walked more slowly, close to the ragged hedge bordering the gravel verge. Then she realised that one of the boys was Jim. He waved at her and she waved back. The others didn't notice, they were so intent on lining up their carts. Once through the front gate she felt safer. Now she could hear the sounds of Mama giving a piano lesson, a five-finger exercise that was being endlessly repeated.

'I'm home, Mama!' Zidra stuck her head around the door of the lounge room. Elizabeth, a girl of about eleven from school, was sitting at the piano next to Mama.

Mama looked around briefly and said, 'You're a little late, darling.'

'Had stuff to do,' Zidra said vaguely, but she needn't have worried. Mama was focusing on the piano keys again; you'd have thought daughters would matter more than an old piano. Maybe she could have stayed out later with Lorna after all, though Mama was probably saving up her complaints ready to tell her off once the lesson was over.

Zidra went into the kitchen. She took the milk jug out of the ice chest and poured a glass. After gulping this down, she selected the largest apple from the fruit bowl on the dresser, and wiped her milky upper lip on the tea towel. Anxiety about Roger did not prevent her from going outside again. Down the back steps, along the side passage and under the hedge without being seen by anyone. Munching her apple, she watched the billycarts race down the hill. Maybe the Cadwallader boys would let her have a go one day but she wouldn't be asking any favours while that Roger was hanging around.

CHAPTER ELEVEN

Jim took the pail from his mother. She gave him a push in the direction of the back door, as if he wouldn't have known which direction to take unless she guided him. 'Feed the chickens, there's a good boy,' she said. She never called the chickens chooks; that was common. His dad never did either, except when she was out of hearing.

'Chook, chook-chook-chook-chook!' Jim clucked, once he was inside the chicken coop, ducking his head because he could no longer stand up in the run. After distributing the food, he refilled the water trough. 'Chook, chook-chook-chook-chook!' he said, and grinned as the fowls clucked back.

His favourite hiding place was under the fig tree behind the back of the run. Well fertilised by chicken manure, the tree formed a dense canopy over an amphitheatre-like depression. He sat down and leant against the trunk of the tree with his legs stretched out in front of him. The ground fell away so steeply that he could see, over the top of the paling fence, the dense bush on the other side of the lane, and beyond that the glimmering of the lagoon. Time to himself was what he wanted. Something was troubling him and he hadn't yet been able to work out what it was.

It had been a lucky thing that he'd come across Zidra and Lorna that afternoon. He'd been scared when he'd broken up the fight. Not on his own behalf but because of what he'd seen on Roger's face. That look of hatred. He returned to it as if he were picking at a scab. Two girls against four boys. A wog and an Abo against four proper Australians.

The ground under him was littered with leaves, through which ants and a small spider were making their way. He placed a twig in front of the spider and watched it change its route. Why he wanted to compensate for what he'd seen on Roger's face that afternoon he couldn't understand. It wasn't his fault. He'd rescued the girls after all, but he felt a need to do something more. Then he remembered seeing Zidra creep under the hedge when he was racing his billycart down the hill. Tomorrow he'd ask her if she'd like a ride on it. Lorna too, if he could find her.

'Jim! Jim!' His mother crashed out of the back door and the screen door slammed shut after her. 'Where is that dratted boy? Time for him to set the table.'

'He'll turn up.' Dad's calm tones could be maddening to Mum when her anger was up. Jim didn't wait for the reaction. So far Mum hadn't noticed his cubbyhole under the fig tree and he wanted to keep it that way. Out of the hiding place he crept, and up the side of the yard. Then he pounded down the side passage as if he'd been round the front all the time.

'Where's your pail?'

'I left it in the chook run.' Jim clattered down the back verandah steps to retrieve it.

'Chicken run,' Mum bellowed after him.

'Jim run,' Jim muttered to himself as he sprinted back up the steps. 'What's for tea?'

'Steak and kidney pie.'

'My favourite,' said Dad, and Mum looked pleased.

The next afternoon Jim took the back route around to Zidra's house. No one should see him inviting her out to play; the last thing he wanted was unnecessary teasing. They'd see her later, if she came out, and that would be soon enough. And they wouldn't need to know he'd invited her; they'd just think she invited herself.

He looked for Zidra under the front hedge. No one there. Then he knocked on the front door and The Talivaldis opened it. Quickly she replaced a surprised expression with a broad smile. 'Master Cadwallader,' she said, 'whom I must only call Jim.'

Jim knew she was laughing at him. Embarrassed, he looked at his scuffed leather sandals through which calloused toes peeped. Brother Andy could bite his toenails; that piece of information would shock The Talivaldis. Now he couldn't think of anything to say. If she were his age and not one of those unpredictable adults who alternated between familiarity and distance, he might make a joke about her name. That wouldn't go down well though; she'd been most particular about his pronunciation when he'd last called, and anyway he wanted to get away as soon as decently possible.

'Perhaps you would like to come inside?'

'Just wanted to invite Zidra out to play.'

'But how kind! She has so few friends and I'm sure that she would love to play.'

Zidra appeared in the hallway behind her mother. 'I've got lots of friends,' she muttered, glaring at her mother. Jim saw the red flush rise up her neck. Once it reached her chin he could no longer bear to look. He glanced again at the mother, who was smiling encouragingly at him. 'Jim would like you to play, Zidra,' she said, eyes now firmly fixed on him as if she thought he might make a run for it.

'Yeah. I could let you have a go on my billycart.' Jim absent-mindedly picked at a piece of loose skin around a fingernail and wished he'd never come. Playing with Andy in the bush or mucking around on the beach seemed like much more appealing activities now.

The Talivaldis clapped her hands. 'On one of those cart things, how wonderful! My darling Zidra, of course you must go!'

Catching Zidra's eye, Jim grinned. She was just about to reply when her mother added, 'But you must not ride down this steep hill, on no account ride on this steep hill. I beg of you that you will take care of her.'

Zidra stayed silent. Probably the best thing to do when her mother was in full flight. Jim surreptitiously licked the bleeding skin around his fingernail. Only when he had promised to take the billycarts somewhere flat did The Talivaldis quieten down. Zidra was forced to wear a floppy blue sunhat below which her hair stuck out like steel wool, and somehow Jim's torn fingernail managed to acquire a plaster. Then they were set adrift into the hot afternoon.

Before they'd even reached the front gate the piano could be heard, as The Talivaldis thumped out some processional march to accompany their flight up the hill.

CHAPTER TWELVE

Ilona had seen the emerald green swimming costume in the Homebush opportunity shop just before leaving Sydney. She had asked the sales assistant if she could try it on in the small cubicle at the back of the shop.

'That's not allowed for reasons of hygiene,' the woman had explained very slowly, as if Ilona were stupid instead of foreign. Her height made looking down her nose seem natural.

'I could wear it over my undergarments,' Ilona had offered. The assistant had refused, as if her undergarments might be unhygienic too. But Ilona had fallen in love with the soft emerald fabric and bought the swimsuit regardless. It was cheap and it looked as if it had hardly been worn, and she could always use her needle and cotton to make adjustments if it turned out to be too big.

This morning, when at last she tried it on, she discovered it was far too large, two sizes at least. It needed drastic needle-work before it was presentable. The side seams would have to be taken in and the straps shortened. In the meantime she could wear it as it was, held in with a couple of safety pins, and hope there was no one on the beach when she went swimming, for she was determined to swim today. It was already feeling hot, although it was only mid-morning, and she had put off going into the surf for far too long.

Now she lingered on the narrow bridge over the lagoon. There was no one around, apart from a distant figure sitting on the steps at the end of the jetty; Tommy probably, fishing as he seemed to do every morning about this time. Putting down the string bag holding her towel, she readjusted the straps of the swimming costume she was wearing underneath a loose dress. The whole day lay ahead, with nothing pressing for her to do until school came out. She noticed, on the beach side of the lagoon, a dilapidated fibro boathouse with a rusting corrugated iron roof. It was barely visible, sheltered from the town by a twist in the river and a dense stand of spiky-leafed trees.

She picked up her bag and walked on. The bridge opened on to a wide track leading onto the beach. Instead of following that as she had originally intended, she took a turning to the right, along a narrow path winding through the bush and which must be the access path to the boathouse. It weaved its way through the trees she'd identified from a library book as melaleucas. Their leaves rustled like sheets of fine paper in the warm breeze. Some unseen bird trilled a single bell-like note. Eventually the path opened into a grassy clearing in front of the boathouse. Through a dirty pane of glass, she could see a rowing boat resting on the sand; at high tide the water would flow right into the boathouse. She walked around the side of the building and saw that the doors of the boathouse were slightly ajar and the tide was starting to come in; the water lapped gently at the sand. A flock of perhaps twenty pelicans stood about in the shallows of the lagoon, as if waiting for some excitement. She walked slowly towards them and one of them sounded a warning, more a growl than a honk. The more timid birds waded away fast, splashing in their haste.

Another narrow path led from the back of the boathouse in the direction of the beach and she decided to take this rather than to return the way she'd come. The path climbed a steep ridge. The melaleucas growing here were thin and rangy. They leant away from the ocean; only their roots, anchored in this inhospitable-looking soil, were constraining them to stay. From the top of the ridge, over a green fringe of bushes, the entire length of Jingera Beach could be seen. Not a soul in sight. She could swim anywhere without fear of being seen in her too-large swimming costume. The track headed straight down into the dunes. She slipped off her sandals, but the beach was even hotter than the air and burned the soles of her feet, so she put them on again to pick her way over the sand.

The sun beat down on her head in spite of the hat, and beads of moisture formed between her shoulderblades and trickled down her back. Above the line of detritus marking the last high tide, she put down her bag and unbuttoned her dress. Almost blinded by the glare, she skipped across the burning sand to the edge of the surf. Straight into the line of breakers she went, until she was wet to halfway up her thighs. Knees bent, she immersed herself to waist-level. The shock of the cold water took her breath away, but after a few seconds the water seemed warmer, and her body began to tingle. For a moment she relaxed, feeling her body shift with the movement of the water that was like a living thing; the dragging of the receding waves, and then the tugging back to shore of the incoming waves; this incessant pushing and pulling. It was as if each outgoing wave were pushing away old cares and each incoming wave ushering in new joys, and she laughed out loud.

Then a harsh noise intruded on her reverie, a loud bellow-ing from the beach. A man was sprinting towards her, arms flapping as if he were controlling traffic, and he was shouting again. And now she could make out the words, 'Don't go in! Don't go in!' He peeled off his shirt as he ran and then his shorts, revealing black swimming trunks, and all the time he continued bawling at her, while discarding clothes onto the sand.

Perhaps she had been mistaken in thinking this was public beach; this must be private land and that explained the shouting. Reluctantly she came out of the water, conscious of her wet swimming costume, the fabric of which seemed to be stretching with the weight of the water and slipping down her legs. Arms hugging her chest, she was reassured that the top of this most unfortunate garment was not wet and that the safety pins were bearing up.

At the edge of the waves, she stood waiting, her heels slowly sinking into the sand as the water eddied around them, shifting the grains.

'You mustn't go in there,' the man gasped, coming to a standstill several yards away. Hands on hips, he had to stop speaking to regain breath.

'I must apologise if this is your beach,' Ilona said, avoiding looking at the dark tufts of hair under his arms and focusing instead on his face. 'I had not intended to cause anyone offence.'

The man puffed ridiculously in front of her, face red with exertion and eyes a cold deep blue, like the almost endless ocean she had crossed to reach here.

'I might have been thinking,' she continued, struggling a little with her English, 'that there is so much empty space here and that one swimmer would not you trouble.'

'You've completely misunderstood,' the man said rather crossly when at last he had regained his voice. Such an unfit – if undeniably good-looking – man should really not be running up and down beaches driving away harmless swimmers but instead should be resting or perhaps engaging in some gentle swimming exercise himself. This was precisely the moment to tell him to take things calmly, and she was about to do so when he interrupted. 'It's much too dangerous here. Surely you can't have failed to notice the strong rip out there?' He pointed towards the ocean.

Following the direction of his finger she saw that the surf was indeed frothing about rather furiously just beyond where she had been standing. It would not have been at all pleasant to be caught up in that. This stranger had perhaps saved her life and she was about to thank him, but now he was glancing at the drooping bottom of her swimming costume; glancing obliquely, it was true, and then averting his eyes. Surely that twist of his lips was a quickly suppressed grin. So the words that came out of her mouth were not those she intended. 'Of course I had no intention of going out that far,' she said, clasping her arms more closely over her chest. 'Only a *nincompool* would do that.'

At this he laughed outright. '*Nincompoop*,' he said when he'd sobered up a bit. 'That's the correct word. You wouldn't have had any choice. You would've been dragged out there by the rip. You're jolly lucky I came along. If I hadn't, you'd have been halfway to New Zealand by now.'

He was one of those men who always had to be right, she decided. Now staring at the sand, she traced out a wide arc with her right foot, aimlessly pushing grains into a small pile. Inadvertently she flicked some of it over his feet. Several wet particles stuck to his ankles, while the rest trickled gently back onto the beach. She felt slightly shocked at this, as if she had made direct physical contact. Looking up again, she saw that he was watching her intently. Gazing as keenly back would help reduce this odious feeling of being caught at a disadvantage.

A few seconds later she turned away, and watched the roiling rip. Her eyes filled with tears. An illusion had been shattered. There *was* danger here, even on this pristine beach, from either the ocean or from men appearing so surprisingly from the bush. She felt humiliated besides, to be seen in a too large costume performing a too stupid action in a too rough sea. How ludicrous I am, she thought. If her rescuer had been homely instead of handsome, her reaction would have been of gratitude and not humiliation. Quickly she blinked away the tears and, after a moment, turned to thank him, the words coming easily now, as if it had not been a battle to be gracious.

'I'll show you where it's safe to swim,' he told her. 'I'm going in myself.'

Once more she thanked him. It was important to learn something from every experience and from him she would learn where it was appropriate to surf. But on no account would she go into the water with this man. Almost better to be at the mercy of the currents than to expose herself again to his scrutiny in this ludicrous swimsuit.

They exchanged names as they marched along the beach on sand firmed by the waves. Peter Vincent; the name sounded faintly familiar. At this point she remembered the man with the Armstrong Siddeley she'd seen on that first visit to Woodlands. 'I've seen you before,' she said. 'At Woodlands.'

The man glanced at her. 'I remember you now,' he said, smiling. 'You were wearing a purple hat.'

It was irrational to feel irritated that he had fastened on that unbecoming hat, and to feel even more irritated when he changed places with her, so that now he was on the ocean side, as if afraid that she might suddenly dart into the waves again. They carried on walking in silence and after a time she began to feel her annoyance ebbing away. There were a number of shells washed up on the beach and she stooped to pick up a pale violet one. Next to it lay a small flat stone. On it was an indentation that looked remarkably like the fossilised remains of something: a small creature perhaps, or a tiny fern. She picked it up.

'Someone must have dropped it here,' Peter said. 'You can find fossils under the headland if you look hard enough. Not so many left now as when I was growing up, but you can still see them in the cliff face.'

'I will give this to my daughter.' Ilona ran a finger over the small impression in the stone. There would be no one to look after Zidra if she were not here to protect her. So in a sense Peter Vincent had saved both Zidra and herself.

When they were almost at the thin trickle of water escaping from the lagoon, Peter stopped. 'It's safe to swim here,' he said, before explaining how the gradual breaking of the waves could be exploited by a body surfer. 'This is where I swim,' he added, giving the place an extra benediction. 'There's a small beach at my place but it's too dangerous. Too exposed. I come here when I want to surf.'

Surreptitiously she glanced at him. Brown body, even browner hands and neck. Clearly he engaged in outdoor work of some kind and probably not in the company of others.

'Where are you from?' he asked.

'Jingera.'

'No, I mean where are you from originally? What part of Europe? I hope you don't mind my asking.'

'Latvia.'

'A lovely place, so I've heard. I've been to Europe but never to that part.'

'Where did you go?'

'Britain, Germany, Holland. I got shot down over Holland in the war and got stuck in a POW camp for two years.'

His voice was as calm as if he'd been stuck in a traffic jam. No sign of emotion; no twitching of lips or eyes, nothing. Never would she be able to say, straightaway to someone she'd only just met, that she had been in a concentration camp. She had to keep all that stuff tightly buttoned up or she would fall to bits. For an instant she wondered what his war had been like and then pushed that thought away. Her heart was starting to pump too fast and she had to change the subject quickly before an anxiety attack could begin. Desperately seizing upon the first thought that entered her head, she said, 'Who owns the boathouse?'

'George Cadwallader.'

'Cadwallader's Quality Meats.'

'Indeed. The odd thing about the boathouse is that it's on the wrong side of the water. There used to be a shack behind it once but it fell down years ago. George keeps his boat there. Goes fishing on the lagoon when he's allowed.'

She was grateful for this long response, to which she only half-listened. Her heart rate was slowing to normal. She was going to be all right. She repeated Peter's words, 'When he is allowed?'

'When he can fit it in.'

'Perhaps I should swim in the lagoon rather than the surf. Is the lagoon safe?'

'Yes, but it's okay to swim in the surf if you choose the right spot. You've got to choose the right day too, and it's best to go in with someone if you don't know the conditions.'

This didn't metamorphose into an invitation and she was almost disappointed not to be given the opportunity to refuse. Peter simply said, 'Better get on with it then.' Nodding briefly, he strolled towards the surf.

For just an instant she looked wistfully after him, for the waves did indeed appear inviting. Then she turned back up the beach. Before long she found a secluded stretch of sand by the lagoon. Like a cautious middle-aged matron, she would swim somewhere shallow and safe.

Once in the still water, her spirits calmed. The water caressed her skin as she glided through it in a leisurely breaststroke. Eventually tiring of this, she turned over and floated, head tilting back so far that her toes broke the water's surface. Far above was the empty dome of the harsh blue sky that was almost too bright to contemplate.

Afterwards she sat in the shade on the bank and, when she was dry, slipped off the swimsuit under cover of her dress. The day was getting even hotter and the bush throbbed with the drumming of cicadas. On the walk back to her cottage, she saw no sign of Peter. He must have passed over the footbridge without her observing him.

Back at the cottage, she placed the fossil on the chest of drawers next to Zidra's bed. A gift for the daughter whose happiness she had threatened by swimming in dangerous surf. After this act of homage, she drew all the blinds and curtains in the cottage, something she should have done earlier, for already the rooms felt baking.

Perhaps it was the heat that was making her feel agitated again, arousing in her a sense of disembodiment. She had a quick shower to rinse off the salty water from the lagoon and hung her costume over the verandah railing to dry. If anything, she was hotter after the shower than before, and more detached too. Lying flat on the sofa and shutting her eyes, she felt as if she were floating outside of herself, floating above herself, an *alien* woman in a foreign land.

A woman with a six-digit blue tattoo on her forearm. Peter Vincent couldn't have failed to notice that when she'd been standing next to the waves with arms crossed over her chest. It upset her – far more than it should have, she thought – to have been recognised as a survivor of a concentration camp by a survivor of a POW camp. Not that the camps were in any way comparable, she knew that. Yet she felt almost as if it forged a bond between them, a link that she didn't want, a link that she would have to fracture consciously. Those old dormant memories, those old suppressed memories, should remain just that and not be reawakened by some chance encounter on a beach. She sighed. Meeting Peter had unsettled her but surely this reaction was far more than was warranted. This *overreaction* must simply be delayed shock after being rescued from possible drowning. That and the terrible heat and the thrumming of the cicadas.

She rolled onto her side. Curled up like the fossilised creature in the stone she'd found on the beach, she fell into a deep but disturbed sleep almost at once. No details of those dreams remained when she awoke an hour later. Only a general sense of disquiet.

CHAPTER THIRTEEN

Peter Vincent couldn't wait to get home. This was always the way. A few hours' absence from Ferndale was about all he could stand and he'd felt that way ever since being demobilised. Apart from the odd week or two in Sydney each year on business, he spent all his time on the land. While running the property in a makeshift sort of way, he was making a decent enough job of it if you ignored the state of the house and outbuildings and some of the fences, although sometimes he had the feeling that his grandparents might not agree.

Now, as he steered his beloved Armstrong Siddeley up the winding coastal road north of Jingera, he thought back over the events of the day. The morning swim at Jingera Beach when he'd rescued the Latvian woman, who didn't seem to recognise how lucky she'd been not to get swept out to sea. Then the entire afternoon in Burford running errands, followed by a brief stop at Jingera pub on the way back, and bit of a yarn with George Cadwallader, who'd dropped in for a middy – that was an unusual event, even Bill Bates had commented on it.

Peter couldn't seem to get Ilona out of his mind. Perhaps he'd been too abrupt that morning. Women had accused him of that before. She'd so obviously wanted to swim in the surf, and if he hadn't wished to conceal from her the state of her swimming suit he might have asked her to go in with him. But no, he hadn't felt like doing that; bodysurfing was a solitary matter requiring his complete concentration. Anyway he'd needed time to put the meeting in perspective. After half an hour in the water, he'd dried himself in the sun before heading back to the car. On the footbridge over the lagoon he'd paused. He'd always loved the view to the west, from the time his grandfather first brought him to Jingera over thirty years ago: tall eucalyptus trees rising to lush farming land and, beyond that, the distant escarpment of the Great Dividing Range. To the east, a flock of pelicans cruised the lagoon near Cadwallader's boathouse. While watching them, his eye was caught by a vivid splash of emerald green, against the dull olive of the melaleuca trees. Ilona was sitting on the shore of the lagoon not far from the boathouse. Quickly he'd moved on, not wanting to be seen watching her.

In spite of her polite words of gratitude on Jingera Beach, it was unlikely that he'd ever be forgiven for seeing her in that ill-fitting swimming costume. It had taken him some time to place her as the woman he'd glimpsed at Woodlands. Colours always stuck in his memory: that's why he'd remembered the purple hat she'd worn that day rather than her face.

Now he pulled into the Ferndale driveway and unfastened the first of the gates. A grumbling in his stomach reminded him of how hungry he was, and after parking the car he went straight to the kitchen at the back of the rambling brick house. At one time the kitchen had been a separate building, but Peter's grandparents had constructed a glassed-in walkway to connect it to the dining room. This walkway never failed to delight him, even when he was at his most morose; its pink and green stained glass panels cast lozenges of light on to the scuffed pine floorboards and the central pane of plain glass framed a view of the sea. When he was not out in the paddocks, he spent most of his time in the kitchen, a large room with whitewashed brick walls and an enormous fuel stove occupying half of one wall. The linoleum floor had seen better days. There were two dressers that extended right up to the boarded ceiling, and on their shelves lay a motley collection of crockery. Running down the middle of the room was a long refectory table that could easily have seated a dozen people. One end of the table formed his desk; it was littered with bills and receipts and other miscellaneous pieces of paper.

He placed a leg of lamb in the baking pan. Accumulated in the bottom was a thin layer of congealed dripping but he wouldn't worry about that. At this moment the phone rang. Cursing, he wiped his hands on a grubby tea towel and picked up the receiver.

'Good news, Peter.' It was Jack Chapman, his old friend from Woodlands, who never bothered with the preliminaries. 'That kelpie pup I promised you is just about ready now. Care to visit us to collect him?'

Peter had seen the tan and black puppies just after they'd been born, and again each time he'd visited Woodlands since. Jack liked to keep his puppies well beyond weaning so he could train them to be good working dogs. Part of the joy of breeding them, Peter knew. Any one of Jack's dogs would suit him but the black puppy was the one he liked best. His own two dogs were getting old now, not that he'd ever get rid of them, but he needed a younger one for work. He suggested collecting the dog the following Tuesday.

'Well, Jude's got a better idea than that. Come for dinner on Saturday week. You could stay overnight and then we could have a game of tennis on Sunday.'

'Sounds good.' But Peter was always cautious about Judy Chapman's weekend invitations; she had a habit of trying to pair him off with unattached women. 'Will there be many other guests?'

'The Sutherlands.'

Peter liked the Sutherlands, local farmers, but he waited in case there were more names on the guest list. Then Jack added, 'And you can have your pick of the three pups I've got for sale.'

'Thanks, Jack.' He would pick the black puppy of course. 'Saturday week it is.'

'Good. Jude'll be pleased.' After a second's hesitation Jack added, rather too casually, 'Grace Smythe will be here as well, by the way. Forgot to mention that. She was at school with Jude. Bring your best togs.'

Only then did Peter realise how neatly the trap had closed around him.

After putting the phone down, he placed the lamb in the ramped-up Aga. It was past six but he felt restless and the thought of the Chapmans' dinner party cast a gloom over the evening. He jammed an old felt hat on his head and went outside, whistling for the two ancient brown kelpies. The grass in the home paddock was bleached almost silver by the summer sun. Under the old trees that encircled the house – the Monterey cypresses and the radiata pines – lay a thick blanket of needles that one day he'd get around to raking up. There was little sign now of the formal gardens that his grandmother had designed. Just a few broken bricks remained where the borders had been; the plants had long since died, choked out by grasses and weeds.

The home paddock was bounded to the east by a low cliff, while to the south it sloped down sharply to a narrow gully that was the only access to the beach. To one side of the gully were some rough stone steps that Peter had built for his grand-parents years ago, on a holiday from school, and which only he and his dogs ever used now.

The dogs dashed down the steps and were already racing along the white sand and barking at the advancing waves when he arrived at the bottom. As usual he left boots and socks on the last step and walked barefoot through the sand. It squeaked as he sank into it, rasping grain upon grain in a countless number of tiny collisions. Life was like that, a series of colli-sions. He walked up the short beach to the northern headland. There he sat, on sand still warm from the sun, and watched the waves swelling in from the Pacific.

Ilona Talivaldis. It was a lovely name. She had a charming accent, although what she'd actually said on the beach this morning hadn't been much to his liking. In trying to avoid glancing at her half-exposed breast he'd focused on her face and arms. A pale face, probably due to the cold water and the shock. Then he'd seen it: that blue tattoo on her left forearm. Not just any old tattoo but a six-digit number. He'd known right away what that meant.

Ilona had survived a concentration camp. Most didn't. He wondered how long she'd been in it. Sad if she'd survived all that only to drown on Jingera Beach. After bawling her out of the water, he'd been surprised to discover that she wasn't grateful, only annoyed and fussing about her swimmers. Once he'd recovered from his initial anger, he'd found it amusing that she should be fretting about appearances when all that really mattered was that she was alive, and not a corpse floating in the waves and being nibbled at by sharks. Her modesty made him aware of what she was covering up, but when he saw that tattoo all amusement drained away. It was shocking to see that right here in Jingera. That reminder of the Nazi concentration camps, the numbers given to the Jews and the gypsies and the agitators when they arrived there. Possessions taken away, clothes taken away, lives taken away too in so many cases.

After all those years of trying to forget, seeing that reminder of the war on Ilona's forearm had shocked him, he could admit that now he was home again and able to think. Seeing it had moved him too, as had Ilona's fleeting expression of defence-lessness that was so quickly replaced with antagonism.

He watched the ocean. Each swell formed a crest, which curled over on itself in a great crash of white foam that, by the time it reached the shore had been tamed by the retreating breakers into a gentle swirl of water. The waves would always roll in like this no matter what people might do to each other. That was what was so reassuring about the ocean's edge, but the surf was dangerous too. You had to know what you were doing before venturing into it.

From the beach, only the homestead roof and the surround-ing trees were visible above the cliff edge. He had always loved Ferndale and his grandparents had known that. They'd left it to him just before the war, when he was no more than an over-grown schoolboy. Returning from England after the war, he found it had been badly neglected. Being honest with himself, it was still neglected, except for the land and the stock and the water tanks. There seemed no point in making any other improvements, no one else would see them and he didn't care about appearances, but just as his grandparents had done, he would live and die here. No other way of life appealed to him. Certainly not a city life; not the sort of life Judy Chapman and her friends led, spending half their time in the Eastern Suburbs of Sydney and the other half in the country.

Although he'd loved big cities as a young man, he soon got over that. In the war he'd witnessed the destruction of too many, spread out beneath the planes before the area bombing began; and afterwards the burning, afterwards the death and destruction. It was still impossible for him to go near a big city now without remembering that. The claustrophobia of burning city streets. And, in his dreams, that terrible sense of falling, falling, falling into a yawning abyss. He always woke at this point, sweating and sometimes screaming.

Now he stumbled back up the beach. Pulling on socks and boots, he noticed a single purple flower blooming on a low-growing plant. Pig's face, that's what his grandmother used to call it. The flower was the exact shade of purple as the Latvian woman's hat that day he'd seen her at Woodlands. Pig's face, purple colour; purple hat. Funny that he should think of that wretched hat again.

He didn't want to think of Ilona Talivaldis. They had Europe in common, they had the war years in common, but he didn't want to be reminded of those memories. He'd spent years putting them behind him. They still resurfaced in his sleep but not in his waking hours. Not until today when he'd seen that blasted number on her arm.

A purple hat. Colours stuck in your mind somehow; colours and flowers. White roses conjured up his first love, Jenny. Reminded him of the white rose she wore when she accompanied him to that last school ball. Sweet Jenny, who had married someone else by the time the war ended. When they'd bumped into one another in Pitt Street, not long after he'd arrived back in Sydney, she hadn't recognised him at first, but they could never have got back together again. He'd known he was a different person to the confident young pilot who'd left all those years before. Quite literally unrecognisable.

At the top of the steps, he paused to roll a cigarette and wait for the dogs, who were reluctant to leave the beach. A sliver of a moon was visible, and a smudge of stars over the darkening indigo sky and he could hear breakers crashing onto the shore below.

He sucked hard on the cigarette. This land was his and it was where he belonged, if only for an instant in a bigger order of things. For now he and the land were as one. He stubbed out his cigarette on the hard ground.

CHAPTER FOURTEEN

'Long, Long Ago', Cherry couldn't get that tune out of her head. She whistled it to herself while she cleaned the upstairs bedrooms of the hotel. Ilona had been teaching her to play it on the piano. So far she was only doing the right hand. The chords would come later, Ilona said, after she had built up more expertise with five-finger exercises and of course the scales. She had talent but didn't seem to be practising as much as she should, or so Ilona had decided at the last lesson. Miss Neville always stayed behind to lock up the school after Cherry finished playing and that tended to eat into the practice time.

It was most important, Ilona had told her, to keep a diary recording meticulously how many minutes she played each day. She hadn't started that yet. It wouldn't make impressive reading. But she did like to play the piano, and to whistle. Over and over she whistled 'Long, Long Ago'.

This morning there was a bit less work than usual because only two rooms had been occupied the previous night, by commercial travellers. So Cherry had some spare time that she could spend doing Bill's office at the end of the upstairs verandah. It hadn't been cleaned for ages. Normally he kept it shut up and she only went in when asked, to give it a quick once-over after he'd tidied it up a bit. Today the door was slightly ajar. She knew he wasn't in there or he'd have been out like a shot to silence her whistling. Couldn't stand her singing either; said she was never in tune although he was tone deaf anyway.

Bill did the accounts in his office every morning for an hour or two, or at least that was what he said he was doing, though she suspected he was actually reading the newspaper. By the time he was ready to harass the cook and open up the bar he always seemed remarkably well informed about the sporting news. Pushing the door slightly open, she stuck her head in. The room was empty. Just as she'd thought, the newspaper was spread out on the desk and open at the sporting pages. Bill did deserve a bit of time to himself, poor bugger, but why he had to pretend he was doing the accounts when he locked himself in here was beyond her.

She pushed the door to again and carried the mop and bucket into the guests' bathroom. Water all over the place and damp towels tossed any old how onto the floor. Surely people didn't act like this in their own homes. It was probably more that paying good money for their accommodation made them think it was acceptable to throw stuff around. Whoever used the toilet last hadn't even flushed it. She yanked at the chain and pushed up the sash window to let in some fresh air. The bathroom faced south and probably had the best view of the entire hotel, right down the beach. If they had spare cash she'd like to convert this room into a sitting room, or perhaps a sewing room for herself.

After cleaning the bathroom, she left the wet towels on the verandah railing and knocked on the door to Bill's office. No response. Then she saw him in the yard below, yarning with old Mr Giles, who seemed to have taken it into his head that it was time for a schooner, even though the hotel wouldn't open for another half hour yet. Mr Giles was getting more and more absent-minded, senile, some might say. Some of his marbles seemed to have got mislaid when he'd lost his wife last year. Married sixty years, now that was a life sentence. She couldn't imagine being with Bill that long but she hadn't worked out yet how to get away.

She got the vacuum cleaner from the hallway and plugged it into the extension lead. Bill's dusty shelves were full of books but none of them were his. They came with the hotel, he'd said when he'd brought her back here after their wedding. He'd been over twice her age and she'd been barely sixteen years old; hard to credit it really. The books were largely do-it-yourself manuals. How to construct a septic tank; how to build load-bearing brickwork four storeys high; how to build a boat; how to do your own electrical wiring. They'd had no use for any of that stuff. She ran a finger over one of the shelves. There was so much dust here you could write your name in it and it would glare right back at you.

When she'd finished dusting, she flapped the cloth out the window and watched with satisfaction as the dust drifted down towards the rough grass below. Then she lifted up the newspaper on the desk and stopped when she saw what was underneath.

The room started to swim and then go black, as if a dark blind was being pulled down in front of her eyes. It couldn't be. Not Bill with this stuff. Surely not Bill. She dropped the newspaper and sat on the floor.

Impossible; she must have imagined it. She'd have to look again. Not now, but when the faintness went. With her head between her knees and eyes shut, she took slow deep breaths.

Her entire body seemed to be pounding: heart, pulses, head. She mustn't think about anything yet. Hopefully Bill wouldn't come back for a bit. No, Bill was still talking to old Mr Giles in the courtyard. Everything was normal, except in her head.

The girl was too young. In and out, she breathed, in and out. Maybe she was only dreaming though. This hadn't happened except in her head.

The faintness passed. She stood up; heart still beating too fast and the palms of her hands sweating. After wiping her them on her skirt, she lifted the newspaper.

The naked young girl was no more than five or six and the man straddling her body was around Bill's age. Wasn't Bill though. She averted her eyes. She'd look again in a moment. Her heart was now hammering like a piston and numbness began to envelope her brain. Clutching the edge of the desk, she swayed slightly and focused her eyes on the bookshelves while willing herself to stay calm.

After another moment she lifted up the picture. Underneath were half a dozen more drawings and photographs. As quickly as her shaking hands allowed, she flicked through them. They were all on the same theme. Men and children. Girls, very young girls. The children too small, the men too large.

Stomach now churning so much she felt as if she could throw up, she gulped air into her lungs. Once more her vision clouded as the room started to swim. She had to get out fast but she couldn't see the door. Fainting wouldn't do; only an idiot would stand here holding the pictures when Bill could come back at any moment. Get out now and get away fast. Go somewhere safe to think before the blackness comes down again.

With quivering hands she put the pictures under the newspaper and smoothed the paper down. Everything had to be left exactly as she'd found it. Bill mustn't know she'd been in here.

She glanced around the office. All that had obviously changed was the removal of the dust and Bill would never notice this. After dragging the vacuum cleaner out of the room, she carefully checked the door to make sure it was exactly as she'd found it, just a couple of inches ajar. She pushed the cleaner back into the hallway and inhaled deeply before going out onto the verandah. She sat on the splintered wooden floor with her back against the wall and tried to collect herself.

Bill liked young girls . . . in a special way. A horrible way. A cruel way. The girls were too small, far too small. What the men were doing to them would hurt. What the men were doing would damage them.

Then it hit her. She'd been small too when she married Bill, although not so small that the act of penetration hurt. Not a child at all but a slender young woman with a boyish figure that had filled out in the first couple of years of their marriage. She'd been a late developer and by then Bill had stopped sleeping with her. By then they had separate bedrooms. The reason he'd stopped sleeping with her was now clear. It was because she was a woman and no longer a child. At the time she'd felt a failure, as if it was all her own fault that he found her unattractive, and it was true that, after a time, she too found him unattractive. Now I understand it all, she thought, and a great sadness engulfed her.

She deliberately made herself think back to the day they'd first met. She'd been fifteen when he came into the haberdashery store in Burford where she worked. Just demobbed, he looked handsome in the uniform. Ignoring her at first, he'd joked with the manageress about employing underage girls. Then Cherry had told him her age and he'd laughed, saying she looked years younger. They'd married on her sixteenth birthday. If there'd been other girls since then, since she'd become a woman, she hadn't known about them. Surely she would have known, what with Jingera being such a small town. Yet maybe not. There were secrets aplenty just in her own family. Her loving the school mistress. Her dad abusing her mum. Her dad walking out on her mum and the pretence that he'd gone west shearing.

And Bill with his child pornography.

Down in the yard he was still yarning with old Mr Giles. She couldn't see them but could hear the murmur of their voices. The leaves of the wisteria climbing up the verandah posts were twisting gently in the faint breeze and sunlight flickered over her. Everything looked just as it had ten minutes ago and yet nothing was the same. Nothing was as it seemed. She was different. Bill was not the man she thought he was. Now she had another secret to conceal from the world and she felt sick at the thought of it.

For a whole day Cherry felt as if someone had died. Unable to function and unable to look Bill in the eye, she told him she was ill and couldn't work. Then she was sick, throwing up into the toilet pan all that she'd eaten, and when that had gone, thin green bile that burned her mouth. After that, she locked herself in her bedroom and began weeping. Falling asleep eventually, she woke up in the small hours screaming. At first she had no idea where she was and then, for a moment, thought she was at home again, with her mother in the next room.

But Bill was in the next room. She could hear him snoring.

It was impossible to fall asleep again. She felt like a wounded animal that needed to crawl off into a hole somewhere and lick her wounds, but the only hole she had was this room. There was nowhere else to go.

Tainted by her association with Bill, she felt as dirty as if she'd been a party to his fantasies, and even if they were still only fantasies, she became afraid of what he might do next. One day he might act them out and destroy someone's life.

Knowing about Bill but not knowing what to do was a terrible strain. Head pounding and throat parched, for hours she tossed and turned, struggling unsuccessfully to come to some decision. At six o'clock she arose and dressed and busied herself about the hotel. By eight o'clock she was on the hotel verandah washing the floor when Miss Neville walked by.

'Come and practise tomorrow,' Miss Neville said. 'You forgot yesterday.'

Although Cherry opened her mouth as if to speak, she couldn't begin to articulate the words that might explain her absence.

'You don't look very well. Anything I can do?'

'No,' Cherry croaked, but Miss Neville there are so many things I want you to do, she thought. If only you loved me enough you'd know what I'm going through and you'd look after me and unwind all these days and take me back to when I was a girl again. Back before I was married. Back before I met Bill. But Miss Neville was a woman not a saviour, and she dismissed her thoughts as childish. She'd gone beyond childish things. It was the child in her that Bill had once loved. Straightening her shoulders, she said, 'No, Miss Neville, thank you for offering but there's nothing you can do. I'm a bit off-colour today but tomorrow I'll come and practise again.'

'Get better soon,' Miss Neville said softly before walking on to the schoolhouse.

For a moment Cherry watched her athletic figure, carrying the basket of exercise books as if it were weightless, and was overcome with sadness. Two small children ran up the hill behind Miss Neville and one handed her a small bunch of flowers. Although I love her so much, Cherry thought, there's a huge part of my life that I can't let her know about or she'll stop loving me. I'm tainted by associating with Bill and I'm unlovable.

She went into the hallway and looked at her reflection in the mirror. A wreck of a face, no wonder Miss Neville thought she seemed ill. Bags under her eyes, unwashed skin, hair a mess. No comb in her pocket or in the drawer so she fingered her hair into shape, powdered her nose, lipsticked her mouth and smudged a bit of lipstick onto her cheeks. A long time ago she'd looked like a painted doll and that was why Bill had loved her, but now she was a raddled old barmaid past her prime. Baring her teeth in an attempt at a smile, she saw smudged lipstick on them.

Once more she wondered if she should tell someone, but who? There was nothing Miss Neville could do except warn the schoolchildren not to talk to strange men, and she did that already, Cherry knew. Anyway Bill was hardly strange; he would be known to most of them. She could tell Mr Davies, the policeman, but there was no reason for him to believe her. The photos would have to be produced as evidence and that seemed far too dangerous. Bill would deny it, maybe even say they'd been planted. No, she couldn't do that. An icy coldness gripped her and her head began to spin. Slowly she went into the bathroom and splashed her face and neck with water.

Perhaps she should confront Bill with this. Tell him she'd seen the pictures when she was cleaning his office. She wasn't supposed to go in there, but that didn't matter. She would tell him that she knew and they would have a row and then she'd leave him, but her pulses began to race again at this thought. He was a big man and she was frightened of him. She was afraid of what he might do. And where would she go if she left him? Although she'd often dreamt of running off with Miss Neville to Sydney, they'd never actually spoken of this. Maybe Miss Neville didn't want to commit to her, and she certainly wouldn't once she knew about Bill. Anyway she'd have to apply for a transfer to move away from here and that would take time.

Cherry gripped the edge of the washbasin. Suppose she applied for a divorce. She'd have to give a reason and then all of this would have to come out in the courts. Bill would twist things around, he was clever with words, and popular. He would say it was her fault and that she wasn't a proper wife to him. Everyone would believe him and she'd be publicly humiliated. At this, her face flushed as if she were already in the dock. Turning on the cold tap, she splashed more water over her face and felt it trickle slowly down her neck and dampen her dress.

The simple reality was that she had no money of her own and couldn't afford a lawyer to defend herself. It was all wrong; it was Bill who should be doing the defending and not her. Now hot tears trickled down her face but she brushed them away. She couldn't afford to be blinded by self-pity. She had to stay calm.

It was obvious that she couldn't tell anyone yet. It was far too dangerous. No one must know. She'd have to watch him all the time, or as much as she could. When he was serving in the bar there wasn't much he could get up to.

It wouldn't be long before she'd wonder if she'd made the right decision, and she would revisit this time and time again.

CHAPTER FIFTEEN

Jim woke up suddenly; alert mind, clear head. Morning already and it was such a special day. Sydney, here I come and I'd better get dressed fast. The striking of the hall clock must have been what woke him up but it was still chiming, far more than six strikes, and there was moonlight visible around the edges of the blind. Back to sleep then, ready for the drive to Burford bright and early tomorrow. There Dad would put him on the express bus to Bomaderry Station and once on that bus he'd be on his own all day until meeting up with the Nevilles at Central Railway Station.

It would be impossible to get back to sleep with Andy making such a terrible racket, each inhalation followed by an irritating click from the back of his throat. And the room felt so hot and airless, and his throat so dry. After quietly opening the bedroom door, he tiptoed into the hall. Now he heard his mother's angry voice, coming from the lounge room. He stood quite still. Her anger induced a sensation in his chest that was like panic, and his stomach tightened and turned. Then he heard his father's low voice, speaking calmly as he always did when Mum was angry. She began to talk more loudly, so loudly that Jim could hear every word, even though the lounge-room door was closed.

'I don't want Jim going to Sydney. I've told you that again and again but you never listen.'

Jim caught his breath. Surely Mum wasn't going to stop him now. He couldn't bear it if she did. Everything was packed and waiting at the back door, except for his toothbrush.

'Of course I listen, Eileen.' Dad was saying each word unusually clearly and slowly. 'I listened to you very carefully and I heard you agree in the end. Anyway, it's far too late to call it off, it would be plain rude. Anyone'd think you'd be pleased the boy might have a chance to go to a top school. You're always saying how fantastic Sydney was when you were growing up there.'

'I agree it's too late to cancel.' Mum had given in and Jim sighed with relief. Then she added, 'But there's just going to be this one trip to Sydney, George, and that's it. Never again. This trip is going to be Jim's taste of Sydney education and then it's off to Burford High next year. It just wouldn't be fair to Andy to split the boys up. Or to me.'

In the hallway Jim grinned, barely noticing that Mum was thinking of fairness to Andy and her, and not to him. She wasn't going to cancel the trip and he'd have his three days away. The outcome of the exam didn't bother him. He didn't expect to get a scholarship; he just wanted this one chance to see a bit of the world on his own. After that, Burford High next year would be just fine with him.

He got a drink of water from the bathroom and crept back to bed. There were no sounds coming from the lounge room now, although his parents were still in there. After shutting the bedroom door quietly behind him, he tiptoed across to Andy's bed. The irritating clicking had stopped although Andy was still breathing loudly through his open mouth. Jim was tempted to roll him onto his side but changed his mind. Andy hadn't

115

said anything much about the Sydney trip and Jim wondered what he thought of it. Nothing at all, probably. His tight circle of friends insulated him from whatever else might be going on.

It was too hot to crawl under the sheets so Jim sprawled on top. Sleep was out of the question, he was far too excited. Then he remembered no more until the following morning, when Dad's touch on his shoulder told him it was time to get up.

From his seat on the bus, Jim watched the trunks of the eucalyptus trees flash by. Tall and straight, dappled white and grey. Between the trees nothing but the slanting rays of early morning sunlight illuminating dark clumps of what he knew to be cycads. A species that had been around even before the dinosaurs, Miss Neville had told him, and was still thriving here between the eucalypts.

On and on the bus went. Through tall forests, past dairy farms, down the main streets of little towns built on rivers, over timber bridges that rattled under their weight. Then at last the bus stopped at the Shoalhaven River and there was the Sydney train waiting at Bomaderry Station. By then he'd eaten all the sandwiches Mum had made for him the night before, and the fruit. There was just time to buy two meat pies from the baker's near the station and then he was on the train. Even now, after travelling for so many hours, he wasn't bored. There was so much to see, so much to think about. He needed to think, otherwise he couldn't absorb what he was seeing. The most trivial thing might have a meaning. Even a random thing could be interpreted if you knew how; he'd seen that in the statistics book he'd chanced on in the library.

While he was pondering this, the train was passing through more trees, trees that allowed you to see right through them to the shape of the land behind. To the bare bones of the land scape, to the folds and ledges of some coloured rock that he supposed was sandstone. Then at last they were on the outskirts of Sydney, proceeding more slowly now, as if they were too early, although they'd been travelling all day and the sun was sinking fast. Past the backyards of houses, first fibro houses, then older brick houses. Mile after mile of them, backing onto the railway line; and now there were many railway lines running parallel with their own. He could look into the backs of endless rows of terraced houses, with tiny backyards mostly filled with rubbish or paved over with concrete. No room for chookyards here, and only occasionally a touch of green.

As the train approached the terminus he became more and more anxious. Everything could go wrong. What if he and the Nevilles didn't recognise one another? What would happen to him then, an eleven-year-old boy wandering around Central Station? Pickpockets, Mum had said, just before he left that morning. Not that he had much in his pockets that could be picked. Watch out for pickpockets, she'd said, get in the right carriage, and don't talk to strange men. There were strange men everywhere, he could see them crowding onto the platform as they passed through Redfern Station and there was only one stop more to go before they were at Central.

The week before Miss Neville had shown him a photograph of her brother and his wife. The brother was tall with smooth dark hair and his sister's sharpish features, but his expression wasn't as stern. Perhaps that was because he'd been photographed with Mrs Neville. She radiated goodwill, you could see it even in the photograph; the beaming face and the skin around the eyes crinkled up with laughter.

But how would he recognise Mr Neville if he'd changed from the photo Miss Neville had shown him? Maybe he'd had his hair cut like Jim's, or possibly even lost all his hair altogether. Jim hadn't thought to ask Miss Neville how long ago the photo had been taken. His stomach churned with anxiety and he began to regret scoffing down those two meat pies that were sitting like lumps of lead in his gut, although he'd eaten them hours ago. Mum and Dad were mad to let him go off like this, to stay with two complete strangers. The Nevilles could be murderers for all they knew. He had hardly any money in his pockets to pay for a hotel room if they didn't turn up, or if he couldn't find them. Perhaps he should have been wearing a red carnation in his buttonhole, or maybe carrying flowers to give Mrs Neville, like the old lady who'd got on the train at Wollongong with a bunch of roses.

With a heavy sigh he stood up on the seat to retrieve the suitcase from the luggage rack. From the case he removed the Jingera school blazer and struggled into it just as the train pulled into Central Railway Station. After a tussle, he managed to slide open the window. Craning out, he found himself peering straight into the eyes of a facsimile of Miss Neville.

'Jim Cadwallader,' the man said, laughing. 'Exactly as Pat described and in the right compartment too!'

Jim got out of the carriage and the Nevilles each shook his hand. Mrs Neville was shorter and rounder than she'd looked in the photograph, but every bit as good-natured. A small battle ensued as to who should assume responsibility for the suitcase, which Jim lost. As they passed through the ticket barrier he was distracted by the great arch of the station and the hall through which the Nevilles were leading him. Forgetting about his shyness he burst forth with a series of questions about the history of the station. The Nevilles spoke as if they were one person: if one paused for breath the other continued effortlessly, only slightly shifting from the original theme. Thus railways led naturally to sheep and sheep to industry and industry to soap. By the time they were at Rushcutters Bay, Mrs Neville was talking about showers, and before long he'd been fed and shunted into their bathroom. There he showered and soon after, although it wasn't yet nine o'clock, he fell into the deepest of sleeps in the Nevilles' spare bedroom.

'Time to get up, Jim,' said Mr Neville, knocking on Jim's door, when it seemed to Jim that he had only just fallen asleep. 'We'll have a spot of breakfast before we head off to Vaucluse.'

He dressed quickly. Mrs Neville prepared a large breakfast of bacon and eggs, although she'd quite understand, she said, if he didn't want to eat it. She herself had never been able to eat anything before an exam, but Mr Neville was quite the reverse, he was always hungry.

Afterwards Mr Neville drove Jim through hilly streets. Everywhere seemed so crowded. Houses jostled against each other, people jostled against one another. It was a relief to reach the space of Rose Bay with its low wall at the edge of the road and beyond, a marina where yachts were moored, their rigging clinking in the breeze like iceblocks in a glass of water. A flying boat came down to land on the bay, but Mr Neville refused to stop the car to look at it, he said they'd be late.

Stambroke College was a collection of sandstone buildings set in neatly clipped gardens and surrounded by more playing fields than Jim had ever seen before. Mr Neville led him through a quadrangle to a lawn where a lot of boys were standing about. Wide steps led to a modern brick building in which the examination was to be held. Some of the boys were wearing Stambroke uniform, grey blazers with blue and white piping, and striped ties in the same colours; and an air of confidence, Jim thought. They were boys from the preparatory school, hoping to get a scholarship to the senior school, Mr Neville told him before he left.

The uniform was too smart and Jim's own clothes seemed so shabby. Not that he cared that much about the clothes; it was the boys' confidence that made him uncomfortable. He'd never win a scholarship here. These boys would be much too clever.

'Where are you from?'

Jim turned. A freckled boy with wavy blond hair, and dressed in the Stambroke uniform, was standing right behind him. 'Jingera,' he said. His voice came out hoarse and he coughed to disguise his nervousness.

'That on the North Shore?'

'No. Down south, on the coast.'

'Lucky you. I love the beach. You live on a property?'

'In a property. In a house.'

The boy laughed. 'You're not a cocky?'

'No.' A moment later Jim realised what the boy meant. Cockies were people on the land. People who made a living from the land, like cockatoos.

'Do you live in town?'

'Yes.' Jim was growing tired of all the questions although he liked the friendliness he felt in the boy. 'Where are you from?'

Men in suits now opened the doors to the building and ushered the boys inside.

'Walgett,' the boy said, as they climbed the steps. 'That's way out north-west. All we eat there is mutton. That's why I'm a boarder here; I need the vegetables.'

The hall was full of desks on which papers were neatly arranged. Jim and the boy took their seats in the row closest to the windows. Once seated, Jim avoided looking at anyone. Instead he stared out of the open window while waiting for the signal to begin. Outside a few older boys in blazers and boaters wandered across the lawn towards some trees, beyond which the harbour glittered. Gazing at the winking blue water, he breathed deeply, feeling almost dizzy with the smell of summer. Of sun on grass and the scent of some flower that was new to him, pungent and sickly sweet at the same time.

Then they were told to begin, and he forgot everything else as he buried himself in a world of numbers and of problem-solving, of comprehension and of general knowledge. The time danced by and before he knew it he'd finished and the papers had been collected. Then he was filled with the excitement that he always felt after losing himself in that way. It was as if he'd left his own body behind and gone somewhere else, and when he came back again he felt liberated by the experience.

The boy he'd met earlier was waiting for him outside the exam room. 'What did you reckon?' he said.

'Really hard.' Jim wasn't going to admit that he'd enjoyed it. 'And you?'

'Terrible. I only sat it because I had to. Where are you staying?'

'With the Nevilles.'

'Not the teacher?'

'Yes, there he is.'

'Time for me to go then.' The boy grinned. 'Hope to see you again.'

He slouched off, hands deep in pockets, with the walk Jim had noticed many of the Stambroke boys affecting. As Jim strolled back to the car with Mr Neville he tried out the Stambroke Walk. It felt funny. Probably required months of practising.

'What do you think of the school?' Mr Neville said.

'Terrific grounds.' These and the exam room were all Jim had been able to take in, and he was starting to feel so very tired.

'They are. Boys who come here are really lucky. I'd better warn you, though, that the exam is very competitive. Didn't want to say that earlier as I didn't want to make you nervous beforehand. So don't get your hopes up too high.'

'Doesn't matter. I'm not banking on it.' Jim had already put behind him all thoughts of winning the scholarship.

———

But on the journey back to Jingera he had plenty of time to think about Sydney. After the exam, the Nevilles had taken him on a ferry ride from Circular Quay to Valencia Street Wharf and back again, the best way to see the harbour, Mrs Neville claimed – she'd grown up in Balmain. The ferry went under the Harbour Bridge, the coathanger, Mr Neville called it, with the great stone pylons at each end that weren't there to hold it up but were simply decoration. 'They're redundant,' Mrs Neville said, laughing. 'As are so many things in life.' Then past Luna Park with its colourful face that was the entrance grinning over the water. Past a row of piers extending like fingers into the harbour. On to various stops whose names he could no longer remember, apart from Long Nose Point, you'd never forget a name like that. In the evening the Nevilles had taken him to see a George Bernard Shaw play in the city. They'd hoped it wouldn't be too dull for him, but he'd loved it. The language, the drama, the way you could be sitting there in the audience between the Nevilles knowing it was all make-believe but at the same time be moved by what you saw on stage. 'Suspension of disbelief,' Mr Neville had explained on the way back to Rushcutters Bay afterwards.

Jim wondered what it would be like having Mr Neville as a teacher. Inspiring probably, he was so enthusiastic about everything. While Miss Neville didn't have that enthusiasm, he knew she was a good teacher. 'How she manages to teach all those different age groups in one classroom I just can't understand,' Mrs Neville had said. 'Originally we thought she'd only stop in Jingera for a couple of years but then she decided to stay on. Likes it there, evidently.'

It was a funny thing how you could want something and at the same time not want it. That's what he felt about the scholarship. If you do want something and also don't want it, the two things should cancel out and mean you don't care either way. Yet he knew that wasn't the case because when he tried convincing himself that he wouldn't get into Stambroke College, he began to feel strangely sad. This was silly when he'd just told himself that he didn't care either way. Next he tried imagining that he'd won the scholarship and this didn't make him feel too good either. Leaving Jingera would mean giving up his old friends and those days spent playing in the bush and on the beach after school, and on his billycart. Not to mention his mother's cooking, and when you came to think of it, even chopping wood and feeding the chooks started to seem quite attractive when you considered the alternative. If only you could gain new things without giving up old things, how much easier life would be. He was jumping ahead of himself though. Mr Neville has said the competition for the scholarships was fierce and he musn't get his hopes up. So he shouldn't even think about it any more. Instead he should think about what he'd seen in Sydney. Almost as soon as he started to replay the ferry ride in his mind, the rocking of the carriage lulled him into a deep sleep from which he awoke only when the train reached Bomaderry Station.

Struggling out of the carriage with his suitcase, he realised how much he was looking forward to getting home. It was good to go away, he'd had a terrific time in Sydney and the Nevilles were nicer than he could ever have hoped they'd be. Yet he wanted to be back where everything was certain, everything was familiar, and he began to think with longing of his bedroom at home.

On the last leg of the homeward journey, on the long bus ride south to Burford where his father was to meet him, he thought again of Sydney. The city was beautiful but the sky there seemed smaller and less clear than down south. In Wilba Wilba Shire the light had a clarity to it. It illuminated things. Sydney was quite hazy really. The views from Jingera were far better than you'd ever find anywhere else: the huge space of the ocean and the sky, and the mountain ranges rearing up behind. He couldn't bear to have to leave that; and he wouldn't be leaving it. Burford Boys' High was a pretty good alternative when you thought about it. Great oval; bus ride there and back a laugh, or so the older boys had said, and you'd meet girls on the bus. Not that he cared that much for girls, although Zidra and Lorna weren't too bad, more like boys than girls.

But Burford High couldn't possibly measure up to Stambroke and he couldn't imagine that any of the teachers would be as kind as Mr Neville.

This faint feeling of disappointment was probably fatigue and hunger – he felt starved in spite of the packed lunch Mrs Neville had made – and he thought of his mother's special shepherd's pie and wondered if she was making it for tonight's tea. Although he'd only been away from home for three days, he couldn't wait to see his family again.

CHAPTER SIXTEEN

The hot breeze twisted the leaves of the eucalyptus trees. They sparkled as they caught the afternoon sunlight and shimmered with a silvery light. Such a lovely glistening that Zidra forgot to watch where she was putting her feet. Stumbling on the rough ground, she nearly fell. Although she moaned slightly, Lorna took no notice. She was striding ahead, hatless. Her scalp was covered with a velvety new growth of soft black hair. Ten days ago she'd been sent home from school with head lice and that was when she'd had her head shaved. Zidra might have envied Lorna's brief absence from school if she hadn't missed her so much. When she returned, Zidra thought how beautiful she looked with that fine head exposed but some of the other children had been cruel. Mama had hidden the tears in her eyes when Zidra brought Lorna home that day for a glass of milk and some biscuits after school.

'Such a humiliation,' her mother said after Lorna had gone. 'Surely there is a kinder treatment.'

'But why did you cry?' Zidra persisted. 'Lorna doesn't really mind.'

'She has grown a hard skin for protection, but anyway it reminded me of things that are best forgotten.'

'What things? Did you have head lice?'

'Things that are a long time in the past, long before you were born.' Her mother hadn't said any more but had started to play the piano, an angry piece with much thumping of the keys.

The sun filtering through the leaves felt hot on Zidra's head, in spite of her hat. The narrow path was littered with twigs and dead gum leaves. Suddenly Zidra remembered about snakes and how they liked to lie in the sun, or at least so she'd been told, for she hadn't seen one yet. Although Lorna was ahead and would surely see any snake first, Zidra started to walk noisily, stamping her feet hard on the ground, pounding the surface to make as much noise as possible.

At last Lorna turned. 'You're frightening all the world. Pretend you're a goanna. You go quieter, you go faster.'

'What's a goanna?'

'Sort of lizard. Very shy, like me.'

Zidra laughed and stopped stamping. The word goanna sounded funny. Go Anna. It would make a good name for someone. She began to copy Lorna's style of walking, a sort of gliding really. She could be a two-legged snake slithering through the bush.

The path became more overgrown as it swung round the contour of the hill and began to drop into a ravine. Now the girls slid and clutched at ferns and low bushes to break their sharp descent. The light, filtering through the dense canopy of trees, was dappled green. Far away a bird called, like a whip cracking. Eventually the path joined a narrow creek that fell steeply, over gold-and-pink-streaked sandstone rocks.

Lorna stopped in a narrow glade where the creek lingered awhile in a sandy-bottomed pool, flanked on the far side by a broad rock tilting down into the water and fringed by ferns.

'Stillwater Creek,' Lorna said. 'I come here sometimes. It's my special place. Not much water now though. Maybe half-full, maybe quarter. That's probably why they call it Stillwater.'

She kicked off her sandshoes as if they were slippers; as usual she had no laces to slow her down. After stepping across some stones, she sat on the rock curving down into the pool. Zidra pulled off her sandshoes and socks and joined Lorna. 'We should've brought our swimmers,' she said. The lagoon was cleaner than this but she felt so hot that any water looked inviting, even water with the greenish tinge of this pool.

'Let's go in anyway. There's no one to see.' Lorna peeled off her shirt and shorts. Wearing only ragged pink underpants, she stood for a few seconds at the water's edge. She turned to Zidra, who hugged her knees to her chest, embarrassed by Lorna's knickers that her mother would certainly have condemned to the ragbag, if not the incinerator.

'There's no one around,' Lorna repeated.

Into the deepest part of the pool she waded and lowered herself into the water. Zidra stripped off quickly. There was just enough water for the two of them to float, and when that palled, to splash and engage in mock fights. After tiring even of this, they clambered out and lay side by side on the worn sandstone rock, with heads cushioned on their bundles of clothes.

Lulled by the running water and the sound of the cicadas, Lorna soon fell asleep. Zidra rolled onto her stomach and watched the dogged progress of a brown ant across the grainy surface of the rock. Soon becoming bored with inaction, she dressed and gathered stones to build up a dam. As she was playing, the shadows lengthened over the glade and abruptly, almost without warning, the whole ravine was cast into shadow.

The bush suddenly seemed noisy. Twigs snapped unexpectedly, the undergrowth rustled for no apparent reason, leaves rasped dryly against one another. Zidra stopped construction of the dam and listened intently. She could hear a louder rustling, which could be footsteps through the dense undergrowth. Perhaps it was just a bird; a lyrebird, or even a kangaroo. The creature seemed to be moving away. Certain now that something or someone had been watching them, she stayed perfectly still and listened until she could no longer make out the crackling noise. Whatever it was had gone. Or perhaps it was frozen as still as she, waiting, watching. She didn't move for another minute. High in the tallest trees, some birds began a mournful conversation, distinct against the background chorus of cicadas.

Only whatever was in the bush knew where she and Lorna were. No one else did, not even her mother; especially not her mother. At this thought, she started to feel even more frightened. Lorna was still sleeping. If Zidra didn't wake her up she might sleep all night. More roughly than intended, she shook Lorna's shoulder. She woke with a start. Gently Zidra stroked Lorna's hair that felt as soft as moss. 'I think someone's watching us,' she whispered.

Lorna looked confused at first, as if she thought she were somewhere else. 'Just a roo or a wallaby, probably.' After struggling to her feet, she dressed quickly. 'Time to go,' she said, as if it was Zidra's doing they were still there. 'You stick close behind me.' She stepped over the stones bridging the creek and led the way up the hillside.

Zidra, puffing along behind her up the steep slippery path, still managed to say, 'Hurry!' even though Lorna was forging ahead. Lorna turned and waited for her to catch up. Grabbing Zidra's wrist, she hauled her along, not heeding the whimpering that was all the protest Zidra had breath to make. Twigs snapped under their feet and the low-growing ferns and bushes lunged at their bare legs, slowing their progress as they battled up the gully. No birds called now and even the cicadas were silent. The bush waited, silent, expectant, for the change from day to evening. The light was fading fast, becoming a dark almost palpable green and Zidra found it increasingly difficult to make out the line of the path. At last it flattened out and Lorna let go of Zidra's wrist.

'It won't be dark for another hour,' Lorna said. 'It's just that the gully's in the shade. You didn't have to panic.'

'I wasn't panicking,' Zidra said crossly, after recovering her breath. She looked around. There was no sign of anyone and, now they were out of the ravine, there was still plenty of sunlight although it was slanting sharply. The sky was pale but blazed golden towards the west. To the east the land fell gently towards the lagoon that glimmered in the distance.

'You didn't look too happy, Dizzy.'

'I'm very happy now. Except I'm sure we were being watched.'

Lorna shrugged her shoulders. 'Need to spend more time in the bush to get used to bush noises. Probably only a kangaroo.'

But Zidra knew that when she'd woken her, Lorna had seemed scared too, although hers seemed to be a different sort of fear. 'She lives on the margins,' Mama had said of her. Maybe that was it, although Zidra hadn't known quite what she meant. At the time she'd thought of Lorna within the borders of her exercise books and she'd laughed.

'Let's have a quick paddle in the lagoon on the way back,' Zidra said. Her legs were coated with dirt and covered in tiny scratches from their rapid ascent.

When they were almost at the lagoon, they heard boys' voices. Although Lorna gestured to Zidra to keep quiet, there was no need; Zidra was already walking on tiptoe and poised to run in case it was horrible Roger, but it was just Jim and his brother Andy, stacking bits of wood on the sand above the shoreline.

'Hello!' Zidra called. The boys didn't seem to hear.

'You're all right on your own now,' Lorna said. 'See you Monday.' Without pausing to greet Jim and Andy, she set off at a fast trot along the lagoon edge, heading south away from Jingera.

Jim lit the fire with one match. Though aware of Andy's envious admiration, he didn't relax his concentration as the flames flickered around the kindling before flaring into a column of fire. This was the moment when you had to keep your nerve; this was the moment when you had to resist the temptation to beat out the flames, because just as suddenly they might die back.

It was when he was putting the potatoes into the ashes of the fire that he heard Zidra call out and there she was, just ten yards away. In the distance he saw Lorna running down the path away from them, as fast as if she was in the hundred-yard sprint. The funny thing was he'd been thinking of Zidra just a few minutes ago, so her turning up was almost like having a wish come true, although it would have been better if it had happened after they'd eaten the spuds. There were only six of them and he could see Andy doing the mental arithmetic of six divided by three instead of two and being unhappy with the outcome.

'We're cooking potatoes and we've only got six,' Andy said.

'You're welcome to share them with us,' Jim said.

Zidra accepted and Jim pretended not to notice Andy glowering at him. When the potatoes were ready, he scraped them out of the ashes and lined them up on the sand to cool. After he'd divided them into three lots of two, Zidra said she only wanted one, so he carefully broke a potato into two to share with Andy. There was nothing more delicious than a mouthful of charred black crust mixed with the soft white pulp inside.

'Why did Lorna run away?' Andy's voice was muffled by the potato.

'I don't know. Maybe she's a bit shy.'

'It's Mum. She doesn't like Lorna.' At once Jim felt disloyal. He shouldn't have said that but he'd wanted to make it clear to Zidra that Lorna's swift departure had nothing to do with him and Andy.

'She's not here. Anyway, why doesn't she like her?'

'Don't know.' But Jim did know. He'd never forget last Sports Day, when Mum had told Dad that Lorna was dirty and it was a disgrace having her at their school. She might be a bit ragged because the family was poor, he'd said, and she'd replied that they were a feckless lot and being poor was only one part of the story. Where she'd come from, the Upper North Shore of Sydney, there weren't any Abo camps and she was jolly glad of it too. Dad hadn't said any more. It was always best not to answer back when she was in one of her volatile moods, but Jim was sure Lorna had heard this exchange. She'd been standing only a few yards away. No wonder she wouldn't stick around.

'When did you get back from Sydney?' Zidra said.

'Yesterday,' Jim said. 'It was a really long trip.'

'I know, I've done it. What was Stradbroke College like?'

'Stambroke not Stradbroke,' said Andy.

'Nice. Very imposing though.'

'*Imposing*,' she said, perfectly imitating his accent. 'You always use such big words, just like my mother.'

Jim felt pleased; this was one of the things he liked about The Talivaldis. When he listened to her speak it felt like he was visiting a foreign country. Strange accent, big words, odd expressions. Zidra had some of it too, that exotic veneer, and he'd several times heard the pair of them speaking in what he supposed was Latvian. He never got much chance to talk to her at school, she was always with Lorna. One day when Lorna was away and he did speak to her, some of the boys started teasing him, so he gave up talking to her in front of the others. It was okay with just Andy though because he liked her imitations, especially of Miss Neville and Mrs Blunkett. He screeched with laughter at these, making them even funnier.

'How was the exam?'

'Okay, I suppose. Pretty difficult really.' He wasn't going to admit he'd found it easy. 'I won't get in though. Mr Neville told me after the exam that there were boys sitting from all over the state, so I wasn't to get my hopes up.'

'You told me you don't want to go to Sydney anyway,' Andy said.

'I don't. I hate the place. Jingera's much better. Aren't you going to eat the rest of that potato, Zidra?'

'It's a bit burnt on the outside.'

'It's supposed to be. That's the best bit. Here, give it to Andy if you don't want it. He's always hungry.' After finishing the last of his own potato, he wiped his hands on his shorts and picked up a couple of flat pebbles from the shore. He tried flicking one of them across the green water of the lagoon. It rebounded a couple of times before sinking. He had more success with the second: it ricocheted off the water four times, as if deflected from a more solid medium, before sinking into the water.

'I never want to leave here, never,' he said. 'It's the most beautiful place in the world.'

'You can't know that,' Zidra said. 'You've only been to Sydney.'

Jim laughed. Picking up another pebble, he flicked it across the water. Five bounces this time. He was getting better.

CHAPTER SEVENTEEN

'Try to keep still, Ilona.' Cherry, mouth full of pins, looked appraisingly at Ilona. Wearing only the green swimming costume, Ilona was standing on the coffee table in the living room of her cottage. 'It doesn't need taking in much,' Cherry said. 'But the length's a problem.' She scooped up the material at hip level to raise the leg line to where it should be. 'We can make a tuck in the material here. Maybe we'll expose it on the outside so it looks as if it's part of the grand design, and it'll draw attention to your nice backside.'

'And away from my not so nice knees,' Ilona said.

After Cherry had heard Ilona's story of the beach rescue, she'd volunteered to alter the swimming costume, picking just before lunchtime when Bill would be busy in the bar. Knowing what she did of both Ilona and Peter, she could easily visualise how embarrassed each would have been at this way of meeting. Peter so reserved and private. Ilona so proud and independent but with that touching vulnerability, although she had turned it into a comic tale that had made Cherry laugh. Desperate for distraction from her worries about Bill, Cherry was especially glad of things to laugh about these days.

Now removing the pins from her mouth, she said, 'Peter

Vincent lives not far north of Jingera, and he hangs about a bit with the Woodlands crowd, Mr Chapman and his wife Lady Muck. Although he's not stuck up at all, unlike that woman. I've served her twice in the Ladies' Bar when she's come in with Mr Chapman, but will she acknowledge me if she passes me in the street? No, never.' Pausing, she made a minor adjustment to the fabric she was pinning. 'Mind you, you hang out a bit with Lady Muck yourself, don't you? Teaching her son the piano and all that.'

'Mrs Chapman is not so bad. She's generous and adores her son.'

'Perhaps she just needs glasses then. The sort that let you see people who don't matter.'

Ilona laughed, before saying, 'He is quite rude.'

'Who – Peter Vincent? No, he's a nice man. Generous too. Always willing to help people, he's got a reputation for that. He sometimes comes into the pub for a middy or two. He probably saved your life, you know.'

'I know that, and of course I am eternally grateful.'

Cherry looked sharply at Ilona. Sometimes she said the oddest things but it was probably through being foreign. Now Ilona said dreamily, 'When I was a girl, my mother used to pin my clothes for me, just like you. Then she would stitch them by hand, for I am not clever with a needle and thread, and always she would say to me, "Keep still, keep still," although of course I never moved.'

Cherry smiled and carried on adjusting the side seams. She stood back to look critically at the effect. 'Where's your mother now?'

'She died in the war.' Ilona's voice shook but she continued. 'After the war I was in a Displaced Persons' camp and then I went to Britain.'

'Just you?' Cherry stopped pinning and sat cross-legged on the floor in front of Ilona.

'Yes. I met my husband, Oleksii, in Bradford. After we married, we rented a room in a terrace house.' Ilona started to move restlessly around on the top of the coffee table. She might have been exhibiting the swimming costume but her expression seemed absent, as if she'd forgotten where she was. 'There were a lot of other people living there too, all refugees of some sort. Most worked in the factory or the hospital. I worked as a cleaner at the hospital. I had hoped to teach the piano but that was not to be.' She paused. Cherry kept silent. The only sounds that she could hear were the ticking of the clock and a bird's chittering in the shrubbery outside. That and the endless crashing of the surf. Then Ilona said softly, 'I am not boring you, am I, Cherry?'

'Never,' Cherry said. 'Carry on. I want to know.'

'After Zidra was born, I arranged with a friend who also had a baby to work on different shifts. We needed always to have someone at home to care for Zidra and her little boy. Oleksii was working very long shifts at the factory, much longer than ours.'

Cherry wondered if Ilona had been happy in her marriage. She must have been; everyone she knew seemed to be happy in their marriage, except for her, although Miss Neville claimed it was mostly a facade.

Ilona was trembling now, even though the room was so hot.

'You're shivering, Ilona. Put this blouse around your shoulders.'

'I'm not cold, I'm hot. The day is so hot, but that winter was so cold. Such frightful weather we had in Bradford then. The grey damp days, the grey damp nights, and the rain, the perpetual rain.' Glancing at Cherry, Ilona blinked as if she was having trouble focusing. Then suddenly she smiled. It was a formal smile, or perhaps a disoriented smile.

'So we decided to emigrate, Oleksii and I. One day Oleksii came home with brochures about Australia. Such a beautiful place it looked and with so many jobs! Zidra would be just the right age to start school. We did not hesitate. A new life for the three of us! And perhaps Oleksii would be able to play in an orchestra and have the time to compose again.' Her voice sounded brittle and her face looked set. 'But that was not to be, Cherry. That was not to be.'

Cherry didn't know quite what to say. Her own troubles faded. Not into insignificance, they were much too worrying for that, but at least into something slightly less pressing. Without thinking, she said, 'How did Oleksii die?' Then she wished she hadn't. Ilona's face assumed a blank look, as if she'd decided too much had already been revealed. Suddenly the bird that had been chittering outside the window gave a loud squawk. A small tabby cat appeared on the windowsill. Catching sight of the women inside, it sprang away in surprise.

'You've had such a hard life,' Cherry said gently. 'I don't know how you've managed to keep your sunny disposition.'

Ilona laughed bitterly. 'My disposition is not sunny,' she said. 'Every day there is a battle to defeat the blackness.'

'But you are brave too, Ilona. Every day you fight and win.'

'Sometimes I do not win, but I will not be vanquished.'

'No, you won't be. Especially not after you survived that.' Cherry gently touched the blue numbers tattooed on Ilona's forearm.

Ilona flinched at the touch and Cherry quickly removed her hand.

'You know what they mean, Cherry?' Now Ilona was rubbing her arm, as if to scrub off the numbers.

'Yes, I know. Miss Neville told me.'

'I will not wear them covered. They are a reminder of what we went through. I cannot yet bring myself to talk of those things, but in time I must.' Her voice broke and she coughed, as if to disguise her emotion. Once this was under control, she said briskly, 'But we must finish our pinning, Cherry, for I know you do not have much time. You are not watching the clock but I am, and I see that soon Bill will be looking around the bar and wondering where you are, and blaming your piano teacher who has been distracting you.'

Bill. Although Cherry knew she had to watch him, she didn't want to think about him. She'd been watching him ever since she'd made that discovery and, so far, he had done nothing out of the ordinary. But Ilona was right, he would be looking for her soon. Not because he missed her, not because he loved her. He would be looking for her only because of the work she did in the pub.

'Keep still, Ilona.' And Ilona did keep very still until Cherry instructed her to twirl around for one last inspection. Then after a final adjustment, Cherry felt satisfied. 'I'll sew it for you on my machine,' she said.

'That is so kind of you. The stitching of the machine will be so much stronger than the stitching of my hand.'

'Machine stitching. Hand stitching,' said Cherry, laughing although she didn't feel much like it.

'And faster too, but do let me come around to do it at your place. You have so little spare time.'

'It'll take me ten minutes at the most,' Cherry said. 'Up one side, down the other, and maybe a nice strip of bias binding to cover the rough edges inside to stop them prickling. Then the French seam around the hips and it'll be done. Maybe we can fix your two frocks later, after my lesson next week.'

'Can I watch you do it?'

'No, Ilona,' Cherry said indistinctly. After collecting all the pins that had fallen onto the floor, she'd started absent-mindedly putting them into her mouth. Taking them out, she jabbed them hard into the silk-covered pincushion. 'Bill doesn't like me bringing anyone home,' she added, but it was more that she didn't want Ilona and Zidra having anything to do with Bill. She would keep her life as segmented as possible. Everyone would be safer that way.

If only there were someone she could talk to about what she had seen in Bill's office. For an instant she wondered if she might tell Ilona, but no, that would be folly; she couldn't possibly burden Ilona with that, especially after all she'd been through. If Ilona knew, she would advise Cherry to tell the police. She was a mother, after all, how could she possibly say otherwise? Then Cherry would have to follow that through, although she knew the police would never believe anything bad about Bill. Even if they did take her accusations seriously, she'd have to go to court and her own secret would come out. She'd thought all this through many times now and she knew she just couldn't bear the humiliation. It might be different if she was brave like Ilona but she wasn't. She was a coward and she knew it.

That afternoon Cherry stood on the hotel verandah and waited until the last child had straggled out of the schoolyard. Only then did she nonchalantly stroll up the hill and pass through the school gate. She would talk to Miss Neville about Bill but first she must practise the piano a little. It was important to keep up the pretence that she was learning seriously and anyway she wanted to please Ilona.

Miss Neville usually offered her a cup of tea to take with her to the piano but today she didn't turn around at the clatter of Cherry's high-heeled sandals on the wooden floorboards. Stopping at the door to the office, Cherry called, in a parody of a schoolgirl, 'Good afternoon, Miss Neville!' But Miss Neville didn't seem amused. Seated at the desk with her back to the door, she noisily turned the page of an exercise book she was marking.

'I'm here! Will I get on with my practice or would you like me to make you some tea?'

'Carry on,' Miss Neville said gruffly, back still turned to the door. Her hair was ruffled as if she'd been running her fingers through it, and her double crown was exposed. Cherry was tempted to take the four steps into the office to smooth her hair but thought better of it. Never before had she seen Miss Neville this unwelcoming. It made her nervous, as if she was a naughty schoolgirl again at Burford Girls' High, waiting to see the headmistress for yet another detention.

She tiptoed into the large schoolroom and shut the door so that she wouldn't disturb Miss Neville's concentration. Perhaps she wasn't really angry but simply doing something very important. The classroom was hot and it smelled musty, of generations of school lunches and the faint sweat of thirty children. Opening the windows would entail first going out into the corridor and asking Miss Neville for the window opening stick. This long broom handle with its metal hook at one end was kept locked away on the grounds of safety. 'Need a bloody licence to operate it,' Miss Neville had said on a better day. 'A teaching qualification at least. Could be used as an instrument of torture in the wrong hands.' There was no way Cherry was going to disturb Miss Neville now just to get hold of that stick.

She opened the piano and began with the scales, using both hands. If only she could induce the left hand to coordinate properly with the right, instead of always being a fraction of a second behind, she could make great strides forward. Stopping, she gazed out the window at the relentless blue sky. It was difficult to concentrate when she'd done something to offend Miss Neville and didn't know what it was. But Miss Neville didn't want to be disturbed so she must be left alone. Back to the scales, up and down the piano she stumbled, faster and faster with less and less accuracy. Eventually she could stand it no longer. Leaping up from the piano stool, she threw open the classroom door, and marched into the office next door.

'What's wrong?' she said loudly, plonking herself down on one of the visitors' chairs that Miss Neville kept in an orderly row at right angles to her desk.

The school mistress closed the exercise book she'd been marking and pushed her glasses onto the top of her head. She turned towards Cherry but instead of looking directly at her, focused on a point slightly to the left of her head. Cherry resisted the temptation to twist round to inspect the wall behind. This manoeuvre must have been perfected by Miss Neville on countless school children and Cherry might find it amusing if she were not so upset. There was a deep indentation to one side of the bridge of Miss Neville's nose where her glasses had been digging in but it would be dangerous to lean over to attempt to smooth it out.

'I popped into the post office this morning,' said Miss Neville eventually. 'It was only to buy some stamps but you know what Mrs Blunkett's like, especially when there's a bit of a queue. Bally woman becomes slower than ever and plays up to the crowd. Gossiping like mad about all sorts of silly stuff. Anyway, what she had to say today I actually found quite interesting. Seemed that Ilona woman was looking for a dress-maker. She'd asked Mrs Blunkett to ask Mrs Jamison next time she came in. Needed to have a swimming costume altered and a couple of dresses taken in.'

She paused, eyes still fixed on the wall behind Cherry's head. Cherry could guess what was coming but waited just in case she'd got it wrong. A small bird flew into the closed window pane behind Miss Neville's desk and fluttered down onto the wide sill where, slightly stunned, it rested a while before flying off towards the radiata pine trees on the far side of the school yard. Miss Neville continued to stare at the wall. Perhaps this pause was carefully judged to give Cherry enough time to blunder in with a lie should she be stupid enough to want to try, or to attempt an explanation. But she wasn't going to do that. Her years at Burford Girls' High had provided too good a training and besides, there was no reason why she shouldn't help Ilona with some sewing if she wanted to.

'Anyway,' Miss Neville continued at last, 'Ilona turned up at the post office last thing yesterday afternoon, just before Mrs Blunkett was shutting up shop. Seemed she'd found a dress-maker. Seemed that kind woman Cherry Bates had offered to do the alterations for her today. Seemed she was going to pop around to her cottage and pin the swimming costume for her.' Here Miss Neville broke into a perfect mimicry of Mrs Blunkett's way of talking. 'Take it in down the seams and shorten it too, for that Mrs Talivaldis is such a little wisp of a thing and that Cherry's so clever, she can turn her hand to anything.'

Miss Neville stopped but Cherry continued to say nothing. Miss Neville was going to have to come clean without any help from her: The truth of the matter was that she was jealous. Jealous of Cherry because this morning she'd had her hands on lovely Ilona's body. Then an unwelcome thought sidled into her mind. Maybe Miss Neville was jealous of Cherry making friends with another woman not because she wanted to see more of Cherry but because she wanted to see more of the other woman. What a ridiculous prospect, there was no evidence for this at all! She was becoming irrational and should drive this suspicion from her mind. There was no point fabricating extra things to worry about. Bloody hell, her whole life would unravel if Miss Neville cared for someone else.

'You're making something out of nothing,' Cherry said, her voice shaking slightly. To steady herself she took hold of the edge of the desk.

'How can you say that? You spend hours with her having lessons and now you're sewing for her as well. You never spend time with me. That's not right and you know it.'

'That's unfair and *you* know it,' Cherry said, her momentary doubt of Miss Neville vanquished.

'I know nothing.'

At this instant the clock began to chime the hour. Cherry knew she'd have to go, or Bill would be complaining again. Complaints here and complaints at home, it was all too much; however Bill complained the loudest and she'd got so much work to do and that other thing to worry about too. Although she couldn't bear to leave the situation with Miss Neville unresolved, she stood up to leave. 'I love you the most in the world. Believe me, I really do,' she said. 'But I've got to go or Bill will kill me.'

Delicate lines creased Miss Neville's forehead and Cherry longed to caress them away. Instead she planted a quick kiss on her tousled hair. 'I'll come around late tonight,' she said. 'Leave the key under the back doormat.'

Then she hurried out, slowing only when she was visible from the street. Today it was a struggle to assume the carapace: Cherry Bates, the good sort. Cherry Bates, the cheerful wife of the publican, sauntering home after practising the piano at the school and ready for another evening pulling beer in the hotel.

Miss Neville being difficult was almost more than she could bear but she didn't want to have to give up seeing Ilona just because Miss Neville was jealous. She needed her friendship more than ever and Ilona needed friends too. Cherry would just have to work harder at reassuring Miss Neville of her affection. The incident upset her though. If Miss Neville could be so easily destabilised it was not at all clear how she would cope with learning about Bill's nasty little secret.

After closing time and the last of the drinkers had gone home, Cherry fabricated a headache and went up the back stairs to their private quarters. She shut the bedroom door and lay down on the counterpane to wait. Soon she heard Bill's heavy tread and the creaking of the floorboards as he blundered around in the bedroom next to hers. Then there was silence. After ten minutes or so she got up and tiptoed into the hallway. Putting an ear to Bill's door, she could just discern the heavy breathing that signified he was asleep. Although going out now meant she wouldn't be able to monitor him, she had no doubt that he would sleep right through the night. Back in her own room, she put a couple of pillows under the bedclothes just in case, although it was unlikely that he would look in her bedroom even if he did wake up; he hadn't done that since they stopped sleeping together years ago.

The night was still warm but she pulled on a dark coat that completely covered her pale dress and squirted some of the scent Miss Neville had given her onto the pulse points behind her ears and on her wrists. Then she picked up a stocking. After pulling the bedroom door, so that it was open only a couple of inches, she put a hand through the opening and deposited the stocking on the floor just inside the door. If it had moved when she returned she'd know Bill had checked on her, although she didn't really believe that he cared enough to do this.

The stairs creaked a bit but nothing would wake Bill once he was asleep. She took the back route to the school mistress's house, through the lane behind Cadwallader's Quality Meats. There was no one around, apart from Old Charlie who was wandering along the lane behind the butcher's, and who paid her no attention even though they passed within several yards of one another. Cherry was used to him and thought no more of it. He often wandered around at all hours, just as she did in her clandestine comings and goings.

She turned into the lane running behind Miss Neville's house. The yellow disc of the moon was so bright that the stars looked almost pallid in the velvety indigo sky. After unfastening the back gate and stepping quickly into the yard, she secured the catch behind her. The dog next door barked several times then subsided into silence. In the distance a mopoke cried. She stayed completely still beside the old timber outhouse. This was where the dunny used to be before people started installing septic tanks, when the cottages were serviced by night-soil men who collected the cans twice a week and carted them off in a stinking truck that you could smell from a mile away. But the dunnies were no longer used and all she could smell was the sickly scent of honeysuckle climbing over the outhouse.

The light was on in Miss Neville's bedroom although it was shielded by the drawn curtains. Cherry moved stealthily up the path and lifted the back doormat. There was no key. Damn it,

Miss Neville was still angry, or worse, had forgotten about her and she began to feel anxious. Hoping not to intercept an insect, she ran a hand over the rough concrete surface. Eventually, just as her anxiety was turning to despair, she found the key under the doorsill. She fumbled for the keyhole and turned the lock. The door opened easily. She stepped inside and then crept up the stairs.

Wearing pale blue pyjamas, Miss Neville was propped up in bed and deeply absorbed in a book. Her glasses lay on the bedside table and the book was only a few inches away from her eyes. Oblivious to Cherry's silent ascent, she turned a page while Cherry stood there watching. Not wanting to frighten her, Cherry descended half a flight of stairs. Here she burst into song and stepped more noisily on the treads. Then she bounced into the room and there was Miss Neville smiling and holding out her arms.

Later Cherry decided that this was the time to tell Miss Neville about the photographs she'd found in Bill's office. There should be no secrets between them. She looked at the dear face resting on the pillow next to her. Surely Miss Neville would know what to do. So practical, she always had a solution for everything. Good no-nonsense advice, that's what was required. Miss Neville opened her eyes. Cherry braced herself for a description of what she'd seen in Bill's office. Struggling to sit up, she at once began to feel nauseated. She gulped and took a deep breath before saying, 'There's something I have to tell you.'

Miss Neville turned away, as if annoyed. 'It's about Ilona, isn't it?' Her voice was sharp.

'No, it's about Bill.'

Miss Neville looked at her again. 'Bill doesn't matter,' she said gently.

'But he does.'

'No, he doesn't matter. We won't let him hurt us. Just forget about Bill.'

'He's dangerous,' Cherry said.

'Listen, Cherry. No one cares about women like us. They don't believe we exist, most of them. There's absolutely nothing to worry about.'

'But what if Bill found out about us? He could blackmail us. Or me.' Cherry attempted a smile before telling Miss Neville about Mr Ryan the maths teacher, thrown out of Burford High because he was a poofter corrupting the morals of children. 'That's what they'd say about you,' she concluded.

Miss Neville considered this. 'Of course we have to be careful,' she said. 'But Bill hasn't got the imagination to blackmail you. Anyway, why on earth would he want to? You're a great little barmaid in his pub, so why spoil that happy arrangement?'

'But what if I found out something bad about him and had to tell someone?'

'Like what?'

Now was her opportunity. Taking a deep breath, she opened her mouth to begin. But it was impossible to unburden herself yet to Miss Neville, she just couldn't do it this soon. Tomorrow she'd do it, or the day after. She said lamely, 'We mustn't do anything to jeopardise your job.' Her voice sounded weak. She *was* weak.

Miss Neville laughed. 'We're not. Don't fret. No one knows about us, but one day I'll apply for a transfer to Sydney and then we'll be together. That is, if you're willing to leave your old man first. No point my being sent somewhere else with you stuck here.'

This was the first time Miss Neville had been so explicit about where their relationship was heading. If Cherry hadn't felt so worried about Bill she might have seized on these words that were more a declaration than a statement. 'We've got to be together,' she said, but she couldn't walk out on Bill yet. He was too dangerous to be left alone. Suppressing a sigh, she knew that she wanted nothing more than to spend all night lying next to Miss Neville in this soft bed, with arms entwined around each other, and the only sound the distant thud of the surf breaking onto the beach.

She left the house by the back gate as usual. Once in the lane, she stopped briefly to listen. She thought she heard footsteps but was mistaken. It was only the silky sound of leaves rustling in the breeze, so she hurried on. Most of the houses were now in darkness, except for the Cadwalladers, where there was still a light shining in one of the rooms, and the Burtons, who had all their lights blazing. Through their uncurtained back window she could make out the figure of Mrs Burton pacing to and fro, clutching a bawling baby to her chest.

There were no lights on in the hotel. Quietly she opened her bedroom door a few inches and stepped in. The stocking was on the floor exactly where she left it. She undressed and slipped between the sheets.

CHAPTER EIGHTEEN

Although it was well after midnight, George Cadwallader knew he had to get out of the house to clear his head. Eileen was already in bed but he couldn't bear the thought of joining her yet. Instead he went onto the back verandah and peered up at the almost full moon. It wasn't a good night for stargazing but it would be lovely out on the river. He would take his dinghy out of the boathouse and row up the lagoon, away from all the houses, away from all his cares. There he would cast out the anchor, or simply drift with the currents, while contemplating the stars.

It hadn't been much of an evening. Over tea, Jim and Andy had quarrelled about some silly thing and Eileen had taken the younger boy's side without first finding out the facts. Afterwards George had sought out Jim, who was sitting at the bottom of the yard, and sat down next to him on the grass.

'She hates me,' Jim had said.

'No she doesn't. She loves you. She loves both of you.'

'Why does she pick on me all the time then?'

George had weighed his words carefully before replying. 'You're older so she expects more of you.' But he suspected it was more than that; he suspected it was because Jim took after his father. Not in intellect, of course, but in character. Having two of them in the one family was too much for Eileen. They looked similar and they had similar temperaments. Slow to anger, logical and steadfast. Qualities that he used to think were good until he'd learnt that Eileen thought otherwise.

'She's very proud of you,' George had added, extemporising. While she didn't seem proud of Jim now, she would be proud of him in the future. She would be proud of him when he'd won a scholarship, as he was almost certain to do, and ended up achieving all those things that George had never accomplished and that Andy, good boy though he was, lacked the ability to attain.

'We're both really proud of you,' George had added. He would have liked to give Jim a big hug but he'd thought he was probably a bit too old for that. So he had contented himself with patting him on the shoulder.

Now, looking up at the stars, he sighed. So much space and beauty up there, and yet down here the four of them were living in disharmony. He couldn't understand Eileen sometimes. She had her priorities wrong, no doubt about it.

He went inside to get a torch from the laundry cupboard. The house was silent except for the relentless ticking of the grandfather clock in the hallway. The little book about the constellations of the Southern Hemisphere, tucked snugly into one of his pockets, bumped reassuringly against his left hip as he walked down the backyard to the lane. The trouble with Eileen was that she just didn't realise that Jim was going to do remarkable things with his life. She needed to have more faith in him, and the boy needed to know now that his mother was proud of him; before it was too late.

Just as he was about to open the back gate, he chanced to see Cherry coming along the lane. He stopped quite still. The last thing he wanted, when he was out for a bit of peace, was to bump into someone he knew. People thought he was a convivial man but that was just part of the job, and anyway it derived more from a willingness to listen rather than from any tendency to gossip. Sometimes he wanted a break from it all, that endless bonhomie with his customers, day in, day out.

In the dark shadow cast by a gum tree, he waited until Cherry had passed by, turning up the hill towards the hotel. Only then did he continue on his way. Perhaps she'd been watching out for the pair of boo-book owls that were nesting in a hollow of one of the gum trees; only the other day he'd heard Ilona telling her about them. It comforted him to think that others might need to spend some time on their own at night. This sighting certainly wasn't something to mention to Eileen though; she had a poor enough opinion of barmaids already.

He made his way along the lane that curved around to join the road down to the lagoon. On the narrow bridge he stood for a while listening to the water lapping against the piers. He wasn't conscious of hearing the breakers beating on the beach, a sound that was so much a part of his life that it was only noticed in its absence, on those rare occasions when he had to go away from the coast. Over the bridge, he turned along the track leading to the boathouse. The moon was so bright it could almost be sunlight were it not for the fact that everything had been robbed of colour. Even his own ruddy hands looked pale and washed out. He switched on the torch anyway; there was no sense in colliding unnecessarily with a kangaroo.

After launching the dinghy, he rowed up the lagoon perhaps half a mile south of Jingera. There he shipped the oars and let the current almost imperceptibly take him back towards the settlement, only occasionally using an oar to guide the craft.

His favourite star was Alpha Gruis, the brightest star in the constellation of Grus. The whooping crane, it was such a lovely translation. He could gaze at that constellation for hours and never grow tired of it. It had been charted on the first Dutch expedition to the East Indies and he liked to think of the sailors on that voyage, seeing stars they'd never seen before, seeing oceans they'd never seen before; what a journey that must have been. The technical details of Alpha Gruis were well known to him: its spectral type and its astrometry; its mass, and its radius, and also its luminosity. But the star meant more to him than a mass of statistics. It meant peace and the insignificance of his own worries, the insignificance of his own imperfections. It meant harmony too, in some way that he couldn't define, and that he'd never attempted to explain to anyone, not even to Eileen in those early days when he'd held such high hopes for their marriage.

He knew better than to tell anyone of things that really mattered. It wasn't just Eileen who'd taught him not to reveal himself. It was also those other earlier collisions when he'd been growing up, those times when he'd exposed his dreams, only to have them shattered by the artillery of that army of realists, his family. That he lacked the academic ability to become an astronomer he'd never doubted, although he hadn't been given the chance to prove this. By his fourteenth birthday, he'd been apprenticed to a butcher, and soon after realised that there was artistry in meat. He'd also learnt to keep dreams to himself. Secrets and dreams were always safe with George, whether they were his own or anyone else's.

Tonight Alpha Gruis was not as brilliant as usual, it was true; that was because of the brightness of the moon. Yet the vast dome of the sky was soothing; he felt comforted by the sense of his own insignificance in the boundless order of things. After about an hour, having drifted back almost to his starting point, he rowed into shore and dragged the dinghy into the boathouse.

On returning home, he undressed in the bathroom and put on the pyjamas that Eileen had left out. He tiptoed into the bedroom and climbed into the double bed. Eileen woke up enough to mumble something about his werewolf-like habits before lapsing back into a sound slumber. Snuggling up to her would have to wait until next Saturday night, although he would have liked nothing better than to hold her in his arms before drifting into sleep.

CHAPTER NINETEEN

Ilona stared hard at the book. Perhaps she should get up and turn on the ceiling light rather than rely on the rather feeble glow of the lamp. The lines of print were starting to look like rows of tiny black ants marching across the page. She blinked and the ants turned into words. If she were not trying to delay the moment when those breakers of fear started rolling in, she would go to bed. Each night she tried to divert the tidal wave by reading anything she could lay her hands on; novels mostly, from the local library. Although the library collection was small, it would take her years to work through it for she read English so slowly. Yet always she would learn; always she would struggle to improve herself and that way, would control her fear.

Reading some more, she halted at the word *peregrination*; she had no idea what it meant. If only she had more energy she would look it up. Her vocabulary was expanding rapidly although she had to be wary of using a long word when a short one would do. Her grammar was possibly impeccable. Those many hours of studying had certainly brought dividends but she suspected her speech was still slightly too formal. In the future she would endeavour to use colloquialisms. When people talked, she listened out for them and stored them away in readiness for the day when she would have enough confidence to employ them. Although despairing of her own accent, she found the local accent far worse, for it was so different from the way that English was spoken in Bradford. Here it was not always easy to understand what people said. Their vowels were different and if she imitated them, they thought she was making fun of them; *taking the piss,* or *making them look a right galah.*

After a while she got out of her chair and tiptoed into Zidra's room. The girl was sleeping on her side with her hair partly concealing her face. The top sheet and blanket had been thrown back, and lay twisted together at the bottom of the bed.

Ilona watched the rise and fall of her daughter's thin chest, clad in white fabric patterned with blue roses. Here in Australia Zidra would be safe, she reflected, safe from the aftermath of the savagery delivered and received by her generation. Not to mention the Red Menace that everyone talked about, although she suspected no one really knew what was happening behind the Iron Curtain. Only a few years ago the Russians were generally regarded as saviours but not in her Latvia. Now they were the enemy and all those former allies were hurling propaganda at one another as if they'd never fought on the same side to defeat the Nazis. She sighed, though not loudly enough to disturb Zidra. If the politicians were to be believed, the biggest peril facing the civilised world was communism. That was what the Prime Minister, Mr Menzies, said and that was what people thought. Propaganda or the truth, there was no way of telling, not until it was all in the past.

Kissing Zidra's forehead, Ilona smelt the sweet scent of clean skin. She knew she would do anything to protect her daughter, anything. She had to; she was the only survivor. She hadn't died when all those others in the camp had died. She hadn't died when Oleksii had died.

Suddenly she found she could scarcely breathe, her throat felt so constricted. A black wave of despair began to wash over her, and might have engulfed her had she not focused on Zidra. Her daughter was her reason to live. Without her, the guilt at surviving would be impossible to bear. Shutting her eyes, she crouched next to the bedside for some minutes, listening to the distant pounding of the breakers and the quicker rhythm of Zidra's breathing. Everything was going to be fine. She had endured that moment, she would get through all such moments. After smoothing a strand of hair away from Zidra's nose, she untangled the top sheet and pulled it gently over her.

Later she made a cup of tea and took it onto the side verandah. The old cane chair felt slightly clammy with the salty air. As her eyes adjusted to the dark, it became possible to distinguish the glimmer of the lagoon and the dark shape of bushland separating the estuary from the beach. Beyond, the crests of the breakers were silvery in the moonlight. She stared up at the stars, so numerous that they formed a great white band they called the Milky Way. It was a soothing sight but not quite soothing enough. Why she'd unburdened herself to Cherry that afternoon she couldn't understand. Perhaps it was because of Cherry's kindness in offering to do those alterations for her; perhaps it was because Cherry had laughed so much at the story of the beach rescue. But another possibility was that meeting Peter Vincent had reawakened some of those old memories she'd spent years forgetting. War and the legacy of war. So many lives lost or blighted. Even in a town as remote as Jingera, the war memorial was covered with the names of locals who'd lost their lives in the last one and in the one before.

So when Cherry had asked about her past, all that stuff about her mother sewing for her and her life in Bradford and their decision to emigrate came pouring out, but nothing about the war. She might think of it but she would never talk of it. And she would avoid seeing Peter Vincent again. He unsettled her.

Cherry had seemed genuinely interested in her story but when she'd touched her tattoo, and such a gentle touch it had been, Ilona had felt as if she might break down altogether and she couldn't have that. Rebuilding her life had been a battle that she was winning, she knew it, but she had to keep control. For Zidra's sake as well as her own.

Long after she had finished her tea, she continued to sit on the verandah. In the distance the breakers rolled in, an endless thud, thud, thud on the shore. An unexpected pleasure of living here was this feeling of closeness to nature, closer than she'd ever felt anywhere before. A large bird flew into the tall eucalyptus tree at the bottom of their yard, one of the pair of owls that lived there. It began to call, a strange boo-book sound that had startled her when she had first heard it, but which was now reassuring. Several doors up the Burtons' baby started bawling again and then abruptly stopped.

Now her attention was caught by a light bobbing along, on the far side of the lagoon, towards the bridge. A few seconds later she discerned a figure walking across the bridge.

A cloud passed over the moon but still she could make out the shape of the man holding the torch. A large man, who now moved on, over the bridge and up the hill towards her house. She slipped inside, locking the door behind her. Peering through the front room window she saw George Cadwallader limping past the house, torch illuminated. Perhaps he too suffered from insomnia. Or perhaps the only time he had for walking was at night.

She struggled on with reading. With three new words collected, she looked them up in the dictionary. *Peregrination:* the action of travelling or of journeying. *Hyssop:* aromatic herb with blue flower. *Heinous:* hateful, odious. *Cherry peregrinates picking hyssop heinously.* It didn't sound right somehow. Nor did it sound better when she substituted George for Cherry, but at last she had wearied herself to the point of exhaustion and beyond.

In bed she lay quiet. In bed she waited for those black breakers of despair to come rolling in from the depths and wash her into a turbulent sleep.

CHAPTER TWENTY

Late the following Saturday afternoon, Peter Vincent began the journey to Woodlands to collect the kelpie pup, and to endure that infernal dinner party Judy Chapman had organised: he'd been dreading it for days.

A mile or two beyond Jingera, he saw Tommy Hunter walking along the side of the road, a bucket and rod in one hand and the other hand half-heartedly thumbing a lift. He'd known Tommy for years; had met him when they were boys fishing in the lagoon at Jingera. Tommy was wearing a pinstriped jacket, the predecessor to Peter's winter-weight suit and which he'd passed on to Tommy some months earlier. It suited Tommy far better than it had ever suited Peter, and he must find it more comfortable too, for he was never without it, even on the warmest day. Peter stopped the car and opened the boot for the bucket.

'You must have half-a-dozen whiting there. Looks like a good dinner.'

'Might've stayed a bit longer if I 'adn't left me dog tag be'ind. Get thrown into the lockup after six without it.'

'Ah, the dog tag.' Peter felt slightly awkward, as if he himself was responsible for those exemption certificates issued to 'deserving' Aborigines who would otherwise be banned from town after sundown. He added, 'But surely the police would recognise you.'

'That don't matter. Only way they know I'm deservun is if I'm wearun me dog tag. Anyway we blackfellas all look the same.' He didn't sound angry about it; it was just a statement of fact, like a comment on the weather.

'How's the family?'

'Good. Littlest goin to school next year, and Lorna's got a new friend.'

'Who's that?'

'That girl whose mother's from overseas.'

'The Latvian woman's daughter?' Peter didn't understand quite why he felt so pleased with this connection. The day he'd first seen the woman with the purple hat at Woodlands, she'd been holding the hand of a young girl with a mop of curly brown hair. Perhaps it was just that he liked the idea of Tommy's oldest daughter befriending the girl. He added, as he did every time he saw Tommy, 'Need some work?'

'No, they're pickun at Prentice's, and the fishun's good.' Tommy laughed.

After dropping Tommy off at the camp by the river, where half-a-dozen kids raced towards him, Peter drove on through the long valley leading to Woodlands. Even here, where the shape of the landscape encouraged clouds to precipitate when they reached the escarpment, the countryside was beginning to look dry.

The closer to Woodlands he got, the more slowly he drove. It was when he got to the top of the first rise that he saw it, and an instant later he heard it: the Tiger Moth aeroplane flying low up the valley. With sweating palms slipping on the steering wheel, he pulled the car off the road and stopped the engine.

He knew what was coming next: that terrible sensation in his breast like a trapped bird flapping around his heart. To forestall it, he gulped the slightly dusty air deep into his lungs. Despite this anxiety, he couldn't help but squint up at the sky. Immediately before the escarpment, just before it was too late, the plane performed several loops upwards. Then it changed direction and flew westwards and out of sight.

It was over, it was gone, and he was panting as if he'd run a mile. Taking out a handkerchief, he wiped his damp hands and neck before getting out of the car. Up and down the gravel verge he marched, breathing deeply all the while. This feeling of panic happened every time he saw or heard a plane. Every time.

Years ago his reactions had been different. Years ago, on a summer's evening just like this, he'd witnessed something that had changed his life. Driving along the Braidwood Road near his parents' property, he'd seen a tiny plane challenging all notions of flying as a means of moving horizontally from one point to another. Instead it had swooped up and down at right angles to the earth's surface. Twisting up like a corkscrew, its fuselage glinting as it caught the slanting rays of the late afternoon sunshine. Then flattening out before plunging straight down, wings tilting first to one side and then to the other. For an instant Peter had thought that it must surely bore straight into the ground, but it had suddenly flattened out and flown conventionally, flown horizontally, for perhaps half a mile. After that, as if fatigued by such monotony, the pilot had twisted the plane up into the sky again and repeated the whole performance. How exhilarating it had looked. How fantastic it would be to defy gravity, to swoop through the air like an eagle, like Icarus. He had longed to try it.

This vision he had kept to himself. Once the Empire Air Training Scheme had started, not long after war had been declared, he had enlisted. Never would he forget the medical inspection, in a shabby barn of a hall that stank of disinfectant and sweaty feet. He'd stripped to the waist and taken his place on one of the rows of benches until it was his turn to be called. Several doctors, who had seemed ancient but were probably no older than he was now, had occupied the examination booths. One by one they'd determined the fate of the men enlisting. Eventually it was his turn. Of course he'd got in. He was the right physical type, the right age, had been to the right school. After that, he'd been sent to Williamtown for training and had been one of the first embarking for Canada, and then for England, to join an RAF squadron.

Now he stopped pacing up and down the verge of the road and looked up at the sky again. An empty sky. As empty as he felt inside, and lonely too. Normally being alone wouldn't bother him; it was what he sought after all; but this was more a sense of isolation and it was a new feeling. Nervousness, he supposed, at the prospect of sitting through Judy's match-making attempt that was doomed to failure from the start. Yet this would only last a few hours and he'd had plenty of experience dealing with her efforts. Feeling calmer now, he looked around him. White daisies flowered along the roadside and, in the paddock beyond, there was a purple smudge of Paterson's Curse that someone should get rid of.

A honking from a car caught his attention. Ian and Joy Sutherland pulled up beside him, in a new-looking Chevrolet covered in a film of pale dust. They ran a property a few miles away and he hadn't seen them for months.

'Broken down?' Joy called through the passenger window.

'No. Just stopped for a breather. Car's running sweet as ever.' Although trying to look normal, he felt he was grimacing rather than smiling.

'Time you got rid of that old thing and got a proper car.'

Peter stroked his Armstrong Siddeley. 'These ones last forever,' he said. 'Aluminium body.'

'Like a plane.'

'Just like a plane.' But the aluminium body was the only similarity, he thought.

'Heading for the Chapmans' dinner party, aren't you?'

'Yes, and I'm picking up a new kelpie too.'

'See you there. Give us a bit of a head start so you're not eating our dust!'

The Sutherlands drove up the valley towards Woodlands. Peter rolled a cigarette while he waited for them to get ahead, and then started up the engine.

———— ·◆· ————

Now he was at Woodlands, sitting with the Chapmans and their other guests in the drawing room. Through the French doors he could see the blaze of gold as the sun sank below the rugged mountains and then the sky faded to a bleached blue. The upright chair on which he perched must be a valuable antique or its lack of comfort would surely have led to its disposal years ago. Opposite him, Judy Chapman and Grace Smythe, elegantly arranged on a sofa, were chatting vivaciously. They might almost be sisters the way they looked alike and spoke alike and dressed alike. But Judy was a little warmer than Grace, who had a hardness about her, a coldness, in spite of the lovely features. Both were wearing dresses of the same clinging silky fabric. Both were striking in an over-painted, over-treated way. He looked obliquely at Grace. Too much make-up, dress too low-cut, too much cleavage on show. Catching the direction of his eyes, she smiled at him. She thought he found her arousing but the last thing he wanted was titillation from this painted lady.

163

Shortly the maid announced that dinner was ready and they moved into the dining room. Peter found himself seated between Judy and Grace. With longing he thought of the peaceful kitchen at home. He wished that Judy had placed him next to Ian Sutherland, who usually had a few good yarns to spin. This was what he hated about dinner parties, being wedged between women who either made fun of him or wanted him to marry their unattached friends. He didn't know quite what was expected of him. Maybe he had once, years ago, but not any more. If he wasn't charming, the women would dismiss him as dull and he wasn't sure he wanted that. His ego was too big, or too fragile. But if he was too charming, amazing Grace might fall for him. That would be far worse; he had to get through the rest of the weekend. He wanted to do it with grace but without Grace. In spite of himself, he grinned.

Judy saw the grin and smiled encouragingly. He reminded himself of the reason he had come: for the tennis the next day and because of Jack Chapman's kelpie. The dinner party was part of the price he would have to pay. Deliberately he asked Grace if she were interested in cattle breeding and saw the smile fade from Judy's face.

The conversation lapsed. At the other end of the table, the others seemed to be arguing about the hydro-electricity scheme. Peter sipped his wine carefully. He had to be careful not to swig it down as if it were the beer he'd rather be drinking. Seeing the jug of water in the centre of the table, he offered to pour for his neighbours. When he'd finished, Grace leant towards him to take the glass and their fingers touched. So too did their shoulders. Suspecting she was deliberately leaning against him for far longer than necessary, he looked at her. Watching for his reaction, she was certainly teasing him. Unfortunately, in his haste to look away, he found he was peering straight down her cleavage. Staring at the far end of the oval table would help to distract him from the blush suffusing his face.

Judy Chapman towards one end of the table, Jack Chapman at the other. The contrast between host and hostess couldn't be greater. Judy's skin so white and her hair so flaming red; Jack's face so flaming red and his hair so white, so prematurely white. Judy so Eastern Suburbs Sydney, Jack so much the farmer: it was a miracle they'd ever got together. Opposites attracted; but it was more that money attracted money. Wiley's Woollen Mills meeting Woodlands Stud Farm. There could be no more blessed an alliance than that of the heirs to the fortunes of each. Little Philip Chapman would be sitting on a pretty fortune when it was his turn to take over and so far there were no brothers and sisters to share it with.

Then Peter realised that conversation at his end of the table had been resumed and it was time to abandon his reverie.

'The Abos are going to be moved on,' Judy was saying. 'That camp's a disgrace.'

'They're not doing anyone any harm there, Jude,' Jack said.

'They've got their own reserve up at Wallaga Lake. What more do they want? That's prime real estate up there, or it will be in a few years' time.'

'They live in such frightful squalor,' said Grace, shuddering. 'And such ugly faces.'

Peter struggled to prevent his distaste from showing as he said, 'Some are quite beautiful. Just as some white people are ugly and others beautiful.' He didn't add what he was thinking, that some people can change from beauty to ugliness in just a few seconds.

'I must tell you about the new piano teacher I found in Jingera,' Judy said, evidently judging it politic to change the

165

subject. 'Such a character. I had her come out for an interview and she insisted on playing the piano to show me how good she is. She did play brilliantly, but do you know what she chose? Shostakovich!' Judy opened her arms wide in a theatrical gesture, as if inviting the others to share in the hapless pianist's folly.

The piano teacher might be the Latvian woman. Peter waited. He could see that the other men at the dinner table looked slightly bemused but the women seemed to know what was expected of them.

'That Russian composer.' Grace was the first to offer an explanation. 'Communist of course. Stalin's poodle.'

'Stalin wouldn't have a poodle. He'd have a Borzoi.'

'You always take things so literally, darling.'

'Do you think she's a Communist, your piano teacher? Exciting to have a Commie spy at Jingera.'

'Hardly. What on earth would anyone spy on there?' Judy dismissed Jingera with a wave of her hand but then recollected that this was Peter's territory. 'Except for darling Peter. I'm sure he's worth spying on.'

'Who is she?'

'Ilona Talivaldis. I've hired her to teach Philip once a week. She's terribly talented. Originally from Poland or Estonia or somewhere. She arrived down here only recently. I was really lucky to find her. It was through Mrs Blunkett.'

'Infernal talker, that woman,' commented Ian Sutherland, the first words he'd managed to contribute for some time. He was sitting on the other side of Grace, who had her back to him the better to talk to Judy on Peter's other side.

Now Grace put one arm on the top of Peter's chair and leant over him for the water jug. 'Sorry, darling,' she said when he tried to help her, but he was not to be caught twice and fixed his eyes on the candelabra in the centre of the table.

'Have you met the Jingera genius?' Grace asked Peter.

'I saw her here a few weeks ago,' Peter said. 'In the yard here, just as she was leaving.' Wherever I go people are talking about her, he thought, and wondered why.

Into his mind sprang that image of her on Jingera Beach, dressed in the ill-fitting swimming costume and hugging her chest. There'd been something touching about that gesture. He'd thought of it again and again but he certainly wasn't going to expose Ilona to the ridicule of the people sitting around this table. Nor would he mention the number tattooed in blue on her forearm. He'd got her number. A new and nasty meaning to that expression. He'd got her number but he knew little about her apart from that.

'You've always been marvellous at finding the right people, Jude. Just look at your divine husband,' Grace said. 'How do you do it?'

'I didn't find Jack, as you know full well. He found me. At the tender age of seventeen at the Hotel Australia, my second ever ball.'

Later, when the guests had either retired to their rooms or gone home, Peter strolled with Jack across the damp lawn in front of the house. The cool air rinsed away the irritation of the dinner party. He accepted a cigarette from Jack. As they sauntered across the grass, a loud scuffling broke out in an oak tree nearby, followed by a carking noise like an old man clearing his throat. An angry possum leapt from the tree to the slate roof of the house, pursued a second later by a slightly larger possum. A territorial fight or a family argument, or perhaps one possum had just wanted to be left alone. A misanthrope like Peter, who was now thinking that a dinner party was like a lottery. You couldn't choose who you sat next to and you couldn't choose when to leave.

He drew hard on the cigarette. Now he thought about it, he'd probably been a misanthrope ever since he'd got out of the camp. Too many human beings, too many inhumane beings. People didn't mention that when they talked of prisoner-of-war camps. Each day petty irritations were magnified by the pain and the hunger and the malnutrition, and the itching skin that made you even more irritable. The fear too, that compounded the jitteriness. The fear you'd die or your mates would die, and that you'd lose all dignity in the manner of your death. It was people who introduced that fear, people who developed that fear.

Only in small groups that he could leave at any time did he feel comfortable. An hour or two at the pub was about all he could stand. There he could listen to a few tales from uncomplicated people he'd known for years, and at any moment he could choose to get up and walk straight out the door. He didn't feel hemmed in there and nothing was expected of him.

In silence he and Jack strolled around the Woodlands garden. Jack was one of the uncomplicated people and he felt comfortable with him.

'Have you ever thought of marrying?' Jack said. 'It's one way to avoid a situation like tonight.'

'No.' Peter looked at Jack who was occupied in striking a match to light another cigarette. Probably Jude had put him up to this; it was the most personal question he'd asked in the twenty or more years they'd known each other. Jack's face, illuminated by the burning match, looked older than it had in the soft lighting indoors. His cigarette end glowed in the darkness.

'I thought you might have married Jenny,' Jack added.

'We were far too young before the war.' And by the time he'd returned to Australia, she'd married an academic whose war had been spent in Intelligence. Not that he'd been faithful to her memory. On his leaves in London there'd been plenty of coupling – in strange bedrooms, in hotels, in a dark doorway one night – with women who wouldn't have looked twice at him in peace time. Everyone loved a pilot; even a colonial one. Marriage wouldn't suit Peter now, he felt sure. Men like him in their late thirties were too set in their ways.

'Get engaged instead,' Jack said lightly. 'It's just as effective but half the cost.'

Peter had nothing more to say. One by one the Woodlands lights were switched off. Jack stubbed out his cigarette and the two men returned to the house.

In the guestroom he'd been allocated, Peter folded down the counterpane and washed his face at the basin. Unused to late nights, he felt wide awake now. That critical hour when his body would switch from wakefulness into slumber had long since passed, probably over the dessert. After opening the window wide, he leant on the sill and breathed deeply the fresh night air. A jasmine vine must be growing somewhere below the window. Its rich scent filled his nostrils and reminded him of that first summer in England all those years ago, a fresh young pilot from the antipodes. That summer when he'd been both innocent and idealistic; that last summer before he grew up.

It was hard to believe that the war had ended so many years ago, when the ripples from its aftermath were still being felt in people's lives. He'd begun his war with idealism and the insouciance of youth. Flying was great fun, the pilots claimed at first, after a drink or three in the mess. Teamwork and initiative were what mattered, they'd all said, and the excitement, the adrenalin. They'd thrived on that, at least to begin with.

Just after he'd been transferred to Leuchars in Scotland, just after they'd given him a new Bristol Beaufighter to fly, something had happened to him. Some fear, planted like a tiny seed in his head, began to germinate. A little fear that was not of death itself but rather that he might choose death. That he might choose to fly his plane as he'd seen that pilot performing near Braidwood. Up, far far up into the sky, and afterwards a quick somersault and into a nose dive. Straight down to earth – spinning, diving, spinning, diving – until at last he would lose control.

It had seemed like such a simple way to go, at a time of his own choosing. That fantasy became a temptation each time he flew out, each time he flew back, palms sweating, hands shaking as he fought this impulse. It was only the responsibility for his crew, who trusted absolutely in his steadiness, that allowed him to carry on. Yet he'd understood that soon something would have to be said. That soon he'd have to tell someone and fly no more.

The day after reaching this decision, he'd flown a mission along the Dutch coast, and a Messerschmitt shot down the Beaufighter. Bailing out over Holland, he and the navigator had parachuted into Nazi-occupied territory, and so no one had ever learnt of that secret fear.

After that he'd never flown again and never would fly again. The panic that was vertigo would never leave him. It was with him in his dreams. Especially in his dreams. This was what was keeping him from climbing into bed here at Woodlands: the dreams that lay waiting for him once he dropped off to sleep.

But he was being stupid and overly introspective. Rarely did he wake up screaming so loudly that others in the house might hear. He wondered why he was thinking of these things again. It couldn't just be the scent of jasmine outside the window. He should think of something else.

A few books were piled up on the bedside table: James Thurber, CS Forester, a couple of battered-looking *Readers'*

*Digest*s, and a book on the history of merino sheep breeding by one JB Langham. He wondered if Judy altered the selection depending on who was using this room. Probably not: music was her thing, as she so often proclaimed. Sprawled in bed, he opened the Thurber and several hours later was relaxed enough to fall asleep.

CHAPTER TWENTY-ONE

J im stood in front of Miss Neville. After school was over she'd called him into the office and now she was staring at him intently. This made him nervous; not that he'd done anything amiss, or at least not that she could know about. Unless she'd heard about that incident with the billycart and old Mrs Beattie.

'I suppose you're wondering why you're here.'

Nodding, he looked down at his shoes. In spite of the polishing he'd given them that morning – a polishing forced upon him by his mother – they were scuffed. They felt tight too; he'd need new shoes before the year was out.

'I received an interesting letter today.'

Jim glanced quickly at her. Just then the telephone rang. While she dealt with it – something dull about the new curriculum – he returned to contemplating his shoes.

After some time she put down the phone. 'Sit down.' She gestured towards the chair next to her desk.

Taking a deep breath, he sat. His bare knees bumped against the desk and he edged the chair back a few inches. The chair legs scraped across the floor but she didn't seem to mind.

'The letter had some wonderful news.' Miss Neville's tone was nicer than he'd ever heard before. 'I'm so very proud of you. You've got in. You've got the scholarship.'

How could this be? There must be some mistake. He'd already decided he wasn't going to get in.

'Are you sure?'

She laughed. 'Yes, absolutely.'

So it was true and, for an instant, he wanted to jump for joy. He'd beaten those other boys; hundreds of other boys. Boys from the Stambroke Preparatory School, boys from all over the state who'd sat the exam. He must be brighter than he'd thought and he glowed with satisfaction, but this lasted only for a moment, and then doubts began to nibble around the edges of his elation.

Maybe all those other boys were just not as bright as he'd thought they were, and the fact that he'd beaten them therefore meant very little. He wasn't really all that clever anyway, there were lots of things he couldn't understand and he began to feel quite daunted by the path lying ahead. He'd have so much to live up to and that would mean he'd have to work harder than he did now. In fact, he barely worked at all. The schoolwork had all been far too easy, but things would be different at Stambroke, there'd be much more competition. What if this exam success was just because he'd had one lucky day? When you tossed a dice sometimes it fell the way you wanted it to and sometimes it didn't. If the only reason he'd got in was good luck, he'd have to allow for bad luck in the future. It was all so risky and he'd have to prove himself by continuing to do well. The thought of failure made his knees weaken. Not only was there that fear, but he'd have to leave Jingera and his family too. That would be hard; he loved it here, at least for most of the time. Sometimes, though, Jingera seemed so awfully small. Increasingly, ever since his trip to Sydney, he'd felt that. It had made him unsettled, although only for some of the time. Most of the time he avoided thinking about it.

He would have to say something to Miss Neville; she was staring at him with a big grin on her face. 'G-g-good,' he stammered at last.

Now a cold feeling began to creep up his bare legs and spread through his whole body, so that he shivered slightly in spite of the warmth of the afternoon.

'Aren't you pleased? Perhaps it's just too big a shock for you. It'll take time to absorb. It's a tremendous achievement, you know. This is the first time ever that a child from this area has won such a distinction.'

'Very pleased,' he muttered, reminding himself again of Miss Neville's kindness in organising the entire thing, even though she'd got it wrong in referring to him as a child. He was a boy, and one who would soon be in secondary school. A tremendous achievement, she'd said, when all he'd done was something he happened to be good at, or that the others were bad at. 'Dad will be pleased as well.' That was an understatement. His father would be overjoyed. At that prospect his glow of pleasure returned.

'And your mother too.'

This was unlikely. He couldn't bear the thought of the rows that would follow once she heard the news. It would mean extra expense, she'd said so often enough. She'd begin snarling at Dad again, and Dad would be patient back, and she hated that.

Maybe he'd wait until teatime before breaking the news. His father would persuade his mother it was a good thing and then he'd go off to Sydney next February, to become a different person. One with a straw boater and a smart blazer, like those boarders he'd seen strolling about the perfect lawns on the day of the scholarship exam.

It didn't bear thinking about any more. Later he'd return to it.

Afterwards, strolling down the hill below the school, he began to feel jubilation at his success and found himself skipping. Remembering that he was too old for this, he stopped and quickly glanced about. There was no one to see. Looking back, he caught sight of Miss Neville standing at the gate watching. Ten minutes ago, being seen skipping by her might have been embarrassing, but now it didn't matter. She smiled and waved, and he waved back. Then he continued down the hill to meet Andy and some of the other boys at the lagoon. They were there already; he could see them clowning on the bridge while they waited.

A light wind was blowing in from the south and a few seagulls wheeled along the river, taking advantage of the direction of the breeze to speed their flight. Just before the bridge they turned north and their cries became barely audible above the thudding of the breakers. That would be him next February, heading north to Sydney and a brand new life. He didn't want to think about this yet. Later, when he was in bed, he would think about it and get used to the idea.

CHAPTER TWENTY-TWO

S tanding on the grass in front of the Cadwalladers' boat-house, Zidra waited for Lorna's response. 'We shouldn't take it, Dizzy,' Lorna said, although her glowing eyes sent a different message.

'Are you going to come wiz me or simply stand there grumbling and drawing attention to yourself?' That's what Mama had said to Zidra in the shop yesterday when she'd wanted to buy some licorice sticks. Hands on hips and eyes narrowed, Zidra found it satisfying to pass on those words to Lorna in Mama's accent. Taking out the boat would be a way of paying her back for her stinginess, and it would spice up the afternoon too. Lorna gave a gratifying giggle.

Zidra and Lorna often sat on top of the boat, beached upside down in the old boathouse, and imagined themselves into adventures. Marauding pirates on the high seas, or ship-wrecked sailors hitching a ride home on the back of a migrating whale. Sometimes the girls crawled underneath the boat and pretended they were inside a hut, hiding from enemies, or surrounded by bandits carrying sharp knives, who were waiting to disembowel them, or worse. Zidra wasn't so keen on that game. Being under the boat made her feel shut in and the salty stink of damp wood made her feel sick, but today they'd have a proper adventure, a real one rather than make-believe. They'd take the boat out onto the lagoon and row away from the town so no one would see them. Only for half an hour or so because she didn't want to be home really late; she didn't want to be home so late that Mama noticed. You could get your own back on someone without them needing to know. That way everyone felt good.

It was hard work overturning the boat but eventually they succeeded, and with only a few scratches. The boat itself was almost beyond damage, a bleached carcass that might once have been painted grey. Zidra took off her shoes and put them on the bench seat in the bow of the dinghy, next to Lorna's scruffy sandshoes. Picking up a rusty old can that was lying on the sand, Lorna threw it into the bottom of the dinghy. 'The boat leaks,' she said. 'I've seen Mr Cadwallader out in it. At night. He has to stop rowing and bail it out.'

'What are you doing roaming about at night?' But Zidra didn't wait for an answer because something more urgent had just occurred to her. 'You can be in charge of bailing,' she said. The alternative was rowing and, though that might be hard work, it was her adventure today and she wanted to be in charge.

'Bet you've never rowed.'

'Have so. Often, but I'll only row to begin with. We can take it in turns after a bit.'

'When did you last row?'

'Sydney.' In fact, that was the first and the last time, with Mama and Papa on the Parramatta River, and then only for a few minutes before her father had seized the oars and said they'd end up being washed out to sea. But now she was so much bigger and stronger, she felt sure it would be easier. 'Have you?'

'Lots of times.' Lorna looked shifty-eyed though, as if she might be lying.

Together they pushed the boat further into the shallow water. Zidra climbed into the dinghy and put the oars into the rusty rowlocks. Lorna pushed the boat further out. 'Get in!' Zidra shouted, anxious that Lorna might be left behind. The boat was floating towards the deeper channel only a few yards away. Here the water swirled around the bend in the river and once in that, she would have to pull hard against the current to move upriver and away from the town. Laughing, Lorna clambered on board, and sat in the stern with the bailing can clenched between her knees. Zidra pulled hard at both oars. One skimmed the water while the other dug in too deep and the dinghy started to change direction.

'Pull equally,' shouted Lorna.

Zidra heaved again at the oars, this time symmetrically. Now they were into the channel and the rapid flow of water pushed the boat around so they were facing downstream instead of upstream.

'The left oar, Dizzy! You gotter right the boat!'

Zidra dragged hard several times with her left oar and the dinghy changed direction again.

'Now both oars. Harder, Dizzy!'

Zidra would have liked to tell her to shut up but had no spare breath. She pulled with both oars and the boat moved slowly forward. Again and again she heaved, and at last they started to move upstream against the current. It was harder work than she'd imagined. She might have asked Lorna to take over if they'd had the time to change position.

'We've gotter get across a bit, away from the main channel,' Lorna said, bossy as usual. 'Head her across so we can row up through the shallows. It'll be easier going there.'

Zidra tried to do this but again dug too deeply with the right oar while the left skimmed the surface. This threw her off balance and the left oar slipped out of the loose rowlock. Lorna lunged forward to catch the oar before it dropped into the water but Zidra was still tenaciously clutching its end. Overbalancing, Lorna fell into the bottom of the boat, which was by now several inches deep in water; her shorts became saturated. Although still clutching both oars, Zidra had stopped rowing. Lorna, now kneeling on the seat next to Zidra, struggled to fit the oar back into the rowlock. With both hands Zidra began to pull the other oar. The boat spun around to face downstream again. Taken by surprise, Lorna and the oar toppled over the edge of the dinghy. While the oar floated for a moment across the current, she vanished under the surface.

Zidra scanned the water for Lorna. No sign of her. Now the paddle end of the oar was slowly pushed around by the flow of the river but, just as the oar started to move downstream, a black hand emerged from the water and grasped the shaft. Next, Lorna's head bobbed up. With both elbows hooked over the oar, she shook the water out of her eyes. Zidra's panic subsided slightly. Although controlling the boat with just one oar was beyond her, she was at least in the boat rather than the water, and she knew Lorna could swim.

'Head her to shore!' Lorna bellowed.

The bow of the dinghy was now pointing downstream. Zidra could see Lorna bobbing about in the water while clutching the oar, which she seemed to be trying to head towards the beach side of the lagoon. Further and further she receded as the current swept the dinghy forward. The shore seemed to be flashing by and soon Zidra would end up at the bridge. She pulled at the remaining oar with both hands, struggling hard against the pressure of the water. At last the boat started to swing around and after several seconds shuddered to a stop. Leaning over the gunwale, she discovered the dinghy was beached in a few inches of water.

And this was the wrong side of the river. Behind was the dense bush forming a barrier between the town and the lagoon. She glanced upriver. The boathouse was several hundred yards away but there was no sign of Lorna. With only one oar she'd never be able to get the dinghy across the channel again.

Carefully she took the oar out of the rowlock and shipped it. After clambering into the water, she tried to push the dinghy further in but it was far too heavy and would not budge. If only they'd thought to bring the rope that was lying coiled up in a corner of the boathouse, she could have tied the rope to the metal loop in the bow and then perhaps pulled the boat back while walking over the pedestrian bridge. Although that would have been in full view of the town, it would be better to be seen than to lose the boat altogether. Harder and harder she pushed but still the boat wouldn't move. She looked upriver again. Still no sign of Lorna. Despite being a strong swimmer, she could have become caught up in the weeds and sucked under, even drowned. Maybe her body would come floating by soon. Zidra would have lost her best friend and she'd have to explain it was all her fault. Tears started to pour down her face.

'Looks like you're in a spot of bother.'

Zidra jumped. Looming above her on the sandy bank was Mr Bates. Now she'd really be in trouble unless she could persuade Mr Bates to help her and to keep quiet about it.

'I've lost Lorna,' she said.

'Lost an oar too by the look of things. If Lorna's the black girl you hang around with, you don't need to worry about her. She swims like a fish.'

'But she fell into the water with the other oar.'

'So I saw, but right now she's standing on the other side of the river waving to you.' He pointed to a spot several hundred yards upriver on the other side. Sure enough, there was Lorna, waving and apparently shouting, although the words couldn't be heard over the distant thudding of the surf. Zidra wiped away her tears with her hands, which were starting to feel blistered.

Mr Bates extended towards her a freckled hand generously sprinkled with ginger hairs. Surely he didn't expect her to climb up onto the bank with him and risk losing the boat once more. Anyway the offer could be ignored now she knew Lorna had survived, though Mr Bates would come in handy for the return of the boat. Somehow it had to be got across to the other side of the lagoon, and returned to the boathouse.

Looking up at Mr Bates, she managed to produce a few more tears. 'I've got to get the boat back to the boathouse. It's Mr Cadwallader's. We shouldn't have taken it but we did. I don't know how we're going to get it back. Mum'll kill me if she finds out.' Mr Bates' figure was blurred by tears; genuine tears now for she was imagining Mama at her most terrifying. But at the same time she knew she looked appealing with head cocked to one side and eyes brimming. She'd admired this effect in the brown-spotted bathroom mirror and been moved by her reflection. Mama was impervious though; she knew Zidra's little tricks.

'That's easily fixed,' said Mr Bates, exactly as she'd hoped. 'We'll row it across. Or rather I'll row it across. I don't think you're much of an oarsman.' Zidra found his laughter quite rude, but was prepared to forgive anything as long as her mother didn't find out.

'I can row across with one oar,' Mr Bates continued. 'We'll go up the shallow bit on this side of the river and cross over at the bend and then make our way back to the boathouse through the shallows on the other side. Then no one'll ever need to know what you've been up to. Especially not your mother.' He winked at her. Mr Bates was being nicer than Papa would have been.

'How kind of you,' she said in her best adult tone. Mr Bates laughed again, as if she'd said something witty.

Now seated in the stern of the dinghy, she watched him roll up his trousers before pushing the boat out of the shallows and scrambling in. It rocked so much that she feared they'd both end up in the water. Mr Bates manoeuvred the dinghy into the fast-flowing river, while she began to bail out the oily-looking water in the bottom. Then he pulled with the oar, first on one side and then on the other. Sprinkling her with water, he pivoted the oar neatly from side to side and now, at last, they were back on the other side of the river. Looking apprehensive, Lorna stood waiting for them. After climbing out of the dinghy, Mr Bates again offered Zidra a gingery paw and this time she took it. It felt hard and calloused. With his other hand, he steadied her as she jumped over the edge into the shallow water. The great splash as she landed darkened his trousers.

While Mr Bates fiddled with the dinghy, Zidra mouthed at Lorna: 'It's all right. He's not going to tell.'

Lorna smiled and splashed across to the boat, and they all dragged it back into the boathouse.

'A good job well done,' said Mr Bates, panting slightly after his exertions. 'But don't do it again, young ladies, or you could get yourselves into even worse trouble.'

Zidra watched him dig into his pockets and pull out four aniseed balls; that meant two each. They were covered with bits of lint but she didn't mind. Perched on a log lying across the edge of the clearing, she and Lorna sucked at their sweets.

Mr Bates stared across the lagoon and panted like a dog struggling to regain its breath.

After a few seconds he turned towards them and smiled. 'You girls are lucky I rescued you.'

'You didn't rescue me. It was just Zidra.' Lorna's cockiness had returned. Zidra could hear her crunching up the last of her aniseed ball.

'And the boat. You could have got into terrible trouble for taking that. It's stealing, you know.'

'No it isn't,' Lorna said. 'We only borrowed it.'

'Try telling that to the police. Especially if you're Aboriginal.'

A sudden churning in Zidra's stomach made her feel quite sick and she heard Lorna's sharp intake of breath. Mr Bates was still smiling so he couldn't have meant his words to be nasty. Quickly Zidra said, 'We did just borrow it. We didn't steal it.'

Mr Bates continued smiling. 'I know that, and you know that, but the police don't know that. If you'd got caught you'd have been in terrible trouble. You might even have gone to jail if Mr Cadwallader pushed charges.'

Zidra began to tremble at this possibility. Being in jail and away from her mother would be terrible, and away from Lorna too. The whole thing had been Zidra's idea, so Lorna wouldn't be in trouble. Unless they thought being Aboriginal made you guilty even when you weren't, but anyway they wouldn't get locked up together. They'd be separated, maybe in solitary confinement. Zidra couldn't bear the thought of that.

'I won't tell anyone about it though,' Mr Bates said. 'You can count on me. It's just our little secret. Mind you keep on being good little girls, but. You especially, Zidra, 'cause I know you can be a bit naughty sometimes. You'd better be a good girl otherwise the truth might get out.' He laughed then, a loud ho-ho-ho like that Santa Claus that Zidra had seen last Christmas at the department store in Sydney. There wasn't any good humour in this laugh though.

'I'm always good,' she said, staring at the sandy ground beneath her feet. Some tiny black ants were dragging the carcass of an insect towards the mound of gravel nearby that was their nest.

'I'm sure you are. Except for today, but.' He laughed again. 'No need to look so sad, Zidra. No one need know except for us. It's our secret.'

'It's our secret,' Zidra repeated quickly. 'It's just between the three of us, isn't it?'

She glanced at Lorna, who produced a half-hearted grin. 'Just between the three of us,' she echoed.

CHAPTER TWENTY-THREE

'Heads you're the policeman and tails I am,' Jim said to Andy, and tossed the penny high into the air. He watched it spin and glint before landing on the path, Queen-side up. This meant he'd be in the role of black tracker and Andy would be Constable Davies. That was good; he'd be in front of Andy for the rest of the afternoon. Barry and Tom, the escaped murderers, were still visible some fifty paces ahead but they'd be scheming to get back to the footbridge without being caught and any second now they'd be out of sight. Then they'd be impossible to find. They could step off the main path and cut through the scrub leading to Dad's boathouse or just hide behind tree trunks and wait till their stalkers had passed by. Assuming his role, Jim began to search the path for clues, for a fallen stick or displaced leaf that might indicate that the quarry had left the path.

'Hurry up,' Andy said. 'You can see they're just ahead but they won't be for much longer if you don't get a move on.'

'It's only a game and you're supposed to be stupid, remember? Mr Davies wouldn't have the wit to say that.'

Andy looked pleased at this. 'I'm in charge so get on with it.' A kookaburra started to laugh. Constable Davies imitated it. Jim had to silence him and how else but with a quick tackle. Rolling on the ground, Andy developed a fit of giggles and, by the time Jim remembered the seriousness of their game, Barry and Tom were out of sight.

Resuming their roles, Jim in front and Andy behind, they followed the path winding towards the sandy strip of shoreline next to their father's boathouse. Halting, Jim held up one hand to warn Andy to proceed quietly. Ahead of them, standing not far from the boathouse, was an intruder who didn't know the rules of the game. Perhaps he'd be able to give some information about the escaped murderers, but they'd have to proceed carefully as he could be an accomplice. Hidden behind a dense clump of bushes, Jim peered at the interloper – a large man wearing a battered canvas hat, navy shirt and cream trousers – who stood with his back to them, staring over the water. Sheltered from sight, Jim slithered along the path with his head well below the top of the dense undergrowth. After twenty yards he stopped. No sign of Barry and Tom anywhere. He crept forward a few more paces. Behind him, Andy crunched some dried bark underfoot and Jim turned, a finger raised to his lips. Andy grinned; he could get the giggles at the most dangerous part of any mission but a stern scowl had the desired effect. Onward they scrambled until they were just a few yards away. Standing, Jim tiptoed across the path bordering the clearing, to the shelter of the bushes on the far side.

Then the man turned. It was Mr Bates. He should have been in the hotel, not standing around the lagoon on a weekday afternoon. Well hidden, Jim stayed absolutely still until Mr Bates turned to look over the water again.

'What do you reckon he's up to?' Andy whispered, creeping up behind Jim and making him start.

'Fishing, I expect.'

'He hasn't got a rod.'

'Probably hidden somewhere.'

'Look, there're those two girls coming around the side of the boathouse.'

'Zidra and Lorna.'

'Your girlfriend.'

'She's not my girlfriend, you twerp.'

'What are they doing in there? That's Dad's.'

Just then Mr Bates called out, 'I'll check the doors. Got to make sure they're secure.'

He vanished around the far side of the boathouse. Looking upset, Zidra and Lorna sat down on a log. Zidra's shorts were wet and Lorna's clothes looked saturated, as if she'd been swimming in them.

Jim started to feel uneasy. There was something not quite right here. Barry and Tom would have to wait. He'd need to check that Dad's boat was safe once the others had moved on and they'd better hurry: the sky was already blazing golden to the west.

Mr Bates now reappeared from the far side of the boathouse. 'All shipshape and Bristol fashion.'

'What does that mean?' Zidra asked.

'Everything's in order. Everything's in its proper place.'

'Your mum'd like that expression,' said Lorna.

'But we're not telling her anything about this,' said Zidra.

'If you want to go boating, you could come out with me one Sunday,' Mr Bates said. 'I sometimes rent a boat and take it out on the river for a spot of fishing.'

'Thank you, Mr Bates,' said Zidra, 'but I'll have to ask Mum first.' She sounded so formal sometimes. That came from being foreign.

'Of course. That's what mums are for.'

'Promise you won't tell anyone what's happened though.'

'Cross my heart and hope to die,' said Mr Bates. Jim wasn't sure if that was a wink Mr Bates gave her or if he was just blinking. Jim couldn't abide people who winked. Grown-ups did it all the time to kids, as if it made them more human somehow. As noisily as possible, he stomped down the path. Mr Bates and the girls started when they saw him. They looked guilty, almost as if he'd caught them doing something wrong.

Zidra was the first to smile. 'Mr Bates's just asked Lorna and me to go fishing with him,' she said.

She was trying to deflect attention from something. Jim stared at her while she inspected her soaking-wet sandshoes. Andy started chattering to Mr Bates about flathead; the boy was obsessed by fish. A fit of giggles overtook Lorna and made Jim feel uncomfortable, as if she was laughing at him. Not that he was going to show it. After strolling across the clearing he peered through the boathouse window. Although his father's dinghy seemed to be lying in its usual spot, he felt sure they'd been messing about in the boathouse. Mr Bates was now relating some complicated fishing tale and Andy was gazing up at him in admiration, as if he was God or something. While Batesy talked, he was gawping; but it wasn't at Andy, it was at Zidra and Lorna, sitting side-by-side on the log.

'Can I come fishing too?' Jim said.

Mr Bates glanced at him in surprise and so did Andy. Maybe it wasn't surprise in Mr Bates' case but annoyance.

'You don't like fishing,' Andy said.

'Yes I do.' Jim glowered at Andy.

'Can we both come?' Andy said eagerly. 'I love fishing.'

'Well, that's pushing it a bit. Not sure I can rent a boat that big. I can take four at a pinch including me but no more than that. I'd need to hire a cruiser if there are too many of you. Jeez, I'm starting to feel like the Pied Piper of Hamelin.'

'I won't be able to go,' said Lorna.

'Why not?' Zidra looked quite put out.

'Family stuff.'

'So Jim and I can come then,' Andy said. In the way that grown-ups seemed to find irresistible, he smiled up at Mr Bates.

'You needn't look so pleased,' said Zidra. 'Lorna was invited and you two just invited yourselves.'

'No bickering,' said Mr Bates.

'It's the truth,' said Lorna. She ran a hand through her cropped hair.

'Better get home now,' said Zidra.

'Remember Mum's the word,' said Mr Bates.

'What does that mean?'

'No telling, drongo,' Andy said.

'Don't you call her drongo, pongo,' said Lorna.

'No telling what?' said Jim.

'Not telling,' said Zidra. She began to chase Andy, who ran off down the track towards the bridge, with Lorna following close behind.

Jim stayed with Mr Bates, who showed no inclination to move. You'd think he might show a bit of embarrassment at being caught skulking around Dad's boathouse but there was no sign of it. After nodding at him, Jim walked around the boathouse to the lagoon side. The doors were firmly latched. Perhaps he could worm out of Zidra what they'd been up to this afternoon, though he'd have to work on it a bit. Bribery might help. Maybe the promise of a billycart ride.

When he'd finished inspecting the boathouse, Mr Bates had gone. No word of farewell. The hostility he felt towards old Batesy was probably mutual and at least they didn't have to walk back to Jingera together. Maybe he'd dashed on ahead to pull a few beers. Mr Bates left too much of the work to Mrs Bates, his father reckoned, but his mother said that was nonsense. Mrs Bates just liked flirting with the customers too much to want to spend time away from the hotel.

Just before the bridge, Jim was ambushed by the two escaped murderers, who leapt out of some bushes waving sticks at him. 'They're guns,' Tom explained. 'We're going to string you up and then hide in the mountains.' Jim's police constable brother was nowhere to be seen. Jim was frogmarched over the bridge where the game officially ended, and all three of them ran home to their tea.

It wasn't until the next day that Jim remembered the scholarship. After school, he popped into Cadwallader's Quality Meats, thinking he might mention the boathouse first and the scholarship next. There were three or four customers waiting to be served. His father was wrapping some sausages but when he saw Jim he called The Boy in from the back of the shop. Wiping his rather bloody-looking hands on his apron, he beamed at Jim.

'Got to talk to my son for a minute,' he said to the world-at-large. 'The Boy'll look after you.' Putting one hand on Jim's shoulder, he steered him out the back of the shop, past the carcasses hanging from hooks suspended from rails, and piles of other things that Jim didn't care to look at too closely, and into the fresh air of the yard.

'Well, well, you have done well,' his father said before Jim had time to open his mouth. To Jim's embarrassment there were tears in his father's eyes, which he wiped away on his sleeve. 'Had a letter from Stambroke College this morning, and

Miss Neville telephoned today too. We're so proud of you, son.' He gave Jim a great hug, squashing him against the stained apron. From a back pocket he pulled out his wallet and removed a five-pound note. 'Don't tell your mother about the money,' he said. 'You'd better go home now so she can congratulate you. You know she doesn't like to feel left out of things.'

Jim went straight to the garage and put the five-pound note into the old cigar box in which his treasures were concealed. It joined his father's military badge from the war with the rising sun above the imperial crown; a couple of fossils he'd found under the headland; the half-sovereign his great-aunt had given him; a newspaper report about the new radio telescope at Parkes and an even older cutting from the ancient newspaper lining his mother's bureau, about the US navy ship sunk by the Japanese off the south coast. The box was kept behind the half-used tins of paint. No one would ever think of looking there, not even Andy.

Then he went into the kitchen. His mother was doing something complicated with the roasting pan and didn't look up immediately but when she did, her habitual frown had gone and she was smiling.

'Well done!' She gave him a quick kiss on his forehead. Her face smelled of Pond's cream and onions. 'Miss Neville will be skiting about you to everyone she meets. Anyone would think it was her child who'd got the scholarship and not mine. Your father said she went on and on when she telephoned the shop this morning!' Before continuing, she pushed some potatoes around. 'You've shown you've got it in you to do well wherever you are. I told your father that.'

Jim waited for a moment for her to add a comment about the extra costs this achievement would entail but she didn't say any more. After putting the roasting pan back in the oven, she suggested he help himself to some milk and a few biscuits before going out again.

Andy was in the backyard, kicking a ball around in a half-hearted manner. When he saw Jim he stopped. 'You'll be going away.' There was accusation in his voice.

'Not for ages yet. Three whole months. We've got all summer. Anyway, she mightn't let me go.'

'Yes, she will, and what am I going to do? There'll be no one to play with.'

'Yes there will be. You've got lots of friends.'

'But no one at home.'

'I'll be home for the holidays. It's only in term time that I'll be away.'

'Nothing'll be the same again.'

Andy was right. Nothing would be the same again. Jim looked at Andy's freckled face and was touched by his anxious expression. 'You can play with my Meccano set while I'm away,' he said. 'Whenever you want.'

Andy cheered up at this. 'What about your train engine?'

'Sure, as long as you're careful with it.'

Andy looked so pleased that Jim wondered for an instant if he'd been over-generous, but better that than the alternative, he decided; and it wasn't as if the toys were going out of the house.

After this, Jim put the scholarship out of his mind. There was the rest of the summer to get through yet before fretting about the future.

In the meantime he wanted to find out what the girls and old Batesy had been up to in the boathouse. That was bothering him still. It wasn't just the boat; it was something to do with Mr Bates' expression and he just couldn't figure out quite what it was.

CHAPTER TWENTY-FOUR

Walking up the hill the following morning, Ilona recognised the solid figure of Mrs Cadwallader coming out of the post office and called out a greeting. Mrs Cadwallader waved and waited for her to catch up.

'Congratulations! I heard the good news from Miss Neville yesterday. You have such a clever son.'

Although Mrs Cadwallader smiled and expressed her thanks, she didn't look as jubilant as Ilona had expected. After a brief pause, she said, 'Actually, I was knocked for six when I heard the news.'

'*Knocked for six*?'

'Surprised. It's a cricketing term for knocking a ball out beyond the boundary. Our expressions must be hard for you.'

'They are and each day I make lists and listen and learn. Jim's done brilliantly. You must be so proud. Miss Neville said no one from this area has ever won a scholarship before.'

Although Mrs Cadwallader looked pleased at this, she said, 'So it seems, but unfortunately Sydney's a long way away from Jingera.'

'That's true, but Miss Neville told me that Stambroke College is a very famous school and that, once a boy gets in, he's more or less guaranteed a place at university.'

At this, Ilona was shocked to see fat tears begin to trickle down Mrs Cadwallader's rosy cheeks. She patted her shoulder and might have put an arm around her too if she'd felt it wouldn't be resented. Although Mrs Cadwallader was always friendly, it was in a distant way and Ilona suspected that, unlike her husband, she was the person one would have to know for years before moving beyond the formalities.

'Jim's young to be going away,' Mrs Cadwallader said, fumbling in her handbag for an elusive handkerchief, which she found eventually. After dabbing her eyes with it, she added, 'He isn't twelve yet, and it's all so unexpected. I'd always thought he wouldn't leave home before seventeen at the earliest. He's such a helpful boy too. Feeds the hens and runs errands and so on.'

'You'll still have Andy for that.' At once Ilona regretted this. Although she'd had yet another troubled night, exhaustion was no excuse for insensitive remarks implying that Jim was expendable or that the two boys were perfect substitutes. 'And Jim will come back for the holidays. I understand the private schools have longer holidays than the state schools.'

'He'll be different though. More critical.'

'He'll appreciate you more. Home-cooking after all that *institutional material* they probably have at boarding schools.'

'Institutional material?'

'Food.'

'But the college is very grand. In an expensive part of Sydney with lots of rich kids.'

'I bet they still serve over-boiled food in the dining room, though, and Jingera is pretty grand too. Glorious views. Complete freedom. He's incredibly lucky to be living here. We all are.'

'Why does he want to leave home then?' Mrs Cadwallader's face began to crumple again.

'Education,' Ilona said hastily. 'You're so lucky to have a bright son.'

'Don't know where he gets it from.'

'Well, he looks like George but he has both of your brains.' Mrs Cadwallader smiled at this.

'You know what I mean,' Ilona said, glad to have made her smile. 'Not that Jim has a double-dose of brains but that bright parents have bright children.' Although she wasn't one hundred per cent sure of this, she did so want to cheer up Mrs Cadwallader.

'A bright boy will do well anywhere. He doesn't need to be educated in Sydney.'

'Well, I've heard that Burford Boys' High is quite good but it doesn't offer the range of subjects that Stambroke does. No music either.'

'He's never shown much interest in music, and anyway, that's a girl's thing.'

Suppressing her irritation at this remark, Ilona said, 'Not at all. Just think of all those composers. How about you – do you like music?'

'I'm not at all musical. I like to sew though. When I was young I used to do a lot of embroidery work and I wouldn't mind taking up tapestry.'

'Maybe you'll have more time for that as the boys grow up.'

'Maybe.' Mrs Cadwallader's face lightened at this prospect and she began to talk of the embroidery prize she'd won at school. Her mother had framed it, and it was sitting in a cupboard in their house somewhere. It was for a tea cloth she'd designed and embroidered, with blue-headed wrens in each corner and with orange flowers decorating the edges.

They chatted some more about other matters before parting. Several yards away, Mrs Cadwallader called out, 'Do please call me Eileen. Mrs Cadwallader sounds so formal.'

'Thank you, Eileen. My name is Ilona.' She'd been wrong about Mrs Cadwallader – Eileen – it had been a matter of weeks rather than years before they'd moved beyond the formalities.

'Goodbye, Elinor.'

Although Eileen Cadwallader had mispronounced her name, Ilona wasn't going to correct her, at least not on this occasion. She felt a great deal of sympathy for her. There was no way that she herself would let Zidra go to boarding school in Sydney, even if she did win a scholarship and was as bright as Jim. But Zidra was all she had, whereas Eileen also had Andy and George. It would be hard to deny a boy like Jim such a marvellous start in life. However the decision would be a difficult one and she didn't know quite what she would do if she were in Eileen's position.

George was set on it though. When Ilona had seen him in Cadwallader's Quality Meats the previous afternoon, he'd discussed Jim's departure as if his bags were already packed.

—•—

That afternoon, Zidra saw the car from Woodlands parked opposite the war memorial. Mr Jones, the chauffeur, was too early again. Now Mama would scold her for keeping him waiting and yet she'd come straight home from school without stopping to talk to anyone. Except for Mr Bates, who'd popped out of the hotel – as he always did when school finished – and who'd shouted a greeting. Recently he'd been joined by Mrs Bates and Zidra was glad of this. Mr Bates never mentioned their little secret in front of her.

It was easier to be on time when Lorna was away. She'd missed school for two days in a row now. Two long days. School was dull without her, for Zidra didn't have many friends. Although Jim was friendly enough, when his mates were around it was usually only in a distant sort of a way, and he'd been acting a bit strange lately, ever since catching them at the boathouse. He'd been hanging around as if he knew what they'd been up to and thought they might do it again.

A few days before, he'd asked outright what they'd been doing at the boathouse. If Lorna hadn't been there, she might have told him they'd taken the boat out. Instead Lorna had suggested that he leave them alone. 'Bugger off,' she'd said. 'We weren't doing any harm and anyway it's none of your business.'

'I asked Zidra,' Jim had said. 'Why don't you let her answer?'

His eyes were green. An olive sort of green like gum tree leaves or like the lagoon on a dull day. No smile either, but intense looking, like Miss Neville when she was really determined or angry.

'Let's go, Dizzy,' Lorna had said, grabbing her arm and leading her away. Looking back, Zidra had seen Jim watching her. Maybe one day she'd tell him. There was no point in him thinking she was worse than she was. But then she'd remembered that she couldn't tell Jim about the boat because she'd promised Mr Bates to keep it a secret, and if she did tell, she could end up in jail.

Now she ran past the war memorial, and the car from Woodlands too. Mr Jones was standing on the front verandah of their house and talking to her mother, who waved.

'I'm not late, Mama. I came straight home.'

'Don't worry, I'm early again,' said Mr Jones. 'I had some errands to do for Mrs Chapman and then your mother gave me a cuppa.'

Taking Zidra's school-case, her mother shoved her rudely into the house and pointed to the bathroom. 'Clean yourself up a bit. There's no time for you to change though.'

Mama must be tired again, she didn't even say please.

The drive to Woodlands took nearly an hour. Mr Jones let Zidra sit in the front on a squashy cushion that was kept in the car for Philip. The car smelled of leather and Mr Chapman's tobacco. Mr Jones seemed to enjoy explaining that the roof of the car was lined with pigskin and the dashboard was made of walnut veneer. Every trip he mentioned this, as if she might forget. Before he had a chance to continue, she reminded him that the seats were made from calfskin and he laughed.

Mama was sitting in style in the back seat. She was usually silent on the trip to and from Woodlands. That didn't matter because Zidra had lots to tell Mr Jones. He was a good listener and only occasionally interrupted to point out some interesting sight. She loved going up the steep, winding road out of Jingera and then alongside the meandering river and up towards the mountain range.

'We could do with some rain,' Mr Jones said, interrupting her conversation. That was what the Jingeroid adults always seemed to say to one another whenever they met, but she let Mr Jones talk about the dryness for as long as it took. If she was especially nice to him he might be willing to stop at the Aboriginal camp on the way home. She'd ask Mrs Jones for a couple of extra biscuits for the return journey so she'd have a little treat for Lorna.

However when they turned off the Burford Road and headed inland she received a terrible shock. The shanties had vanished and even the fireplaces had gone. The rocks that once surrounded them had been scattered. A few piles of ashes were all that was left of the settlement, apart from some sheets of rusty corrugated iron piled up next to the road.

'They've gone,' she said, fighting back the tears. 'They've gone and Lorna never even said goodbye.'

'Moved on,' said Mr Jones.

'Where to?'

'To the Sutherlands' place for the picking, I heard.'

'Where's that?'

'We passed the drive into it a couple of miles back. The Sutherlands have got some pickers' quarters. They'll be better off there than here.'

'Closer to Jingera than here?'

'Definitely.'

'So Lorna'll be coming back to school then.'

'I reckon.'

Zidra didn't feel reassured though. She looked out of the window so Mr Jones couldn't see her face. Pulling a handkerchief out of her tunic pocket, she wiped away the tears.

'Far easier to get to the Jingera school from the Sutherlands' place than it is from here,' Mr Jones continued. 'The school bus stops at the bottom of their drive.'

'Has Lorna been away from school again?' Mama called from the back seat.

'Yes,' said Zidra rather irritably. 'I told you yesterday.'

'But not today. We have not spoken since you got home. I expect she's unpacking. It is certainly not an easy task to move home, however little one has. Although it is important in life not to become too attached to places and things.'

Zidra wondered if Lorna took the little green elephant with her. The pink shell Lorna gave her was still in her pocket. Whenever she touched the shell she thought of Lorna. Her friend would have the elephant with her and might be thinking of her even now. Tomorrow surely she'd be back at school; unpacking stuff after the move couldn't take all that long. Zidra ran her fingers over the ridges of the shell before putting it away again. Next to the shell was the tiny fossil her mother had given her. Today she would give that to Philip Chapman and that way the giving would be complete. He had given her an elephant that she had given Lorna. Lorna had given her a shell. She would give Mama's fossil to Philip so he had something to remember her by too.

And that was guaranteed to bring Lorna back to school.

Glad of Mr Jones' silence, Zidra blew her nose. Soon they reached the wooden bridge over the river. Clank rattle rumble went the loose boards as the car's tyres rode over them. Mama hummed a little; off in her world of music again. At last the car turned onto the dirt road to Woodlands and bounced over the cattle grid. Zidra loved the bumping of the car over the uneven surface of the dirt road. It was full of what Mr Jones said were potholes. She also loved the faint smell of dust that entered the car, even though they'd now wound up all the windows. But most of all she loved the long shadows that were starting to creep across the paddocks and that made the valley seem more solid somehow. Soon they reached the white fence surrounding the Woodlands home paddock. Mr Jones turned the car off the main driveway and drove around the side of the house, where he parked right outside the kitchen door.

'Mrs Jones promised we'd make chocolate fudge squares today,' Zidra said, opening the door too early and almost falling out.

'Not so hasty, Zidra. That way you will not an accident cause.'

Mrs Jones was waiting outside the kitchen door and Philip was standing behind her. Today he was wearing a pair of long trousers. This was the first time Zidra has seen him out of knickerbockers. With his legs hidden from view he looked less vulnerable somehow.

'I've got you a present,' she said to Philip, after Mrs Jones and Mama had started on one of their lengthy conversations.

'W-w-what is it?' He looked slightly jaded as if nothing could surprise him, although he still managed to stutter.

'Something special.'

'W-what?'

'Shut your eyes and put out your hand.'

He did so and she placed the fossil on his palm. Opening his eyes, he looked down. 'It's b-b-b-beautiful,' he said, a bit doubtfully though. For an instant she regretted handing it over. Surely he could show a bit more enthusiasm about such a gift.

'It's a fossil. The remains of a creature from thousands of years ago, Mama said. It's been petrified in the rock.' She wasn't too sure what petrification meant and hoped Philip wouldn't ask.

He didn't say anything but ran his fingers over the indentations. 'A f-f-fish or a sh-shell,' he said slowly. 'I th-th-think it's a shell.'

'Whatever.' Zidra wasn't going to argue about it. It looked a bit like a prawn to her but it could have been anything.

He nodded and struggled to spit out the words. At last he managed, 'Th-th-thanks.' Then, for the first time in all those weeks they'd been visiting, he smiled at her. His face changed. The cut-off look had gone. In its place was a sort of glowing appearance, as if he'd switched on a light behind those strangely coloured eyes.

'It's a pleasure,' she said and blushed slightly.

'Now it is time to make music!' Her mother, emerging from the chat with Mrs Jones, appeared not to have noticed the transfer of the fossil. Sneaking a quick look at Philip, Zidra saw that he looked as embarrassed as she felt. Later Zidra would have to tell Mama what she should have said, that it was time to play the piano.

———◆———

Ilona's peripheral vision had become well-developed with maternity. While apparently focused on Mrs Jones' conversation, she was also able to witness Mr Jones engaged in flicking a feather duster over the car; a rather futile exercise given that he would be chauffeuring them down the dirt track again in just over an hour's time. After this he beat the duster against the kitchen wall and looked at his reflection in the shiny paintwork. By shifting her head slightly she was also able to observe Zidra in the act of giving to poor Philip the little fossil Ilona had found on the beach the day she might have drowned. Philip's smile was radiant as he slipped it into his pocket. Zidra's pleasure was manifest. Darling Zidra, who had so little to give, had been generous to this boy who had everything and nothing.

That was when Ilona said, 'Now it is time to make music!' Her fatigue forgotten, she gave Zidra a quick kiss before sailing into the house. She glided through the entrance hall, with Philip in tow, leaving Mrs Jones and Zidra behind. So confident did she feel after Zidra's act of generosity that she might almost have owned the house.

The drawing room was deserted but the piano was open and Philip's music was on the top. Ilona and Philip sat side-by-side on the long piano stool. 'We shall begin with our five-finger exercises,' she said, and watched Philip place his fingers on the piano keys. Though long-fingered, his hands were small, but that did not matter. What mattered was that he cared enough to perform even these simple exercises with passion. After finishing, he played the scale of C, which he executed perfectly with both hands. Then Ilona played a simple tune for several minutes. 'Do you know what that was?'

'N-n-no.'

'It was from a symphony that Beethoven wrote a long time ago. It was such a happy piece. Next I shall sing it for you, just tra-la-la. Afterwards we shall sing it together, you and I. Together we shall let our spirits fly up into the heavens, and then we shall sit together for a few moments' quiet before we shall start on a new piece that you will learn. All in the scale of C.'

Again she played the short excerpt from Beethoven and sang while she played. Afterwards she played it once more and Philip sang with her. His voice was clear and thin and, as she had hoped, he didn't stutter when singing. He had a good ear and did not hesitate.

When they stopped, she glanced out the bay window. Green lawn, in spite of the drought, and the deciduous trees were decked out in the dense greenery of summer. They might have been in Europe instead of in an Australian homestead.

'You have such a lovely voice,' she said, looking at Philip and smiling. 'Next we shall try a new piece. It is a song.' She pulled out of her bag a rather battered sheet of music and placed it on the music stand. With her right hand she played the first few bars of music, very slowly, pointing to each note on the page with her left hand. Then she played it through again, afterwards instructing the boy to play. She was impressed that he was immediately able to play both hands together.

She had no doubt that Philip practised. Although Mrs Chapman seemed devoted to her son, Ilona guessed that the boy was too intimidated to do anything that might displease her, and neglecting to practise would most certainly do that.

Ilona was glad that Mrs Chapman, whose glamour was so formidable, appeared only rarely on the days for the piano lessons at Woodlands. Each visit Ilona simply slipped in and out of the back entrance like the tradesperson that she was in the Woodlands world.

CHAPTER TWENTY-FIVE

Later that afternoon and some miles south of Jingera, the Woodlands car began to splutter. Zidra struggled to make out the interesting new words Mr Jones was muttering but it was impossible against the coughing of the engine. Then there was silence until Mr Jones pulled on the handbrake and climbed out, slamming the door.

'You can get out too but on no account say anything,' Mama advised. 'It is always best to be quiet when motors exhibit mechanical problems.'

Zidra hopped about a bit at the edge of the road. There was nothing to do and she soon started to feel bored. Crossing to the other side of the bitumen, she sat down with her back against a large rock. Below her stretched paddocks and then the sea but there wasn't a single farmhouse in sight.

Mr Jones carried on fiddling under the bonnet for a few more minutes and then stood up straight, stretching his back. 'Could be the tappets. I'll have to get the old girl towed into Jingera. Someone's bound to come along soon. We can thumb a lift.'

After what seemed like a very long time Zidra heard the thrum of a motor coming from the Burford direction. A minute later, when a low grey car appeared, Mr Jones stepped forward and held up his hand. The car stopped and a tall man got out. Recognising him, Zidra glanced at her mother. Face like a mask. Always a bad sign, although you'd think she'd be pleased that the man they'd seen at Woodlands that first visit was going to rescue them.

Mr Jones was happy though. 'It's Mr Vincent,' he said and immediately began to talk about tappets.

'If that's what's wrong I'd better give you all a lift into Jingera.' The man grinned at Zidra. His deep blue eyes looked at her as if she was a proper person instead of just someone's kid. 'What's your name?'

When she told him, he made no comment about it, unlike almost everyone else she'd met. 'Looks as if you and your mother will be finishing your journey in my old car. Old but reliable.' Fondly he patted it, as if it was a horse rather than a lump of metal. A panting black dog now had its head out of the side window.

'He wants to get out,' said Zidra.

'And I'm not letting him,' said Mr Vincent, smiling. 'He's still only an overgrown puppy and a very obedient one, but I'm not taking any chances.'

'What's his name?'

'Spot.'

'That is a very original name,' said Mama in a not very nice tone of voice. 'Especially as there's no spot on him.'

'That's the humour of it.'

Patting the dog's velvety coat, Zidra pretended not to see Mama blushing. She said, 'I'd love to have a dog.'

'I will not let her,' said Mama. 'Dogs tie one down so terribly. It is they who tether their owners to one place, when it is their owners who think they are tethering the dog. It is too much.'

Zidra looked at her in surprise. Anyone would think Mr Vincent was offering them Spot. She wasn't herself today. She must be annoyed about the tappets.

'You'd better sit in the front seat,' Mr Vincent said to her mother. 'Spot always sits in the back on that rug and I'm afraid it's covered in dog hairs. I'm sure old Jonesy and Zidra won't mind though.'

'I too am not frightened of a few hairs of the dog,' said Mama. 'Or even of the dogs from which the hairs drop.'

Mr Vincent laughed – his laugh seemed to come from deep in his chest – but Mama didn't. Spot welcomed Zidra into the car by licking her hand and then stuck his head out of the window again. Zidra told Mr Vincent about her afternoon at Woodlands. She didn't forget to mention the fossil she'd given Philip.

'I think I saw your mother pick up that fossil on Jingera Beach.'

'You did indeed,' said Mama. 'Zidra loved that fossil but she chose to give that boy something he didn't have.'

Zidra smirked at this. After Mr Vincent dropped Mr Jones at the garage on the outskirts of Jingera, she said, 'I expect Spot needs watering.'

'I do not think one waters dogs,' said Mama doubtfully. 'Horses perhaps, but not dogs.'

'I'm sure Spot would appreciate some watering,' said Mr Vincent. 'I wouldn't mind some watering either, I can tell you. I'm looking forward to a cup of tea when I get home.'

'You can have some tea at our house, can't he, Mama? He's been so kind, rescuing us.'

'It is indeed teatime,' said Mama, in a not very welcoming sort of way.

'It's too late for a cup of tea,' said Mr Vincent rather hastily. 'I don't want to spoil your evening meal.'

'Not at all,' Mama said, staring straight ahead. 'You must come in.'

After Mr Vincent agreed, Mama added, 'We are very simple people.'

Zidra snickered at this but quickly turned it into a hum.

'I too am a simple man,' said Mr Vincent, also staring straight ahead. 'Simple in tastes although not, I like to think, in terms of intellect.' He laughed and Zidra did too, although she didn't understand what he meant.

'It is my poor English that causes you so much amusement,' Mama said.

Mr Vincent drove the car down the hill and stopped outside their house. The orange flowers growing over the front verandah were glowing in the fading light. Mama and Mr Vincent struggled with their doors but Mr Vincent was out first. Zidra watched him race around the car to the passenger door but he was too late. Mama was through the front gate before he was anywhere near. She must be very tired to be behaving like this. Perhaps having Mr Vincent to tea wasn't such a good idea after all.

'You can open my door if you like,' she said. After he'd done so, she said very quietly, so that Mama would not hear, 'She sometimes gets like this when she's tired.'

'I think we all do,' he said seriously, holding the gate open for her. 'But thank you for letting me know.'

Without allowing Peter time to hesitate, Ilona guided him into the only armchair with decent springs. The chair squeaked when he sat on it. Even as she watched for his reaction, she was wondering what there was to offer with the tea. His head almost mechanically swivelled from one side to the other, like one of those Aunt Sallys she had seen at the fairground. She followed the direction of his eyes: on the mantelpiece was a jar crammed full of banksia flowers cut from the garden, in the centre of the room lay the faded floor rug, there were the uncurtained windows – the week after moving in she'd taken down the abundantly flowered curtains and folded them away – and there on the far side of the room was the piano.

'What a lovely piano,' he exclaimed.

Not for a moment did she believe that his interest in the piano was genuine; his exclamation had been that of a man with no conversation seizing any prop to support him. However she said, 'I inherited it from my husband, Oleksii. It was the only thing I shipped from Sydney, apart from a few books.'

'And my games too.'

Zidra, now sitting on the rug by Peter's feet, might have been a dog, so doting was her expression. At once she began an inventory of her games. For a moment Ilona stood listening, intent on ensuring that the conversation should remain general. Although it was she who had given away information about Oleksii to this unwanted guest, she did not wish Zidra to offer more. She herself did not want to make any more contact with this man. Any exposure of her past to him could be too disquieting.

Now Zidra was becoming animated about a card game in which Peter had expressed an interest, so it was safe to leave them talking together. Preparing the tea in the kitchen, Ilona listened to their laughter and the murmur of conversation although it was impossible to discern the words over the hissing of the kettle. She searched the pantry cupboard and found that there were no biscuits to serve with the tea; both tins were empty. Zidra must have eaten the last of them without telling her but that hadn't stopped the girl inviting Peter into the house. Back in the living room she put the tea tray down on the low table between the armchairs. Quickly she caught up some sheet music littering the floor and this week's *Burford Advertiser*, still open at the letters page. While proud of her achievement, she had no intention of exposing to Peter's scrutiny the letter she'd published about the Soviet presence in Hungary.

Zidra must have interpreted her return as an excuse to leave the room; Ilona could hear her tuneless whistling from her bedroom and longed to call her. Come back, darling Zidra, I forgive you for taking the last of the biscuits and I have nothing to say to this man, come back and entertain us. The awkward silence left behind was now broken by the rumbling of Peter's stomach. The poor man must be hungry but he would have to remain that way and she would offer no apology for the lack of biscuits. Tea is what he had been invited for and tea he would certainly have.

'The view here is magnificent,' Peter said.

She handed him a cup and saucer. Keen to avoid contact with him, she let go too quickly and, although he adroitly juggled the saucer, a small amount of spilt liquid collected in it. 'So clumsy of me,' he murmured.

'The view here is indeed wonderful.' She watched him take two spoonfuls of sugar and stir the tea noisily with the tarnished sugar spoon. 'That's why I decided to come here. Or one of the reasons. I knew the McIntyres in Sydney and they raved about Jingera.' The McIntyres never raved; they were a diffident but kindly Scottish couple and she regretted that she was starting to affect Mrs Chapman's manner. It was because

Peter was part of the Woodlands world but she was not and never would be. Recalling now the many contacts he might have in that world, she continued, 'But the real reason we came was that I wanted to find a peaceful town in need of a piano teacher. For that is how I earn my living.'

'Do you have many pupils yet?'

'Five, but more will come, I am sure, through words from mouths.'

'Word of mouth.'

So automatic was his correction he might have been a teacher rather than a farmer. The silence that followed this soon expanded and threatened to fill the room. Sidelong she glanced at him and intercepted his steady gaze. After a moment he blushed slightly and looked away. Now that she had disconcerted him, it was her turn to stare. His hair was too long and *foppishly* it fell over his forehead. Restlessly she began to tap her fingers on the saucer she was still holding.

At last he spoke. 'Perhaps you will play something for me on the piano.'

This was indeed one way of passing the time. She put down her teacup and moved to the piano stool. 'I shall play you some Shostakovich. I do so love the preludes and fugues.'

She opened the piano and began to play. After a few minutes she forgot all about her tiresome visitor and became caught up in the music, but some time later a brief cough reminded her of his presence. She had no idea if this interruption was deliberate or not. Perhaps he was trying to get her to stop; she did have a terrible propensity for getting lost in music. He was probably desperate to get away to find something to feed that growling stomach of his. This speculation was sufficient to destroy her concentration so completely that she made a mistake – and she never made a mistake with these preludes, never, for they were so simple and she had practised them for years. Shocked, she abruptly stopped playing.

'I am so sorry,' she said. 'I am playing badly this afternoon. I mustn't bore you any longer.' After shutting the piano more loudly than intended, she again sat in the armchair opposite him.

'You play beautifully.'

A Woodlands comment, she thought even as she thanked him. Facile and meaningless. After a pause – this man had absolutely no conversation – she said, 'Today we noticed that the Aboriginal camp near Woodlands has been moved.'

'The police move the Aborigines on periodically.'

'But that is terrible.' For some reason that she could not understand she was suddenly even more annoyed with Peter. It was almost as if he was condoning what the police did.

'They come back again after a while,' he said. 'Then the police leave them for a bit before moving them on again. They're supposed to be at the reserve at Wallaga Lake.'

'Zidra's best friend Lorna Hunter lived at that camp.'

'She'll be back.'

'What makes you so sure?'

'They always come back.'

This seemed to Ilona such a callous comment when Zidra was missing her friend so badly. She'll be back, they always come back, was all he could come up with. As if Lorna was a cat who could always make her way back and not a young girl who was Zidra's best – her only – friend. Barely suppressing her indignation, she glanced obliquely at the clock and found that this interminable visit had in fact lasted only thirty minutes, but it was more than enough. He was an impossible man and she didn't want him in her house any longer. She stood up and began to collect the tea things.

She would not catch his eye as he handed her his cup and saucer.

'I must go,' he said.

'Indeed it is getting late, and alas, soon Zidra must go to bed.'

Now Zidra appeared. 'Are you going already, Mr Vincent?'

'Yes.'

'Give Spot a pat for me.'

'I will.'

'Spotless Spot,' said Zidra and began to giggle.

The child is being deliberately provocative, Ilona thought. Without waiting for their laughter to subside, she opened the front door and stepped aside to allow Peter by. Still she could not bear to look at him.

'Goodnight, Ilona. Thank you for the tea.'

'Goodnight, Mr Vincent.' Never would she call him Peter, never. 'Thank you so much for your help today.'

Then she shut the door firmly behind him. For a moment she rested her head on the doorjamb while listening to the sound of his car starting up and then fading away.

'He didn't stay long,' Zidra said, staring at her with that penetrating look she adopted sometimes.

'Long enough, and now I must make supper.'

Only as she began to peel the potatoes did it occur to her as odd that Zidra and Peter – now he had gone she could be less formal – had got on so well together when she herself simply couldn't abide the man. It must be because Zidra talked so much that she made people feel at ease. If Zidra hadn't left them alone the visit might have gone more pleasantly. Of course not only was he lacking in conversation but he was arrogant too. He hadn't offered to let her surf with him on Jingera Beach and although she would not have accepted, this was another example of his insufferability. Just because he had rescued her, twice, didn't mean she had to like him. So many were his annoying traits that she began to catalogue them. First was the implication that she had no sense of humour. Then there was the way he had sat almost comatose in her armchair, only occasionally coming up with some trite comment. Magnificent view; lovely piano; and laughing at her English when his own speech was so inarticulate. Then he had coughed and put her off the prelude. Why she was even thinking of him now she had no idea. He'd only agreed to have tea in the first place because Zidra had made it difficult for him to refuse.

It was not until later, when Zidra was tucked up in bed and Ilona had pulled out of her shelves the book of English usage, that she realised why he'd laughed when she'd said hair of the dog. She blushed at her gaffe. Dog hair, hair of the dog. Who could guess that they would mean such different things? The trouble with that man was that he enjoyed making her seem like a *right proper galah*. Her irritation lasted several more hours. After it wore off, she began to wonder if she had been rude to him and if today's awkwardness had been partly her fault.

Soon after this bout of self-criticism ended, she suddenly thought of how much she would like to cut his rather beautiful hair. At this point she realised it was time to put away such silly fantasies and to seek distraction in a good book.

It hadn't been a happy evening, Peter reflected as he steered the Armstrong Siddeley along the road towards Ferndale. True, he'd been able to rescue Jones and his passengers. When someone was in distress you couldn't simply pass them by on the other side of the road with your face averted and at first he'd been really pleased to see Ilona. Ever since Cherry Bates had sung her praises when he'd last visited Jingera pub, he'd been unable to stop thinking of her, and this was in spite of his earlier resolution to avoid such thoughts. But he'd offended her this evening and he didn't understand how.

Funny that stepping onto someone else's territory could change things completely. That's why some animals marked out their area; step over this and you're dead. That way their equanimity wasn't disturbed. Only ever meet on neutral ground; he should have thought of that before accepting the invitation to tea, although he couldn't really have refused. It was one of those situations where you knew you'd lose whatever you did. If he hadn't accepted, she would have been offended. Yet when he did accept he'd felt so awkward in her space that he hadn't been able to think of anything to say apart from that banal nonsense about the view.

Another reason for accepting was curiosity; he'd wanted to see inside her house, he'd wanted to learn more about her. If only Zidra had stayed with them while they had tea the outcome might have been different.

Perhaps not. He reminded himself of how annoyed Ilona had been when he'd coughed. He just couldn't help that; he'd tried to suppress the tickle in his throat for as long as possible. Then she'd glared at him and soon after seized his teacup before he'd quite finished, and had more or less thrown him out. How the woman had such a lovely daughter he couldn't fathom. A prickly woman. An impossible woman.

Maybe that was not surprising given her past. You might manage to survive an impossible situation but you wouldn't be unaltered. Bits of you were mutilated, bits of you were destroyed. Though the damage might not be visible, it was there all the same.

Yet there was some quality of her face, her expression, that wouldn't let go of him. That mixture of vulnerability and challenge. He'd noticed that at their first meeting on the beach and had revisited it again and again. Now his first impressions had been confirmed; she was looking for confirmation of the worst in people. Or perhaps only in men; it was clear she adored her daughter. The girl Zidra, with those sharp eyes that missed nothing and that air of wanting to please. 'She gets like that when she's tired.' He'd liked the way she'd said that.

And he'd especially liked her appreciation of spotless Spot, who now gave a short yap as Peter pulled up at the first gate on the drive into Ferndale. Once free, the dog raced ahead of the car to the next gate and then back again. Only after Peter had driven through the last gate did Spot stop running. While Peter sat on the running board to roll a cigarette, the dog lay down at his feet and salivated onto his shoes.

Later, after feeding the dogs lumps of mutton, Peter ate cold lamb chops and a few potatoes left over from the night before. He should really have begun to work through the unpaid bills waiting in a pile on the kitchen table but instead he went to bed early, too tired even to draw the curtains. The bills could wait. Everything could wait apart from making sure the animals were looked after, and he always did that.

It must have been after midnight when he woke screaming from that old dream of falling. Falling into an abyss with no bottom; falling knowing there was no way out. Falling, fearing that he might have chosen the abyss from other alternatives that he could no longer recall. It took some seconds for him to realise where he was. Not falling out of a plane over occupied Europe but in his bedroom at Ferndale. Bright moonlight streamed through the window and illuminated the mother-of-pearl inlay on the old brass bedstead. The dream was wrong.

There was no way out of his life but forward. Second following second, hour following hour.

Getting up, he washed his face in cold water. His reflection in the bathroom mirror looked like that of a stranger, and one who was years older than he. Outside, the dogs stirred but only Spot followed him around the verandah and across the paddock to the cliff edge. He sat on the top step of the stone stair leading down to the beach and watched the breakers roll in. Strange how that regular motion could drain all thought from your mind, leaving it vacant if not soothed. That was why he had to be close to the sea, but close to the land too. He had to have something to anchor himself firmly to.

Eventually Spot got tired and lay down at his feet. At this point he remembered Zidra sitting on the floor next to him while she described her games, and he smiled. Meanwhile the moon moved imperceptibly across the sky and when it had vanished behind the pine windbreak, he returned to the house. He was tempted to let Spot inside to sleep on his bed but dismissed that impulse as sentimental.

CHAPTER TWENTY-SIX

Cherry Bates felt shaky and unwell. Half the night she'd spent fighting with her sheets and pillow, trying to get comfortable, and the other half in complicated dreams of great urgency: she had to get somewhere, she had to do something, and everything was conspiring to stop her. Because of this she was ready far too early. Although she had plenty of time for tea and toast, she was so nervous she couldn't eat anything. After Bill left – he was going to pick up Les Turnbull's boat and take it round to the jetty to collect the children – she put on a sundress and her make-up and headed towards the lagoon. Probably looking as if I don't have a care in the world, she thought; amazing what a nonchalant stride and a bright red lipstick can do. In her beach bag were sandwiches and a towel. While Bill didn't know it yet, she'd decided to accompany him on this boating expedition.

Passing by Ilona's cottage, she heard voices from inside. Ilona was shouting something in her foreign lingo and Zidra called back in her high clear voice. Cherry slowed to a leisurely walk and looked around. The sky was opalescent and the air was cool and fresh. The early morning light accentuated the folds of land forming the northern headland, which crumbled down into the sea, frilled at the cliff base by white foam. The morning was so still that between the thudding of breakers she could hear the faint hissing of waves. Tranquillity everywhere except in her head. There'd been no peace there since Ilona had told her about the boat trip and that was a few days ago now. Yesterday Cherry had mentioned it very casually to Bill and he'd laughed at her. Asked if she wanted to pack a hamper for the kiddies. When she agreed he said Ilona was going to do it and told her to spend a nice relaxing Sunday with her feet up. As if.

There were several dinghies moored at the jetty but no sign of anyone yet. She sat on the railing and glanced at her watch. Twenty-five past eight. The lagoon water slapped and sucked at the underside of the boats and a black cormorant stood on a spit of sand at the beach end of the lagoon. It had spread its wings out to dry, like a rampant eagle on some flag she'd seen, a Russian or German flag perhaps, or a flag from one of those other European countries that she was never going to visit.

At last she heard the sound of voices. Turning, she saw Zidra and the Cadwallader boys running down the hill, followed at a slower pace by Ilona. Then the putt-putt of a motor and there was Bill rounding the bend of the lagoon in the launch. He didn't see her at first, didn't see her till he'd tied up the boat. Then his smile faded.

Looking away at once, she glanced at Zidra's bright little face aglow with excitement. She glanced at Andy's freckled face squinting up against the glare, and at Jim's darker face that looked almost guarded, as if he didn't want to be here either. Giving his shoulder a quick pat, she smiled and said, 'Rather be sleeping in, Jimmo?'

Seeming more like the carefree boy she was used to seeing running about the place, Jim smiled back. 'I'll wake up once we get going,' he said. Then he looked at Zidra and she saw the smile erased from his face like a chalk drawing wiped off a blackboard. He was worried about something, that was clear. It couldn't have been much fun having Eileen for a mother, so up herself she was unable to see what a terrific hand life had dealt her. That boy would be out of here as soon as he could. Scholarship lined up to a boarding school in Sydney, and Cherry wouldn't be surprised if he never returned to this dump of a place after that. She wished she could get out too.

But Bill would have to be dealt with first.

She looked around her, at the points of light dancing on the surface of the lagoon, at the unsurpassable loveliness of the morning, and felt a sudden emptiness.

Turning to Ilona, she said, 'I hear you're going to provide the music for the Christmas dance.'

'Mrs Turnbull asked me. I am delighted at this honour,' Ilona said in that funny way she had of speaking. But she wasn't stuck-up like Lady Muck from Woodlands, who spoke as if she had a fishbone wedged in her throat. With Ilona it was just that she hadn't got the hang of the language yet. 'Daphne Dalrymple and I will take it in turns to play the piano, so that in between we can dance. If we are asked. As well, somebody from Burford is coming with an accordion.'

'That'll be Billy the Fish. Used to be a fisherman until he lost his foot to a shark in a freak accident. Pulled the shark on board and it snapped his foot right off at the ankle and swallowed it whole.' Cherry saw how shocked Ilona looked, and added, 'There aren't any sharks in the lagoon though. And Billy's got a lovely pink plastic foot that he'll show to anyone who asks him and some who don't. Ruined his fishing career though. He works in the fish and chip shop now. Getting his own back on the sharks by chopping them up and battering them.'

Laughing as if she didn't believe Cherry's story, Ilona climbed onto the jetty railing to sit next to her. 'Are you going on the boat too?'

'Yes,' Cherry said loudly.

'First time you've mentioned it,' said Bill, looking up at her. His eyes were a hard blue, like the sky on the hottest of summer days.

'It's such a lovely day and we never go out together,' she said, forcing a smile. 'I thought it would be a nice surprise for you.'

'No room for any more than four,' he said at once.

How could she not have thought of this? She inspected the boat. He was right. Deliberately he'd hired a boat that would only take four and for an instant she wondered if he knew of her discovery in his study. No, that was impossible; she'd left everything just as she found it that day.

Maybe yesterday she should have told him she was going to accompany them; she'd agonised about that countless times, but she'd known he wouldn't let her; that was precisely why she'd left it to the last minute to announce she wanted to go. Now it was too late, she could see that. It had never occurred to her that there wouldn't be enough space on the boat.

'Bad luck, old girl. If only you'd told me yesterday that you'd wanted to come. Then I could've tried to get hold of a bigger boat.'

Then you would have done nothing of the sort, Cherry told herself. She glanced at Ilona, who didn't appear to have noticed anything.

Bill added after a moment's thought, 'Otherwise I'd love to have the old girl on board, but we can't spoil the kiddies' fun now, can we?'

'So good of you to take them out,' said Ilona. 'You must be a bugger for punishment.'

The children laughed while Cherry began to chew one of her fingernails.

'A *beggar* for punishment,' Zidra said. 'You mustn't use bad language. You know it isn't nice.'

So excellent was Zidra's mimicry you might have thought Miss Neville was on the jetty with them. Cherry gave the girl a sharp look but she saw on Zidra's face only amused affection for her mother.

'It's a long time to be out on the water,' Ilona said anxiously.

You might have thought she'd only just noticed it was going to be a long day. Cherry wondered again if she should warn Ilona; if even now she should try to call a halt to the day's outing. No, she couldn't. What could she possibly say, here on the jetty with Bill listening to her every word? She should have made a stand earlier. Days ago she could have said something to Ilona. It needn't have been about Bill; it could have been about the weather or the heat or the bushfire threat. Playing up any one of those dangers might have been enough to stop the trip.

What could possibly happen when the Cadwallader boys were going along too? She clung to the thought that the children would be together all day. No harm could possibly come to them then. 'Keep an eye on the younger ones,' she whispered to Jim. She meant Zidra of course. Keep an eye on the little girl. 'You all stick together.'

'We've got Mr Bates to look after us,' said Jim, loudly enough for Bill to hear.

In that stupid way of his, Bill grinned. 'We'll be back by five sharp,' he said to Ilona. 'And I'll make sure we spend some of the time in the shade. We won't get too hot then.'

'You will keep your hat on, won't you, darling?' Ilona said, but Zidra wasn't listening any more. Chased by Andy, she was racing up and down the jetty and the entire structure shook with their motion. 'You will keep your hat on!' Ilona cried out again.

'Yes, Mama,' Zidra shouted.

An overexcitable girl like her mother was how Miss Neville described her. Bright but slightly spoilt. She was wrong though. For a fleeting moment Cherry felt a pang of envy for Ilona. A lovely daughter and no husband; she could go anywhere; she could choose what she did with her life. Quickly she pushed that mean-spirited thought away. You couldn't envy someone who'd been through what Ilona had. Taking Ilona's arm, she squeezed it, as if to apologise for her unstated thoughts. Ilona looked surprised but pleased too, and squeezed Cherry's arm back.

'Your husband is so kind,' she said. 'I worry about so much.'

'The kids will have a lovely day,' Cherry said. 'Don't you worry about a thing.' It was herself that she was reassuring though. She added, 'Jimmo's going too and I think we can rely on him, don't you?'

When she winked at him, he didn't wink back although he smiled again. For an instant she wondered if he was humouring her but put that idea out of her head. My worries are over, she told herself, at least for the time being. There isn't anything Bill can get up to, provided the kids stick together, and they'll have to. They'll be together all day in the boat.

———

Zidra sat in the bow facing backwards, so she could wave at Mama and Mrs Bates. Mama's hand went from side to side and Mrs Bates' up and down. Then Zidra felt silly sitting backwards and swung her legs over the bench so she was facing forward. Her sandaled feet rested on the damp coil of rope. Once around the bend in the river and out of sight of the jetty, she took off her hat.

'Hat on!' shouted Andy.

'I can do as I please.'

'You promised,' said Mr Bates, but nicely though. 'And I promised your mum too. She'll never forgive me if I take you back looking like a boiled lobster.'

'I don't go red,' Zidra said, but she put on the hat again and secured the elastic under the hair at the nape of her neck.

'You go a lovely golden brown,' said Mr Bates. 'You're so lucky to have olive skin in this climate, you and Jim both. Poor Andy and I are the ones who should have been left behind in northern climes.'

'What are climes?'

'Northern parts,' said Jim, keen as always to show off his knowledge. 'Europe, where we all came from.'

'All except the coons,' said Andy.

'Don't call them that. They're Aborigines,' said Jim crossly.

'Don't snap my head off. Otherwise we'll dump you ashore, like they used to do with people who mutinied, didn't they, Mr Bates?'

'They shot some of them,' said Mr Bates. 'But I don't think we need to do that with Jim just yet.'

'How come you never had any kids, Mr Bates?'

'Not allowed to say how come,' said Zidra. 'You've got to say "How was it that you never had any kids?"'

Mr Bates didn't seem interested in such distinctions. 'Never happened that way. Wasn't meant to be. I'm very happy when I'm allowed to borrow other people's, but.'

'Probably best,' said Jim, who seemed to be thawing at last. 'Then you can send them back home to their parents when you've got sick of them.'

'And you don't have to feed them either,' said Andy. 'Mum said kids are a terrible expense. Eat you out of house and home. Did you bring any lunch, Mr Bates?'

'We've got lunch,' said Zidra. 'Mum made enough sandwiches for everyone. On proper white bread from the baker's and with Burford Cheddar.'

'I've brought along a cake too,' said Mr Bates. 'A proper bought cake from the baker's, none of your homemade stuff.'

Although Zidra loved bought cake, she bristled on Mrs Bates' account. 'Mrs Bates makes lovely homemade jam,' she said. 'And Mrs Jones out at Woodlands makes yummy homemade biscuits.' Mentioning Woodlands shut everyone up for a bit. She'd noticed this before. Just drop the name into the conversation and no one could think of anything to say.

Remembering Woodlands made her think of Philip and his toys, and that led naturally to the little green elephant that she'd given Lorna. Putting one hand in the pocket of her shorts, she felt for Lorna's pale pink shell. She missed Lorna, whose absence had left a great empty hole in her life. Wherever she was, Lorna would still have the elephant with her. It had gone into her pocket that fast when Zidra gave it to her; the best gift ever, she'd said.

Last night after midnight, Zidra had woken up feeling as if Lorna were right next to her in the bedroom and trying to tell her something. She'd turned on the light to check if Lorna had somehow managed to get into her room but there was no sign of her. Nothing under the bed apart from an old hairball and nothing in the little wardrobe either, apart from clothes. She'd gone into her mother's room. Although Mama said she never got any sleep, she was in the deepest of slumbers. At first Zidra hadn't wanted to wake her but she did in the end. If she didn't tell her mother she knew she'd never get back to sleep again.

'That was telepathy,' Mama had said at once, almost as if she'd been waiting for an opportunity to bring out this word. 'One person communicates with another without their being anywhere near each other.'

'Like a telephone?'

'Just like a telephone. Only without the handset. Mental communication. Your Papa and I sometimes felt we'd communicated telepathically, but that was before he had become so cut off with his illness.'

Zidra didn't want to hear of Papa's illness again; it made her feel uncomfortable and sad. She wanted Mama to focus, to pay full attention to what she was saying. Then Mama added, 'Perhaps it's because of Lorna's move. Mr Jones said she's moved from a humpy to pickers' quarters on a farm. I expect she'll turn up soon and no one will tease her any more, because she'll be able to wash herself like all the other children, in a proper bathroom instead of in the river. You're probably worrying too much.' Mama put her hand on Zidra's forehead as if she might have a temperature. 'Perhaps you felt this telepathy simply because she was thinking of you, and thinking that she loved you.'

Zidra shut her eyes and concentrated hard to send a message back. Lorna, I love you. Lorna, I love you. After that, she started to feel better: Lorna loved her enough to telepath her and she'd telepathed back. She snuggled up to Mama, who put her arms around her and held her tightly. Eventually she carried her back to her own bed again and stayed until who knew when: she must have dropped off to sleep not long after.

Now, cruising up the lagoon, these thoughts of Lorna fluttered again across the surface of her mind, like the flickering sparks of light that danced across the surface of the water.

She sighed. The day was lovely but it would be better with Lorna here.

The boat puttered past the Cadwallader boathouse. The doors were firmly shut and a new and very large padlock held them together. Maybe the boys had told Mr Cadwallader that she and Lorna had been hanging around the boathouse. She turned around to check on the others. Mr Bates was staring straight ahead. Andy and Jim were sitting side-by-side on the middle seat. Andy was leaning over the side of the boat and trailing his hand in the water while Jim was staring into the distance with that faraway look he got sometimes. 'That boy is a dreamer,' Mama had said of him. 'And practical at the same time, but I do not think he will follow in his father's footsteps. A butcher he will not become.' Zidra rolled the last sentence around in her mouth. She would love to have spat it out in Mama's voice but, without Lorna here, there was no one she trusted enough to tell. The only person who was allowed to laugh with her at Mama was Lorna.

'Would you like to steer for a bit, Zidra?' Mr Bates called out. She clambered down the length of the boat and sat next to him. 'Put your hand on the tiller like this.' Resting his hand on top of hers, he showed her how to pull the tiller to the left or the right, so that the rudder moved and changed the flow of the water. It was easy to do. Although she hoped Mr Bates would move his hand from hers, he didn't. His skin felt calloused and his palm slightly sweaty. Glancing down she saw, between the freckles, golden hairs covering the top of his hand and running right down to the first joint of each finger. Hurriedly she looked at the river lying ahead. Eventually she said, 'I've got the hang of it now. Can I do it on my own?' Laughing, he moved his hand away.

After a few minutes, when Zidra had negotiated the next bend of the river, Mr Bates whispered to her, 'You haven't told anyone our little secret, have you? You taking the boat out when you shouldn't have.'

'No,' she said, her voice quavering. She coughed, so Mr Bates would think it was hay fever rather than nerves, and wished he hadn't raised this, especially with the two boys in the boat. They'd agreed it was to be their secret and here he was whispering about it with Jim and Andy only a few feet away. But she added, 'Did you see the boathouse is padlocked now?'

'Can't say I did. It's a good thing if it's going to stop certain people from taking the dinghy out and nearly drowning themselves, but.' He chuckled a bit at this, but not loudly enough to be heard by the boys over the puttering of the motor.

'Maybe Mr Cadwallader saw us. Or Jim and Andy told him.'

'Probably just coincidence. They didn't see anything and I didn't tell anyone. It's just a secret between you and me.'

'You and me and Lorna.'

Just then Jim turned around. 'Can I have a go now please, Mr Bates?'

After Mr Bates agreed, Zidra changed places with Jim. Watching the dark green water slip slowly past, she started to feel hungry. Perhaps they could have some of Mr Bates' cake soon.

Andy must have been thinking along the same lines. He said, 'Where are we going to have lunch?'

'There's a nice little beach further upriver,' Mr Bates said. 'I thought we could stop there and have our lunch on dry land, and maybe have a bit of a swim after our lunch has gone down.'

'Mama says you should wait at least an hour after eating before you swim. Otherwise you get cramps.'

'Then that's what we'll do,' said Mr Bates. 'We must do as your good Mama says.'

Jim made a sort of snorting noise. Zidra looked at him closely to see if he was making fun of her but he was staring over her head at the river.

———

Ilona, sitting in the old cane chair on the side verandah of her cottage, heard a squawking and looked up from the book she was reading. Half-a-dozen grey and pink cockatoos flew over the backyard and swooped around the eucalyptus tree before joining a larger flock heading south along the river. Flying low, they soon vanished, hidden by the fringe of dense forest. By now the birds would be flying over Zidra, and she too would be watching them.

Ilona's watch showed one o'clock. Nearly four and a half hours since the boating trip had begun, and only ten minutes since she had last checked the time. Perhaps her watch had stopped but it was still ticking when she held it up to her ear. It was almost impossible to concentrate. It was not that the book she was reading was dull, but more that she was distracted by other thoughts. The heat and the folly of allowing Zidra out for so long, and whether or not she had given Zidra a big enough bottle of cordial to drink.

Putting the book on the verandah floor, she went inside and turned on the radio. Too late for the one o'clock news but just in time for the local weather forecast. A fine day. Temperature expected to reach ninety-two degrees Fahrenheit. The bushfire danger level was high and a total fire ban was in force right across the state.

At least Zidra would be safe from fire in a boat. Water water everywhere. No fire danger there.

Hoping to find some music, Ilona twirled the dial of the radio. A church service was being broadcast from somewhere in Sydney. The singing was appalling, far too slow. Although the organist was playing at the right tempo and the choir following the organ, the congregation had a mind of its own and *en masse* was lagging behind.

She retrieved her book, but knew she would not be able to concentrate on it. A niggling little anxiety gnawed away inside her. Even the beauty of the lagoon, coruscating in the sunlight, could not distract her. It was not really the heat or the fire danger that was worrying her. It was Zidra's sadness, which seemed to date from when Lorna had left, and she didn't know what to do about it.

Last night, when Zidra had slipped into her bed and talked about communicating with Lorna, Ilona had remembered how she used to feel that she and Oleksii communicated by telepathy when they were apart. Just as Zidra claimed she did with Lorna. Her own communication with Oleksii had been nothing concrete, of course; just a sudden deep feeling of warmth and understanding. A sudden intuition that Oleksii was thinking of her with affection, with love. He too had claimed he felt it, that there were times when he had felt that she was transferring her thoughts to him.

But that was a long time ago. That was years ago now.

A fly landed on her nose and she brushed it away impatiently. She should face it; her marriage to Oleksii had ended long before his death. One had to be realistic and confront the truth. One should not *pull the wool over one's eyes*.

Sighing, Ilona picked up her book again, and the sheet of paper and pencil that she always kept to hand when she was reading English. There were so many words whose meaning she did not yet understand and she refused to skip over any of them. She gathered them in sets of five nowadays, although to begin with it was in sets of three, and then consulted the dictionary. Today she had deviated from that practice to look up one single word. *Sunstroke*: collapse or prostration, with or without fever, caused by exposure to excessive heat of the sun.

Again she hoped she had not been unwise in allowing Zidra to spend all day out of doors. If anything happened to her daughter, she didn't know what she would do.

Jim saw the cockatoos screeching over the strip of bush lying between the lagoon and the ocean. Their noise drowned out the conversation of the others as they flew closer. Before heading in the direction of Burford, they traced out a wide semicircle overhead – a mass of pink and grey and white.

'Never seen galahs this close to the sea before,' Mr Bates remarked. 'Must be the dry weather driving them east.' The four of them were sitting, in the shade cast by some she-oaks, on a tartan rug that Mr Bates had spread out on the grass. Andy and Zidra were still munching apples; they were such slow eaters. Below their picnic spot lay a narrow strip of white sand and beyond that the boat lay anchored several yards from the shore. 'Those birds are almost as noisy as the schoolyard at lunchtime,' added Mr Bates. 'We can always tell when school's out by the din.'

'That's what Mum says about the pub,' said Andy, who was getting a bit overexcited. 'You can always tell when it's closing time by the racket.'

Laughing, Mr Bates stretched himself out full-length on one end of the rug with a hat over his eyes. 'Reckon I'll have a nap for a few minutes,' he said. 'All this sunshine makes an old cove like me pretty tired.'

Jim was beginning to get a headache and, much as he disliked being close to Mr Bates, decided to stretch out on the other end of the rug. That way he'd kill two birds with the one stone: keep an eye on old Batesy and maybe get rid of the headache at the same time. Zidra and Andy scrambled down onto the beach and started to play in the sand, constructing a castle with a moat around it.

The sunlight, glittering through the leaves above, made a dancing red pattern on Jim's closed eyelids and he sat up again. Mr Bates appeared to be asleep and the moat the others were constructing was becoming larger. Taking the tea towel in which the fruit had been wrapped, he folded it into a little rectangle, cool and slightly damp. With the folded towel covering his eyes, he lay flat on his back and listened to the soothing sound of the breeze whispering through the she-oaks and the lapping of the river water against the little beach. And the faint murmuring of Andy and Zidra as they endlessly talked.

When he awoke, he was alone in the glade. Thinking for a brief moment he'd been left behind, he sat up too suddenly and, through swimming eyes, saw that the picnic things were still scattered on the rug and the boat was anchored just a few yards off the beach. The sun had moved over though; the trees cast longer shadows across the grass and the beach.

He stood up, and at once felt even dizzier. The trees and the sky twisted around and he nearly fell over. Grabbing hold of the gnarled trunk of a she-oak, he waited until the surround-ings stopped shifting before shouting, 'Andy! Zidra! Andy! Zidra! Mr Bates!' There was no response. His heart was racing so fast he could feel blood drumming in his ears. What a fool he'd been, he should never have fallen asleep when charged with looking after Andy and Zidra, never. Wherever they were now, he had to catch up with them and fast.

There was a narrow, rather overgrown path at each end of the glade. Quickly pulling on socks and sandshoes, he took the southerly direction, upriver away from Jingera. Occasionally stumbling, he ran along the path, which became even more overgrown the further south he got. Now he started to wonder if it was a path at all, rather than a slight bending back of the long grasses and low bushes that might have been made by the passage of animals, kangaroos perhaps. Slowing to a walk, he fought past the increasingly dense bush. The river he made sure always to keep in sight; it wouldn't do to end up getting lost himself. Just as the point when turning back seemed the only option, he thought he could hear distant voices. Rounding a thicket of low-growing wattle, he saw ahead, in a clearing by the water not five yards away, two bodies lying on the ground.

He gulped and stood still, and his heart seemed to stop beating. Then the bodies moved. The bodies of a man and a woman. On a tartan rug that was not dissimilar to Mr Bates', they lay entwined and red-faced, and staring at him in surprise. He didn't know them though; they must have come downriver from Burford. It was the kissing rather than embarrassment that brought such a rosy glow to their faces and he felt himself blushing on their behalf.

'Have you seen anyone?' he asked, staring resolutely towards the river, where a small motorboat was moored. Out of the corner of his eye he observed the woman pulling down her dress and the man sitting up awkwardly.

'No, can't say we have,' the man said. 'Apart from you, that is. Are there many more of you wandering around?'

'Yes. A man and two kids. Have you seen them?'

'We've been here an hour or two, and we haven't seen a soul.'

'Sorry to disturb you,' Jim muttered, feeling even more awkward. 'They must have taken the other path.' He turned and started walking back the way he had come.

Once out of sight, he started running again, hammering along through the undergrowth. His headache was returning, a relentless thump-thumping in his temples. High in the tallest trees, a group of magpies carolled, their clear wailing calls distinct against the thrumming of the cicadas.

There was no one in the glade, but the picnic things were still there and the launch still at anchor. He took the other path, north towards Jingera, along the river edge. Faster and faster he ran, the pounding of his feet in time with the banging in his head. Although beginning to feel slightly dizzy again, he went on, over the unyielding earth, the vegetation becoming dryer as he moved into the sclerophyll forest. Tripping over a rock, he fell hard onto the ground, grazing a knee. It began to bleed but he barely noticed in his haste to carry on. After several hundred more yards, the path opened into another small glade next to the river.

And there were Zidra and Mr Bates, sitting side-by-side on a rocky shelf at the river's edge, with their feet dangling into the water. Neither of them seemed to notice his arrival. There was no sign of Andy anywhere. Leaning towards Zidra, Mr Bates now put an arm around her shoulders and pulled her close. At this point Jim strode across the grass, which muffled his footsteps, and stood behind them.

'What are you doing?' Both Zidra and Mr Bates jumped. Mr Bates had his left hand over Zidra's, just as he had on the boat.

'I'm showing her how to attach a sinker to the fishing line.' Mr Bates removed his hand, revealing Zidra's small hand that was indeed clutching a fishing line wound around a piece of cork.

'You've been asleep for ages,' Zidra grumbled, putting the fishing line down on the rock. Her face was tinged with green but it might have just been the light filtering through the trees.

'Where's Andy?' he shouted. 'Andy, where are you?'

'Right here.' Andy emerged from the bushes. 'Do you want to fish?'

'No, I hate fishing all the time,' Jim said crossly. 'What were you doing?'

'What do you think? Having a pee, of course.' Andy grinned. 'Then I got a bit distracted by the cicadas. Look, I found a Black Prince!' He held out a clenched fist. Slowly opening it, he revealed the dark locust. Without interest, Jim gave it a perfunctory glance. His head was thudding and he desperately wanted to lie down.

'If you don't want to fish,' Zidra said, 'you can help me finish the sandcastle. It needs more work.' She jumped up and stood by his side. Fishing or building sandcastles, he didn't know which was worse. Puzzled by what he'd seen, he nonetheless didn't understand why. Batesy was showing Zidra how to fish, that was all.

'Well, are you going to help me finish the castle?' Zidra said.

'Okay.' He thought of what Mrs Bates had said that morning and added, 'We should all stick together, you know.'

'Were you scared?' asked Mr Bates, standing up. 'We'd never have left you alone if we thought that.'

— ◆ —

At last they were back in the boat and heading towards Jingera. Soon the sun would sink below the escarpment and Jim could hardly wait for that moment. His head was throbbing even more now, and every flicker of light seemed like a spear piercing his skull with a sharp point of pain. The relentless putt-putt-putt of the launch's motor didn't help, shattering the peace of the bush and the river, and the stink of the diesel fuel made him feel even sicker.

There was something strange about the way Mr Bates looked at Zidra. He fawned over her too much and he stared at her all the time, as if she was a little doll or something. As if he worshipped her. Might be because he didn't have a daughter of his own, that could be the reason. Some men wanted daughters rather than sons and Mr Bates didn't have either.

Jim pulled at the top of a fingernail that had got snagged on his fishing line that morning, and yanked it right off. The pain, as the nail tore off below the quick, distracted him for a moment from his anxiety and nausea.

He was desperate to get back home. A boat was a pretty claustrophobic thing. The others seemed tired too. Everyone had gone very quiet now. Even Zidra, usually so talkative, seemed subdued.

At last the jetty was in sight. Two figures were standing side-by-side, looking out for them. Mrs Bates and The Talivaldis began to wave when they saw the launch. Mrs Bates up and down, The Talivaldis from side to side as if she was royalty. Jim was glad Roger wasn't on board to make fun of that.

Jim glanced at Zidra just as she glanced at him. In spite of his headache and general irritation, he smiled. He wasn't going to allow her to think that he might find her mother ridiculous. Or that he was worried about Batesy fussing over her all the time.

CHAPTER TWENTY-SEVEN

Another Saturday night. George finished his bath and dried himself slowly. After donning pyjamas, he carefully combed his wet hair and wondered if Eileen would forgive him for that argument after dinner. It was the worst row they'd ever had. The boys had gone out in the yard to play after tea and he and Eileen had bickered again about the scholarship. *It isn't fair to Andy* was her latest war cry. She'd abandoned the previous one – *just think of the expense* – only days ago.

However it was Saturday night and he would try to make love to her. Surely it was one way of making up their differences, although he didn't feel much like it. For once, thinking of her naked breasts wasn't arousing. Shutting his eyes, he pictured her cleavage as he'd seen it over dinner, on display in the V-neck of her dress. He imagined sliding his hands down into that cleft and unbuttoning the dress-front and gently releasing those lovely breasts, and afterwards sucking at the nipples, those strawberries that he so loved to roll around his tongue, and lick and tease, though tonight the images didn't help. There was not even the slightest tingling in his groin.

There was nothing for it now but a spot of manipulation. Opening his eyes, he undid the tie on his pyjama bottoms and picked up his penis in his hand. Lifting it and rubbing it had no effect: it remained as flaccid as a condom. They would have to be reconciled before he was able to make love to her again. Maybe he'd never be able to make love to her again. Suppressing a sigh, he refastened his pyjamas and went into the bedroom.

Eileen had left the bedlamp on but she had her back to him. Although the night was still hot, she had drawn the sheet right up to her chin and tucked it firmly under her, so he had to untuck his side of the sheet to climb in next to her.

'I'm sorry about our disagreement,' he said, and he *was* sorry. If only she would quietly give in.

'So you ought to be.' Her voice was muffled by the pillow but he was heartened she had deigned to reply.

'I hate it when we argue.' Her dark hair was spread on the pillow next to his. Several white hairs he had never noticed before moved him strangely but he couldn't afford to become distracted. He switched off the lamp.

'Jim's not going, George.'

'Yes he is, Eileen.'

'He's not. *It isn't fair to Andy*.' That was it, out with the new war cry, and her tone was so savage. 'Andy would feel he was second-class if Jim went to Stambroke.'

'Why should he? You've said yourself they're different.' He just couldn't see Andy being bothered by this, or at least not in the sense that Eileen was suggesting. Andy would miss Jim, no doubt about that; but he had lots of his own friends and wasn't exactly lacking in confidence.

'Andy's just as talented as Jim. You only have to look at his artwork to see that.'

'Even you have to admit that he isn't that good at his books,' George said, his resolve sharpening to such an extent that he no longer minded what she thought of him. Taking a deep breath, he said firmly, 'Jim's going to be allowed to take up the scholarship come what may and you can just put that in your pipe and smoke it.' This was perhaps the unkindest he had ever been to her in their entire married life.

She didn't seem unduly perturbed. 'We'll see about that,' she said, and within a few minutes she was sound asleep.

Lying awake next to her, George felt his heart racing. So that was it. The end of communication between them.

Nothing was going to stand in the way of this dream. Nothing.

Once he had convinced himself of his resolution, and this took some time, he too fell asleep; only lightly, visited by strange fancies that drew him in and out of consciousness.

CHAPTER TWENTY-EIGHT

Peter was awoken by a bell ringing. Not the phone. Not the old dinner bell outside the kitchen that was occasionally used by his few visitors. Must be the front doorbell that hadn't been rung in years. Easing himself out of bed, he picked up a dressing-gown on the way into the hall. The doorbell rang again. Moonlight washed into the hall through the fanlight over the front door and illuminated the wall clock. Its hands showed ten to two.

He turned on the verandah light and opened the door. Old Charlie stood there, blinking. His appearance was even more dishevelled than usual, and there were leaves and grass seeds on the greatcoat that he wore regardless of the season.

'You'd better come in.' Peter knew Old Charlie would come to his house only if something really bad had happened. He led him down the long hallway and into the kitchen. Charlie didn't smell the best and it was a hot night, so he opened the outside door before offering his visitor a cup of tea and trying to get him to sit down at the kitchen table. The old man avoided the chair and attached himself to Peter's dressing-gown sleeve instead.

'You've got to come with me.'

It was the first time Peter had ever heard Charlie speak more than a couple of grunts or a mumbled g'day and he was surprised at his coherence. 'Can't it wait till morning?' he said gently. Nothing could be so urgent that it had to drag a man out of his bed on Saturday night, when the morning after was the only time all week he could sleep in a bit.

'No.'

For an instant Peter wondered if the old man had been drinking, even though rumour had it that he'd never touched a drop. Peter sniffed and couldn't smell any alcohol although there were lots of other odours emanating from Charlie's person. 'What's up?' he said.

'You'll see.' Charlie was starting to look upset now and if Peter was not mistaken, a couple of tears spilled out of his rheumy eyes.

'What will I see?'

'Come with me.'

'I've got to change first.'

'I'll wait on the back verandah,' Charlie mumbled. He shuffled outside and parked himself on the step.

Peter pulled on trousers and a shirt, and slipped on his boots. No socks to be found so he'd just have to go sockless. Before joining Charlie on the verandah, he retrieved a torch from the cupboard underneath the sink.

But the moon was almost bright enough for them not to need the torch. Charlie led him down the driveway and onto the narrow path through the dense bush to the north of Ferndale. For someone whose gait was usually more of a shuffle than a walk, he could move remarkably fast.

Peter thought of his comfortable bed and wondered why on earth he was following a mad man through the bush when he could be fast asleep. He grabbed hold of Old Charlie's great-coat to slow him down. 'Where are we going?'

'Tommy Hunter.'

'What about Tommy Hunter?'

'Got to see him.'

'Well I'm not walking all the way up to Wallaga Lake. We'll go by car.'

'Not far from here. Two, three miles north.'

'Of here?'

'Yes.'

'We're driving then.'

They retraced their steps. Peter unlocked the car and wound down the window before standing back to let the old man in. Now Old Charlie seemed a bit daunted. The shock of having to ride in a motor vehicle. Peter helped him into the car and shut the door behind him.

In silence they drove several miles north of Ferndale.

'Stop here,' Old Charlie said, pointing to the edge of the road. 'Look.'

Then Peter saw, in a clearing at the side of the road, a crouching man. He appeared to be holding something and was rocking to and fro. Peter stopped the car at once and retrieved the torch from under his seat. He directed the beam so that it illuminated the figure. It was indeed Tommy Hunter.

'What's up, Tommy?' he said. 'What have you got there?'

'Lorna's cardigan,' he said, holding up a dark bundle. 'And look what was in the pocket. That green elephant she carries round. Must've dropped the cardigan in the struggle. Welfare's taken her.'

'Maybe she just dropped that when she was walking here.'

'No. Look at them scuffle marks. They dragged 'er into the van, just like they did the other kids at the reserve.'

'When was that?'

'Yesterday. Welfare took lots of kids. Missus told Lorna to run and she did. Thought she'd got away till now.'

'When did you find this?'

'Three, four hours ago.' Tommy's voice broke and he coughed.

'You've been here all that time?'

'Yes. Old Charlie said 'e'd get you.'

Peering around for Old Charlie, Peter saw him crouching motionless nearby, a squat dark shape, and breathing heavily through his mouth. The trees seemed to be looming in, squashing them, so it was becoming a struggle to breathe. 'I think I'd better go to the police. See if I can find out what's happened. You want to wait here?'

'She won't come back. Won't let 'er back.'

'But she's a . . .' Peter didn't know quite how to express what he was thinking. If both parents were full-blooded Aborigines she shouldn't have been removed. It was the mixed-race kids they took away.

'Missus 'ad 'er by whitefella when she was fifteen.'

'I see.'

'I'm comin' with you. Old Charlie wait here in case.'

Old Charlie nodded.

Peter opened the car door for Tommy, who was still clutching Lorna's cardigan. The drive south to Burford seemed interminable but it was probably only half an hour. The Burford streets were deserted. Peter parked right outside the police station with its depressing blue light illuminating the entrance. Tommy refused to get out of the van. ''Aven't got m' dog tag on,' he said. 'They'll lock me up.'

Inside, Peter found a bored policeman slumped at a desk, a red-faced man in his late forties. So happy was he to see some break in the routine that he almost embraced Peter, but his expression altered when Peter explained why he was there.

'A half-caste Abo. Yes, they've been taken away.'

Peter felt disembodied, as if it were someone else, and someone he didn't know all that well, standing in the police station.

'Lorna Hunter's ten or eleven. The daughter of a good friend of mine,' he said.

'Not your daughter then?'

If Peter hadn't felt so shaken he might have resented the man's patronising tone.

'No. Can you check your records?'

The officer went into the back of the police station, leaving Peter alone in the waiting room. He could hear the murmur of voices from out the back. Pacing up and down, he occasionally stopped to check on his car parked outside. The last thing he wanted was for Tommy to get arrested for being in town after six without his tag.

Presently the officer returned. 'Take a seat, mate,' he said. 'It'll be a few minutes before my colleague finds the file.' Peter sat down on one of the hard wooden benches.

'Want a cup of tea?' The man took a thermos flask from under his desk.

'No thanks.' Peter stared glumly out the window.

'Abos were moved on from here last week,' the man said, taking a noisy sip of tea. 'We started shifting them up by Jingera and then came back here to move the local buggers on.'

'Where to?'

'Where they're supposed to be. Up at Wallaga Lake Reserve.'

'That girl Lorna Hunter went to school in Jingera.'

'She probably wasn't there much. Terrible truancy rates the Abos have. Kids in and out of school, it's no wonder they're not educated.' Putting his feet up on the desk, he rocked the chair back and forth. 'We moved the Burford coons on after the Welfare Board took the half-caste kids. I reckon Welfare will have their hands full.' He laughed.

Peter tried to imagine what it would be like to lose someone you loved and found there were tears in his eyes. Becoming emotional would never do. Looking out the window again, he blinked rapidly several times. 'Where did they take them?'

'The Gudgiegalah Girls' Home or the Kinchela Boys' Home.' The man paused before adding, 'It's for their own good. They'll have the blackness bred out of them in a generation or two. Once the half-caste kids were gone, we moved on the full-blooded Abos. They'd been fouling up the land, doing their business anywhere and everywhere. Public Health had to close the conveniences at Burford Oval because the niggers'd been using them all the time. They were that filthy no white person could bear to go in.'

'They've got to go somewhere,' said Peter.

'Yeah, Wallaga Lake.' The officer now emptied the last of the tea from the thermos into his mug.

'No, they've got to go to the *toilet* somewhere. If the Council shuts up the public toilets in the park, the Aborigines have got to do their business somewhere.' Peter's head was starting to spin. It must be the fatigue; maybe he should have accepted that offer of tea but it was too late now.

'Nah, they do it anywhere even when they've got proper toilets. Not a nigger-lover, are you?'

'I reckon they're people just like you and me.'

The officer laughed indulgently. 'You see another side of life in this job,' he said. 'And it isn't too nice, I can tell you.' He got up and went into the back of the station again. A few moments later he returned.

'Yes, Lorna Hunter's gone. She'll be sent to the Gudgiegalah Girls' Home. Ain't nothing you can do about it, mate. Sorry about your friend, but that's the long and the short of it.'

CHAPTER TWENTY-NINE

Containing himself, distancing himself. George had been doing that all morning. Occasionally, when he least expected it, it came rushing in at him again, threatening to overwhelm him. Then he had to stop whatever he was doing and take deep breaths until he was strong enough to push it away from him once more. He wasn't going to give in though.

Mentally gauging the length of each log, he stood in front of the wood pile. They were uniformly eighteen inches long and he planned to rearrange them so the pile was even more orderly than usual. The whole afternoon lay in front of him. He would stack the logs in the timber frame he had constructed the previous Sunday.

He began to arrange the logs between the constraints, with their rough sawn edges facing out. Or facing in, it all depended on your perspective, and he feared he was losing his. The growth rings, year after year, were exposed to view. The big logs he would stack first and afterwards he'd slot between them the more slender pieces of wood.

The day was hot and the woodpile was in the sun. He took off his felt hat and wiped the sweat from his brow with a handkerchief. Eileen was indoors having a rest. He could do with one himself but he had to keep his exhaustion at bay, just as he had to keep his loneliness at bay too. He drove himself on, not heeding the splinters, not heeding the heat.

After several hours he heard the fly-screen door slam but he didn't turn. He knew it was Eileen. She didn't say anything and he didn't stop working. He didn't even turn around, but he was aware of her standing on the verandah, watching him.

'Quite a work of art, that,' she said at last. 'Reminds me of the Royal Easter Show.' Her voice was not unkind.

He stopped at this, at the memory of those piles of fruit and vegetables, and the beautiful arrangement of the more colourful vegetables into the coat of arms of New South Wales. The background to his meeting with Eileen all those years ago. He felt a prickling behind his eyes. Eileen's kindness was not what he needed at the moment, and it wouldn't be genuine, it would be part of their war of attrition. *It isn't fair to Andy*. He could hear again the savageness of her tone the previous night.

He had to hold himself together, he had to be self-contained. Taking a deep breath, he turned slowly to look at his wife, who was standing on the verandah and smiling at him.

'Nice to see you being tidy, George.'

For once he was glad of the veiled reproof. It would stop him falling apart. He thought of the shopfront window of Cadwallader's Quality Meats. Of the exquisitely arranged display of chops and steaks, of the orderly rows of sausages and the mounds of tripe decorated with sprigs of fresh parsley. He knew he was always tidy but Eileen would never look at that display.

'Would you like a cup of tea?' she added.

She brought it out to him in the old enamel mug with the chip on it right where his mouth went. Unhygienic it undoubtedly was, but it was his favourite mug and had belonged to his father before him. Gratefully he took it but didn't look at her face. When she'd gone back inside, he sat down on the stump he used as a chopping block and again wiped the sweat from his brow.

That morning Peter Vincent had telephoned to tell him the news about Lorna Hunter. He knew about this policy in the abstract but it had never before happened to anyone he knew. Never to a kid who was in the same school as his sons. It must be a mistake and he was going to phone the Burford police himself this afternoon. That sort of thing couldn't be allowed to happen in a civilised place like Wilba Wilba Shire.

Yet if Peter was right, what would it be like to lose your family? He couldn't bear to lose his. They meant more to him than anything. Without warning he began to weep. For the callousness of authorities who would take away half-caste children, their families were only Abos after all. For Jim, whose cleverness meant that Jingera was not big enough for him. And for Eileen who no longer loved him, he was quite sure of that now.

Putting the half-empty mug down on the ground, he rested his head on his hands. Softness and love, that's what might have been. But not for the likes of Lorna Hunter, if Peter was correct. Not for himself either, as long as he refused to yield to Eileen. He knew that soon he'd have to resume constructing his barrier. There was no meaning to life, there was no order to life, unless you imposed it.

Only at this instant did it occur to him to put himself into Eileen's shoes. Maybe it wasn't just the expense that was bothering her. Maybe it wasn't fairness to Andy either. Maybe she was thinking she was losing a part of her family; in a way she was. Even though the scholarship was the right thing for Jim, and George was absolutely convinced of this, the children were Eileen's life and now unexpectedly part of this life was about to be removed. At such a prospect Eileen might well be feeling a sense of loss. Or even of anger, and what better way to manifest this than to refuse any physical contact with him? How insensitive he'd been not to think of this before.

On the other hand he wasn't entirely to blame. If only Eileen had been able to say to him, George I'm going to miss Jim terribly, if only she'd been open with him. Then they could have talked things through and avoided this awful alienation. He would have to tread more lightly with her. Although Jim was going to be allowed to seize this opportunity, he himself would need to work harder at understanding Eileen's point of view. She might never soften but he had to try to understand what she might be going through.

At this point he rubbed a handkerchief over his face. It was as wet as if he'd just washed it and his mouth felt dry. Picking up the mug of tea again, he deliberately sucked at it, slurped at it, something he would never do if he were not alone. When the tea was finished, he carried the mug to the back verandah and left it on the splintered planks. Constructing the wall of logs was allowing him to put things in perspective. Constructing the wall was holding back the worst of his unhappiness.

———

Jim, washing his hands in the bathroom later that same afternoon, wasn't aware that his father was on the phone until he came into the hallway. Dad had his back to him and was holding the receiver up to one ear and a cupped hand over the other ear. The radio in the lounge room sounded quite loud, even through the closed door, but Dad was speaking softly in spite of this. Jim might have gone straight past him and into the kitchen if he hadn't heard him mention Lorna Hunter. He stopped still. This wasn't exactly eavesdropping, he just wanted to know more.

'I'm phoning about Lorna Hunter,' his father repeated, rather more loudly this time. 'Can I speak to the officer in charge? . . . Surely you can put me through.' There was a pause and then he continued, 'What about the parents? No one in Jingera seems to have heard anything . . . Oh, I see, well I won't hold you up then. I'll try again some other time. Thank you. Goodbye.' Muttering something about the police all being stupid fools, he put the receiver down before noticing Jim standing in the hallway.

'News about Lorna?' Jim said, trying to give the impression that he'd only just come out of the bathroom.

'There's some news about Lorna,' Dad said, looking worried. 'But I don't know if it's true. That's the trouble, son. I don't know enough yet.' He glanced at his watch. 'Time you fed the chooks, isn't it? We don't want your mother rousing on you again, do we?' Before limping down the hallway, he gave Jim a distracted pat on the shoulder. Into the lounge room he went and shut the door firmly behind him.

Jim stood still for a moment longer, puzzling over his father's conversation.

There was something unusual about Lorna's absence, that much was clear. Perhaps the rumour he'd heard from Zidra was wrong and Lorna hadn't moved to the Sutherlands' property. Another report had it that the whole family had been shifted back to Wallaga Lake, but perhaps Lorna had run away instead. Perhaps she'd become a Missing Person and that's why Dad was on the phone just now. Although wanting to ask his father more, he guessed from the overheard conversation that he didn't know anything much.

And it was the first time ever that Dad had told him to feed the chooks.

Jim went outside anyway, although he'd already fed the chooks that day. Needing some time to think, he went straight to that favourite hiding spot of his, under the fig tree below the chicken run.

CHAPTER THIRTY

The day of the Christmas dance was stinking hot. Jim mooched around at home, trying to keep out of his mother's way. Her entire morning had been spent baking stuff for the dance at the church hall and by early afternoon she was at her grumpiest. You might have thought she'd be glad to let him and Andy outside to play but she wouldn't have a bar of that, and she wouldn't let them near the kitchen either. *Hanging around getting underfoot* was how she put it. Eventually they shut themselves in their bedroom and started a game of Monopoly. By late afternoon a light breeze sprang up that cooled the house and their mother's temper. She was almost back to normal when it was time to head off to the hall to get preparations underway. The boys also had to go to help carry, for their father had gone on ahead in the van to collect the trestles. She wouldn't hear of Jim and Andy dragging her pots and plates along on their billycarts, so they headed off balancing trays, a much more precarious undertaking.

The hall felt stifling, even though all the sash windows on each side were wide open, and Jim was glad the kids would have the backyard to play in once the dance started. After they'd put down the trays in the kitchen at the back of the hall, and grabbed a couple of sausage rolls when no one was looking, Jim and Andy went outside. Around the back of the hall, some of the boys had started a game of French cricket with a bat and tennis ball. They weren't allowed cricket balls here after that time Andy lobbed a ball through the rectory window and smashed it.

Then Jim saw Roger O'Rourke pick up something from the back of the incinerator. Holding it behind him, he came running across the yard. 'Here's O'Rourke coming in to bowl,' he shouted and lobbed whatever he'd been holding straight at the batsman. It missed and went through the window of the shed at the back of the hall, shattering it into a hundred pieces. Roger shrieked with laughter. 'It was a cricket ball,' he shouted. 'Gotya! I'm batsman now!' He seemed as unaware of the broken window as he was of several fathers advancing down the side passage, rolling a keg of beer in front of them like a drum announcing their arrival.

Roger's father was the first to notice his son racing around the yard holding a cricket bat and ball, and the pile of broken glass in front of the shed. 'That's enough,' he shouted, advancing down on him, red hair bristling. Roger swung around and his father yanked the ball from him. 'Where did you get this from? You know cricket balls aren't allowed here any more.'

'Nowhere,' said Roger.

'Nothing comes from nowhere.' Roger's dad was red in the face now as well as the hair.

When Zidra heard the crash of breaking glass followed by shouting, she ran down the back steps of the hall. Roger

O'Rourke being bawled at: she couldn't stop herself smirking at the sight. Staring at the ground, Roger looked miserable but he was certain to have deserved it. Mr O'Rourke continued rousing on Roger. She might have felt sorry for him if he hadn't tipped ink onto the cover of her exercise book yesterday afternoon. Miss Neville had blamed her and she'd accepted the blame. Although she could have told on him, she didn't. But that hadn't seemed to make him feel grateful.

Roger started to kick with one foot at a clump of grass. This made Mr O'Rourke even angrier. Now Mrs O'Rourke appeared in the yard and marched across the rough grass to her husband and son. Zidra followed close behind and was unable to prevent her smirk from turning into a grin.

'Where did you get that cricket ball from?' Mrs O'Rourke's voice was sharp enough to cut through a stale loaf.

'Behind the incinerator.' Roger waved towards the back of the yard. They all stared at the incinerator for an instant.

'What was it doing there?'

'How would I know? I s'pose someone left it there after the last game.'

All the boys snickered a bit at this and Zidra grinned too, but Roger carried on watching the grass grow.

'What are you gawping at, the lot of you?' Mrs O'Rourke said, turning on them. 'I'm going to get rid of this and I don't want you playing with cricket balls here again. Plus you're going to have to pay for that pane of broken glass from your own pocket money.'

Roger looked up and saw Zidra standing behind his mother. He grinned defiantly. Seeing the grin, Mrs O'Rourke cuffed his ear. Now Zidra grinned more widely. She followed Mrs O'Rourke into the kitchen and saw her stuff the cricket ball into the garbage bin. It wouldn't stay there long, she knew.

Just then Mama swept through the door from the hall and gave a little shriek. 'There you are, darling Zidra! I have been looking all over for you.'

Squirming with embarrassment, Zidra wanted to tell Mama to speak like a normal person, not a foreigner. Instead she said, 'We Australians are given to understatement.' It was her best imitation yet of Miss Neville. 'You won't find us an emotional lot, Mrs Talivaldis.'

Mama laughed, though Zidra could tell it was in spite of herself. So too did some of the other ladies. Zidra's spirits lifted. She liked an audience, even if it was only mothers and not the children she really wanted to impress. Looking around quickly to see if Miss Neville might have heard, she was relieved to see that she was nowhere in sight. One or two of the older ladies were glaring at her though. 'Too clever by half,' one of them muttered. 'If she were mine I'd give her the strap.'

Mama chose to ignore this, or perhaps she hadn't heard. 'You will help Mrs Bates with distributing the knives and forks across the tablecloths in the hall,' she told Zidra while giving her a hard shove, her equivalent of the strap.

***

It was late afternoon by the time Peter shut the main gate into Ferndale and turned the car onto the road heading south towards Jingera. It was still several hours before sunset but the western sky was beginning to glow golden through a thin red haze that looked almost like dust. He'd wound down the car windows to get some air but he still felt unpleasantly hot. Accelerating to generate a cooling breeze, he almost missed seeing Tommy Hunter walking along the verge of the road heading north – the very man he'd wanted to see. Immediately he stopped the car and backed up to a patch of shade.

'G'day,' Tommy said. He didn't smile though. It was almost as if he hadn't wanted Peter to stop. 'Where are you off to?' His voice was listless.

'Jingera. The Christmas dance.' Peter got out of the car. 'Can't say I'm all that keen though.'

'Could've fooled me. You was goin' like the wind. Flyin' along. Think you was still up in the air?' Tommy took off his old felt hat and fanned himself with it.

'Where're you heading?'

'Wallaga Lake. The missus and kids are still there.'

When Peter had last seen Tommy's family, his wife – a small shy creature in a baggy floral dress – had five children in tow. All with brilliant smiles and a willingness to look straight at him, unlike their mother, and now there were only four children. He wondered if their smiles were still as brilliant. 'How's the family coping?' he asked.

'Pretty crook.' Tommy fanned himself once more with his hat. 'Missus in tears plenty often and little kids too.'

'I checked again, Tommy. With the Welfare Board this time. I drove in to see them yesterday. I'm afraid the police were right Welfare has taken Lorna.'

It had been a hopeless visit. The woman he'd spoken to, a tall blonde who'd spent too much time in the sun, had been adamant it was for the children's own good. Got any children yourself? he'd asked her. No, she'd replied but if I did I'd want them to have the best start in life, and then she'd smiled in that mawkish way people did sometimes when they were talking about kids in the abstract. Now he hesitated before adding, 'And there's nothing we can do about it, Tommy, but at least we know for sure where she is – Gudgiegalah Girls' Home.'

'That's what Welfare told the Missus when they tookem other kids.'

Peter felt helpless. He didn't tell Tommy what he'd also learnt from the woman at the Welfare Board. That the children weren't allowed to keep in touch with their families. There was little chance of Lorna seeing her family again, or at least not until she was older, fourteen or fifteen, but Tommy probably knew that already. 'I'm so sorry,' he said. Lame words, but it was better by far to say something, anything, than to ignore Tommy's distress.

He sighed. Lorna was a bright kid and maybe she'd do all right in Gudgiegalah. She'd get an education and maybe make a life for herself. Though from what he'd heard she was more likely to end up as housemaid to some rich property owner out west, far from where she belonged.

Tommy, gazing into the distance, appeared to be staring at the range of mountains to the west. Or staring beyond the range, as if he could see as far as Gudgiegalah. 'Gotter get on,' he said eventually. 'Gotter get back.'

'Would you like a lift?'

'No,' Tommy said so quickly that Peter wondered if he had interpreted his offer as pity, but it was probably more that he needed to be alone.

Although the car was now as hot as Hades, Peter sat in it for a few minutes. In the rear-vision window he watched Tommy's reflection, a shabby figure trudging along the dirt verge. It was a long way to Wallaga Lake if you had to walk.

Eventually Peter started the engine and drove on, more soberly now, towards Jingera. Occasionally he caught glimpses of the ocean that was so smooth it looked like faintly rumpled silk. Silky like a woman's skin. Although he didn't especially want to go to the Christmas dance, particularly after seeing Tommy's sad face, he knew that Ilona would be there. Over the past week or so he'd experienced no more nightmares and he'd come to the conclusion that Ilona hadn't intended to offend him that afternoon; *she gets like that when she's tired*, Zidra had said. Instead he'd found his own conduct wanting. It wasn't his coughing during the Shostakovich prelude that now bothered him but his laughter at her misuse of English.

Initially he'd wondered if she lacked a sense of humour. That would explain why she found correction difficult, but it was one thing to be corrected, quite another thing to be laughed at. Learning new idioms was hard enough without being mocked and he wanted to make amends for that.

The fleeting hope that she too might want to apologise he dismissed as a wild fantasy.

Chapter Thirty-One

B y the time Peter reached Jingera the temperature had
cooled by several degrees. The paddock opposite the
church hall was so full he parked the Armstrong in a side
street where there'd be little chance of it being knocked later
by some inebriate. The noise from the hall ratchetted up even
in the short time it took him to walk from car to hall.

Most of the people he knew by sight if not to talk to.
Farmers like himself, with their wives in brightly coloured
dresses and helmets of curled and shining hair. A few fisher-
men who lived in Jingera although the port was some miles
further south. Some forestry workers, and all the Jingera trades-
people out in force. In the near corner he could see Mrs
Blunkett holding court. She was talking nonstop. It was a
miracle she managed to absorb all the gossip that she did when
she never seemed to listen.

Seeing Ilona coming out of the kitchen, he was struck by
how lovely she looked: her normally wild hair was restrained
by a wide black ribbon and she seemed paler than ever, apart
from two circles of colour on her cheeks. Her fragile expression
belied what he suspected was a core of steel. A core covered in
barbed wire that he might never be able to get close to. Yet

in spite of this he began to push his way through the throng.

Only at this point did he see that his old acquaintance Jeff Heath was also heading in her direction and would get there first. Good-looking Heath, *accomplished polo player*; and womaniser too – although the *Burford Advertiser* never mentioned that bit. Already he had her elbow in a proprietorial grip and was leaning forward to whisper in her ear. Imagining those seductive silver words, Peter felt annoyance stab his breast, and now, as if Ilona were incapable of making her own way, the polo player was steering her through the knots of people towards the tables. Worse even than this sight was that she didn't seem to mind; indeed, she was laughing up at him. Peter's displeasure metamorphosed into a novel emotion that he recognised was jealousy. Clearly he'd have to rescue her and might even offer an apology. How to do this was not obvious but he knew that most of his character traits were unforgivable. Curtness. Bluntness. Directness. Humour. At this point he almost gave up. No, he couldn't possibly leave her to dreadful Heath. She had to be saved from that.

Through the crowd he wended his way. Only occasionally did he stop to talk to people, when it was absolutely necessary to avoid giving offence. Always keeping an eye on his goal. His goal and quarry, for he was determined to separate them. When he had almost reached Ilona and Heath, a whisper arose that it was time to eat. Had he not been so resolved to reach Ilona, he might have stood back. But here she was, holding two empty plates, and good heavens, she was smiling at him and handing him one plate and Heath the other.

Smiling first at her and then at Heath, he imagined for a moment that he'd hidden his true feelings until Heath said, 'You're looking a bit out of sorts, old man. Parties not really your thing, are they?'

So intent was Peter on Ilona that he overlooked Heath's comment. In some indefinable way, she looked altered. It wasn't just that she was dressed so differently, in a sleeveless dark green dress of some shiny fabric. It was more her open expression and incandescent eyes. Turning to see if there was anyone behind who was the focus of this beacon of light, he could see only Jim Prior's leonine head inclining towards Dalrymple's shiny pate, and behind them the shabby cream wall.

'I adore parties,' Ilona said.

So that was it. She was wearing a social smile. Never before had he seen her at a public gathering so how could he have known that this radiance was something she put on like a piece of jewellery for a gala occasion.

'So do I,' said Heath. 'I love dancing.'

'I too like to dance but it's the music that I really love,' said Ilona. 'Tonight I will be playing the piano for some of the time. Daphne Dalrymple and I will take it in turns, and also there will be Billy the Fish.'

'Perhaps you'll save a dance for me,' Peter said quickly.

'And one for me,' Heath said.

Damn the man; it was a struggle for Peter to conceal his irritation. But Ilona wasn't looking at either of them. Instead she was staring at Cherry Bates beckoning from the kitchen doorway.

'Perhaps it's about Zidra,' Ilona said. 'Or the sausage rolls.'

For an instant Peter thought she rested her hand on his arm as she slipped by. Although she might have, he saw only Heath's hand pushing him aside to allow someone access to the table. The woman seemed a little unsteady on her feet. It might have been that someone had just nudged her although she did seem to reek of sherry. He could do with a good slug of something strong himself.

'Who's Zidra?' Heath enquired casually.

'Ilona's daughter.'

'She's got a child?'

'Yes. She's widowed.'

'How old is the child?'

'She's about nine or ten I'd say. Haven't you heard about her? I thought everyone knew what everyone else was doing around here.' His voice sounded nastier than he'd intended.

'I've been overseas. Got back last week.'

Heath's immediate dissipation of interest gladdened Peter's soul. If he hadn't felt so happy for himself, he might have been embarrassed for Heath's transparency. The man just melted away and a few seconds later Peter saw him heading for a group of unattached women of the type that attended the Bachelors' and Spinsters' Ball. Beautifully dressed and coiffed and with minds as vacant as a church on Saturday. Any one of them would make a perfect match for Jeff Heath.

He wouldn't take any chances though. By the kitchen door, he waited for Ilona to return. Although a reasonably good dancer, he was probably not good enough for her and she could add that to the list of his failings. This possibility did not, however, affect his appetite. Institutional living had that effect. You ate what you could as soon as it appeared and you ate it fast. To fill in time he had a second helping. When that had gone, he peered through the door into the kitchen and saw her deep in conversation with Cherry Bates in a room full of women. Beating a hasty retreat, he found a clean plate and made a selection for Ilona from the fast-vanishing food on the trestle tables before returning to his post just outside the kitchen door.

❦

Once Ilona and Cherry had agreed on the oven temperature, Cherry said, 'You be nice to him, won't you, darl.'

'Who?' Ilona helped herself to another asparagus roll from the plate on the kitchen bench.

'Peter Vincent. And watch out for that Jeff Heath.'

Ilona smiled. While initially tempted to suggest that Cherry was fussing too much, she now decided that she liked this attention. 'I will. I know Heath's type, and anyway he's flirting with those smart women in the far corner. They both asked me to dance, by the way.'

'I thought Peter would. I saw the way he was looking at you.'

'I hope his dancing is better than his conversation.' Ilona now took two sausage rolls.

'Don't be too quick to jump to conclusions. He's a good man, just a bit shy.'

'He's arrogant.'

'He's the least arrogant man you could meet. Personally I find him very easy to get along with.'

'You should dance with him then.'

'Perhaps I will, if he asks. He's a beaut dancer, by the way, I saw him at last year's dance.'

Although Ilona now experienced an unreasonable twinge of jealousy, she certainly wasn't going to ask who Peter had danced with.

'But tonight he's only got eyes for you, Ilona, and I've got a great topic of conversation for you. It'll probably last several dances at least. Just ask him what he found out yesterday in Burford. He popped into the pub in the late afternoon and told me all about it.'

'What was he doing in Burford?'

'You can find out yourself. It'll give you something to talk about.' And with that Ilona felt Cherry's gentle push in the direction of the hall.

Holding a laden plate, Peter waited just beyond the doorway. 'I got this for you. I thought you might be hungry and the food's going so quickly.'

'Thank you, how nice.' Only now did she notice his haircut. No longer did his hair fall foppishly forward but it sat neatly on either side of a sharp parting. Far too neatly, it might almost have been painted onto his skull. Although in the kitchen she had already consumed three sausage rolls, four cocktail frankfurters and two asparagus rolls, she accepted his offering. The source of the irritation she was now feeling was surely this overloaded plate rather than disappointment with his dreadful haircut.

As she started to eat, she became aware that he was watching her carefully, as if she were an invalid who hadn't eaten for some time. 'I can never take very much before I play the piano,' she said. 'Although Daphne will play first.'

'Nerves?'

'Not so much nerves as anticipation that swells up inside me like a dried apricot in water.' She was about to put the plate down but he took it from her.

'Do you mind if I finish it?'

He ate neatly with his lips together and she was glad of that, although why, she had no idea. This man was nothing to her apart from being a source of irritation. He unsettled her. She'd known that was the trouble with him from the day of the beach rescue and that annoyed her, for she didn't want to feel unsettled.

It really was too bad about his haircut. In the right hands – her hands, for Oleksii had always said that she was very good at cutting hair – Peter's thick straight hair could be shaped to look quite sculptured. Of course cutting his hair was out of the question. She would dance once with him out of politenesss and afterwards she would play the piano, and at this thought she smiled.

After Peter had finished eating, he said, 'Are you going to play Shostakovich?'

'No,' she said at once, wincing slightly. 'Too modern.'

'The jazz suites perhaps. Maybe "Tea for Two"?'

She had forgotten those. This, and her suspicion that he might be trying to make amends for that unfortunate afternoon tea, made her feel almost favourably disposed towards him. She said, 'I don't think that would be appropriate. Though of course it is lovely music. Being associated with Russia isn't good these days. Not that I am, of course, but since the Hungarian revolution everyone from a Soviet Bloc country is vanished by association.'

'*Tarnished* by the association.'

Correcting her was something he simply couldn't resist and she was tempted to retaliate by changing her mind about the first dance. But no, she must not *cut off her nose to spite her face*. She really wanted to dance, even with this unsettling man. Then unbidden came the thought: *particularly* with this unsettling man. After dabbing at her mouth with a serviette, she repeated, 'Tarnished by the association. I could, of course, be a Commie bastard.' Right away she realised she'd failed to get the Australian accent right. It wasn't from her that Zidra had inherited a gift for mimicry.

'I know you're not,' he said, laughing.

'But probably people make rumours about me because I am foreign.'

'People start rumours about everyone, foreign or not.'

Start rumours, not make. She filed away the correction.

'That's human nature,' he continued. 'We talk about one another.'

'Cherry said just now that I should ask you what you were doing yesterday in Burford.' Leaning against the doorjamb, she waited.

'I went to see the Welfare Board. Tommy Hunter told me last week that Lorna had been taken away by the police. I had to check if he was right, and he was, I'm afraid, and she's going to be sent to the Gudgiegalah Girls' Home.'

'Surely not. That's a long way away. You said only the other day that she'd be back.'

'I thought she would be. The Aborigines regularly get moved on and then they come back, but this is the first time they've taken away the kids from this area, the half-caste kids that is.'

She listened carefully while he explained what had happened. You wouldn't think this possible in Australia, she said when he'd finished. In Europe during the war, and before the war. But not now, not in this country that was supposed to be such a safe haven. Only after he'd repeated everything once more could she believe it. Poor little Lorna. Poor Lorna's family. It's the assimilation policy, Peter explained, but it was more that they thought the Aborigines were no good. Aboriginality had to be bred out of them and the taint of blackness removed. It was not so very different to what had motivated the fascists. Get rid of the Jews, get rid of the gypsies. Although here at least the children taken away were being educated, or so Peter had said.

'Can't anything be done?'

'I'm afraid not. It's government policy and they're sticking with it. Believe it or not, they think they're doing the right thing.'

'There may be a right policy for the wrong reason but there's no such thing as a wrong policy for the right reasons,' she said firmly. 'In Europe I may as well still be.'

'In Europe I'm glad you're not.'

She already knew how it felt to lose your family, she didn't have to imagine that. And a dance was not the place for these thoughts; her hands started to shake and her heart to pound.

Only now did she realise how wrong she'd been about Peter. He was kind and considerate and not the arrogant person she'd thought. He'd gone out of his way to help an Aboriginal family and to try to intervene on behalf of Lorna with Welfare. She'd misinterpreted what he'd said about Lorna that afternoon of the tea. He wasn't dismissing her at all. Just as Cherry had hinted, she'd been far too quick to judge him. Let's face it, she'd felt grumpy that day, annoyed that the car had broken down and that Zidra had talked nonstop ever since seeing that Lorna's camp had gone. And even though Ilona had been dropping with fatigue and there were no cakes or biscuits in the house, she'd felt obliged to go along with Zidra's ill-timed tea invitation. That had felt like the last straw but it was such a small thing. His comment about Lorna, that suggestion she would always return, had been an excuse to hate him. Converting all her frustration into anger, she'd made him the target for her indignation with the world. He hadn't deserved it, this much was now clear. He wasn't callous at all. Suddenly she wanted to unburden herself and to her surprise found she was willing, indeed she wanted, to tell him not only how she had mistaken his comments about Lorna that day when he came to tea but also how she had been taken away herself.

Perhaps he had been thinking along the same lines, for he said, 'Where in Latvia are you from?'

She did not resent this question as she might have a few weeks ago. 'Riga originally,' she said. 'When the Nazis came, my parents and sister and I were taken to a labour camp. Is that what the Gudgiegalah Girls' Home is like, a labour camp?'

'It's a boarding school, Ilona. However much one might hate this policy, it's not a labour camp or a death camp.'

'It's an internment camp.'

'Yes, I'm afraid that's exactly what it is.'

Now she glanced at him. He was watching her. His eyelashes were short and straight, and the dark blue of his irises was flecked with a paler blue. At some stage while they were talking he'd ruffled his hair. Funny how a tousled bad haircut could impart such an endearing boyishness.

'You were telling me about Latvia,' he said gently.

It was impossible to look at him and simultaneously relate her history, which she now felt compelled to do. Instead she focused on his shoes. Brown riding boots, the countryman's footwear, even for a dance. How strange that her brain could register that, while at the same time her heart was beating rapidly and the palms of her hands sweating at what she felt obliged to relate.

'We were taken to a concentration camp in 1942. They sorted us. For some reason I was chosen for life and the others for death. None of my family survived except for me.' Now she was finding it hard to draw air into her lungs. That old panic was starting. She was guilty of surviving when all those she had ever loved had died. It was almost as if, by choosing to love someone, she was condemning them to death.

But no, there was Zidra, lovely Zidra.

Again she tried to take a deep breath but the air got lost somehow, as if her trachea was lined with sponge. Although she could hardly breathe, she started to speak very fast. There was a yawning chasm in front of her but it was imperative to have this conversation and she would leap right over the chasm, and leap over the detail of those war years too; she could not describe those, even to a man as sympathetic as she now felt Peter to be. 'After the war was over, I was selected from the DP Camp to go to England. I ended up in Bradford. I didn't want to go back to Riga because of the Communists.'

From the jug on the table, Peter poured a glass of water and passed it to her. Her hands were shaking. His touch as he gave her the glass was as reassuring as if he were reaching out his arms for her to catch hold of. She might have grasped his wrists if she had not now been clutching the glass.

'I met my husband-to-be, Oleksii, in Bradford. He too was Latvian, although we had never met before.' At this moment Daphne Dalrymple started to play the piano, loudly and fast. For once Ilona cursed music. It became hard for her to speak above the sound of people's voices competing with the melody. Although she raised her voice, Peter bent his head towards her so that his right ear was just inches from her mouth. It was a large ear, resting flat against the side of the head.

'Oleksii was a Catholic and after a while I too became a Christian. Notionally at least, for I am not anything in fact. I am only myself, or what is left of myself.' Sometimes she doubted she was even Ilona Talivaldis, rather than a shell left behind by some once-living creature. Yet tonight she knew who she was, and perhaps even where she was going. She added, 'Though I do observe the rituals from time to time. When it is convenient.'

'The marking of life's passages,' Peter said.

Averting her eyes from the delicate whorl of his ear, she stared at the tongued and grooved floorboards. 'Oleksii was very musical,' she continued. 'Much more so than I. He composed as well as played. He was destroyed by his talent because he could not develop it, and in due course he died.'

'It can't have been easy for him in Bradford.'

'Or in Sydney,' she said, and then wished she could bite the words back. She did not want to cause offence to this man who was hearing her confession.

'It can't have been easy in Sydney either,' Peter said gently. 'You can be an outsider anywhere. Even in your own country.'

The noise level around them dropped as people began to move onto the dance floor. At the same moment that he shifted his head to look straight at her, she glanced at him. 'Is that you? Are you an outsider?'

'Sometimes. Especially since the war. I was lucky to survive the prisoner-of-war camp. A lot of the others didn't. Now I feel I belong only at Ferndale. There I'm a part of the land.'

'Ferndale is your farm?'

'My property, yes. It's where I belong.'

Daphne Dalrymple started to play another piece on the piano. Peter held out his arms to Ilona and she moved into his embrace. He held her lightly while she lifted her head high. This was the first time she had danced for many years. Cherry was right, he was a *beaut* dancer. At first she thought she was imagining the violin. But no, there was a man with a fiddle standing next to the piano. Billy the Fish was now accompanying Daphne.

CHAPTER THIRTY-TWO

Kids were running around everywhere but wherever Zidra went she was in the way. The whole evening all she'd heard was *watch it*, or *scram*, or *where's Lorna*. She might as well go home, no one would even notice. Then someone turned on the fairy lights that were strung along the eaves of the hall and over the lower branches of the pine tree and everything changed. The hall was the vast cabin of a ship sailing across the ocean and the yard became the decks crowded with people. Beneath the tall mast of the pine tree was a dark space where she would take shelter. She could lie on this thick carpet of needles and never be seen.

But she was wrong.

'Great spot you've got here,' said Jim. 'Mind if I join you?'

He sat cross-legged next to her and immediately she began to feel more cheerful. Just as he'd opened his mouth to say something, Roger O'Rourke came barging up. Right away she knew Roger wanted to get even with her for laughing when his parents roused on him. Bracing herself, she waited.

'Wotcher doing here, eh? Got any smokes, Jim?'

'No. We're just talking, that's all.'

'Jim loves Zidra. Zidra loves Jim.' Roger danced around them, chanting.

If she ignored him, maybe he'd go away. She sneaked a quick look at Jim to see how he was taking it. You could see he didn't care. 'Bugger off, you little twerp,' he said.

In spite of this, Roger didn't seem to want to leave. He leant against the rough tree trunk and idly kicked at the pine needles while simultaneously picking at a scab on his elbow. 'I heard your Ma talking to Mrs Bates,' he said to Zidra.

'What about?' Her voice came out even sharper than she'd intended.

'Menzies and stuff. She's a Commo, your Ma.'

'No she's not,' Jim said. 'She had a letter published in the *Burford Advertiser* about Hungary. How can that make her a Commo? She's against the Reds not for them.'

'My dad said she's a Red.'

'You're a Red,' said Zidra. 'Red hair; red freckles. Red, red, red Roger.'

'Reds under the bed,' said Roger giggling. 'Better watch out for yours.'

'Yours more like.'

'I'm in the top bunk and Johnno's in the bottom.'

'Reds under *your* bed then,' said Jim. 'Johnno's hair's even redder than yours.'

Grinning, Roger pulled off the scab and flicked it into the long grass next to the fence. 'Sure you haven't got any smokes, Jim?'

'Mum would skin me alive if I did, and put me through Dad's sausage machine.'

Zidra smiled although it wasn't much of a joke. Especially as she wouldn't have put it past Jim's mum to lose her temper and carve him up if she caught him with a cigarette.

'Betcha don't know where Lorna is,' Roger said.

'Bet you don't either,' Jim said. She could tell without looking he was checking on her reaction.

'Do so. Just heard she's gone to an orphanage.'

Stupid Roger, thought Zidra, and decided to leave the questioning to Jim. He didn't let her down. 'How can she go to an orphanage when she's not an orphan?' he asked.

''Cause she's an Abo,' Roger said defiantly.

'That's no reason.'

'Ask Dad then. That's what he said, and she'll never be able to go home.'

'Where is this orphanage?'

'Gudgiegalah Home.'

'That's not an orphanage.'

'What is it then?'

'A home for girls.'

'What for, if they're not orphans?'

'It's for Aboriginal girls whose families can't look after them.'

'Lorna's family look after her,' Zidra said, unable to keep quiet any longer.

'Half-caste girls.'

Zidra now felt completely confused. Lorna had gone to the Sutherlands', that's what Mr Jones had said. Then Mrs Bates had said she was at Wallaga Lake. And now stupid Roger had made up another story, just to upset her; he knew what good friends she and Lorna were. Then to say Lorna was half-cast instead of being fully and perfectly cast was too much. 'There's nothing wrong with Lorna,' she said. 'She's beautifully cast. She can run faster than anyone.'

'Not cast, *caste*,' Jim said quickly. 'It means race.'

'What's half-caste then?'

'One parent black, one white.'

'But her father's black, I've met him.'

'He's not her father,' Roger said, smirking.

'How do you know?'

'Just do.'

He was wrong about everything, the idiot. She glared at him but already he'd lost interest, his eyes fixed on a game of tag that someone had started up. Once he'd gone, she said to Jim, 'Have you heard anything about Lorna?'

'I heard Mrs Dalrymple tell someone just now that the Welfare had taken her.'

'Not to the Sutherlands'?'

'No. To Gudgiegalah Girls' Home, like Roger said.'

'Everyone says something different.' Mrs Dalrymple and Roger must have got it wrong.

'That's probably 'cause they don't know. It's all rumours.'

She waited to see if he had any more to say. Above their heads, the fairy lights twinkled from the pine branches. She watched him start to gnaw at one of his fingernails. In spite of the warmth of the night air, she shivered. Funny how you could feel so alone even when you were surrounded by people. Maybe she'd wake up and discover Lorna hadn't gone at all.

'It's not as bad as you think.'

'But she'd be away from her family.' She didn't add that school would be intolerable without her. The loneliness. The teasing. The taunts.

'Think of it as if she's going away to school. If she has gone. Like me next year. Off to a new school.'

'But she can never come home, that's what Roger said.'

'She'd be able to come home when she's grown.'

'That's years away.' Years and years, an eternity. She felt as if she'd been punched in the stomach and her eyes began to water. Surreptitiously she wiped them with the back of her hand. Only when she felt that her voice wouldn't quaver did she add, 'All my friends are going away. When are you coming home?'

'Every holiday.'

But there'd be that everlasting term in between holidays. Blinking away more tears, she looked over the yard. Some of the younger kids were beginning to get tired. Quarrels were breaking out and little ones starting to throw tantrums. That's what she'd like to do: stamp and bellow and hurl herself on the ground, and then to shout *don't* and *no* and *why Lorna?*

Yet she'd felt a bad thing was coming. She'd felt it ever since that night before the boat trip, when she'd woken up thinking Lorna was telling her something. The telepathy was real but Mama had been wrong about its meaning. A variety of emotions now battled within her. Anger with her mother for misinterpreting that dream. Rage with the world that she was losing Lorna. Anxiety for what Lorna must be feeling, and worst of all, this terrible feeling of sadness. Struggling to retain control of herself, she was but dimly aware of Jim's awkward pat on her forearm.

Ilona's head was spinning, not with alcohol for she had not touched a drop all evening, but with music, with dancing, and – she was at last willing to admit it – with the intoxication of Peter's presence. Standing next to her at the piano, he was turning the pages of the music at exactly the right time. Not that she needed this assistance, she was perfectly capable of turning the pages herself, and indeed she felt so confident tonight that she could have played these pieces blindfolded. Plus Billy the Fish was making the violin sing like a human being accompanying her playing; an unexpected talent that added to her pleasure in the music.

On finishing her last piece, she glanced up at Peter. He smiled and rested a hand lightly on her shoulder. Before he had a chance to withdraw it, she gently put her hand over his and watched his face light up. Then she remembered Zidra.

'I am such a bad mother,' she said, jumping to her feet. 'I must find Zidra. I had almost forgotten about her.'

She weaved her way through the packed hall, and into the kitchen that was empty now apart from piles of dirty plates and a ragged-looking dog chewing at a bone under the table. She clattered down the back steps of the hall and stumbled a little on the rough grass at the bottom. Bill Bates, part of the knot of men wrapped around the beer keg, caught her and Mr O'Rourke seized her other arm.

'Steady on,' O'Rourke said, as if she might be intoxicated when it was he, she suspected, who was shickered.

'My heels,' she explained, laughing and extricating herself from the men's steadying grip. 'Have you seen Zidra anywhere?'

'Sitting under the pine tree,' O'Rourke said. 'I'll show you.' He led the way across the grass, as if she might have trouble distinguishing it from the other trees, all eucalyptus, encircling the yard.

'Zidra!' she called.

'We're here, Mrs Talivaldis!' Zidra and Jim were sitting side-by-side on the pine needles.

'I wondered how you were getting on,' Ilona said. 'I have finished playing the piano and wondered if perhaps you might be feeling neglected.'

'I want to go home now, Mama.' Zidra's voice sounded strained. The excitement had been too much for her.

Ilona crouched down next to her. 'Don't you want to hear Billy the Fish doing his solo?' she said gently.

'Billy the Fish is terrible,' said O'Rourke. 'You oughta go home before then.'

'But he is a wonderful musician,' said Ilona. 'He plays the fiddle with so much passion.'

'You haven't heard him on the accordion, but,' said O'Rourke. 'Terrible songs, those, and rude too. That's why he's on at the very end. So the kiddies won't hear.'

It was the singers rather than the musician who were so terrible, Ilona suspected. 'I'll take you home now, darling,' she whispered to Zidra, putting an arm around her shoulders. Even in this dim lighting, her face looked washed out. 'Are you staying, Jim?'

'I've got to wait until Mum tells me to go home,' he said.

'That'll be as soon as the singing starts,' said O'Rourke, laughing. 'My missus'll be heading off with our lot then too.'

'We shall make our farewells inside the hall,' said Ilona.

'Say goodbye, you mean,' said Zidra, quite crossly.

'We shall say goodbye,' Ilona continued, 'to our friends in the hall.'

But Ilona's attention was distracted, so she did not hear Zidra's whispered words to Jim. She had caught sight of Peter, who was just emerging from the kitchen. He was standing on the top step and peering down the yard.

He was looking for her. He was looking out for her.

CHAPTER THIRTY-THREE

Horrible Roger had smeared red jam on Zidra's seat during the lunch recess. It wasn't until all the kids started laughing when she got up to go home that she'd realised something was wrong. Even then she mightn't have known if little Lyn Cross hadn't told her. The humiliation! How she'd blushed at the discovery and that had made horrid Roger laugh all the more. 'Started your periods, have you?' he'd said. While having no idea what he meant, she knew it couldn't be nice. And there was no way she could wash the jam off either, with the toilet block being out of bounds once school was out. If Lorna were here she would have sorted out Roger. Now there was nothing for it but to take the long way home, creeping along the back lanes so that no one would see her with the red sticky mess on her tunic.

She wasn't even sure that she wanted to go home today. This afternoon Mama was giving two lessons, one after the other, and wouldn't have any time to spare, no time even to listen to the story about Roger. Then there'd be all that thumping on the piano, that endless ping-ping-ping-ping-ping up the keys, and ping-ping-ping-ping down again. Five-finger exercises were so good to develop coordination of the hands, Mama said, but she didn't think of her daughter's ears. If Zidra didn't get home until after the piano lessons were over, she wouldn't even notice.

Zidra hung around for a while in the school playground, until Miss Neville came out to tell her to go home. Soon after, she heard the sound of Mrs Bates banging out scales on the school piano. Pianos everywhere; she'd rather hear the birds any day. That's what Lorna had taught her, how to listen to the bush. How to hear the music that was all around you, music that you just blocked out unless someone told you about it. If only Lorna were here; she'd make Zidra's jammy skirt an excuse for an adventure and not a retreat.

She trudged along the back lanes leading down to the lagoon. Once or twice she thought she heard a sound behind her and turned to look, suspecting Roger might be tracking her, but there wasn't a soul about. No one to see her, no one to taunt her; she'd be able to sponge the stuff off her skirt in peace.

She hid her school-case in the spot near the bridge that she and Lorna had made their own, and took off her shoes and socks. Avoiding the few sickle-shaped jelly fish beached on the edge of the lagoon, she waded into the water. A wet handkerchief would surely do the trick. The sticky mess on the back of her skirt came off easily; maybe there was still a bit of a mark but that was probably just from the lagoon water.

Through the cool clear water, her feet were visible and appeared bleached to a stark white. Blue veins stood up prominently on the top and the edges of her toes were a ruby red. Distorted by the water, her legs appeared shorter than in reality. Wriggling her toes, she dislodged some of the brown slime covering the sandy bottom. This swirled around and sank again, some of the particles settling on her feet. She felt more alone than ever before. If she stood here long enough, her feet would become invisible. She might become invisible too, or turn into a discarded log like that old tree trunk lying at the water's edge that Lorna claimed had been left there by some long-ago flood.

Eventually she stepped out of the water and dried her feet on her tunic skirt. It was too early to go home; her mother would still be giving lessons. Instead she'd walk along the edge of the lagoon; maybe as far as that spot where Stillwater Creek trickled into the lagoon and Jim and Andy had baked those potatoes in the days before the total fire ban.

———

After the last customer had left Cadwallader's Quality Meats, George and The Boy began the evening liturgy. The Boy had performed his ceremonial duties with greater efficiency if not devotion since his pay rise several months ago. Today he was even more zealous than usual and by ten past the hour George was ready to go home. Normally he'd return by the back lanes but today he decided to leave by the front door.

It was then that he saw it. Someone had stuck a label on the flank of the painted cow adorning the top of the shopfront window. Peering up, he could just discern the writing on the label. Batty Beattie. If he didn't view the painting as a portrait of his wife he might have smiled at this but as it was he felt only annoyance. The cow was much too young for this sobriquet.

He unlocked the shopfront again and went out the back to fetch a stepladder and a pail of water. Standing on the step-ladder, he could just reach the label. It peeled away easily, but then he discovered that it had been attached with a couple of pieces of chewing gum that were unwilling to part company with the cow. Although he tried sponging the gum with water, it wouldn't come off. Something must be able to remove it but he couldn't think what. Not methylated spirits because that might remove the paint. Brown paper and a hot iron, he was almost certain now he'd heard Eileen recommend this. If she hadn't disliked the cow so much, he might once have asked her to do it. Perhaps late at night; she didn't like making an exhibition of herself. But it was impossible to ask such a thing of her now. They were barely speaking to one another, although the exchanges they did have were of exquisite politeness, and he'd tried so hard lately to see things from her perspective. These days she refused to talk about the scholarship at all. If he raised the matter, she stonewalled him, and when he tried to explain that he understood what she was going through she'd simply laughed in his face. How can you understand, George, you are a man, she'd said. As if being a man was something to be ashamed of.

After descending the stepladder, he inspected the painting from pavement level. The two dabs of gum didn't look so bad from this distance. A couple more spots weren't all that noticeable on a Friesian cow. It would have been worse if he'd commissioned a painting of a Jersey all those years ago. Maybe he'd leave well alone for the moment. Better than having to discuss the matter with Eileen. It was possible anyway that the paint might come off with the gum. It wouldn't do for the cow to have holes in its flank.

He felt upset nonetheless. The cow had been without blemish and the comfort of it lay in its perfection. So disgruntled did he feel that he decided to stroll down to the lagoon before going home. The river was always soothing and maybe a quick look at his boat would calm him. Although it hadn't calmed him a few weeks ago when he'd found the dinghy was lying the wrong way up and the bailing can was missing. He'd put a padlock on the boatshed doors after that.

You never used to have to worry about locking things away. Nothing seemed quite the same as it used to. Nothing was safe any more. Not his boat, not even his cow that was in full view of half the town. After crossing the bridge over the lagoon, he headed along the track to the boathouse. The bush was drier than ever. No longer sparkling in the light, the leaves of the scrubby trees drooped sadly, quite still, and the sparse undergrowth was a uniform drab olive. The path was baked hard, and littered with the detritus of the bush; the twigs, nuts and dead leaves that took so long to decay but that would burst into flames with just one match.

After several hundred yards, out of sight of the settlement, he stopped and stared at the lagoon. A flock of pelicans floated at the water's edge. Most held their heads high, necks fully extended. Three or four had turned their heads a full one hundred and eighty degrees and buried their beaks into their feathers. That's what he'd like to do. Bury his head in something soft and cocooning that would obliterate his unhappiness.

Beyond the pelicans, on the western side of the lagoon, folds of land fuzzed with bush dropped down to the path just above the waterline. Further back, the bush had been cleared for farming. Behind this, the tall straight trunks of a forest of eucalyptus trees looked like nascent telegraph poles topped with broccoli heads.

At this moment his eye was caught by a movement near the water's edge, not far from where Stillwater Creek entered the lagoon. It was a girl sprinting towards the town. After a moment he recognised her. The Latvian girl Zidra was running so fast it wouldn't surprise him if she turned into a bit of an athlete, like Jim and Andy. Not so long ago she would have had Lorna with her. He glanced at his watch. Ten minutes to six. Perhaps she was late for tea as he might be too if he didn't get a move on. The boys were at cricket practice and he'd promised Eileen to be home in time to feed the chooks in Jim's place. He was going to have to hurry. An angry Eileen on top of everything else would be too much. Tea at six o'clock sharp, that was her rule.

He turned back the way he had come and so he missed seeing Bill Bates walking, ten minutes later, along the same path as Zidra.

CHAPTER THIRTY-FOUR

Ilona puzzled over her daughter's behaviour. For some days she'd seemed out of sorts. Tired and irritable, and on three nights in a row had woken up screaming.

'What's the matter, darling?' she said, holding her daughter close after the most recent nightmare.

'Nothing's the matter.' But Zidra's body was shaking and Ilona could feel her heart beating wildly inside her rib cage like a bird struggling to find a way out.

'What did you dream of?' Ilona pushed Zidra's hair off her face and gently stroked her flushed cheek.

'I've forgotten.'

'Was it Lorna again?'

'No.'

'Was it something that happened at school?'

'No.'

'Not Roger?'

'No.'

Ilona lay down next to Zidra and held her tightly until at last the sound of steady breathing indicated she was asleep. It must be Lorna, or rather Lorna's absence, that was causing such a change in her daughter. Extricating herself from Zidra's embrace, Ilona tucked in the sheet around her and sat on the edge of the bed to watch the regular rise and fall of her chest.

Too many nightmares, too many worries. Zidra had lost friends before; Zidra had left behind friends before. Not in Bradford, for she was too young to have had friends there, but in Homebush. There must be more to her unhappiness than simply missing Lorna. Anyway, Lorna was not her only friend. There was Jim. Admittedly a year or two older, though that was a good thing for it surely made him more responsible. If there were something wrong at school Jim would know what to do about it. Yet he was only a boy and had other friends, boys who occupied most of his spare time. It was no good asking him if he knew what was wrong, just as it was no good asking Zidra if she knew what was wrong. There was nothing else to do but to arrange to see Miss Neville, to find out if Zidra was being bullied at school.

Ilona tiptoed out of Zidra's bedroom and, heaving a great sigh, sat in an armchair in the living room. She did not want to see Miss Neville. The school mistress alternated between cordiality and animosity for reasons that Ilona could not fathom.

However the next day, after all the children had left school, she knocked on the door of Miss Neville's office. Looking up from some papers as Ilona entered the room, the teacher gestured to a hard wooden chair next to the desk. Her expression was unwelcoming, her demeanor slightly dishevelled.

'I'm here about Zidra.' Ilona nervously twisted her fingers together.

'Of course you are,' Miss Neville said rather abruptly.

Just then Ilona heard a trill of scales from the adjacent schoolroom. Two octaves perfectly played by two hands. 'How lovely to hear Cherry practising!' she exclaimed.

Miss Neville looked at her coldly. 'Mrs Bates practises every day,' she said firmly, as if Ilona had made an accusation.

Mrs Bates to you but Cherry to me, Ilona reflected. 'I suppose that you know I am teaching Cherry. She is making good progress. It was so kind of you to allow her to practise here. I know she does not have much free time at the hotel where there is not even a piano.'

'I am perfectly aware of that,' said Miss Neville, 'and that is why I invited her here. It was almost entirely my own idea.'

'An inspired idea,' said Ilona, experiencing a sudden flash of intuition about the cause of Miss Neville's prickliness. She was jealous of Ilona's friendship with Cherry, that was it. 'Quite inspired.' She glanced beyond Miss Neville. Outside the sky was a blazing blue, too blue. 'But of course it is Zidra about whom I wish to talk to you.'

'As you said. What do you want to discuss? Your daughter's rapidly catching up with her arithmetic now she's finally mastered the multiplication tables.'

'They are a little like the scales then. Practice makes perfect. But it is not my daughter's academic progress that is causing me anxiety, Miss Neville. Rather it is the suspicion that I harbour that she may be being picked on.'

'Picked on?'

'Have you noticed any change in her behaviour since Lorna left?'

'She's become quieter. More introverted perhaps,' said Miss Neville. Next door Cherry moved on to a scale in another key. 'Aboriginal children come and go from school. The other children are used to it, but maybe Zidra isn't. It's a great shame about Lorna being taken away from her family. Such a bright girl but maybe the schooling's good in Gudgiegalah. I have to say that I haven't noticed any other change in Zidra apart from a general quietness.'

'She's waking up with nightmares. Screaming, night after night.'

'I'm so sorry to hear that. Perhaps it's because of your past.'

'But the screaming is only recent. That's why I'm here. To ask if you think someone might be humiliating her.'

'No. I don't allow any humiliation at my school.'

So firmly did she say this that Ilona almost believed her. 'I am delighted to hear it.' But she was not, for she would feel better if she could find the cause of Zidra's unhappiness.

There was another brief pause. The piano in the next room stopped. Then there was a clicking of high heels on polished wood and into the room swept Cherry, wearing a sleeveless floral dress with a full skirt, and lips painted an even brighter red than usual.

'Mrs Bates!' Miss Neville raised her hand. 'I am in a meeting with Mrs Talivaldis.'

'So sorry, darl,' Cherry said breezily. 'Hello, Ilona, didn't expect to see you here, but you will have heard me practising.' She laughed. 'What do you reckon? Any signs of improvement?'

'Not a single mistake.'

'Must get back to it, then. I get so little time. Where's Zidra?'

'Out in the schoolyard.'

'Oh? I might go and say hello. Not good to have her hanging about on her own feeling lonely. Ta ta, Miss Neville!' Out of the room she clattered and a moment later her voice could be heard summoning Zidra.

'Perhaps we have finished now,' Ilona said after Cherry had shut the door behind her. 'I am reassured to know that you have not observed any bullying of my daughter.'

'It's not that I haven't observed it,' said Miss Neville. 'It's that it doesn't exist in my school.'

Ilona felt tears of frustration filling her eyes and blinked them away. Bullying existed everywhere but this fool of a teacher wouldn't recognise that. 'I suppose you do not call tipping ink onto the cover of someone's exercise book bullying.'

'If that happens, the children should report it to me at once.'

'And if they don't?'

'What proof would I have that it happened?'

Ilona recognised that the interview was leading nowhere. 'Thank you for your time,' she said, rising to leave. 'I shall of course see myself out.'

'I'll let you out.' Miss Neville's voice was almost kindly now. 'You mustn't worry too much about Zidra. She'll grow out of whatever's frightening her now and emerge the stronger for it.'

'I do hope so,' said Ilona, stepping out into the harsh sunlight, but she didn't feel reassured.

'I'll watch out for her,' Miss Neville said, as Ilona was about to call Zidra. 'It's not possible for me to be everywhere at once and I may have missed something.'

Ilona glanced quickly at the school mistress, who was staring at Cherry and Zidra. They were sitting side-by-side on a bench in the uneven shade of a gum tree. As soon as Zidra saw them, she stood up and ran to her mother. Ilona embraced her and waved at Cherry, who did not seem to be in a hurry to resume her practising, for she stayed seated where she was.

Ilona took her daughter's clammy hand in her own and together they descended the hill in silence. Maybe she would talk to Peter about Zidra next time they met up. Some time in the next week or two, he'd suggested at the dance.

Then it hit her, what she feared most of all: that Zidra might be developing Oleksii's tendency to melancholia.

Cherry watched Ilona and Zidra as they walked slowly down the hill. Beads of sweat trickled down her back and the under-arms of her dress were saturated. Greatly agitated, she ran through the conversation she'd overheard between Miss Neville and Ilona. Zidra waking screaming at night! Zidra quiet in the daytime! It didn't bear thinking about.

Once she'd suspected that Zidra might not be with Ilona in Miss Neville's office, she'd felt even more troubled. After Miss Neville's denial of bullying at her school – and Cherry had absolutely no doubt that this sort of behaviour would be stamped on – she'd burst into the office where they were talking. She was right: Zidra wasn't there. Although Miss Neville was clearly irritated at the interruption, Cherry hadn't cared. Rushing into the playground, she'd been terrified that the girl might have gone. But there she was, sitting on one of the swings that were now in the full sun. Apparently oblivious of the heat, she seemed so preoccupied, so dejected-looking that she wasn't even pushing herself on the swing. That was when Cherry had called out; the child had jumped off the swing and come to her. Together they'd walked across the burning hot bitumen and into the dappled shade of the gum tree, and sat down on the timber bench. There were dark shadows under Zidra's eyes and she looked tired. But worse than that, her usually mobile face was completely lacking in expression, so that it seemed almost like some mask that she had put on. Cherry wanted to ask outright if Bill had been pestering her but couldn't think of how to phrase this. Bill had become obsessed by the girl, this was her suspicion. This would also explain his generosity in taking the children out on the launch that day. Not to mention his regular presence on the hotel verandah each afternoon when school came out. Hers too; she never let him go out there alone these days.

'You look a bit tired,' Cherry said to Zidra, as they sat together in the school playground. Lightly touching the girl's hand, she was relieved that anxiety did not feed into her voice. 'Anything bothering you?'

'No,' Zidra said faintly. A quick glance up at Cherry and then away again, as if embarrassed to meet her eye.

Knowing that she was the last person in town Zidra could talk to, Cherry sighed, but there was no way that she could allow Zidra's welfare to be threatened or that of her mother. Bill had to be stopped and she would tell him so this very evening.

Staring at the ocean, she wondered what she might say. The view brought no inspiration. Just off the beach some board surfers were visible, dark dots on the water's surface, but underneath them lay who knew what sort of menace. Sharks or a sudden change of current, anything could happen. Above the distant crash of the surf she could hear seagulls crying and the monotonous chanting of a small child from one of the houses below the school. A child of perhaps five or six, a vulnerable child.

At this moment Cherry's dislike of Bill turned into hatred.

Some moments later, she got up from the seat and went inside. Tip-tap, her high heels went on the floorboards. Tip-tap right past Miss Neville's office and into the schoolroom. She sat down on the stool in front of the piano and ran through a few scales, but it was impossible to concentrate. After a while she banged both hands down hard on the keys – such discordance, such frustration – and rested her elbows on the edge of the piano and her head on her hands.

'What's the matter?' said Miss Neville, coming into the room and putting an arm around her shoulders.

291

'I don't feel well. I'm going to have to give up for today and go home.' Cherry felt unable to tell Miss Neville of her worries, or at least not yet. She was glad of her touch though. It made her feel stronger.

'It's probably the heat, Cherry. Can you rest when you go home or will the Taskmaster make you carry on working?'

'Probably.' Cherry sighed. The bar would be filling up now as the men came in after work and she didn't feel like making the good-humoured banter that everyone expected of her. Not until later that evening, after closing time, would she be able to talk to Bill.

However by closing time that evening Bill was drunk, for the first time in years, and it was obvious he wouldn't be able to comprehend anything she might say. Only a few seconds after he'd stumbled into his bedroom, loud snoring reverberated through the hallway. She'd have to speak to him the next day whenever she could get him alone.

CHAPTER THIRTY-FIVE

Peter spent the days after the dance surveying Ferndale and wasn't too impressed. Not with the landscape but with his stewardship of it. For over a decade he'd been here and there was so little to show for it. Methodically he catalogued his omissions of care and soon filled half-a-dozen sheets of foolscap paper. But his affinity with Ferndale was growing day by day.

Sometimes, though, he forgot what he was doing. The jagged mountain range would capture his attention. Or the tiny blue flowers on the shrubs hugging the top of the cliff, which he'd never noticed before, or the cracks in the dry earth. It was only Spot jumping up on him that reminded him of what had to be done. Then he paused to wonder if a sense of faith was being restored to him. Faith in what, he was unsure. The land. The light. The possibility of loving.

On the last day of the survey, he took a satchel containing lunch down onto the beach below the homestead. Even here it felt hot. There wasn't the slightest stirring of air, in spite of the crashing breakers. Hat tilted against the glare, he sat in the shade of a large rock. Gnawing on hard bread, on which he'd arranged lumps of even harder Burford Cheddar – he'd forgotten to replenish the pantry and was having to make do with what he could scrounge – he felt he now had a future. A future beyond mere survival.

Ilona must visit Ferndale. Tomorrow he would drive into Jingera and persuade her to come. How would the place seem to her? Squinting, he glanced around. At the northern end of the short beach, the fissured cliff face was dotted with lime green and olive-coloured bushes that were stunted by their southerly exposure. Below the headland, waves washed around some jagged pinnacles of rock. Two black cormorants, perched on the highest rock, surveyed the sea. It was a dangerous place to surf but Ilona knew about dangerous water after her experience on Jingera Beach. He wouldn't need to convince her that she couldn't swim here.

After finishing lunch, he returned to the homestead. That was at least structurally sound, although undeniably dilapidated. The verandahs needed reroofing and the woodwork needed repainting. Several hundred yards distant was an agglomeration of sheds, yards and water tanks. They jostled around the bleached weatherboard cottage that had once housed the manager.

Perhaps, when he got the place going properly again, he'd find another manager. He'd been reluctant to do that before because he'd wanted to be alone. Maybe now he was getting ahead of himself; he should leave the manager idea for a bit and proceed incrementally. First he'd hire some casual labour and see how things worked out. It wasn't a shortage of funds that had been hampering him but a shortage of motivation.

The main house felt baking hot inside. Before leaving that morning he'd forgotten to shut the windows against the heat. After closing them, he drew the curtains; they were shabby velour things that needed replacing. The outbuilding that was the kitchen seemed even hotter than the house, the fuel stove making the room almost unbearable. After making a pot of tea, he put it on a tray, together with a cup and saucer. In the glassed-in walkway connecting the kitchen to the main house, he paused. There was something strange about the lozenges of light cast by the stained glass panels; they were too yellow somehow. The light outside was queer too, an almost luminous yellow. He glanced at his watch. Only three fifteen and far too early for the sun to set. A strong wind had sprung up in the short time since he'd come indoors and was buffeting the Monterey cypresses and radiata pines surrounding the house. The highest branches whipped back and forth, as if they were made of some flexible wire rather than brittle wood. The sky was now covered with a thick layer of dark grey cloud tinged with orange. That must be red dust scooped up from somewhere out west; they had no earth that colour around these parts.

At this moment a streak of lightning sliced the sky, followed a second later by a crack of thunder so loud that the walkway windows shivered. On the verandah, Spot began to howl and even the two old kelpies whimpered a bit. He let the dogs inside. Gently he stroked quivering Spot: this was probably the first thunderstorm he'd ever experienced. Flashes of lightning and claps of thunder formed a syncopated entertainment. When Spot began to whine, he shut him in the dining room and returned to the walkway, his exhilaration growing. This would be the first rain for months.

But when it came it was mainly dust. Dabs of fine mud splattered the windows and stuck there, leaving penny-sized circles of red ochre. Soon there were so many that it was hard to see out and even the flashes of lightning were barely visible through the fine layer of mud covering the glazing.

Then, as suddenly as the storm had started, it ceased. The wind dropped and the red-tinged clouds drifted slowly eastwards.

He released Spot from the dining room and went outside with the dogs. The house and ground were coated with red dust. More precious tank water would have to be used to clean the windows. There wasn't even a scent of water on soil and the temperature must still be pushing a hundred. Although the trees were intact, half-a-dozen branches littered the patch of weeds that were once called a lawn.

But he'd ask Ilona and Zidra to visit anyway. They could see Ferndale at its worst.

CHAPTER THIRTY-SIX

It got Jim worried, Zidra trailing round after him all day as if she wanted to tell him something and her face so miserable that tears couldn't be far off. There was no chance of them finding anywhere quiet to talk though, with the other kids milling around at recess and Roger the nong saying that Zidra was his girlfriend. Once school was over, and everyone was streaming out of the school gates, she remained close to him. Still not a word as they walked side-by-side down the hill. Past the pub, Mr Bates standing there as usual to say *g'day* with Mrs Bates right next to him, and all the time Zidra so close that she kept bumping into his schoolbag. But instead of turning to go down the hill, she turned right as if she'd invited herself back to his place and he was glad of that. Finally, when the other kids had peeled off and Andy had dashed ahead, he said, 'What's up?'

'I want to talk to you.'

'What about?'

'Not here.' Her face crumpled like screwed-up tissue paper, she looked furtively around, but there was no one to hear them, just Andy some yards ahead and out of earshot.

'We can talk in a hiding place below our chookyard if you like. No one'll see us there.'

The branches of the fig tree formed a thick canopy over the hollow in the ground. Jim perched in his usual spot against the trunk of the tree while Zidra sat cross-legged next to him. He watched her face assume a greenish tinge in the dense shade. Straight ahead she stared, at the bush beyond the back lane and the glimmering of water in the distance.

'What's the matter?' he said. 'You can spill the beans now. No one can hear.'

'It's hard to tell.' From her pocket she pulled out a handkerchief and started to twist it around her fingers.

'You mean you don't know what's the matter or you don't know how to explain it?'

'Don't know how to explain it.'

'Just start at the beginning then.'

'It's about Mr Bates,' she said.

'What about him?'

'He frightens me.'

'I thought you really liked him. You know, like he was your dad.'

Pulling at the edge of the handkerchief, she seemed reluctant to continue. 'I bumped into him the other day,' she said eventually. 'It was after Roger'd put the jam on the back of my tunic and all the kids were laughing at me. So I took the long way home through the lanes.' Although her voice broke, she continued. 'Mama – Mum – was giving some piano lessons so I thought I'd have a bit of a walk through the bush. You know, down to that spot by the lagoon where you cooked those potatoes that day.' Again she stopped and fiddled with the handkerchief.

'Near Stillwater Creek,' Jim said.

'Yes.'

Tears were beginning to trickle down her face. Tempted to put an arm around her shoulders, he thought better of it; she'd surely shake it off. 'Then what?' Hoping his mother or Andy wouldn't appear, he cast a quick look behind them. All he could see were a few chooks scratching around in their yard in spite of the heat.

'I met Mr Bates and he gave me a whole bag of lollies and we sat down and ate them.'

Jim started to feel uncomfortable. 'And . . .?' he prompted.

'He asked if I'd told anyone about our little secret, when Lorna and I took out your dad's boat.'

He'd been right, the two girls and Batesy had been up to something down by the boathouse and he'd suspected that all along. His father had noticed too; the padlock had appeared on the boathouse doors not long after.

As if to gauge his reaction, Zidra glanced quickly at him.

'Who cares about the boat?' he said gently. 'Dad wouldn't, as long as you put it back.' This was a lie but he'd never before seen Zidra look this vulnerable.

'Mr Bates said I could go to jail.'

'They'd never lock you up for something like that. No way.'

'You sure?'

'Yeah, I'm sure.' He watched Zidra scrubbing at her tears with the twisted-up handkerchief. 'There's nothing to worry about.'

'There's more though.'

'What?'

'Mr Bates pulled out some pictures.'

'What of?'

'Can't say.'

'Got to say.'

'You know . . .'

'Please tell me, Zidra.'

'Rude things.'

'You don't mean . . . ?'

'Yes. I didn't know what they were at first.' She swallowed and wiped the hanky across her mouth. Then so quickly he could barely make out the words, she said, 'Then he took out his thing.'

'What thing?'

'You know, in there.' She pointed to Jim's fly.

'No.' Shocked to the core, Jim felt himself blushing deeply and his hands started to sweat.

'Yes.'

A wave of nausea swept over him but he managed to say, 'And he didn't . . .?'

'No.'

'And then?'

'I ran away as fast as I could. I'm much quicker than he is.'

At this point she was overcome with sobbing and he patted her on the shoulder. Although he'd known something was wrong, he hadn't guessed it was this. Couldn't have guessed it was this, although ever since that awful boat trip he'd wondered why Batesy had fussed over her all the time.

Now he knew.

'You mustn't worry,' he said, surprised that his voice sounded so calm. 'But you've got to keep out of his way for a bit while we work out what to do.'

'I'm doing that, but I'm frightened of him coming out of the pub. He's always there on the verandah.'

Of course she was right, Batesy was always there, smiling and nodding at the kids, and fawning over Zidra, the creep. 'I'll walk home with you after school. All the way to your house.'

'What about when you're at cricket practice?'

'I'll walk you home first.' But he wouldn't always be able to walk her home. There'd be some days when she'd be on her own and by the end of the summer he'd be off to his new school. Then anything could happen. He started to chew at his thumbnail.

'I can't tell anyone else,' Zidra said. 'No one else would believe me.'

'I believe you. I'll think of a way of dealing with this.' Indeed, an idea was already forming in his mind.

And the idea would develop, together with his anger, over the next few hours.

———◆———

Cherry watched Bill all evening to make sure he wasn't drinking. That night, when the last customer had left and the doors of the hotel had been locked for the night, they were alone.

'Have a good practice yesterday afternoon?' Bill said, rather too casually, Cherry thought.

'Not too bad.' This was the time to confront him. For a day she'd been formulating what to say but now the words vanished from her mind. She began a routine inspection of the ashtrays. The bar stank of stale cigarette smoke and beer, and the room was hot and stuffy. The little speech she'd prepared was forgotten but something had to be said. She opened her mouth to speak but Bill got in before her.

'I saw the Talivaldis woman go up to the school yesterday afternoon after school was out. Elinor or Ilona or whatever she calls herself.' So hard was he scrubbing at the bar top you might have thought he was sanding it. 'Zidra's not ill, is she?'

'No, Bill. She's not. Or at least not as far as I could see. Ilona went to see Miss Neville.' She picked up a damp cloth and, with trembling hands, folded it into a small square.

'Do you know why?'

'I've got a fair idea. I'm not sure Ilona has though.' She wiped out the inside of an ashtray with the cloth, which turned black. It was disgusting. Putting down the cloth, she braced herself for what had to be said. 'You haven't been interfering with the girl, have you, Bill?'

He stopped scouring the bar counter and stared at her. A slight twitch under the right eye gave him away. She'd got through to him and her heart began to race as fast as if she'd been on a long run.

'I don't know what you're talking about,' he said.

They remained staring at one another. She was not going to look away first. His face had become even more scarlet than usual and against this heightened colour, his eyes were the palest blue.

'I think you know exactly what I'm talking about,' she said slowly, observing the slight twitch again. 'I'm talking about little girls, Bill. I'm talking about you wanting to do things with little girls.' With fists clenched so tightly that the fingernails dug into her palms, she was glad of the pain: it would keep her to her purpose. 'It's got to stop or I'm going to tell everyone.'

'There's a thing or two I could tell people about you, old girl.'

Her heart jumped. Surely he couldn't know about Miss Neville: they had been so careful! A hot flush suffused her face and neck, but she was angry rather than ashamed. 'I really don't care what you tell anyone.' Her words were like bullets, cold and hard. She could no longer bear to look at him. Instead she stared at the reflection of the back of his head in the strip of mirror behind the bar. Blond tufts of hair framing a shining red dome and, above this, a frieze along the top of the mirror advertised Tooth's Beer.

'Well, you should. I saw you kissing Pat Neville. On the mouth, in the classroom. I don't think that would go down well with the Education Department, do you?'

In that instant she realised that she no longer cared what people thought about her. After all, she was an adult and could make her own choices, and take the consequences too. She thought again of Mr Ryan losing his job at Burford High School all those years ago but he was a man and people wouldn't believe that two women would do such a thing, and if they did believe it, so be it. 'I'm not going to be distracted by that nonsense,' she said, though her voice was shaking.

'Don't think I haven't noticed.'

'I don't fancy little girls like you do. Now I know why you lost interest in me all those years ago. It was because I'd grown up. I'd become a woman and you wanted a girl.' The pain of this realisation was still with her. She glanced at his face, a fleeting look. His features were swollen with anger and she couldn't bear the sight of him. Children weren't in any position to make their own choices and that was why men like Bill had to be stopped. What really mattered was protecting children from people like him.

'You and Miss Neville, you'll be the laughing stock of town. Once they've finished lynching you.'

'No one would believe you,' she said slowly and distinctly, but she was beginning to feel frightened. 'All I care about is that you lay off Zidra and any other kids you might have your eye on. Do you understand?'

Who could tell what he might do next. A big man, he could easily knock her down, just as her dad had knocked down her mother all those times when she was growing up. She gauged the distance to the doorway into the hall. Three yards at least but she was lighter on her feet than he was and she wouldn't be cowed. Deliberately, unhurriedly, she walked towards the door. There she turned. Bill was standing in the same position, as still as a block of stone. Once she might have felt pity for him – not any longer. Although at this instant he was immobile, as soon as he recovered from the shock anything could happen. He'd never hit her yet but he was cornered now.

She ran up the stairs two treads at a time. Once she'd locked the bedroom door, she took the key out of the lock and put it in her handbag. Only after pushing the heavy chest of drawers against the door did she begin to feel reasonably secure. Her hands were still shaking and her voice box hurt. This lingering tension in her throat made her realise how loudly she must have been shouting at Bill.

Tomorrow she'd go to the police but he was unlikely to guess that. She'd been docile for years and he'd think she was going to stay that way. Or that's what she hoped now she'd decided to leave.

After pulling a small suitcase out of the wardrobe, she began to pack. She wouldn't take much, it would be easier to travel light and it would be less conspicuous too. Just a few under-clothes and dresses, her sponge bag and of course her make-up. Tomorrow before seeing the police she'd have to let Miss Neville know what was going on. First thing in the morning she would drop into her house, going as usual down the back lanes where the dunny cart used to go, and that way she wouldn't be seen. If she was seen it wouldn't matter, not any more, not now she'd made up her mind to leave. After that she'd go to Burford. It would have to be the Burford police that she told, not Jingera. That local man Davies was too thick and knew Bill far too well and would never believe her.

Now she'd made this decision she felt a little better. No less anxious or nervous but at least she knew that she was doing the right thing at last. Miss Neville would help her all she could because she was a friend. After that, what might eventuate was anyone's guess. It was no good hanging around waiting for things to happen, waiting for the situation to get resolved. She had to act herself to settle it. Now she'd determined what to do she was more comfortable with herself, although still apprehensively listening to the noises of the hotel, the creaking that a wooden building always made at night, and listening for Bill's tread.

At this point she remembered the photographs and pictures. They were evidence and hidden away in Bill's study. But she wasn't going to try to get in there and retrieve them now. It would be too dangerous with Bill out there still. Anyway if she did take them there wouldn't be any evidence. She had to leave them where they were so the Burford police would be able to find them after she'd told them everything.

She stayed alert for a long time. An hour or so after she'd packed, she heard Bill treading heavily up the stairs and was aware of him standing on the floorboard that squeaked just outside her bedroom. Heart thudding, she wondered if the door would hold if he tried to break it open. Then he moved on to his room and she heaved a sigh of relief as his door clicked shut. For hours more she lay awake, fully dressed, all ready for the morning getaway. Not long after the sky began to lighten and the first bird calls could be heard, she fell into a light and troubled sleep.

CHAPTER THIRTY-SEVEN

Ilona couldn't settle to anything. It was too hot to read, too hot to do the ironing, too hot even to play the piano. In the hope of getting some cool water to drink, she ran the kitchen tap for several minutes but still the water came out tepid. After filling a jug she put it in the ice chest and went out onto the side verandah. It was even hotter outside and the air was so still. Too still. Even the distant surf seemed sluggish, as if it was an effort to break on the shore.

She picked up yesterday's newspaper lying on the wicker table and flicked through it. Nothing much in it that she hadn't already read. After folding up the paper, she fanned herself with it. The heat produced by this effort seemed greater than the cooling effect of the tiny draft generated and she soon stopped. If only a breeze would come up. This place was supposed to have a temperate climate, not such frightful heat. It was supposed to be a safe haven too, or that's what she'd hoped. A shiver ran through her and she turned suddenly cold at the thought of poor Lorna's fate before once more being enveloped by the oppressive heat.

Although more than a week had passed since the Christmas dance, Peter still hadn't called in to see her, and she was starting to wonder if she had imagined all that had passed between them. Leaning over the verandah rail, she stared up at the sky. It was a most peculiar colour, quite jaundiced-looking. At this point her eye was caught by the shiny corrugated iron shed in next door's backyard. It was glowing strangely, reflecting the yellow light. Like a religious painting, she thought. Light did that to things; it gave them meaning, even when they had none.

And there was a strange smell in the air, almost as if someone had decided to burn off their rubbish in spite of the total fire ban. Yes, she could definitely smell smoke and possibly also the faintest scent of burning eucalyptus leaves. Blowing in from Bournda Forest, probably; she'd heard on the news that lightning had started a number of fires there.

Jim put the tin of blue paint back on the shelf in the garage where he'd found it. He could hear the sound of the radio coming from his parents' bedroom. That was good. Mum must be having a rest and the radio would disguise any noise he might make. It was bad enough that he'd skived off from school in the lunchbreak. Even worse would be if she found out what he'd been up to.

Spattered with blue paint, his hands were trembling. Angry still, he was not angry enough to forget what he'd been taught about cleaning a brush after use. With an old rag he wiped the surplus paint off the brush. He put it into an empty jam jar, tipped in some turps and jiggled the brush around to clean the bristles. It was hard to see in the garage; the dust storm had made the windows that filthy, but turning on the light was too risky. The last thing he wanted was Mum bursting in, thinking he was a burglar.

MR BATES IS A PERVERT, that's what he'd painted onto the side of the Masonic hall. But he'd have to go back to the hotel; without some incriminating evidence, no one would believe Zidra. Batesy was too popular. Everyone said good things about him, even Jim's parents and they weren't too fond of the pub, especially his mother. Everyone would think Zidra had made it up. He'd have to get some proof.

When the bristles looked reasonably clean, he removed the brush from the jar. He dried it off by wiping it up and down on the section of garage wall kept clear for that purpose. After cleaning his sticky fingers on a turps-saturated corner of the rag, he stepped out of the garage into the heat and shut the garage door quietly behind him. Things seemed different somehow. Maybe it was the birds, or the lack of them. Not a single bird call. Not a sound apart from the faint thudding of the surf. He glanced up at the sky. That looked funny too. Although there wasn't a cloud to be seen, the usually deep blue had a distinct yellowish tinge to it, the way it had looked before the dust storm. There was probably another storm coming; that would explain it.

He headed along the unpaved lane leading to the back of the hotel. Still not a soul around. No one would see him. He'd been lucky before and he'd be lucky again; the heat kept people indoors. Slinking through the gate leading into the brick-paved courtyard of the hotel, he heard voices coming from the bar. The men in there wouldn't see him though, not if he was quick and quiet. He crept around the boarded-over well in the centre of the courtyard and up the back staircase to the Bates' private quarters.

Still no one around.

The floorboards upstairs creaked under his weight but no one came. The handle of Mr Bates' office door turned easily.

The door was unlocked and the room was empty. After tiptoeing in, he shut the door behind him. It would be silly to lock it though. If anyone was coming he'd hear them and then he'd duck behind the door as it opened and race out. Going straight to the big desk, he pulled out the middle drawer. It shot out so easily that he stumbled backwards and the drawer contents spilled onto the floor. Nothing of interest there though, just a few old pens and pencils, and what looked like old racing scores. Back into the drawer they went, higgledy-piggledly, no time to waste on leaving them in any order. He began to work his way methodically down the bank of drawers on the left-hand side, rummaging through the mess to see what could be found. Still nothing of interest. Then he opened the top right-hand drawer and removed some sheets of writing paper. Eureka, this was it!

But the picture was disgusting. He put it back as fast as if it was burning his fingers. Glancing quickly around the room, he tried to focus on something else. The old leather armchair, rows of bookshelves, piles of old newspapers on the floor. A quite ordinary room. Yet the picture was there in the desk and it wasn't ordinary at all.

Maybe he'd just imagined it. Maybe he was making a mistake; he had to have another look. After lifting the pile of photographs out of the drawer, he shuffled through them. The ones towards the bottom were the worst. He felt like puking and wished he hadn't looked. Throwing them onto the desktop, he took several deeps breaths.

Something had to be done with this stuff though. He should take it away. Even as he thought this, his hands were picking up the top photograph and scrunching it up. The picture was too stiff and came undone. Just then he heard footsteps in the hall outside. Heavy footsteps, it could only be Mr Bates. Heart thumping faster now, he thought of hiding behind the door. That was cowardly though, especially with the evidence all over the desk. He had to confront him; that was the only thing to do.

The door opened and Mr Bates stood there. Jim saw his face turn red and twist with anger. Bang went the door behind him; thump thump the boots as he advanced across the room; thud thud Jim's heart as he glanced at the open window. It was tempting to escape that way but the drop to the yard was too great, and anyway he'd resolved to stand his ground.

'What are you up to, my lad? Stealing's a crime, remember. I don't think your fancy new school in Sydney takes criminals, do you? Defrocking the scholarship boy, now that's a strange image, isn't it?'

'Porn's a crime too, remember.' Only the week before Jim had heard on the news about a raid in Sydney. 'Dirty postcards, especially ones showing "Daddy's Little Girl". You'll get years in jail, you pervert.'

Mr Bates laughed. 'That's a big word for a little boy,' he said, moving closer to the desk.

Jim spread his hands over the pictures. They were proof and he had to keep hold of them. But Bates leant over the desk, grabbed hold of his wrists and threw him backwards. Losing his balance, he fell to the floor, hitting his forehead on the corner of the bookcase. Head smarting, backside hurting but he had to stop Batesy removing the evidence. By the time he was on his feet, Bates had scooped up the photographs on the desktop and was pulling a box of matches from his pocket.

'Here goes your evidence, boyo,' he said, opening the matchbox. 'Think anyone would believe your word against mine? I doubt it.'

If only Jim could distract his attention for a moment, just long enough to grab the photos and escape. Got to be quick though: say something, do something. Tell Batesy he knew about Zidra, that should stop him.

'There's Zidra's word too.'

He was right, that halted Bates. Though not for long enough and he didn't let go of the picture. Yet that sure was a sharp look he gave Jim just before striking the match. The edge of the paper blackened and glowed red, and then ignited into flickering flames. Got to get closer, sidle around the desk, creep up on him. Maybe while he's distracted by the flames Jim could grab the rest of the photographs. But no, Batesy put the burning postcard on the desk and lunged out with his foot. Who'd imagine that a blow to the stomach could hurt so much and make Jim double over with fiery pain? And just when he'd got his breath back and managed to stand up, Batesy set alight two more photos. Damn it, the evidence was going up in smoke right in front of them. Just then a sudden gust of air from the open window fanned the flames of the postcard burning on the desk. For an instant, petrified, Jim watched them flicker and flare. Then the gust became a hot wind blasting through the window and blimey, the flames now leapt from the burning postcard to the other papers scattered over the top of the desk, and almost instantly they were on fire.

No time to waste, he has to get away, and fast before the exit is blocked. Jumping over the leg that Batesy extends, he dashes to the door, wrenching it open. Down the hall, faster and faster, shouting all the while, voice becoming hoarse and then breaking, 'Fire, fire!'

And so frightened that not once does he pause to look back.

———

Ilona took the jug of water out of the ice chest. It was only slightly cooler than before but she poured herself a glass and drank it. Turning on the wireless, she twiddled the dial to try to find the local radio station. It was broadcasting some tedious program about wool prices. She glanced at her watch. Still some minutes to go before the half-hourly news headlines.

After unplugging the radio, she took it into the living room and reconnected it. The room was a little less warm than the kitchen but still uncomfortable. The wool-price piece had ended and there was now a program about bovine mastitis. *Mastitis is complex; there is no simple solution to its control. Some aspects are well understood and documented in the scientific literature. Others are controversial, and opinions are often presented as facts.* She might have found this interesting had she not wanted so desperately to hear about the local fires. Although perhaps it was reassuring that there were no fire bulletins. Perhaps there was nothing for her to worry about.

Then the mastitis program ended and the news began. She turned the volume up. *Around one hundred firefighters at the Bournda Forest fires near Burford are preparing for a challenging afternoon as they work around the perimeter of a number of fires that started with lightning strikes on 10 December. While the fires are not immediately threatening properties at this time, the risk to scattered landholdings today is significant and residents and visitors of Burford, Jingera and the Lower Burford River Valley are advised to prepare. Gusty high winds are forecast from the mid-afternoon and temperatures are already over the century.*

At the end of the news item she switched the radio off. What preparations should be made she had no idea, apart from collecting Zidra after school rather than letting her make her own way home. Thinking of Peter alone on his *landholding*, she remembered that Ferndale was well north, so perhaps he would not be at risk. But Jingera residents were *advised to prepare*. She would have to ask someone what this meant, her neighbour Mrs Robinson perhaps, or Mrs Blunkett.

After putting on a wide-brimmed hat, she went out onto the front verandah. A wind had arisen in the short time she'd been indoors and it nearly lifted the hat off her head. The sky was now even more yellow; a luminous yellow mixed with grey, like an enormous bruise. Something was wrong though, for there wasn't a cloud in sight. She sniffed the air. It didn't smell right. She sniffed again.

It was burning wood she could smell, as if the bush was on fire. Then she heard the clanging of a bell from the direction of the town centre. Over the top of the hedge she caught a glimpse of a fire engine wheeling around the war memorial. At the sight of a spiral of smoke arising from the northern part of the square, her heart began to pound. A fire here, right in the heart of Jingera! The hotel perhaps, or the old hall opposite it. Both buildings flanked the road up to the school. Zidra might be caught there, all the children might be caught there. Ilona had to get up to the school somehow and the quickest way must surely be the back way, along the lane behind the houses opposite.

As she opened her front gate, she noticed Peter's Armstrong Siddeley parked outside the post office. Why he hadn't called in to see her she couldn't understand. Although she wanted to see him, she hesitated not even for a fraction of a second. After crossing the road, she walked rapidly up the narrow alleyway between the houses opposite. There was no time to lose. The column of smoke from the direction of the hotel was expanding and spreading out to form a dense cloud over the town. Once she had reached the lane leading up to the headland she broke into a run.

Peter had spent the last hour sitting in the shade at the edge of the lagoon with bare feet immersed in the water. It had been his intention to visit Ilona as soon as he'd arrived in Jingera but when he'd reached the front gate, he'd realised it was right on lunchtime. Not a good time to call unannounced. That's what he'd told himself anyway as he marched down the hill, and cut through the bush on the western side of the lagoon just before the footbridge. Here he'd found a comfortable place in which to sit out the lunch hour. At two o'clock he'd go back to Ilona's place, or maybe just before.

At precisely ten minutes to two he removed his feet from the water. The wind that had sprung up was so hot he barely needed to dry them; the water evaporated within seconds. While pulling on his socks, he heard the clanging of the fire engine bell from the centre of Jingera. Hurriedly pushing feet into shoes, he struggled back through the undergrowth to the road leading to the town. Black smoke billowed up from the vicinity of the pub. Smelling the acrid scent of wood burning as the westerly wind blew the smoke in his direction, he began to feel alarmed for the town. Many of the houses leading down to the lagoon were summer cottages but people were coming out of those that were occupied. This time he had no hesitation when he reached Ilona's house. The front gate was open although it had been closed when he passed by earlier. Its rusty hinges protested as it swung back and forth in the wind. Fastening it behind him, he knocked loudly on the front door. There was no response, but the door had not been properly shut and his knocking pushed it open. He called out Ilona's name but there was no reply. It occurred to him that she might be sleeping. She probably felt the heat terribly coming as she did from Northern Europe, even though that was years ago.

'She left a few minutes ago, love,' a voice said. Turning, he saw Mrs Robinson, an elderly woman with a thick thatch of grey hair, peering at him over the side fence.

'Where did she go?'

'Don't know. Can't see over the hedge. Where's the fire?'

'Looks like it's from the pub. I'm going to find out.' He shut Ilona's door without locking it, just in case she didn't have the key with her. Anxiety was nibbling at his gut.

After securing Ilona's front gate, he glanced westwards. There was smoke coming from outside the town now. It looked as if the forest between the town and the farmland was also on fire. He took a deep breath and ran straight up the road towards the square.

CHAPTER THIRTY-EIGHT

Sniffing, George stood in the yard behind Cadwallader's Quality Meats. Something was burning. Bushfires somewhere and not all that far away. There was a pall of reddish-brown smoke extending from the north-west right down to the south. Overhead the sky appeared almost misty, as if veiled in yellow gauze. As he watched the hazy yellow sky above turned a sullen grey and sparks began to drift through the air. Hurriedly he stumped into the shop, where The Boy was wrapping up a parcel for a customer. Trying to tune into the local station, he fiddled with the dial of the radio. Although the static was awful, he'd just about picked up a signal when the clanging of the fire bell drowned out the crackling of the radio. It sounded close, as if the fire engine was pulling into the square. He limped across the sawdust to open the shopfront door for the customer and would have followed had Mrs Blunkett not blocked the way. Her light blue eyes were popping and her usually neat hair was dishevelled. 'The pub's on fire,' she shouted, as if George were yards away rather than inches. 'The fire brigade's here! I've shut up the post office.' The shop door banged behind her as she fled.

'Fewest words she's ever uttered,' George said, trying to quell his trepidation. The fire engine was parked in front of Bates' hotel and firemen were directing their hoses on flames that were ripping through the building. Dense black smoke began to drift down towards him and the roaring of the flames was frightful.

The drill in a bushfire was to stay inside with the doors and windows shut and rolled-up wet towels across the bottoms of the doors to stop any sparks getting in. Yet this wasn't a bushfire and he had to get the boys out of school fast. He had to find Eileen too and The Boy had to get home.

He locked up the shop behind them. No time to worry about rolled-up wet towels now. People were running everywhere, coughing and spluttering and shouting. Davies, the Jingera policeman, and a couple of his cronies were guiding people towards the road to the lagoon. The smoke was so dense George couldn't see the way up to the headland. Fear flowered inside him and he broke into a sweat. Somehow he had to get past the hotel and up the hill to the school to find Jim and Andy. Sidling by people running down the hill to the lagoon, he headed for the vicinity of the road leading up to the headland. At this point the way was blocked by a volunteer fireman with a blackened face, whom George recognised as Taffy Hughes. 'Can't go up there, George. The road's been cut. The pub could collapse on that side any moment.'

'Got to get to my boys. They're in school.' George was joined by a few other anxious-looking parents.

'The school's already been evacuated. The teacher's taking all the kids down to the beach through the back lanes. Don't worry, they're all right.'

Davies now came running up, stuttering in his excitement. 'You've got to get onto the beach. Get over to the lagoon as fast as you can. The Bournda Forest fires are pretty well out of control, they reckon, and they've shut all the roads out of here.'

Back past the shop, George limped around to his house a few hundred yards beyond. Eileen already had the hose connected to the rainwater tank that supplied the kitchen sink and was hosing down the roof. 'Thank God you're here, George,' she said, voice rising. 'The kids are already on the beach, Mrs Burton told me, and I didn't know whether to stay or to go. I've had the radio on and they say we've all got to get out. Jingera is ringed by fire.'

'It's not ringed by fire,' George said calmly, although this wasn't how he felt. 'It's only Bournda Forest that's burning. The hotel's caught on fire as well, God knows how. It looks pretty much under control, though it could spread.'

Together George and Eileen stumbled along the path and out the gate. As they crossed the square, he glanced at his shop and the bakery next door. Both were intact but he wondered for how much longer. The hotel was still burning fiercely, flames leaping into the sky and debris blowing towards them. The street was full of people, all running in the same direction, and forming a stream that flowed down towards the lagoon and across the footbridge onto the beach. George and Eileen hastened past the post office. Although Peter Vincent's distinctive car, the grey Armstrong Siddeley, was parked outside there was no sign of him.

Halfway down the hill George thought he saw two rows of schoolchildren lined up on the beach close to the surf, and felt a flicker of relief. Then a cloud of dense black smoke swirled down from the hotel or the bush, and obliterated the view. Spluttering, and with eyes watering so much he could hardly see the way, he pulled out a handkerchief. He gave it to Eileen to tie over her face, before removing his apron, which, until now, he'd forgotten he was still wearing. Even with this held over his mouth and nostrils, the acrid smoke still tore into his lungs at each breath and he began to cough. Please God, may my boys be safe, he pleaded to the celestial being in whom he didn't quite believe.

'Pull yourself together, George,' Eileen said, and only then did he realise he'd been voicing his pleas aloud. Despite this lapse, she took his hand and semi-dragged him along. His gammy leg, aching in the spot where it had broken years ago, hurt with each step.

At last they were over the bridge and stumping along the short track to the beach. Still hand in hand, they staggered across the sand, and there were the children in two rows by the water's edge, just as he'd seen them in his vision on the hill. They were sitting cross-legged, as if they were in a school assembly. Catching sight of his parents, Andy waved, and George's heart turned over. But Jim was nowhere to be seen. Miss Neville and Ilona Talivaldis were roaming around the children as if they were herding sheep or cattle. George went straight up to the school mistress.

'Where's Jim?'

'Can't find him anywhere. He didn't return after the lunch break. I thought he might have been with you.'

'He's not.' George now began to feel deeply alarmed. After collecting Andy, he hurried back to Eileen.

'That bally boy!' Eileen shouted. 'I'll skin him alive when he comes back.'

'I'll find him,' said George. 'Keep Andy with you.'

George could feel sweat pouring down his back and soaking the waistband of his trousers. Jim had no idea of how dangerous a fire could be and for an instant George hated his son for destroying his peace of mind. And for putting at risk his own bright future: the brilliant scholarship, the science degree, the radio telescope. Jim's stupidity could hardly be credited. To play truant today of all days.

Stumbling from group to group, George asked if anyone knew where Jim was. No one had seen him, not since lunchtime at school. The heat was searing and the air so dry it was hard to breathe. Gusts of wind shifted sparks, and soon there were so many specks of debris whirling about that it was almost as if a swarm of locusts had descended on the beach. Then the wind metamorphosed into a westerly gale and there was an abrupt thundering sound, as if planes were flying low overhead. Turning, George was just in time to witness a great ball of fire jump the lagoon, leaping from the treetops on the Jingera side of the river to the treetops on the beach side. An instant later the crowns of all the trees in the strip of bushland between the river and the beach exploded into flames. The sky turned red as the flames burned higher and higher.

Panic rising inside him, George found it increasingly hard to see through the clouds of black smoke billowing across the beach. People who had been spread across the sand now ran towards the surf and formed an uneven line along the breakers' edge. George's heart was hammering as he edged his way past, searching for his beloved son.

CHAPTER THIRTY-NINE

Peter Vincent had been reluctant to leave the town. He'd searched every street and every lane looking for Ilona. Only when he'd learnt that all the children had been evacuated onto the beach did it occur to him that Ilona would also be there. Then he'd sprinted straight down the hill and over the footbridge.

It was when he was running over the sand dunes that he heard what sounded like a squadron of bombers flying low overhead. Immediately he fell flat on his face. There was no raid, though. There would be no shelling from the ocean, no bombing from overhead. He was lying on Jingera Beach hemmed in like all the other refugees between the burning bush and the sea. Brushing the sand from his face, he looked at the bush between the beach and the lagoon. The treetops were blazing like a torched city after the planes had dropped their bombs. The roaring he'd heard was from the fire jumping across the lagoon. Black smoke belched across the beach and the sky was almost as dark as a moonless night. The only illumination was provided by the burning trees that were, as he watched, transformed into an orange wall of flame.

Ilona had to be here somewhere. Please God, she was here somewhere. He couldn't bear to lose her but he had to avoid thinking of that. He had to keep his nerve and move methodically from one group to the next until he found her.

It was then that he heard someone call his name. Someone who couldn't pronounce it quite correctly, someone who put equal emphasis on each syllable. He felt a lurching in his chest and a prickling behind his eyes. She was here. She was safe.

Changing course, he ran towards the line of breakers. There she was, standing not far from the edge of the surf. Just before reaching her, he stumbled and might have fallen had Ilona not stood up and taken his arm.

'Thank God you're here,' he said. 'Where's Zidra?'

'With one of the O'Rourke girls.' She pointed, and Peter saw the two children standing next to a partially constructed sandcastle and staring at the burning bush.

'Thank God you're both safe.'

She put her arms around him and held him close. So close that he was able to bury his face in her hair that reeked of eucalyptus smoke and tickled his nostrils. For a few moments they remained like that. He could hardly believe this miracle: that he had found her, that he was able to hold her, and that she had reached out for him first. When she looked up at last, he saw in her fine brown eyes something that was unmistakably affection, something that might even be love. For weeks he'd hoped for this although never had he admitted it to himself, never until now. And the amazing thing was that for years he'd thought of himself as unlovable and, on his worst days, as incapable of love. How wrong he'd been though, he could see that in her eyes and feel it in his heart. How tired he was of being alone, tired of having only himself and his dogs and Ferndale to watch over. He cared for Ilona Talivaldis and wanted to protect her, and he began to murmur this into her ear.

When he eventually paused for breath, she whispered that she had become fond of him too. The moment she'd first realised this was when she'd heard about the trouble he'd taken to check with the Welfare Board about poor Lorna. That's when she'd recognised that he was a good man, a kind man, one whom she could trust. That's when she'd decided that he wasn't just a handsome face with *nice* hair that was in desperate need of a good haircut in a style that she herself could easily administer.

He laughed at this. 'Samson and Delilah. I'm not sure I should let you cut my hair.'

'Your strength is not in your hair. It's in your heart and your head.'

'My arms are quite strong too.'

'All the better to hold me with, and now it is time for your *embrocation*.'

'My embrocation?'

'Yes. When you tell me when you began to care for me.'

'Ah, the embrocation.' Not for an instant was he tempted to suggest that reciprocation might be more appropriate, nor to laugh. 'Let me see. I began to fall for you ages ago. I can even tell you exactly where.' Down the beach he pointed, although the spot where she'd been about to venture into the rip all those weeks ago was not visible through the dense smoke haze.

'But I was impossible then.'

'You were but it was your lovely face that hooked me.'

Never would he tell her that it was that metamorphosis of vulnerability into antagonism that had awakened his interest, nor would he reveal how delightful was her use and misuse of long words. Let her think it was her beauty and charm that had won his heart. At this moment he noticed on her left cheek a dark smudge that he tried to brush away, but his fingers were also covered with dust, and the smudge became larger. This gave her a clownish appearance that once he might have found amusing but now found added greatly to her loveliness.

She put a finger on his mouth and traced its outline and he had just placed his lips on hers when he heard someone calling his name. It was George Cadwallader, staggering towards them and shouting.

It was hard to distinguish his words, what with the surf thundering onto the sand and the fire crackling in the bush beyond the dunes. When George reached them, he took hold of Peter's arm. Normally unflappable, he was in a terrible state. His eyes were staring and he was so breathless he could hardly fashion the words. 'It's Jim. He wasn't in school when the kids were evacuated. He's gone AWOL.'

'What's AWOL?' asked Zidra, who had abandoned watching the fire and was now plucking anxiously at Peter's sleeve.

'Absent without official leave,' said Peter. 'Where have you looked, George?'

'All over the place. Can't see him anywhere.'

'I'll help you find him. You do the beach and I'll see if I can get back into Jingera.'

'I'll help,' said Zidra.

'No you won't,' said Ilona, grabbing hold of her hand.

'Yes, stay with your mother,' Peter said. 'She needs looking after too. I'll find Jim and you make sure your mother doesn't go missing again. I've been searching for her since lunchtime.'

Zidra didn't smile.

'Promise me you'll keep an eye on her,' Peter added.

'I promise.' Zidra didn't look at him though. She gazed behind him, at the burning bush that illuminated her worried face.

CHAPTER FORTY

To love Peter and be loved in return was such a wonderful thing that Ilona might have danced with joy, right there by the waves, had not her delight been tempered by the new worry of Jim going missing. Instead she sat on the sand next to Zidra and put an arm around her shoulders.

'You're too hot, Mama,' Zidra said, shaking her off. 'Why couldn't you let me help?'

'It's too dangerous. They will find him soon, rest assured.'

Zidra grunted but said no more. After a time one of Ilona's pupils, a tall inarticulate boy of thirteen or fourteen, appeared with a baby kangaroo swaddled in a towel. He'd taken the joey from the pouch of its mother who had died further down the beach after escaping from the bush, he said, and wondered if Ilona would like to look after it. Ilona unwrapped it. The creature was a tiny hairless thing, just a few inches long. The miracle of a new life. The miracle of a new love. 'We'll look after it,' she said, grateful for the distraction, although she had no idea how they would care for it. Gently she gave it to Zidra to hold, but she didn't seem much interested in the bundle, and soon sank back into lethargy.

Ilona felt as if the moisture in her body was being sucked out by the heat. Thankfully the smoke was beginning to lift a little and it would be easier for Peter and George to see where they were going. She traced her lips with her forefinger, as if still feeling the gentle touch of Peter's lips. Ever since that night at the Christmas dance, she'd suspected that she was beginning to feel more than ordinary affection for him. But it was only this afternoon, only half an hour ago, that she'd been willing to countenance the possibility that she could fall in love with him. Immediately before the fire had leapt across the lagoon, when she'd been standing with her back to the ocean, she'd seen him running over the sand dunes. A moment later, the fireball had roared from the treetops on one side of the river to the treetops on the other. At once he'd dropped onto the sand and, for one terrible instant, she'd thought his body was burning. Then he'd stood up and carried on walking across the sand and her heart had filled with love for him, for at last she made the connection. He was used to hurling himself away from danger, that's what he'd done in the war. He was used to being bombed. He was used to conflagrations. He was even used to internment. Released little more than a dozen years ago, he'd lived through an experience that, perhaps in some respects, was not so dissimilar to hers, and that was an extra bond between them. At the Christmas dance she'd told him a little of her past but had neglected to ask about his. She would when she was ready. She would when he was ready.

At this point she was distracted by Zidra pulling at her arm. 'How much longer are we going to have to stay here?'

'Till the fire dies back and the firemen say it is safe.'

'Where do you think Jim's gone?'

'I expect he's just exploring.'

'You should have let me help look.'

326

'I'm sure they'll find him soon.' But she wasn't sure at all and began to feel more worried. It seemed as if anything could happen on this blazing afternoon. She stood up to look at the bush behind the sand dunes. Certainly the smoke was continuing to lift. The boles of the trees were gently flickering like candles. The understorey had been burnt out, so that now she could see between the tree trunks the glimmering lagoon behind. Jingera was still shrouded in smoke.

'Will the house be okay, Mama?'

'I don't know, darling. We shall find out.' She thought of Oleksii's compositions and their few clothes. Yet possessions did not matter, she'd learnt that years ago. Food mattered, love mattered.

She was startled by a hubbub. People were jumping up from their positions on the sand. A woman shouted and pointed to a man stumbling across the footbridge carrying a large object. Everyone began to run towards the bridge. Once on the beach the man lost hold of the bundle, and awkwardly it fell to the ground. He bent and gently rolled it over. Immediately it became obvious that it wasn't a bundle at all. It was a human body lying face up in the sand.

Ilona experienced a fluttering sensation in her chest and began to feel faint. She might have fallen had she not been clutching at Zidra's arm. Please God not Peter or Jim, she thought. It surely can't be Peter, and it was too big to be Jim. Her heart was beating rapidly and the palms of her hands were sweating. The body was the same size as Peter's, and the blue shirt he'd been wearing was exactly the same shade as the shirt shrouding this body. Despair threatened to sweep over her but she wouldn't succumb to it. Not here, not yet, not with Zidra needing her. Tears trickling down her face, she glanced at her daughter whose face was now a ghastly shade of white.

Perhaps Peter had only fainted though. Brushing away her tears, she said, 'Come, Zidra,' and tried to take her hand. Instead Zidra gave her the little bundle containing the baby kangaroo.

Just then she saw Eileen running along the beach, dragging Andy behind her. 'It's my boy!' she shouted, 'I know it's him!' Weeping, she pushed her way through the crowd. 'It's Jim. Oh, please let me through!'

Zidra, with one quick movement, wriggled free of Ilona and followed close behind Eileen. People began to jostle forward and Ilona could no longer see the body, or where Zidra had gone. Panic clenching her stomach, she tried to follow.

Then she saw Zidra squatting on all fours, peering between the legs of the people surrounding the kneeling man and the body slumped in front of him. Ilona pushed between two elderly women, forgetting to apologise in English rather than Latvian.

'One man's dead, apparently,' one woman was saying. 'Asphyxiated, but Davies is okay.'

Ilona's stomach began to churn so much that she thought she might throw up. She took a deep breath before wriggling further forward. The figure kneeling on the sand was certainly Davies. Next to him was the body. Tears now blinded her. Although her heart was hammering, she felt that peculiar numbness and detachment that was shock. After taking several more slow deep breaths, she wiped away her tears with the back of her hand and glanced quickly at the faces of the people around her. In detail she saw them, as if they were her real concern rather than that blurred shape in her peripheral vision. Not far from her was Cherry Bates, standing with Miss Neville. Next to them stood Eileen and Andy, and there was George beside them.

And all these other people too, with their curious faces, enthralled faces. People averse to death but fascinated by it too.

Suddenly she found she could scarcely breathe, her throat felt so constricted, and despair began to sluice over her. Yet she had to look at the body once more and when she did she was just in time to see Mr Davies and George lifting the shoulders. Now they were wedging coats under the head, and she held her breath until they had finished the task and she could see the face.

But this wasn't Peter at all, and not Jim either. It was old Mr Giles who lived up by the cemetery and she couldn't imagine how she could have been so mistaken. This frail body bore no resemblance to Peter; and thank goodness, Mr Giles wasn't dead after all; he was struggling to sit up and even now starting to sip at the flask of water that George was holding to his lips. There was hope yet and she almost laughed out loud with relief.

'Is there anyone else left in town?' George asked Davies. So close were they to her that Ilona could hear every word although he was speaking very softly.

'No. We searched everywhere.'

'You didn't see Jim or Peter Vincent?'

'No. Everyone's evacuated except for the firemen who are still there.'

'How much damage?' said a loud voice from the crowd.

'Just the pub, and all the bush between here and the south side of the town.'

'When can we go back?'

'Probably in a couple of hours. The firemen will let us know when. Now settle down all of you and tell me where I can find Cherry Bates.'

'Here she is.'

Davies motioned her over. 'Bad news, I'm afraid. I'm really sorry about this, Cherry.' There was a short pause before he added, 'We couldn't get Bill out in time. The roof caved in and blocked the way out, and he's dead, I'm afraid. Asphyxiated.'

Shocked, Ilona heard the collective 'Aaah' from all around. Jovial Bill Bates dead, killed defending his property, and poor Cherry a widow too. Although Cherry had her back to the crowd so her expression was hidden, Ilona saw her sway slightly, as if she might faint. Quick to react, she leapt forward, but not before Miss Neville who was even now wrapping her arms around Cherry's shoulders and holding her close.

At this point Ilona glanced at Zidra's face and was struck by its queer expression. Perhaps it was a trick of the poor light but it seemed almost a smile. The poor dear child; Ilona bent down to give her a kiss and a hug. It must be the shock of hearing of Bates' death and the worry about Peter and Jim.

Now everyone started talking so loudly that Eileen's sudden shriek went almost unnoticed. Ilona heard it though and saw Eileen start to run towards the rocks at the northern end of the beach. Close behind her was George, almost crab-like in his effort to get along with his lame leg. And there, not more than a hundred yards away, were Peter and Jim trudging along the sand. Joy suffused Ilona's body. She took Zidra's hand and together they ran along the beach towards them.

Chapter Forty-One

'I'm so glad to see you!' Eileen said, giving her older son the biggest embrace George had ever seen her bestow. Now it was George's turn to hug Jim. 'My boy's back again,' he said, and then held him at arm's length for an inspection: grey face, grey clothes, and a fine layer of ash powdering his hair. But he was alive and seemed unharmed.

'I can't believe you'd do such a stupid thing, son,' George said. 'You must have been mad to stay on the headland, and what were you doing out of school anyway?' At this point he became so overwhelmed with relief that he had to look away. He barely registered what he was looking at: the water meandering between the lagoon and the ocean, and next to it groups of people sitting on the beach. He barely registered either the sounds of voices as people shouted to be heard over the drumming of the relentless surf. All he could focus on was his joy that Jim had been found. Passing a sleeve across his tired eyes, he turned to Peter. 'I can't thank you enough for finding him,' he said, voice cracking with emotion that even a brief fit of coughing couldn't disguise.

Peter shrugged, as if his efforts had been minimal, or perhaps he was simply giving George time to recover. 'He was hiding in a cave till the fire passed over.' After a pause, he said very quietly, 'There's something else we need to talk about, although you mightn't want Eileen to hear this just yet.'

George followed Peter and Jim and sat on the sand a few yards away, while Eileen was engrossed in telling Ilona and Zidra about how worried she'd been.

'What's up?' George said.

'Tell your father what you told me, Jim.'

Jim began to talk. He talked so fast that George occasionally had to ask him to repeat details.

'I see,' said George slowly

'The fire wasn't my fault, Dad.'

'Of course it wasn't, son. You were lucky to get out though.' He knew it would take him time to absorb this information. Days probably. Bill Bates that way inclined, whoever would have believed it.

Later George sat down a little awkwardly next to Eileen, with his bad leg extended in front of him. To his surprise, she took his hand.

'You're right about Jim,' Eileen continued. 'He's a very special boy. I realised that when I thought we'd lost him. Andy and Jim are both special in their different ways.' She squeezed his hand and wriggled her bare toes a bit.

He looked at her feet. They were pretty feet, in spite of the bunion that was developing on one big toe. He hoped she wasn't going to tell him that Jim was so special she'd decided she couldn't allow him to take up his scholarship. She hadn't even ordered the uniforms he'd need, although it was nearly the end of the term and he'd be starting at Stambroke College in early February.

He held her hand a little awkwardly in his own. He wasn't used to this hand-holding business. This was the second time in one afternoon she'd done this, and in public too. Although he liked Eileen's new demonstrativeness, he was even more determined than before that Jim was going to take up his scholarship, come what may.

'Yes, Jim's a very special boy,' Eileen repeated, and then stopped. He braced himself for what was coming. 'So, George,' she continued, 'I really do think we should give him the best start in life that we can.' His heart sank. So this was it. *The best start in life that we can* would be a good family environment while Jim attended Burford High.

'The best we can,' George repeated, parrot-like, and waited.

'Yes, we should give him the very best start in adult life that we can. So, George, you're right about the scholarship. Jim must be allowed to take it up.'

He noted the way she said *Jim must be allowed*. It was as if someone else, and not she, had been blocking Jim from the Sydney school, but he also knew that what she had just said would not have come easily to her. *George, you are right.* It must be years since she had said such a thing without at once qualifying it with a criticism. Although perhaps that was yet to come. *George, you are right but you are wrong.* He waited, not saying anything.

'So I wanted to say that I'm sorry. You've been right all along about the scholarship.'

Only now did he dare to hope. Glancing at her, he saw she was smiling. He grinned back but couldn't think of anything to say that wouldn't seem overly triumphant. He had won though.

'And who knows,' Eileen said, 'what might happen with Andy? Maybe he'll turn out to be a great artist.' She looked oceanwards, as if gazing into the future.

And still she was smiling.

George began to feel a little peace descend upon him. Now that Jim was safe, now that Eileen had been willing to make a compromise, he would be able to keep going. His family was lucky but others weren't quite so fortunate.

'Andy could become a great artist,' he repeated slowly, for his wife's benefit. 'Anything is possible, Eileen.'

But nothing would ever be quite the same again, he knew. Too much had happened. The pub was gone. Bill Bates was dead. You just never knew what people were really like. Jim had taken the initiative by raiding Bates' office and only now did George begin to feel proud of his son's behaviour. Although he'd been foolhardy and his life had been endangered, he'd done the right thing.

Now Eileen had agreed that Jim should be educated in Sydney, he could start talking normally to her again. Maybe the armistice that they'd just reached would mean they could rub along together a bit better in the future. Of course, she'd have to be told everything that had happened, or nearly everything. Maybe not right this minute, he didn't think he could face that yet, but certainly tonight.

Unbidden, an image sprang into his mind. It was the advertisement he'd seen in the *Burford Advertiser* the previous Saturday. The newspaper would have gone already, probably wrapped around the garbage that he carried out to the bin each evening after tea was over. But he could recall every detail of the advertisement, including the telephone number. The six-inch telescope was quite a few years old and needed some work. Nevertheless, as soon as the lines were repaired, he'd telephone the owner about it. The telescope was probably in pieces and that's why it was so cheap, but if he put his mind to it and had all the parts, he reckoned he could have a go at fixing it. He didn't think Eileen would try to prevent him from doing that now.

CHAPTER FORTY-TWO

Cherry, sitting on the sand next to Miss Neville, struggled with a range of conflicting emotions. Fear that someone in Jingera knew about Bill's inclinations when they didn't need to now he was dead. Pity for Bill and the terrible way he'd died. But most dominant of all was the feeling of relief that he and his photographs had gone. Weeping was all she could manage for the moment to reconcile these feelings.

That morning, after she'd awoken from a brief restless doze, she'd crept out of the hotel and down the dunny-cart lanes to Miss Neville's house. Seeming both joyful and surprised at seeing Cherry with her small suitcase in her kitchen, Miss Neville had said, 'Stay here as long as you like, dearest. Treat it as your home.' Soon afterwards she'd dashed out the front door to open up the school. Although Cherry had planned to catch the next bus to Burford, due to depart at two o'clock, the fire had put an end to that.

When the alarm had sounded she'd hurried out of Miss Neville's house but hadn't immediately seen that the hotel was on fire, so distracted had she been by the activity in the square: the fire engine, the milling people, the impression of panic.

Once she'd realised that the pub was blazing she wasn't in the least tempted to return. The few material things that she cared about were in her case at Miss Neville's. Never for even an instant did it cross her mind that anyone would still be in the pub, least of all Bill. At that point the large blue letters painted on the side of the hall had seized her attention. *MR BATES IS A PERVERT.* Somebody else must have known what he was like and this meant that Bill must have done something. Shown his disgusting photographs to someone probably. That person had painted those letters onto the wall of the hall only this morning. Once the townsfolk were allowed to leave the beach and go back to their homes it wouldn't be long before they'd all be gossiping about it. Maybe sooner, if they'd seen what she'd seen.

And she'd known about it, she'd known about it for weeks and hadn't told anyone.

'Dearest Cherry, please don't cry,' whispered Miss Neville, putting an arm around her shoulders.

'I've got nothing left.' This wasn't at all what she'd intended to say, especially as she still had her suitcase and her make-up.

'Bloody hell, Cherry, you've got me.'

'Yes, I've got you,' Cherry said, smiling now.

'And you can live with me forever and ever.'

Cherry took Miss Neville's hand and squeezed it.

'And we can buy you new clothes and say you're my lodger. And maybe I can apply for a transfer to somewhere bigger than here, where people won't gossip and where you can forget about all this.'

'Sydney perhaps. You should have done that years ago.'

'But then I wouldn't have met you, and once I'd met you, how could I leave?'

'I might have gone with you.'

'But you might not.'

'You never asked me.'

'You never suggested it either,' Miss Neville said.

'We've kept too much from each other.'

'Yes.' There was a brief pause before Miss Neville added, 'This question might seem a bit callous, but were you insured?'

'No idea. Bill looked after all that. We probably were, and I'm pretty sure he had some money stashed away in the Commercial Banking Company.'

'Dry your eyes, pretty one. We've got a great future ahead of us.'

But Cherry was now remembering those blue letters and what she had to tell Miss Neville. Perhaps she should just sneak out later that night with a tin of paint to go right over them. It would take several coats. That bright blue would be hard to cover up. Bill was dead now so there was no need for people to know. 'Do you have any house paint?' she asked.

'Yes, but what the blazes do you want that for? Not planning to paint my house, are you?'

'Someone painted something nasty on the side of the hall. You know, that corrugated iron thing opposite the pub. I want to cover it up.'

'Bill didn't set the hotel on fire deliberately, did he?'

'Not to my knowledge. Someone just painted the words 'Bates is a pervert' in blue letters a foot high. People will know it meant Bill.'

'People can think of really nasty things. Bill mightn't have been all that sensitive but he was the last person anyone would think of as a pervert. I'd know. Being a teacher makes you very aware of those things.'

'You're wrong there. He had all sorts of obscene pictures and drawings.'

'Really? You can't just buy these things, you know, Cherry.'

'Don't you believe it. There's a black market out there for dirty postcards. Haven't you read about all those raids the police have been carrying out in Sydney? Anyway, he might have got them in the war.' Pat had led a sheltered life, she decided, and realised that, for the first time, she'd been able to think of Miss Neville as Pat.

'Well, bloody hell, I find that quite shocking. Why didn't you tell me?'

'I was going to a few weeks ago and then just couldn't. I should have, I know. Then I was going to tell you today. That's why I came around this morning, but there wasn't time.'

'Of course you bloody well should have told me! Just think of all those kids in my charge. You should have told me as soon as you had any suspicion. Now I come to think of it, he was always hanging around outside the pub when school came out. I thought that was just part of his "hail-fellow, well-met" stuff. It never even occurred to me he could possibly be that way inclined.'

'I'm sorry.'

'Well, so am I, the bastard.'

'As soon as we go back into town, I want to paint over the letters.' She wanted to blot the pictures out of her head too.

'Leave them there, Cherry. It really doesn't matter now that he's dead.'

Perhaps Pat was right, and, with Pat by her side, she would be strong and she would no longer need to care about what people might think. Indeed they should know her husband was a pervert. It might make them more watchful in general and that would surely be a good thing.

Zidra, standing with Jim on the hard sand next to the surf, stared at the thick haze of smoke over the ocean. The water looked more grey than blue. If Mr Bates hadn't died in the fire she'd still be feeling frightened. She shuddered. She didn't like thinking about him, dead or alive. But being dead meant he couldn't ever return, so she was safe now.

'I wish Lorna hadn't gone away,' Zidra said. She fingered the pink shell that she carried in her pocket ever since Lorna had given it to her.

'She'll come back one day,' Jim said.

Zidra wondered if she would. Mrs Bates had told Mama yesterday that it might be possible for them to visit the Gudg-iegalah Girls' Home. Thinking of Mrs Bates reminded her of Mr Bates again. She still found it hard to believe that he was really dead. 'Mr Bates was a horrid man,' she said. She paused. Maybe it was the shock that was making her feel so strange, so numb.

'Quite horrid,' Jim said.

'Mama said you shouldn't say that of the dead. They can't answer back.'

'It's hypocritical to say that you shouldn't speak ill of the dead.'

'Hypocritical?' He just couldn't resist a long word when a short one would do and Mama wasn't hypocritical whatever that meant.

Jim shrugged. 'Hard to explain. Say one thing when you mean another. Or when you think you're above criticism but you're too lazy to form an opinion.'

'Mama always has an opinion.'

'No, not your mum. It's a saying, stupid. That you shouldn't speak ill of the dead. It's like a proverb. Or an old wives' tale.'

'I'm not stupid.' But she knew Jim didn't mean it. Without him she couldn't have got through the past few weeks. Protecting her was something he'd done ever since the time she and Lorna were being stoned. 'Anyway I'm glad he's gone.'

'So am I.'

The tide was turning. She retreated as a wave advanced towards her bare feet. Jim stayed in the water though, letting it wash his grubby legs. 'You don't have to worry about all that stuff any more,' Jim said. 'And neither do I.'

'I know I don't have to worry.' Now that she'd said it aloud, the fear that she'd been living with for days began to seep slowly away. 'But why were you worrying?'

'I was worrying about you, obviously.'

She felt pleased by this. While knowing that Jim looked after her, she hadn't known he *worried* about her. That was something rather more special.

'And I was worrying about what would happen to you after I go. Now I don't have to bother so much.'

'You'll be coming back for the holidays, though. You can worry about me then.'

'Yeah. I'll be grown up by then, though.'

'You'll be able to worry about me even more. That's what grown-ups do. Just think of Mama.' Glancing in her direction, Zidra saw that she was still sitting with Mr Vincent. That was nice. 'And anyway,' she told Jim, 'I'll be pretty grown up myself.' She felt her old spirit returning. She wasn't going to let Jim come over all superior just because he was nearly two years older. 'I'll be ten by then.'

Jim laughed. 'Very grown up,' he said.

And then she forgot about Mr Bates and ran into the waves after Jim, splashing him with water.

Ilona and Peter were sitting side-by-side on the sand. On her lap, Ilona held the baby kangaroo cradled in the towel that created the illusion of a pouch. The joey might not live, Peter had warned her. As if she did not already know the dangers of getting attached to anyone, but she would try to keep the baby kangaroo alive.

Peter now began to tell her everything that had taken place since he'd gone to look for Jim. When he had finished, she said, 'It's hard to believe such a thing could happen in Jingera.'

'Jim's a brave boy,' he said.

'So the pictures were pornographic?'

'Probably not what you're thinking of, Ilona. The pictures were of men and young girls.'

'But how disgusting!' The shock made her feel quite nauseous and her mouth dry. Surely jovial *respectable* Bill Bates would not have such tastes. 'Are you sure?'

'Yes, Jim was quite certain of that, but I'm afraid it gets worse, Ilona.'

'Tell me.' Her voice cracked and she licked her dry lips.

'Bates showed Zidra the photos.'

'No!'

'Yes. That's how Jim knew.'

'She told him?'

'Yes.'

'But she didn't tell me.'

'Perhaps it's easier to say those words to another child.'

A horrible thought crept into her head and almost made her retch. 'Did he touch her?' If Bates had interfered with her daughter she would have killed him personally. He was dead though, and she was glad of it. Glad of it.

'I asked Jim that too. He said no. Bates showed her the photos and then she ran away.'

She ran away. She was a fast runner. That was just as well. Maybe seeing the photos had caused her nightmares. No wonder the poor child had woken up with bad dreams. Ilona clenched and unclenched her hands.

Later, when she felt less agitated and they were alone, she would talk to Zidra. 'I wish she'd told me,' she said at last.

'She probably will. Try not to worry, Ilona, he never touched her.' Putting an arm around her shoulders, he gently pulled her close.

'Are you quite sure?'

'That's what Jim told me.'

For a moment she rested her head on his shoulder. Then he said, 'Jim went off to the pub at lunchtime. He had some idea of finding the photos and using them as evidence against Bates.'

'Brave boy.'

'A very brave boy – and Zidra so brave too. She's a strong character like her mother.'

Suppressing a sigh, Ilona watched Zidra and Jim standing at the edge of the breakers. When she spoke to Zidra about all of this she would have to be very careful. She shouldn't make too big an issue of it. After all, Zidra was safe from Bates now. He could never harm her. Never.

'Things happen to kids,' Peter said, 'and they walk away from them and put them behind them.'

'The ones that survive do,' she said.

Now she knew that Jingera wasn't quite the sanctuary she'd been looking for. It hadn't turned out to be a safe haven. Perhaps there was no such place and she would have to stop looking for it.

'Zidra's a survivor, Ilona, and we'll look after her.'

She noted the plural and turned to look at him. Gazing at the ocean, he seemed tired and there were fine lines around his eyes that she hadn't noticed before. The lines moved her deeply. They made him seem vulnerable. When she reached out to touch his cheek, he took her hand in his. It was warm and dry. Perhaps he was a safe place: she was going to find that out.

She also kept a watchful eye on Zidra, still standing with Jim above the line of the surf. They seemed sober, like middle-aged folk, but today almost everyone was subdued. Subdued by the heat; subdued by all that had gone wrong; subdued by the fire and then by the death of Mr Bates. As well, the knowledge that Bates was a paedophile was probably even now beginning to circulate among the evacuees. Whether or not it would be believed was another matter.

Shortly she would go and get Zidra. But for the moment she stayed where she was, watching the waves and the dense smoke that was very slowly dispersing.

Now she noticed that Zidra had begun to push at Jim and they were flicking water at one another. She is a little better now, Ilona thought. For a moment, she has forgotten her troubles, but she will need to be closely observed.

Peter said, 'I came to see you today. That's why I was in Jingera. I wanted to ask you if you'd like to come out to look at Ferndale.'

'I should love to see Ferndale,' she said gently. 'It sounds very beautiful, from what you have told me. Although on no account am I to swim in the sea on your beach.'

He laughed.

'Perhaps you will show us how to care for Joey who has lost his mother. A big loss. So many will have lost so much today.'

'But the town is saved and the bridge is still standing. The fires moved around Jingera without affecting any of the buildings except the pub. Incredibly lucky, but the power will be out for a day or so and the roads to the south are still shut.'

'How is your farm?'

'Seems as if the fire didn't get that far north. I'll be driving back this evening, I hope.'

'Perhaps you would like to have something to eat with us first. If we can go back home tonight. It is too far for you to drive without first having the meal of the evening, and you can show Zidra how to feed Joey.'

'You could do with a baby's bottle. The Burtons might have a spare. Or if they don't, an old eye-dropper might do.'

Together they watched the waves slowly advance up the beach. 'It's coming,' Peter said after some minutes.

'What is?'

'The southerly change. You'll feel it any minute.'

'How do you know?'

'Instinct.' Smiling at her expression of disbelief, he pointed south. An army of purple and black clouds was advancing north, driving in front of it the pall of smoke. Then the wind hit them, a blast of cool air. 'What did I tell you?'

'The southerly change.'

'It will pour in a few minutes. That will put out the last of the fires.'

The temperature dropped so rapidly she started to shiver and hugged Joey to her. All over the beach people began to cheer. Zidra and Jim ran up the sand. 'I'll take Joey,' Zidra said. 'Jim and I'll look after him. Jim said his mother has a bag we can put him in.'

Ilona handed over the little creature, still sleeping in the towel. As the children hurried along the beach to find George and Eileen, she felt the first heavy drops of rain on her bare arms and face.

'It's over,' Peter said. 'And now for some wonderful, wonderful rain.'

344

In the meantime she sat on the roof, her stomach rumbling with lack of food. The minutes passed, the hours passed. The sky was now swathed with stars. Big mob stars. Years ago, her mother had told her the story of how they'd formed. Once the sky had been dark, darker than anything she could imagine. Darker even than her claustrophobia. Dark until two ancestors had sailed up the river and into the sky, and transformed themselves into stars to shine down on their people. And from that time the spirits of the earth mob after death went up into the sky, and made a river of shining stars.

Tears filled her eyes. She desperately wanted to see her mother again. It had been four years since the last time. Worse even than this was the manner of their parting, without a proper farewell. How she longed to see her, to feel her warm arms around her, to rest her head on her shoulder, to smell that scent of sunlight on clean cotton. And to feel loved. *I love you*, she whispered into the warm night air. *I love you, Mum.*

CHAPTER 1

An instant before the doors of the school bus clanged shut, Zidra Vincent hopped down the three steps and onto the pavement. She'd just caught sight of her parents' car parked near the hotel, which meant they must be here in Jingera. Ahead of her were the other Jingeroids, the girls and boys who, like her, travelled to and from Burford each day. Among them was her friend Sally Hargreaves, whose family had moved to Jingera last September. Though, at fifteen, Sally was a year older than Zidra, they'd struck up a friendship on the school bus.

'Want to come home for a while?' Sally asked. She had freckled skin, blue eyes and long dark hair, and a laugh that could make even the grumpiest of people smile.

'Thanks but I might miss my lift. Saw Dad's car there and thought I could avoid an extra ten minutes on the bus with the Bradley boys.' Once the Jingeroids alighted, the Bradley boys were the only other kids on the bus. Living on a property a few miles north of where Zidra lived, their idea of sport was baiting her until she could get off at the entrance gate to Ferndale.

Now she strolled across the square in Jingera, around the war memorial with its wreath of red paper poppies from Remembrance Day, and down towards the post office. For a moment she stood next to the car, a vintage Armstrong Siddeley, and looked around. The new pub that had opened three years ago was a hideous building, everyone agreed on that. Walls an ugly brick, as yellow as jaundice, and a speckled red-and-ochre-tiled roof that fortunately could be seen only from the headland. There was a new clientele too, the surfer boys who, a year or two back, had got the message that the surf at Jingera beach had a good curl to it.

The car was unlocked but her parents were nowhere to be seen. She scribbled a note on a scrap of paper from her school-case and left it on the dashboard, before placing the case on the floor in front of the passenger seat, where they could see it.

After strolling by the war memorial, she accelerated past the post office – hoping Mrs Blunkett wouldn't catch sight of her, otherwise half an hour would be lost in idle chatter – and turned into the unkerbed street leading down to the lagoon. Weatherboard cottages lined the road; some were semi-concealed by hedges and others had no gardens at all. Several hundred yards down the hill she stopped at a gate, on each side of which was a glossy-leafed hedge studded with sweet-scented white flowers. She used to live with her mother in this cottage. She still thought of it as theirs, even though they'd stayed there for less than a year. They'd moved out nearly four years ago, after her mother's marriage to Peter Vincent and the adoption that had made him her legal father. The house, what you could see of it behind the vines, seemed shabbier now. Someone from Melbourne had bought it as a holiday cottage but it wasn't much used. Its windows gazed blankly at her without even a glimmer of a welcoming reflection.

She opened the gate and walked up the brick path. It had been several months since she'd last visited the cottage, and the verandah floorboards seemed more weathered and splintered than ever. Yet she found it reassuring that they still squeaked in exactly the same places as when she'd lived there. Though she loved everything about Ferndale homestead, visiting the cottage felt like coming home. She sat on the verandah's edge. The only sounds she could hear were the surf thudding onto Jingera beach and seagulls wailing.

At this point, Zidra saw her father passing by the front gate, marching purposefully up the hill. He had a rolled-up towel under his arm and wet hair.

'You've been surfing. You could have taken me!' she called, leaping up from the verandah.

'You were at school,' he said, giving her a hug. 'Anyway, what are you doing hanging around this place? You've got a new home now, remember?'

She laughed.

'Your mother and I decided to come into Jingera on an impulse. So I thought I may as well have a swim after collecting the mail. There are two letters for you today; they're in the glove box of the car.'

'Good. Where's Mama?'

'Seeing Mrs Cadwallader.'

'Oh, that means she'll be ages yet.'

'She said she'd be back at the car by 4.30. I think one of your letters is from Jim Cadwallader, by the way.'

Zidra tried to conceal her delight, and to saunter to the car rather than rush at it as she really wanted to do. She took the letters from the glove box. She wouldn't open them yet. She would postpone that pleasure until after she'd thoroughly examined the envelopes.

The first letter had a Vaucluse postmark and *Zid Vincent, Ferndale nr Jingera* scrawled across it in Jim's spiky handwriting.

He'd started addressing her as Zid from the time of his first letter to her, after he'd gone off to Stambroke College in Sydney as a scholarship boy. She knew it was to make all his new friends think that Zid was a boy.

She looked at the second letter. Her name and address were written in block capitals sloping from left to right, in a hand that she didn't recognise. ZIDRA TALIVALDIS, LAGOON ROAD, JINGERA. The old address and her former surname, but Mrs Blunkett had known which postbox to put the letter in. The envelope was of poor quality paper and very thin. There couldn't be more than a page inside and there was nothing written on the back of the envelope. She squinted at the postmark that was faint and smudged, and tried to decipher what the letters said. Her heart lurched as she made out the word GUDGIEGALAH.

Lorna Hunter had written at last.

Or maybe it wasn't from Lorna at all. That backward sloping printing wasn't in Lorna's style. The message must be *about* Lorna, and a little worm of anxiety turned in her stomach. Glancing around her, she saw that her father was heading across the square and into Cadwallader's Quality Meats.

With shaking fingers, Zidra ripped open the envelope and pulled out the single sheet of lined paper that had been roughly torn from an exercise book. The pencilled message was sloping from left to right for only the first few lines and after that the writing changed. It was now unmistakably Lorna's hand, although still written in cramped capital letters. Lorna must have been in such a hurry that she'd given up the attempt at complete anonymity.

WE'RE GOING BY BUS TO JERVIS BAY FOR A HOLIDAY WEEKEND 16th–18th FEBRUARY. TELL MUM AND DAD TO GO THERE TOO. I'M <u>BANKING</u> ON YOU. THEY

CENSOR EVERYTHING HERE AND I'M NOT EVEN SURE IF I'M GOING TO GET THIS LETTER OUT. I'LL TRY TO POST IT TOMORROW. WE'RE ALLOWED OUT SOMETIMES TO THE SHOP TO BUY LOLLIES, BUT I'M GOING TO BUY A STAMPED ENVELOPE INSTEAD. THOUGHT IT SAFER TO WRITE TO YOU AND ANYWAY I DON'T EVEN KNOW IF THEY'RE STILL LIVING AT THE SAME PLACE.

I REALLY MISS YOU, DIZZY. IT'S LIKE A PRISON HERE. I'M ALWAYS GETTING INTO TROUBLE – THAT'S NOTHING NEW – AND THEN I GET LOCKED IN THE BOXROOM. THEY DON'T KNOW I CAN GET OUT THE ROOF LIGHT AND SIT ON THE ROOF. HA HA.

CAN'T WAIT TO SEE MUM AGAIN. <u>PLEASE TELL HER TO GET TO JERVIS BAY SOMEHOW</u>. I'VE HAD NO NEWS ABOUT THE FAMILY SINCE NANA CAME TO SEE ME A YEAR AGO AND DON'T KNOW HOW THEY ARE.

WITH LOVE

Lorna used to attend Jingera primary school with Zidra in the days before the Hunter family had been sent to the Reserve. Soon after that, Lorna had been taken to the Gudgiegalah Girls' Home. She was a half-caste, that's what they called her, and Tommy Hunter wasn't her real father.

Zidra read the letter again. There were no names to identify the writer, or the recipient either, apart from *Dizzy*, and who would realise that this was short for Zidra? Yet if the message had been intercepted at Gudgiegalah Girls' Home, anyone would have been able to guess who'd written it. Zidra wondered how many letters had already been written and never gone out. The girls there were banned from all contact with their past.

According to the postmark, this letter had been posted less than a week ago. It was several months until the bus trip to Jervis Bay. She'd have to figure out how to get the message to the Hunter family, though like Lorna she had no idea if they were still at the Wallaga Lake Reserve.

'What are you reading?'

Her mother's voice startled her. For a moment she'd forgotten where she was and now felt irritated at being distracted from her thoughts. Her mother opened the back door of the car and sat down on the seat next to Zidra. She made a face to herself, but not so that her mother would see. It was doubly annoying that there was no *Hello darling, have you had a nice day at school?*

'Hello, Mama,' she said, kissing her on the cheek and folding over the letter. 'Have you had a good day?' Mama's hair was pinned up in some sort of topknot and her even-featured face, without its usual frame of exuberant fair hair, appeared tired. Zidra would tell her about Lorna later. She needed to digest the contents of the letter herself first.

Her mother smiled, apparently oblivious of Zidra's veiled reproof. 'It was *bonzer*.'

Zidra winced. An expression like this sounded ludicrous when spoken in a thick Latvian accent. After nearly a decade in Australia, her mother had acquired the local slang but not the diction. You'd think her musical training might have made her more receptive to the rhythms of speech.

'I just had tea with Mrs Llewellyn and Eileen Cadwallader,' her mother continued. 'Where's Peter?'

'At the butcher's.'

'What for? He killed a sheep only two days ago.'

'Same reason as you went to see Mrs Cadwallader and Mrs Llewellyn,' Zidra said. 'To have a chat.'

Her mother's grin was reflected in the car's rear-vision mirror above the windscreen. The brown dress she was wearing was almost the same colour as her eyes.

At that moment, Peter opened the front passenger door and settled himself into the seat. Her mother climbed out of the back seat of the car and into the front. After she turned the ignition and preselected first gear, the car kangaroo-hopped several feet before stalling.

'Foot on the change gear pedal,' Peter said mildly.

You weren't allowed to call it a clutch. That was because the Armstrong Siddeley Whitley was so special that all its parts had different names to ordinary cars. Zidra knew this because Peter had also been teaching her to drive around the home paddock, and she reckoned she was already a better driver than her mother. But it would be two years at least before she could sit for her driving test.

Her mother muttered something in Latvian that was almost certainly indecent, and turned the ignition key again. She'd been driving for three months so you'd think she'd have got the hang of it by now. She insisted on practising, and Peter didn't seem to care. In fact it was almost as if he enjoyed it, in spite of all the jerking and stalling.

Zidra's mother began to drive so slowly along the Jingera to Ferndale road that soon there was a queue of cars behind them. When Zidra mentioned this, Peter suggested that she give her mother a break. When she's had more practice she'll get her speed up and on no account are you to pressure her to go any faster. Fat chance of that, Zidra thought. Even the bus with the Bradley boys might be better than this slow crawl north.

Once home at Ferndale, Zidra went to her room in the attic. It had originally been used as a boxroom until she'd persuaded her parents to have it painted and insulated and made into her bedroom. Three dormer windows illuminated the space, which was large with steeply raked ceilings. Each window was rather small, but together they shed sufficient light that the room never seemed gloomy, even on the most overcast of days. One dormer looked to the east and the ocean, the other to the north with Mount Dromedary rearing up in the distance, and the third to the west. That was her favourite view, of the folds of hills rising to the distant mountain range, all framed by the pine trees that had been planted when the house was built in the late nineteenth century.

After throwing her school-case onto the bed, Zidra stripped off the Burford Girls' High School uniform – the navy blue tunic and white shirt – and put on old trousers and a shirt. She glanced quickly at her reflection in the wardrobe mirror. Several months ago she'd decided that she might actually be quite good looking – she'd been lucky to inherit her mother's regular features and even that high forehead could be disguised by allowing her dark curls to fall forward. Curls that periodically her mother said were just like those of her real father, *poor Oleksii*, whom Zidra herself always thought of as *Our Papa Who Art in Heaven*.

With the two letters now in her pocket, she clattered down the stairs and out to the kitchen, where the family's outdoor boots were lined up, in regimental order, near the door to the back verandah. Her piercing whistle summoned the two dogs, Rusty and Spotless Spot, who knew without being told that she was off to the stone stairway leading down to the beach. Here she perched on the top step while the dogs bounded down to the strip of white sand below.

Carefully she unfolded Lorna's letter and read it again. She had no idea whether or not the Hunters were still at Wallaga

Lake. She certainly hadn't seen any of them in Jingera lately. Glancing around her at the vast dome of the sky and the ocean in front of her, she thought of how much Lorna must loathe being incarcerated at her school. Training Centre was how it was described. Mama had snorted when she'd learnt that. Training to be domestic slaves, she'd said.

Zidra put the letter away and slit open the fatter envelope from Jim. Three sheets of closely written paper, which she began to peruse with great eagerness. After reading a couple of paragraphs, however, she puffed out her cheeks in exasperation. It wasn't that liking cricket was evil as such, it was more that inflicting lengthy descriptions of it onto others was deeply inconsiderate, especially when he knew how boring she found team sports. She skimmed through the letter until she reached the final paragraph.

> *I was interested to read in your last letter that you want to be a journalist. That would suit you, Zid, with your love of writing and history. One of the teachers told me that newspapers offer cadetships, so you might want to check up on that. By the way, did I tell you that my good friend Eric Hall is coming to stay with us in Jingera for a week or so towards the end of the Christmas holidays? He comes from near Walgett and you might remember I visited his family's property last year. Flat as a pancake out there, so he'll think he's in paradise at Jingera.*
> *I'm really looking forward to coming home.*
>
> *Yours sincerely,*
> *Jim*

She laughed out loud at the *Yours sincerely*, wondering how long she would have to know Jim before he could write anything a bit more affectionate. She always made a point of signing her letters to him *With love from Zidra,* just as she did with all her friends. *With love from Zid* mightn't go down so well if people thought she was a boy, though.

Jim's abbreviation of her name was nice and no one else ever thought to use it, although it wasn't as nice as Lorna's name for her, *Dizzy.* Together the nicknames made a good combination, she thought: *Dizzy Zid.* There was something glamorous and light about the name Dizzy.

Now she found that thinking about Lorna was bringing back all those feelings she'd been keeping squashed down ever since reading her letter and, having forgotten a handkerchief, she sniffled into her hands.

Lorna had been taken from her family almost four years ago. Zidra remembered waking from a nightmare at that time, convinced that Lorna was telling her something. Telepathy was how her mother had described it. Of course Zidra hadn't known then that Lorna was being taken away, only that she was in trouble. After that, Zidra's own life had become difficult. It wasn't just the loneliness and fear that she felt after her best friend vanished, but also the vulnerability. It was only Jim's friendship that had kept her going.

And she hadn't spoken to Lorna about any of this. Although longing to, she hadn't seen or spoken to her for years.

her parents to have it painted and insulated and made into her bedroom. Three dormer windows illuminated the space, which was large with steeply raked ceilings. Each window was rather small, but together they shed sufficient light that the room never seemed gloomy, even on the most overcast of days. One dormer looked to the east and the ocean, the other to the north with Mount Dromedary rearing up in the distance, and the third to the west. That was her favourite view, of the folds of hills rising to the distant mountain range, all framed by the pine trees that had been planted when the house was built in the late nineteenth century.

After throwing her school-case onto the bed, Zidra stripped off the Burford Girls' High School uniform – the navy blue tunic and white shirt – and put on old trousers and a shirt. She glanced quickly at her reflection in the wardrobe mirror. Several months ago she'd decided that she might actually be quite good looking – she'd been lucky to inherit her mother's regular features and even that high forehead could be disguised by allowing her dark curls to fall forward. Curls that periodically her mother said were just like those of her real father, *poor Oleksii*, whom Zidra herself always thought of as *Our Papa Who Art in Heaven*.

With the two letters now in her pocket, she clattered down the stairs and out to the kitchen, where the family's outdoor boots were lined up, in regimental order, near the door to the back verandah. Her piercing whistle summoned the two dogs, Rusty and Spotless Spot, who knew without being told that she was off to the stone stairway leading down to the beach. Here she perched on the top step while the dogs bounded down to the strip of white sand below.

Carefully she unfolded Lorna's letter and read it again. She had no idea whether or not the Hunters were still at Wallaga

Lake. She certainly hadn't seen any of them in Jingera lately. Glancing around her at the vast dome of the sky and the ocean in front of her, she thought of how much Lorna must loathe being incarcerated at her school. Training Centre was how it was described. Mama had snorted when she'd learnt that. Training to be domestic slaves, she'd said.

Zidra put the letter away and slit open the fatter envelope from Jim. Three sheets of closely written paper, which she began to peruse with great eagerness. After reading a couple of paragraphs, however, she puffed out her cheeks in exasperation. It wasn't that liking cricket was evil as such, it was more that inflicting lengthy descriptions of it onto others was deeply inconsiderate, especially when he knew how boring she found team sports. She skimmed through the letter until she reached the final paragraph.

I was interested to read in your last letter that you want to be a journalist. That would suit you, Zid, with your love of writing and history. One of the teachers told me that newspapers offer cadetships, so you might want to check up on that. By the way, did I tell you that my good friend Eric Hall is coming to stay with us in Jingera for a week or so towards the end of the Christmas holidays? He comes from near Walgett and you might remember I visited his family's property last year. Flat as a pancake out there, so he'll think he's in paradise at Jingera.
I'm really looking forward to coming home.

Yours sincerely,
Jim

She laughed out loud at the *Yours sincerely*, wondering how long she would have to know Jim before he could write anything a bit more affectionate. She always made a point of signing her letters to him *With love from Zidra,* just as she did with all her friends. *With love from Zid* mightn't go down so well if people thought she was a boy, though.

Jim's abbreviation of her name was nice and no one else ever thought to use it, although it wasn't as nice as Lorna's name for her, *Dizzy.* Together the nicknames made a good combination, she thought: *Dizzy Zid.* There was something glamorous and light about the name Dizzy.

Now she found that thinking about Lorna was bringing back all those feelings she'd been keeping squashed down ever since reading her letter and, having forgotten a handkerchief, she sniffled into her hands.

Lorna had been taken from her family almost four years ago. Zidra remembered waking from a nightmare at that time, convinced that Lorna was telling her something. Telepathy was how her mother had described it. Of course Zidra hadn't known then that Lorna was being taken away, only that she was in trouble. After that, Zidra's own life had become difficult. It wasn't just the loneliness and fear that she felt after her best friend vanished, but also the vulnerability. It was only Jim's friendship that had kept her going.

And she hadn't spoken to Lorna about any of this. Although longing to, she hadn't seen or spoken to her for years.

Acknowledgements

Warm thanks to Peter Bishop, Catherine Blyth, Karen Colston, Beverley Cousins, Chris Kunz, Sara Maitland, Kathy Mossop and Lyn Tranter for their many helpful suggestions, and to the staff at RHA. I am especially grateful to Maggie Hamand and Kirsten Tranter for their perceptive comments about the structure of the manuscript. Part of the book was written while I was on a Varuna Longlines Fellowship, awarded by the Eleanor Dark Foundation.

Background reading came from the book by Mark McKenna (2002), *Looking for Blackfellas' Point: An Australian History of Place,* Sydney: UNSW Press, as well as from the Australian War Memorial research website for the history of Australian pilots' involvement in the Second World War.

Alison Booth was born in Victoria and brought up in Sydney. After over two decades living in the UK, she returned to Australia in 2002. She currently holds joint academic appointments at the Australian National University and the University of Essex. She is married with two daughters.

Stillwater Creek is her first novel. The sequel, *The Indigo Sky*, is set four years on in 1961. Alison is currently engaged in writing the final instalment of the trilogy.

Q&A WITH ALISON BOOTH

One of the great strengths of the novel is the powerful description of the landscape, and the impact that it has on the principal characters. What does the township of Jingera represent to each of the main characters in the novel?

Each views the town differently. For Ilona, it's the last refuge, and somewhere to eke out her dwindling savings and earn a living. For Peter, it's somewhere to surf, drink a few beers at the local hotel and then escape, when he is fed up with people, back to his isolated property. For Zidra, the town is a mixture of freedom and exposure to prejudice, but it allows her to form an important new friendship with the Aboriginal girl Lorna. For Jim, Jingera also offers freedom to run wild in the bush and on the beach, but it is also somewhere from which he must get away if he is to develop. For Cherry, the town has brought her happiness through an illicit love affair that can only flourish if she leaves. For George, the town and its environs are his love and his livelihood. He represents the goodness of small-town life.

Jingera seems almost like a character in its own right. Did you intend this to happen and is Jingera based on a real place?

Jingera is a fictitious town, although there are many small townships on the southern coast of New South Wales to which it could be related. The book is about the arrival of a new family into this apparently peaceful coastal town, and how this triggers a series of events that profoundly affect the lives of many of the people living there.

While originally Jingera was intended simply to be the setting of the novel, it developed a life of its own. Each character responds differently to the distinct beauty of the place, and the story also explores how the relationship to the land and other aspects of the natural world can heal and sustain the spirit of some of the characters. One example is George and his stargazing, another is Peter and his relationship to the land.

The novel is set in 1957. Does the choice of year matter to the narrative and, if so, why?

I chose 1957 because I wanted a time period in which child pornography and abuse were not on the social radar, and in which part-Aboriginal children were being taken from their parents by a paternalistic regime. In part this was because I wanted to focus on the moral dilemma arising when a woman discovers her husband has a collection of child pornography, and this raises her suspicions that he might engage in paedophile acts. The additional moral dilemma is about forcibly removing children from their families. Both are closely linked in the novel, not only because each concerns the rights of children but also because the removal of the Aboriginal girl Lorna makes it possible for her close friend Zidra to become threatened by the paedophile.

An additional reason for choosing 1957 was that some of the adult characters were still bearing the scars of the war and the enormous upheaval it caused in peoples' lives. This made it easy to compare the lives of immigrants with Aborigines, both of whom were on the fringes of society. While this could of course be done in the present time, because we are still a society in which both Aborigines and asylum-seekers might be thought of as fringe dwellers, I wanted to tell the story historically. I really like the long view that an historical setting affords. In part this is because the broader events are better understood, at least to my mind, when they are in the past than in the present.

One of the main themes in the novel seems to be the human flaw of prejudice. How does the paedophilia relate to this prejudice?
That's a good question. The police officer's prejudice means that he doesn't see Aboriginal people as human beings. Prejudice is also there in the reduction of people to names – wogs, dagoes, reffoes, and Abos – and most evil of all, tattooed numbers – that downgrade their humanity. But the way people feel about paedophiles is not a form of prejudice like racism. Judgement of paedophiles is based on the unjust action, and not on the person's status or skin colour.

Another great strength of the novel is its profoundly humanistic vision and the tenderness with which the characters are portrayed. Are any of them based on real life?
No. They bear no resemblance to anyone I've met. They're entirely fictitious and turned up on the page unannounced. Some of them even brought friends, whom I turned away!

READING GROUP QUESTIONS

1. Music is extremely important to Ilona as a means of self expression. Does music serve any other purpose in *Stillwater Creek*?
2. Discuss the importance of the scene of the two girls, Zidra and Lorna, borrowing George Cadwallader's boat, getting into difficulties and being rescued by Bill Bates. Do you consider this is a pivotal scene in the story?
3. Lorna's point of view is never explicitly given and yet she is a vital character. Why do you think the author chose not to present Lorna's point of view?
4. What role does the little green elephant play in the plot?
5. The novel is written from six different viewpoints. Did you want to hear from more of Jingera's townfolk? Who do you think gave you the most insight into the town, and why?
6. What are the obstacles that each of these six characters must overcome?
7. In what way does the Christmas Dance develop the narrative?
8. Discuss how each of the characters have changed by the end of the novel.

THE INDIGO SKY

By Alison Booth

It is the spring of 1961, and the sleepy little town of Jingera is at its most perfect with its clear blue skies, pounding surf and breathtaking lagoon. But all is not so perfect behind closed doors.

George Cadwallader – butcher by day and stargazer by night – is loved by everyone, except his wife. He only wants the best for his family – yet it's all falling apart.

Philip Chapman is a sensitive young boy, a musical prodigy – and a target for bullies. But with his wealthy parents indifferent to his cries for help, his entire future is at risk…

Then there's Ilona Vincent and her daughter Zidra, former refugees, now fully-fledged 'Jingeroids'. When a voice from the past reaches out to them, they're soon in a race against time to reunite a family that has been cruelly torn apart…

Once again weaving together the enchanting stories of Jingera and its townsfolk, Alison Booth offers up a heart-warming sequel to the critically acclaimed *Stillwater Creek*.

Read on for an extract…

PROLOGUE

No bulb in the light fitting. No water, no food. The room hot and airless, the only furniture a battered iron bedstead with a thin mattress and stained cover. The palms of her hands felt sticky. Moisture trickled down between her shoulderblades and into the band of her knickers. Her shift was damp and clung to her skin. There were no windows, apart from a small roof light. Through this she saw the occasional lonely cloud drifting across the pale blue.

Although without a watch, she knew by the whitening of the sky that it was almost evening. The others would be at dinner and she wouldn't be there to look after them. This would be the second meal she'd missed today. After running her tongue over dry, cracked lips, she took a few deep breaths to stem her rising panic. She couldn't bear the thought of being enclosed in this small space once it was dark. Already the walls seemed to be pressing in on her, as if they had a life of their own; a living breathing organism that would crush her once night fell. She could die in here and no one would know.

The fading light began to turn greenish, as if filtered through leaves that she could not see. She inspected the roof light. Nothing more than a vertical glazed panel where part of the ceiling slanted up at an acute angle. Again she tried the door. Still locked of course, and bolted too. She'd heard the click-click of the two barrel bolts being pulled across after she was pushed inside all those hours ago. She rattled the door and put her shoulder against it; a futile gesture as the door opened inward.

Once more she looked around the room, and up at the ceiling. Closely she inspected the roof light. Maybe that glass panel wasn't so fixed after all; it looked as if there might be a handle halfway up the sash. She'd never be able to reach this though, in spite of her height, in spite of standing on her tiptoes. Again the walls seemed to be pushing towards her, and her heartbeat was becoming frantic. Slowly, deeply, she inhaled and exhaled until the panic started to abate.

Of course there was the bedstead, she thought. Although it was heavy, she was easily able to push it underneath the roof light. Standing on it, she tried to reach the handle, but it was still too far away. Doubling the mattress over would give her an extra few inches. Quickly she rolled the mattress up, struggling with the lumpy old kapok. Soon she was climbing up onto it. Just as she was balancing there, she heard footsteps approaching along the corridor outside. She had to get down fast. The bed had to be back in its proper place against the wall. No evidence; that would only mean more punishment.

Clip-clop, clip-clop. The footsteps passed by the door without a pause. *Clip-clop, clip-clop.* Straight down the hallway to the far end, where they stopped. A door was opened. After a few moments she heard it shutting again, and the footsteps returning.

'Let me out,' she shouted, banging on the door. 'Let me out!'

There was no response, apart from the clicking of metal-tipped heels, straight past the room in which she was imprisoned, and down the corridor. Then there was only silence. And with it she felt the return of her claustrophobia. Heart pounding, palms clammy, mouth so dry it was hard to swallow.

She wouldn't give in though.

She pushed the bed back under the roof light and again rolled up the mattress. After climbing on top of it, she balanced precariously, arms stretched out to each side until she felt stable enough to raise her hands above her head and slowly stretch towards the roof light handle.

Now it was within reach. She turned it and felt it move. A slight push, and cool air washed in. She gave the sash a harder shove. Hinged at the top, it opened outwards. After placing one hand on each side of the opening, she hauled herself up. *Lucky I've got arms like an ape*, she thought. That's what they'd said about her when she'd been brought here first, after they'd stripped her and washed her in carbolic soap and scrubbed her all over until her skin hurt.

As she pulled herself up and over the sill, she heard the plop of the mattress as it unrolled onto the wire bed-base. For a moment she sprawled on the metal roofing. The corrugated iron was still hot, although the sun had now set. Above her, a crescent moon hung low in the washed-out sky and the first few stars began to appear.

This was the furthest she could escape to, she knew that already. From the top of the three-storey building, with its steep roof dropping away on all sides, there was no way out. Although there were some trees nearby, they were too far from the building. She would never be able to reach their branches. For a moment she wondered if she would only break a leg if she were to jump over the edge of the roof. Probably not. She'd break her spine or her neck too, or be dead on impact. The choice was always hers to try. Not tonight though; not yet.